Richie the Caseworker

Christopher Febles

First published in 2022 by
FARAXA

www.faraxabooks.com
info@faraxapublishing.com

Richie the Caseworker

© 2022 Christopher Febles

Interior design / pagesetting by Faraxa Publishing

Cover illustration by Delanie Pon

EDITED AND PROOFREAD BY *Editizing*.COM & Faraxa Publishing

ISBN 978-99957-925-5-7

For Shirley and Rosie

There are no grown-ups. Everyone is winging it; some just do it more confidently.

- Pamela Druckerman

Table of Contents

Prologue: The Call-Up 7

The Delivery...19

The Replacement Player 69

Welcome to the Show 93

Follow Through 117

Spring Training..141

Budding Prospect..165

Hot Streak..193

The Slump..225

The Push 269

The Wildest of Cards..331

Epilogue: Getting the "W"...383

Notes 393

Acknowledgements..395

About the Author..399

Prologue: The Call-Up

October 1982

*T*en year-old Richie McGinn, sitting in the backseat of the family's bulky '71 Buick Regal station wagon, didn't hear yet another yelling fit from his mother. His hands were pressed against the window, and his light green eyes were as wide as they could be, as he took in the majesty of his favorite place on the corner of River Avenue and East 161st Street.

"Yeah, yeah, Jesus Christ, officer, I'll move!" yelled his mother. She waved her cigarette out the window at the cop in the street.

"Ya gotta move that car, lady," the tall cop bellowed.

"This is good, Mom," Richie's fifteen year-old brother Pat said, as he opened the door. "Come on, Richie, grab your glove and let's go."

Richie grabbed his first-baseman's glove, a hand-me-down from Pat, and bolted from the car. He was so excited he nearly ran into a crowd of people on the sidewalk. Pat grabbed his jacket and pulled him back.

Through the car window, their mom asked, "What time is this over?"

"I don't know, like, ten-thirty, eleven? Kinda depends on what happens in the game, Mom," Pat said.

"Oh, screw that," she said, putting her cigarette between her lips and fumbling through her purse. "Yeah, YEAH! I'm moving! Gimmie a goddamn minute!" she said to the cop, now at her window. She produced two subway tokens and put them in Pat's hand.

Richie saw Pat's smile disappear as he looked in his palm. "Really, Mom?"

"Oh, please," their mother said. "I took the subway all the time when I was a kid. Just walk from Woodlawn."

As Richie watched the sun disappear behind the towering outline of the Stadium, he realized they'd never had to walk home from a night game. It was a long walk from the last stop on the #4 train to their apartment on McLean Avenue, just over the Bronx border in Yonkers, and they'd have to do it in the dark.

"Grow up, you'll be fine," she said. "No way am I coming all the way back here in five hours." Richie had begged to go early to see batting practice, so it was just getting on six o'clock. The shutters of the Stadium were still closed.

Pat sighed, exasperated. "Thanks, Mom," he said, not looking at her. She u-turned illegally and drove back up River Avenue.

Richie saw Pat's face instantly change from a frown to a huge smile. "Come on, Richie! I got a surprise for you."

They jogged together down River, passing the shuttered entrance to the bleachers. Richie lagged behind, as his skinny legs could never keep up with Pat's.

"Hey, wait up!" he said.

"This way!" Pat yelled. "Come on, slowpoke!"

They came to a stop outside Gate 6. Breathing hard, Richie stammered, "We're...we...no bleachers?"

Pat smiled. "Nope. That's the surprise. Check it out." He carefully took two tickets out of the frayed front pocket of his jeans and handed them to Richie.

Printed on blue fancy card stock were the words "Loge Level," along with "Oct. 1," "Boston," and "Game 79." It was the first time Richie had ever held a ticket that wasn't for the bleachers. All of a sudden he felt the weight of the tickets, now terribly scared they'd blow away or get stolen.

"Holy geez, Pat!" he said. "These are ours?"

"Yup," Pat said, grinning.

"But –"

"Traded for them with Billy Camareri."

"With what?"

"My Reggie Jackson rookie card."

Richie's eyes bulged. "What? Pat, that was your best card! It's worth a fortune!"

Pat lifted his palms. "S' OK. It was Dad's, anyway. He'll never know."

Only a few fans, all of them male, waited outside the gate, an imposing steel shutter. Richie saw an old man smoking a cigar, a huge guy eating a meatball hero, and a skinny guy who turned out to be a scalper ("Who needs tickets, who needs tickets?" he chanted).

As they waited, he tuned out the deafening sound of the elevated train overhead, and thought about what it would have been like to have been here just one year earlier. They'd been so close – so close! – to going to Game 1 of the 1981 World Series. Their dad had promised to get them tickets – he "knew a guy," apparently – but came home empty-handed. When Richie screamed and cried, their father had said, "Oh, grow a pair, and stop being such a goddamned baby. It's only baseball, and I got good money for those shits. You can watch it on TV." When

9

he ran to his room, crying into his pillow, he could hear Pat yelling and arguing with his parents. Later, when he fell asleep with his sorrow, Pat came in to check on him. He pretended to sleep, as he was too upset to talk to anyone, but he could feel Pat's hand stroking his hair, saying, "I'm sorry, man, I'm so sorry. I'm so sorry."

Just a few days later, in the middle of the night, their father moved out. In the year since, Richie heard from him only once, a forced encounter that ended in Pat once again yelling over the phone. The absence wasn't a surprise, however, as "he'd shacked up with some broad again," as his mother slurred.

"Good riddance to bad rubbish," Pat had said.

Pat shook him into the present. "Hey, come on, they're opening the gates!"

The shutters rolled open with a loud crash. The boys raced ahead, finding a spot in the front row of the right field's main section. Pat explained to Richie that they could hang out there during batting practice, at least until someone showed up for their assigned seats. "This is a prime spot to catch a BP home run ball, man," Pat said.

This was the first game Richie had been to all year, since their mother had no interest and money was tight. Pat was the one who'd always taken him, who showed him how to keep score, who told him about the Yankee greats: Ruth, Gehrig, DiMaggio, Mantle, Munson, Jackson. Richie was scrawny and uncoordinated, and kids made fun of him for always striking out in Little League. So he walked away from his dreams of Yankee glory, and lived vicariously by watching every game on WPIX, following their statistics in the paper, keeping score in his own little notebook, and watching Pat play. Pat, though only in ninth grade, had made his Varsity baseball team, manning first base. Richie trudged to the dusty field whenever he could and sat right behind first base so he could watch him in action. His daydreams were odd by daydream standards: he dreamt of Pat playing in the pinstripes, not himself.

With the fading twilight glistening off the shiny blue seats, the Stadium was almost empty. The shouts of the few fans there echoed like off the walls of a canyon. No one at all was in their section except someone selling scorecards, which Pat bought with three crinkly dollar bills. On the field the batting cage was set up. One player at a time took his swings as his teammates looked on, chatting or playing catch. A few players were in the outfield, shagging flies. From where the boys sat it was hard to tell who was at bat, but some of the right-handed hitters smashed towering shots into the left-field seats. The hair on Richie's neck stood on end as he heard the thundering crack of the bat.

After a few minutes, Oscar Gamble, a left-handed outfielder, hit one that bounced off the warning track, perhaps on its way into Richie's hands. He leaned over the rail, but the ball didn't reach.

"Oh, no!" he said. "My lucky pen!" It had fallen from behind his ear and onto the field.

Pat said, "Oh, so close! Just be careful next time, OK?"

"But, Pat, my lucky pen! That's the one you gave me."

"Aw, I'll get you another one, Richie," Pat said. "I found that on the field one day. You —" He stopped short, as one of the Yankee bench players shagging flies came over to the rail.

The player was short by major league standards. He had narrow eyes and a floppy haircut, and wore his cap low on his forehead. He jogged to the track and picked up the pen.

11

"Hey kid," he said. "This yours?" He held it up, a silver Arrow pen, worse for wear from having been trampled by high school ballplayers.

Richie was speechless. He was thrilled that a Yankee was talking to him, but he had no idea who he was.

"Go ahead, Richie, tell him," whispered Pat.

"Oh! Uh, yeah, that's my lucky pen. Sorry I dropped it."

"That's OK, kid, it happens." He was young, fresh-faced. Richie even thought he could have been Pat's age; they were about the same height. The player examined the pen carefully with his left hand.

"Say, this is a nice one. Your lucky pen, you say?"

Richie said nothing. Pat nudged him in the ribs.

"Oh, uh, yeah, uh, h-he gave it to me," he said, pointing at Pat, who waved and smiled.

The player continued to look at the pen. "You know," he said, "I could use some luck. I'm trying to make the team here, and I don't have my first hit yet." He looked at Pat, then Richie. "Tell you what. You let me have this pen, and I'll get you an autographed ball. What do you say?"

Richie looked at Pat, who mumbled, "Are you nuts? Say yes!"

"O-OK," he said.

"Great!" said the player, who took a ball from his glove, signed it, and tossed it to Pat. Pat's mouth gaped as he handed the ball to Richie, who was struck dumb.

"Richie!" hissed Pat. "Say 'Thank you'!"

"Oh, uh, Th-Thank you," he said.

12

"Thank you, Richie. I need all the luck I can get. Enjoy the game!" And he trotted toward the dugout, as Yankees BP had ended.

"Hey, good luck, forty-six!" Pat shouted. The outfielder turned and waved briefly, then continued on his way.

"Oh my God! That was so cool! Look at your ball!"

Richie looked at it. The signature was illegible.

"Orn...Morringer?" he said.

"Hmm," Pat said. "Maybe it's in the program." Richie checked, but there was no number 46 for the Yankees listed.

"Probably one of those September call-ups,"[1] Pat said. "But still cool," Pat reassured him. "A Yankee talked to you, man! He has your lucky pen!"

"Wow," Richie said, still stunned.

They stayed for all of batting practice, only reporting to their Loge seats when the seat holders arrived a little before first pitch. Though he'd been to a few games before, he'd always sat in the bleachers, which weren't connected to the rest of the Stadium. As they walked to their seats, Richie gazed wide-eyed at the concession stands, the souvenir shops, the long ramps. A cool autumn breeze swirled through the tunnels, lifting the wings of his Yankees jacket. The sounds of the Hammond organ mingled with the hum of the pre-game crowd. He closed his eyes as they walked through the tunnels, taking in the smells of hot dogs, popcorn, and pretzels. More than once Pat had to grab his hand to get his attention. He felt like a big-shot as an usher – a real-life usher with a red jacket – took their tickets and walked them to their seats, brushing them off with a cloth. "Enjoy the game, boys," he said, smiling and waving off Pat's meager tip.

13

Richie spent the first inning open-mouthed. Never had he been this close, even if it was one level up from the field. The players' uniforms gleamed. He could hear the pitches hit the catcher's mitt with a loud "thwack!" He stared at the constellation that was the digital scoreboard. He could even see the contours of the players' moustaches, the batting gloves in their back pockets. He never took off his glove, worried a foul ball would come their way, and he wouldn't be ready to catch it. He even held the scorecard with it.

After nine innings the game was tied. As the tenth inning started, The Voice of God, Public Address Announcer Bob Sheppard, said:

"Your attention, please…ladies and gentlemen…Now playing first base for the Yankees…Number forty-six…Don…Mattingly…"

"Hey, that's your guy!" Pat said to Richie.

Richie said, "He plays first, just like you!"

Pat explained the story to the strangers in front, and they beamed at Richie. He blushed.

Then, in the eleventh, with the ball in Richie's jacket pocket, Mattingly lined a ball into right field for a single. On the amber-and-black scoreboard appeared the words:

"THAT WAS DON MATTINGLY'S FIRST MAJOR LEAGUE HIT. CONGRATULATIONS!"

"Hey!" Pat said, elbowing Richie in the ribs. "You did it! You got the guy some luck! Way to go, Richie!" The strangers turned and shook his hand. They asked to see the ball. Richie looked at Pat first, who nodded that it was OK.

"Wow, that's great," said the older of the two men. "Hang onto that. Who knows, maybe this kid is good one day."

"Way to go, Don!" Richie yelled as loud as he could, hoping he could hear. Pat shook his shoulder and cheered. In his scorecard, Richie put a star next to the box with Mattingly's hit, his personal touch to note a special play in the game.

The Yankees lost in the twelfth, Mattingly flying out to end the game. Richie was disappointed, but both teams were eliminated from the playoffs anyway, and his brush with fame more than made up for the loss.

"Don't make eye contact, and don't let go of my hand," Pat sternly told him as they put their tokens in the turnstiles. It was probably a childish gesture given their ages, but Pat's huge, strong hand made him feel a little safer among the sweaty and imposing throngs. He did what his brother said, just looking at a gum spot on the floor, thinking about what he'd experienced that night.

"I can't believe that happened," he said as they trudged up the long, lonely stretch of Jerome Avenue toward home.

"It did, man," Pat said. "That was incredible. Don Mattingly, huh. Wonder if he'll make the team next year."

"Think that'll be you one day?"

Pat laughed. "Yeah, probably not."

As they walked up Jerome, the street became more and more deserted. On their left was the dark forest of Van Cortlandt Park, and on their right was the menacingly silent Woodlawn Cemetery. They saw a stripped and burned-out car, covered in graffiti. Richie shivered, trying to look straight ahead, staying close to his brother.

"We're almost there," Pat said, reading his thoughts. But they still had quite a ways to go.

"Think he's any good?" Richie asked, hoping the small talk would help.

Pat shrugged. "You never can tell. He's kinda small for a first baseman, kinda skinny, too. But he made some good plays at first. Who knows? Kinda depends on luck, too."

"I wonder if he'll use that lucky pen."

Pat turned to him and smiled. "I would."

They kept walking. Richie said, "Why didn't Mom come get us, Pat?"

"Pfft. Hell, I don't know."

Richie didn't respond. Pat took his shoulder just as they went to cross Van Cortlandt Park South.

"Hey, Richie?" He leaned down, looking him in the eye. "I think…I think it's me and you for a while, OK?"

"What do you mean?"

Pat sighed. "I don't know. Mom's…busy, I guess. In and out, not always home. You noticed, right?"

Richie nodded.

"So, look. You can always come talk to me, OK? Some bully comes and bothers you, find me. You wanna go to the game? We'll scratch some money together and sit in the bleachers. We'll make those PB&J sandwiches, just the way you like 'em. You and me, together. Bleacher buddies forever. OK?"

Again, Richie nodded. They crossed the wide avenue.

16

Finally, they reached their apartment. Pat turned the key and they tiptoed to their room. Their mother was snoring in hers.

As soon as Richie reached their room, he mounted the ball on his dresser between two Matchbox cars. As they tucked themselves into their beds, Richie said again, "I can't believe that happened."

"Yup," Pat said. "You helped a guy. Nice job."

As he drifted to sleep, he thought: just five months to spring training. Then we'll know if he made the team.

17

The Delivery

February 1995

Richie McGinn groaned as the door to the enormous Pelham Manor mansion opened. Why these people called Pizza Palace when there were plenty of pizza joints much closer he had no idea. He'd gotten lost because he didn't realize there was both a Poplar *Drive* and Poplar *Court*. He guessed wrong and had to ask for directions at the gas station on Gramatan Avenue, and had to wait ten minutes while the attendant was using the can.

The guy who opened the door looked like he'd just walked off a Ralph Lauren ad. Blond, tall, athletic and blue-eyed. He was wearing a starched white shirt, argyle sweater vest, tweed jacket, and a handkerchief in his breast pocket.

"Richie?" the guy said, clearly recognizing him.

"Ah, hell," Richie muttered.

"Hey, Richie! How are you?" He extended his hand.

"Hey, Trevor." He had four cold pies in his hands, and could only offer a pinky. Trevor balked, then shook it awkwardly.

Richie and Trevor were roommates in college at George Washington University in DC. Trevor made it well known that GW was his "safety" school. He'd tried twice to transfer to Dartmouth with no success. He was a middling student at best, but he met with more success in the work world, having secured a Wall Street job in his sophomore year. Richie regularly kicked the shit out of him in Nintendo baseball.

"What have you been up to?" he asked Richie.

He thought: *What's it look like?*

"Uh, you know."

"Oh. Right. Hey, uh, thanks."

Richie handed him the pies. "Yup. That'll be $37.50."

"Right! Uh, here you go." He dropped the coins on top of the bills. "Hey, do you want to come in, man? I, uh, we're having a party. I, uh, got into Wharton."

"Mmm, business school," Richie said, still looking at the money. "Awesome, congrats. No, you know, I gotta get back and all…"

"Hey, sorry I haven't called. You know, busy studying for the GRE's and working at the firm and stuff. You know how it is."

Sure, I read the Great Gatsby, douche. Tell Daisy to kiss my ass.

"Sure, I know. No problem."

"Well, uh…I gotta go. They've been waiting for the pizza back there, and – well, I'll see you around, OK, Richie?"

Yeah, see you at the next cricket match, asswipe.

"Yup. Thanks again."

Richie walked back to the car. He looked in his palm. There it was: $37.50 in exact change. Including ten nickels.

Richie lay his head on the steering wheel as a sea of red lights on the Bronx River Parkway appeared in front of him. He knew he should've taken local streets. This job had just gotten worse and worse. Parking in Yonkers was impossible, his ass constantly hurt from the worn vinyl seat, and when he made a mistake with an address, he was sure to be cussed out. Someone once called him a "motherless bitch bastard." At least once per night he'd get completely stiffed on the tip, either from spite or forgetfulness, or from people who truly had no idea that you're supposed to tip the delivery guy. He smelled, almost all the time, like a calzone.

Tony diStefano was his boss at Pizza Palace, the place he and Pat patronized since childhood, and they loved him. He was 6'3", 240 pounds, had a bouffant haircut, mutton chops, and most days just wore a white t-shirt with a pack of Marlboros rolled up in the sleeve. If it weren't for the pencil mustache and the heavy New York accent, he could be Elvis. He loved to chat and had a colorful way with words, which was to say he'd augment every sentence with fascinating curse words in two languages.

One night, six months earlier, when Richie had walked in to pick up a Sicilian pie, Tony had said, "Yo, Richie. You ain't workin'. Why don't you do deliveries for me? You could help me out, eh?"

Tony was right: he wasn't working. It had been a fruitless summer after an aimless year in college. He'd finally settled on history as a major after switching four times, from biology, to sociology, to philosophy. He'd also bounced around from different part-time jobs and internships in his college years, including a stint on Capitol Hill in Senator Pat Moynihan's office. He spent three years lifeguarding at the fitness center for $5.50 an hour, but let his certification lapse. He spent three summers working inventory at the A&S at the White Plains Galleria for $5.75, but it was so tedious he

21

contemplated hanging himself with all the crappy imitation silk ties he'd counted, and it had been shut down in 1994, anyway.

His best experience was through satisfying a service requirement at a food pantry near Dupont Circle. While they had made him do all the heavy lifting as the youngest volunteer there, he'd often got to interact with the people, hearing their stories and helping them pick out different foods. Even when the requirement was satisfied, he'd kept working there. He'd also helped at the accompanying community center, working on street fairs, voter registration, recreation, outreach, and of course, lots of lifting and moving large objects. Many of the neighborhood residents had gotten to know him by name. But they weren't hiring, and it paid less than pizza delivery anyway.

As senior year had drawn to a close, he'd been to Career Services, but nothing seemed to work out. Either he didn't have the qualifications, or whatever jobs they referred him to seemed boring. In one case, the boss of a printing company said at the end of an interview, "You don't wanna work in this shithole." When Richie said to his Career Services counselor that he liked working at a community center, he replied, "You're gonna make a living doing that?" He scanned the want ads (looking in the New York papers only) and saw nothing that interested him.

He'd come back to Yonkers after graduation and justified a little vacation. He didn't see himself behind a desk, or taking on the added expense of grad school, and dreaded the prospect of filling out an application at the local Waldbaum's.

So when Tony had offered him the job, money was tight, and he was going stir crazy. "Sure, Tony," he'd said. "I'll help you out."

22

But after six months, Richie began to realize that Tony was a lousy businessman. He sent Richie home earlier and earlier, sometimes as early as eight PM. He was basically a weekend guy ("Anybody wants pizza delivered on a fuckin' Monday, I say *mafankulo*," [2] Tony said). He also didn't admonish Richie when he was late or when someone called to complain. "That guy was a fuckin' *mameluke* anyway," he'd say. Instead of making pizzas, he'd often go into ten-minute anecdotes peppered with curse words about some stupid cousin. Richie wondered how the place even stayed in business.

When Richie returned from Trevor's house, Tony was on the phone. "Yeah, yeah…uh-huh…sure, sure, I will…No problem, boss…OK." He hung up. Speaking to the phone, he said, "And fuck you, you fuckin' *stronzo*."

Richie dreaded to ask, but he said, "Everything OK?"

"*Maron, che palle*," Tony said. "The fuckin' balls on these people, eh? Nah, don't worry about it. Some little *bastardo* complained about his pie being late."

"Trevor?"

"Yeah, that's him. How the hell did I know? Poplar Drive, Poplar Court, Poplar *Fongoul*, whatever. Don't worry about it. He tip you?"

"Nope."

Tony shook his head. "*I coglioni, mafankulo*." He opened the register and took out some bills. "Here, I got you, cuz. Tell you what, take a little extra. And you could go home, OK? Serve them *puttanas* right, no pizza for them."

23

Richie looked down in his hands at the $49. It was a little more than the $8.50 per hour he and Tony had agreed upon in August. He must have included Trevor's nonexistent tip. It was 7:30.

"You sure, Tony?"

"Yeah, yeah – oh!" He picked a box off of the top of the oven. "Here, for you and your brother, and that little *carina* he got."

This is the worst-run business I ever saw, Richie thought. He picked up the box. "Uh, thanks, Tony. Sure it's OK?"

"Yeah, yeah, whatever. You a good kid, Richie. Enjoy your night. Don't take no shit off no fuckin' *mamalukes* like that fuckin' *stronzo* Trevor."

Richie parked just up the street from the apartment he and Pat shared. It was the first floor and basement of a huge multi-family house in Yonkers, a few blocks away from where they grew up. It was owned by a New York City firefighter named Charlie, who lived in Orange County and who'd inherited the house from his mother. Their apartment was a totally illegally subdivided unit: Charlie just clumsily slapped doors with locks in the foyer. He insisted on being paid the $1,200 monthly rent in cash, which would be delivered on the first of every month in a safe in the basement. It was reasonable by market standards, but it represented a good chunk of Pat's paycheck as a low-level bank employee.

"Richie?" He heard Pat's voice as he took off his slushy boots. He answered by sighing loudly.

"Heyyyyy," Pat said on seeing the pizza box. "Yes! Tony's the MAN!"

"Nice to see you, too, you *stronzo*."

Pat started. "What's that mean?"

"I don't know, but it sounds awesome, doesn't it?"

"Yeah, it does. Maybe I'll use it in the bleachers on some Italian player or something. Anyway, you're back early."

"Another banner day for Richie McGinn," Richie said, lowering himself onto the couch, rubbing his brow.

"Sorry, bro. You know, you can quit that job if you want. I know how bad it sucks."

"No, Pat. No. We need the money, right?"

"Well, sure, but I don't mind. I can cover us while you look for something that… that doesn't suck so bad."

"Well, I love Tony. I don't wanna quit on him. And, well… you know. Every little bit helps, I guess." He pulled out the bills, and poured a pile of nickels on the table. "What should I do with this?"

Pat cocked his head. "I don't know. Whip 'em at cars? The bills, you keep."

"What about gas, and groceries?"

"Yeah, pay for gas, and you keep the rest."

"OK," Richie said, spreading himself on the couch. "Oh, yeah. Saw Trevor. Delivered there. Pelham."

"One of the dudes from your apartment?"

"Uh-huh." He related the story.

Richie would have loved to have cracked Trevor over the head with his own polo mallet, since Tony probably wouldn't have fired him, anyway. The delivery had been the most interaction he'd had with his junior and senior year roommate since they'd graduated. Trevor was the only one from the New York area; Tommy and Marky were from Brookline, Massachusetts, and Stanislaus "Skrub" Skrabanek, a computer engineer who was even nerdier than Richie, came from California. They all played in a fantasy baseball league,[3] and at the end of sophomore year Trevor asked him if he wanted to share a bedroom in an apartment in the Adams-Morgan district with Tommy, Marky and Skrub.

But it turned out that Trevor was hardly ever there. He spent weeks during the school year at his uncle's brokerage house on Wall Street, paying others to take notes for him in the classes he missed. The others were likewise busy, working on Capitol Hill and in the lab. They couldn't be convinced to make the two-hour haul to Baltimore to see the Orioles' new ballpark, and tickets were either sold out or priced out of range anyway. He eventually realized that he shared no interests with them other than fantasy baseball, and they all pulled out before long, as he crushed them all year after year. Thus, he went back to Yonkers every weekend and every break he could. Pat had expressed his concern at his return, at first ("Don't you have friends there?" he'd asked), but after a while he'd stopped.

So after graduation they had made promises to stay in touch, which Richie knew were hollow. Sure enough, they returned his "How are you doing" messages late, or not at all. The calls made him uncomfortable, anyway, as they had no choice but to expound on the early successes they all enjoyed in business, politics and engineering. Trevor was the next Bernie Madoff; Tommy and Marky the legislative aides for Ted Kennedy; and Skrub (or "Steve," as he now preferred to be called), a developer at Apple in California. Richie was none of those things. Pat encouraged him to stay connected, playfully telling him to "get a life," but the calls began to feel like homework. So before long he'd just given up.

"Oh yeah, Marilyn knows Trevor's family," Pat said. "Said they treat the help like shit and pay them the same way. Straight-up assholes."

Richie looked at the TV. ESPN was on. They were talking about the ongoing baseball strike. The labor strife had halted the 1994 season in August, cancelling all remaining games including the World Series. No headway had been made between the owners and players since.

Richie pointed at the screen and said, "What's gonna happen with this? Players coming back or what? Spring training's supposed to start soon."

Pat opened the box and took a slice. The Sicilian pie was still steaming. Neither of them used a plate. "They're gonna use scabs."

"Scabs? Seriously?"

"That's what I heard. Replacement players."[4]

"Oh, forget that. A bunch of has-beens, scrubs that couldn't even cut it in the minors? Putting on the Yankee uniform? That's blasphemy. No way."

Pat sighed. "I always wanted to take you to your first playoff game, man. To make up for what Dad did to us. I thought last year was gonna be the year. It's been fourteen years, man. Long time, we're due. YOU'RE due."

27

"We're ALL due," Richie said. "Donnie Baseball, he's SERIOUSLY due. A Yankee through and through, never won a World Series. Not even the playoffs. It's not right. Just not right."

"Got that right, bro," Pat said, raising a beer in a toast. Richie tipped his own.

The Yankees had had a great 1994, cruising in first place all year. It'd looked like Richie and Pat would finally get to the playoffs, maybe even the World Series, thirteen years after their father had reneged on his promise. So would Donnie Baseball, who'd enjoyed a wondrous twelve-year career without a single playoff game. But the strike had blown all that away.

Going to the Stadium was one of the only things that made life tolerable for Richie. None of his friends were around or even interested, but Pat dutifully accompanied him as often as he liked. They sat in the bleachers, of course, them being the cheapest seats in the house.

The faded plastic blue seats delivered instant back pain. The most exotic food at the meager concession stands were the peanuts, as they were obviously named by someone with a loose grasp of English and an even looser sense of irony: they were called "Uncle Jesse's Nuts." In the dead of summer the place became the Sahara, absorbing enough solar energy in just a three-hour ballgame to power the scoreboard for a season and a half. And, as Richie well knew, all the other seats were inaccessible. Once Pat had a buddy sitting in the Main section who wanted to meet up; he'd told him to come over to the right field upper deck seats around the third inning and wave.

But truth be told, there was nowhere else they'd rather sit. Yes, the Yankees were finally competitive again. Don Mattingly was good – no longer the star of the team, but the beloved team captain – and Richie made everyone around him shut up whenever he came to bat. But the charged atmosphere, the fierce heckling of the other team, and the wild personalities of the "Bleacher Creatures" were as much part of the game as Cracker Jacks.

They'd clap and chant when an elderly gentleman named Ali would play a delectable salsa beat on his cow bell to start the game or induce a rally. They'd boo and jeer the fans of any opposing team, the Red Sox and Mets in particular. They'd cheer on "Queen Tina," all four-foot-eight of her, the spiritual leader of the "Bleacher Creatures," when she'd challenge an opposing fan to a fight. They'd encourage anyone peering over the side of the upper deck (including Pat's buddy) to "Jump! Jump! Jump!"

And at the end of Ali's beat, they'd yell, "Yankee Baseball, Mets Suck!"[5] (Some would add, "[Opponent] sucks, [opposing right fielder] sucks, box seats suck, everybody sucks except the Yankees.")

When the lockout hit, Richie moped around the house, no interest in football or any other sport. He dragged his way through long, meandering books and watched way too much network TV. Six months later, there was still no progress. No baseball, no Yankees, no Donnie Baseball. Just lousy replacement players.

"Sorry, man," Pat said. "About the job, the strike, Trevor. I can't believe you were friends with him. What a *stronzo*."

A few nights later, as they were closing up shop, Tony blew on his hands and said, "Yo, Richie. I meant to tell you: I'm movin'. Sellin' the place."

"What?"

"I'm movin'. My cousin has a place in North Carolina, some *pezzo di merda* town down there with a Pizza Hut franchise. I'm bleeding money in this goddamned place, so I'm hightailing it outta here."

"Oh, shit. For real?"

"For real. Got a buyer for this place, and they're gonna keep it a pizza parlor. God bless 'em, maybe they'll have better luck than me. I'll put in a good word for you if you want, but it's a family thing, and I think they want their kid to do the deliveries."

Richie put his hands on his hips. He shook his head. "When?"

"End of next week."

"Wow, that's fast."

"Yeah, I know. They need me down there ASAP. We're gonna pull in like three times what we make here. Yeah, it's shitty pizza, and they're a bunch of backwater fuckin' *mamelukes* down there, but we're gonna try to do our own thing." He paused. "Hey, look, I'm sorry, Richie, I –"

"No, no, that's OK. You gotta do what you gotta do."

"Yeah, but I didn't mean to leave you in the lurch like that. Especially last-minute and all. *Maron*, but this thing was only temp for you, right? I mean, you're a college grad, you're super smart, you got something lined up, right?"

Richie sighed. "Yeah, I got some irons in the fire. I'll be fine."

Tony scoffed. "You don't wanna be doin' this fuckin' *merda* your whole life, anyway. Believe me. Go out and, you know, DO somethin'. You got brains, use 'em."

They walked out, Tony locking the door behind him. He extended an ashy, hardened hand, which Richie took. "Well. We got one solid week and change. You could stick it out for that time?"

"Yeah, sure," he said, shrugging his shoulders, hands in pockets, thinking, *I got nothing else going for me, so why the hell not.*

Tony lit a Marlboro with one hand using a shiny steel lighter. "Thanks. Not for nothin', but you been a real help, a real help. You're a good guy. If there's anything I can do for you, I'll do it, *capisce?*"

Trevor had said basically the same thing to him at graduation. "OK. Thanks."

"*Buona fortuna*, Richie. You'll be fine."

"Yeah, I know. See you tomorrow."

After Tony drove away, Richie looked at the Escort. Pat was probably asleep, so there was no one to talk to. So he decided to drive around for a few hours.

He took the Sprain Brook Parkway, a straight, darkened path to nowhere. The steering wheel of the Escort shivered when he went over sixty,[6] so he slowed down. *Not like I have somewhere to be, anyway,* he said to himself.

31

As a few flurries glanced off the windshield, he thought about Trevor, on his path to conquering Wall Street. He thought about the Brookline boys, budding power brokers. And Skrub/Steve. Designing space-age computers. And he couldn't even hold a low-level pizza job. Couldn't even help himself make ends meet.

Now I'm gonna need even more help, he thought, shaking his head.

When he walked into the apartment, it was 1:15 AM. He heard a voice: "Richie?"

He saw Pat walk into the living room. He looked wide awake.

"Hey, man, where were you? I was worried."

"Oh, just out driving. Sorry about that." He flopped down on the couch.

Pat looked askance at him. "Everything OK?"

He sighed. "Tony's is closing."

"Aw, no," Pat said, sitting in the easy chair. Just like all the other furniture, they'd gotten it off the street on bulk pick-up day. They had only disinfected the chair *after* they'd both gotten rashes.

"Shit," Pat continued. "That's too bad."

"Yeah, well," Richie said, "kinda saw it coming. I love Tony, but he's no businessman."

"Mm," Pat murmured. "When?"

"End of next week."

"Pretty quick."

"Yeah, I know."

"I'm sorry, Richie. Tough break."

"Well, maybe it's for the best," Richie said. He sat up a little. "Hey. What's this gonna do to us?"

"What do you mean?"

"You know. Our finances."

"Oh. Ah, well, don't worry about that. Like I've always said. I'm here for you. I'll take care of you as long as I need to."

"No, Pat. It's not fair, I –"

"Yeah, I know, Richie, I know," Pat said, waving his hand. "But really, it'll be OK."

Richie looked at the floor. Pat said, "Hey. Look at me."

Richie looked in his eyes, a shade of green a little darker than his own.

Pat said: "Remember way back when? The summer before you left for college? Mom – well, Mom basically abandoned us, right? Moved to New Hampshire with Joe," he added with derision. "And I said, no, no way. That would have broken us up. No way was I gonna let that happen. I wanted you here, with me. Your home is here, right here."

Pat shifted in order to face Richie a little better. "No, it hasn't been easy. Yeah, we've had to scrimp and save. I'm not gonna lie: supporting two people on my salary is tough. But you and me, Richie? We're the only family we've got." He paused, took a deep breath. "So look, we'll be OK, money-wise, OK? We'll make it work. You? You just focus, get a job, use that brain of yours, find something you like. And me? I'll be fine, I don't mind putting in the hours. I don't care how long it takes. You hear me? You're my family, Richie, I'll be here for you."

You're my family, Richie. The phrase took him back to that anxious day Pat mentioned. Their mother, reeking of Jim Beam, had announced to them that she was marrying her boyfriend of five months, a musician named Joe, and moving to Berlin, New Hampshire. Pat, who'd just landed a Manhattan bank job, could "do whatever he wanted." But Richie, who was going to college in the fall, would have to come home to their rural bungalow during holidays and summers. His heart sank, thinking how he might never see Pat, or the Stadium, ever again. But it was Pat who'd erupted. He'd pounded the dinner table like a dictator, shouting that he wasn't about to allow Richie to "work at the feed store in Bumfuck, New Hampshire". They'd screamed and yelled, he about her past abuse and she about the boys' ingratitude, Richie a timid spectator. He'd thought the skirmish had ended when both parties retreated behind slammed doors. But then he'd heard Pat approach his mother's room, exchange some words, and then storm out of the house, bellowing, "You bet your ass I can!"

The next day, Pat had given him his graduation gift: a ticket to the bleachers. After the Yankees had been retired in the third, Pat had turned to him, gripped his knee, and told him his plan: Richie could come live with him. It would be tough, but it could be done, if they were careful with money. With tears in his eyes, he'd said:

"Richie. Please stay with me. Please live with me. You're my family, Richie. You're all I have."

34

The very next day he moved into the place Pat had found; two bedrooms, so Richie could have his very own room for the first time in his life.

"This is your home, now, Richie," he'd said. "Whenever you come home from college, you come here, got it?"

Then, Pat had sat him down on the creaky, used couch and told him that although his mom refused to help them if they lived away from her, Pat would make sure they'd be OK. Richie had a partial scholarship, which helped, and Pat said he'd help pay for his books, expenses, and whatever loans his aid didn't cover. Pat still had five years of student loans of his own to pay off (getting a five-year MBA from Fordham was a good long-term plan, but put the hurt on his wallet in the short-term), and the rent might have been cheaper had he just found a one-bedroom or a studio. But he insisted it would all work out. "It's gonna be great – living the bachelor life with my little bro," Pat told him, crushing him in a hug. He just asked that if Richie needed something, he would call him, and not their mother. They shook on it, and celebrated with a Sicilian pie from Tony's place.

After that, they'd made an effort to stay in touch with their mother. But she was nasty and irritable every time. "Whaddya want?" she answered when they called. They sent a Christmas card but didn't get one back. Finally, on Mother's Day, Pat got into a loud shouting match with her over the phone, one that ended with, "We don't need your sorry, drunken ass, anyway!" From then on there was no response from their mother at all. The phone calls and letters got to be too much work. So they didn't even try anymore.

Back in the present, eyes weary from the long hours of driving, Richie said, "OK, Pat."

Pat smiled. "Great. Now," he said, sitting up a little straighter. "I wanted to talk to you tonight. I haven't decided anything, 'cause I wanted to talk to you first. It's late, but…"

Richie looked at the cheap, Caldor digital clock, clicking closer to 2 AM. "It's OK, Pat," Richie said. "It's you who has to get up early."

"Oh, I'm fine," Pat said. "This is kinda important, so here goes."

Richie looked at Pat. He was only twenty-seven, but he looked older. He still had all his hair and the athletic build that had made him a standout ballplayer in high school. But the rings under his eyes looked darker every year, and his shoulders stooped a little lower.

Pat cleared his throat. "This internet company, Tac-Net? One of the guys who used to work in computers with my bank, well, he started it. You know, they hook people up with email, dial-up services, World Wide Web access, stuff like that. It's really cool, you'd be really into it. Anyway, they got a big investment from some big shots, and they're expanding, and they want an MBA guy with experience to manage the business side of things. They want me to be the CEO and CFO. Basically, in charge of everything that's not computers. They have a feeling this thing is gonna take off, be huge."

He paused, his hands folded in front of him.

"Wow, Pat," Richie said. "Sounds cool."

"Yeah, I know. That was a thing for me, you know? Starting my own business. Kind of a pipe dream, like I'd be, I don't know, creating something, not just moving money around. Well, you know, the idea isn't mine or anything. But I can get behind it. This Web thing, it's gonna be big someday. I'd love to be one of the people who… brings it to people? I like that idea."

Richie looked at Pat. His face was neutral, almost frowning. "I like that idea, too. So what's the problem?"

Pat scratched his chin. "I don't know. It's risky. Pays less. Well, I get a salary and a shitload of stock. So if the company does well, I do well. Kind of an incentive, you know?"

"Yeah, I get it."

"And look. We'll still be OK, money-wise. You can kick in, once you get a steady job. But once I sell this stock, shit, I could pay for you to go to grad school, know what I'm saying?"

"Seriously?"

"Yeah. Well, you know what I mean. That's the kind of money we're talking. Long-term. I mean, it's dodgy, but it'd be great experience for me, cutting edge. But hey, I won't do it if you aren't comfortable with it. I don't want to put any pressure on you. Understand?"

Richie thought about Pat's job. He'd never been there. He'd never watched him at work, never really asked what he did beyond the day-to-day. Pat rarely complained, and never mentioned anything about any aspirations beyond his bank job. Thus, Richie felt a sudden pang of guilt: never had he even known that Pat had such dreams of entrepreneurship. He just worried about his own needs, his own self-exploration. Pat had punched a clock, day-in, day-out, for five years, without ever pursuing his dreams, while Richie goofed off and wasted precious time.

So, there was no way, *no fuckin' way, evah,* as Tony would say, that Richie was going to stand in the way of anything Pat wanted to do.

He said, enthusiastically, "Hell yeah! My brother, CEO. Awesome!"

Pat grinned. "Thanks, man. That means a lot to me. I'll let 'em know."

A few days later, Tony sent him home at seven with a stunning-looking white pizza. As he and Pat ate yet again out of their hands, the phone rang. Pat answered it.

"Hello? Oh, hi, honey! Yeah, it was OK, how was yours? Oh, really? Aw, I'm sorry…Yep, we saved a few slices for you…Uh-huh, he's here…Yeah, I will…No kidding…Yeah, we'll talk tonight…Oh, yeah, yeah, I'm ready…No, I'm dressed, sorta…Oh yeah, no, I'm ready…OK, love you, too…Bye!"

"Marilyn says hi," Pat said. "She's coming over in a bit. We're going to the movies. Cheaper on weekdays. I gotta get dressed." He went to his bedroom.

"What're you seeing?" Richie asked.

He could hear Pat groan. "'Before Sunrise.'"

"What the hell is that?"

"Some movie about…I don't know. Love, I guess. Ethan Hawke's in it."

"Ha-ha!" Richie cackled. "You gotta go see a chick-flick." He made the "whip" sound.

"You're a tool," Pat said, coming back into the room.

"I'm just breaking your balls, bro. Hey, I heard they're givin' away free pantyhose."

Pat ran over and punched him in the arm. Richie guffawed, rubbing his arm.

"Ow! Just kidding, man, just kidding. I love Marilyn, OK?"

Richie had gradually come to like Marilyn, Pat's girlfriend of nearly two years. She was a pretty brunette, a one-time track star whom Pat had met at Fordham. Though in her skirts and pantsuits she looked every bit the hard-boiled corporate lawyer she was, she matched Pat's outgoing and personable nature. She was very smart, very well read, and confident without being cocky. She came from a stable, wealthy family that lived in a cavernous home on a hill in Eastchester, but occasionally enjoyed sitting in the bleachers with the boys and drinking pint after pint at the local pubs. She'd taken an instant interest in Richie, asking him about the history courses he took, the books he read (that she read, too), and even arcane baseball stats. She'd only been dating Pat for a month before she bought Richie a Christmas present: an "away" Yankees jersey in exactly his size. She rented a place with her girlfriends in White Plains, but since Richie had come back from college, she had been spending more and more time in their apartment, often sleeping over.

When he thought about his own romantic situation, it was no better than his vocational one: he'd not dated successfully since junior year. None of his girlfriends found his vast knowledge of baseball a turn-on, and eventually they ran out of things to talk about. His prospects for the future weren't a selling point, either. Molly, a marketing major from Bunker Hill, had broken up with him by telling him she faked liking baseball the whole time she was with him. "Yankees suck!" she yelled over the phone. That had definitively ended any chance of reconciliation.

But Richie was happy Pat and Marilyn were going out to the movies, so as not to be the third wheel again. Theirs was a small apartment, and the displays of affection, the nuzzling on the couch and light kisses, made him terribly uncomfortable. They included him in dinners at nice restaurants or family events at Marilyn's parents' house, but lately he'd been trying to fake an illness or claiming to have to go to work. He also noticed in his brother more and more the telltale signs of premarital comfort: fixing his tie, wiping a lipstick smudge from his cheek.

Just after Pat tucked in his shirt, the doorbell rang. Pat greeted Marilyn at the door. She had her curly brown hair down around her shoulders, and she wore stylish jeans with what looked like the blouse and jacket she wore to work.

"Hi, Richie!" she said, kissing him on the cheek. She looked at the TV he was watching. There was more bad news about the baseball strike.

"Sorry about the baseball thing," she said. "That sucks."

He shook his head. "Total bullsh- crap."

"You can say 'shit,' Richie. It is, it's total bullshit."

Pat draped an arm around her. "That's my gal. She's a keeper. Here, lemme get you a slice."

"Do you have decent beer this time?"

"Yeah, for once." He pointed at Richie. "Blame him for the crap you usually get."

"Could I have a plate, please?"

"Oh! Oh, of course, your majesty!" Pat bowed. She threw a pillow at him, a direct hit to the face. He giggled and left for the kitchen.

She sat in the easy chair. They had never told her where they'd gotten it. Every time she sat there, Richie got nervous.

"So, uh," he said. "How's work?"

"Ugh," she said, massaging her forehead. "Totally sucks. The things these corporate douchebags worry about all day, ugh. And let me tell you…" She looked around to make sure Pat wasn't in the room, and leaned forward. "I get hit on like every day there. Total pervs. I gotta find a new line of work." She sat back.

Pat came back, handed her a plate, and set a beer on the table for her. She took a bite and said, "Oh, Tony, he's on a roll lately. Hey, I heard they're closing. Sorry about that, Richie."

"Eh, whaddya gonna do, *che palle, foncoul*," he said, poorly pantomiming Tony.

Marilyn nearly choked on a bite of pizza. "What the hell does that mean?"

"Son of a bitch, or something like that. I'm gonna miss Tony most of all."

"Well," Pat said. "Like you said. Maybe it's for the best, right?"

"Yeah, Richie," Marilyn said. "I like Tony, too, but you're too good for that place."

Richie blinked. "Huh?"

"You know. Delivering pizza? You can do better."

"Hey, Mar," Pat said, "cut the kid some slack, OK?"

"Oh, no," she said. "I didn't mean it like that. Just, you know, Richie's so smart. You know, he could be, I don't know, working in an office or something."

"Yeah, Mar, I agree, but you know, he needed to earn some money for himself. Give him some credit."

"Yeah, I know, but maybe it's time, you know, to start looking for a career or something. Use that brain of his."

"Oh, sure, sure. I'm sure he'll make more money someday, find a career he likes, but –"

"Excuse me," Richie snapped. "Do you mind talking to ME, please?"

Marilyn dropped her head, picked it up again. "You're right. I'm sorry, Richie. I didn't mean anything by it. I – we – just, you know, want to help, that's all."

We?

"Yeah, Richie," Pat said. "I'm sorry, too. She's got a point, though. Maybe now you're free to do something, I don't know… more… substantive?"

"You know what?" Richie said. "Let me just get through the next few days, OK? I'll find something else. I'll throw some applications out there, who knows. All I know is I don't like not having money, not contributing. At this point I don't give a shit what it is, OK? And yeah, I hate seeing Trevor and those guys conquering the world when I get shit-canned from a pizza joint. But... let me figure it out, huh?"

Both Marilyn and Pat were silent, sad looks on their faces. After a few beats, Pat said, "You're right, Richie. I'm sorry, we're sorry.

You take your time, don't worry about us." He turned to Marilyn. "Ready to go?"

"Yeah. Good-night, Richie," and she kissed his cheek again as they left.

Richie finished every last slice in the box.

His last week was pretty light. He helped Tony pack up a lot of the stuff they wouldn't be needing after Sunday. He finished *20,000 Leagues Under the Sea* in all the down time.

On Valentine's Day, Richie was packing boxes when he heard Tony answer the phone. "Pizza Palace...Oh, hiya, Francis...Oh, yeah, I know...That's OK, don't worry, we'll be fine...What's that? Oh, sure, sure! Ooh, that's kinda far...Oh, I see...Right, right, I understand...Oh, sure, for the kids, that'll be great...Sure, sure, we can do that...No, that's OK, just, uh..." as he searched for a pen. "Right, six plain, one pepperoni, one sausage. Wings, sure...uh-huh. We got Diet Coke, is that OK? Right...6:00...What's the address? Yeah, yeah, it'll be OK...Eh?" He looked over at Richie. "Yeah, I think I got a guy... Richie....Oh yeah, he'll be fine, he's a good guy, college guy. Sure, he'll be great. I'll pay him a little extra...no problem, no problem. 6 to 8, yeah, OK...Yeah, Sunday's our last day...Eh, whaddya gonna do, it's all for the best." He looked again at Richie. "Yeah, shouldn't be a problem. And yeah, you could have him for the night. No problem. Awright, take care, Francis."

He hung up the phone. "Hey Richie, you heard of some homeless shelter? Housing Solutions America, in Greenburgh?"

Richie shook his head. "A homeless shelter? In Greenburgh?"

"Uh-huh. Well, my cousin Francis works there. They got this big order, you heard. Some Valentine's Day party."

"Geez. That's up there, like a half-hour drive, right?"

"Uh-huh. Might as well take it, though. Not much other business. And nice to do something for those poor kids."

"A homeless shelter for kids?"

"For families. Why not? Do some good for a change."

"Don't they have pizza places closer to them?"

"*Maron*, fuck if I know. Who cares? It's a big-ass order, and I'm doin' a favor for my cousin, so why argue?"

"OK, no problem. 6:00?"

"Yeah. Here's the thing: they want you to stick around for the party. Until about 8:00, 8:30. They have a cake and stuff, and they want someone to help serve. Kinda like catering."

Richie huffed. "We do catering?"

"*Fongoul*, I wish. Hey, whatever. I'll pay you a little extra on top of what these folks give you. All right?"

"Sure, Tony. No problem."

Richie said this, but as he drove his hands were clenching the wheel. He didn't think any of the people at the Dupont Circle pantry were homeless. It was a happy place: families were always grateful for the help, and he worked alongside many of them at food drives and play dates for the kids. But homelessness? That seemed different. He'd read about it in a public policy class, and in his forays into Manhattan he'd come across plenty of downtrodden men asking for change on the 4 train. He imagined men in rags begging for a dollar, wild women shouting at one another, a stinging odor in his nose. He thought he could handle that. The idea of homeless children, however, made him cringe. He had an image in his head: dirty-faced, bulgy-eyed, emaciated children looking back at him, like a UNICEF ad. He inched just a little over the speed limit so the pies didn't get cold, and the Escort quaked in protest.

His exit was a bucolic one, far from either Yonkers, Tarrytown or White Plains. On the south side of the highway was a strip mall, on the north, office buildings, and beyond that, woods. The signs pointed to Westchester Community College, where he'd never been. The houses were modest but with huge lawns. A golf course, a ubiquitous Westchester sight, stretched on his left. In fact, he thought maybe he'd pulled into a golf course parking lot when he'd reached the address. He picked up the menu on which he'd scribbled the directions and squinted. Yes, he'd gotten it right. But behind the tasteful iron fence were classic lampposts illuminating well-manicured lawns and pleasant sidewalks, dusted with the faintest snow flurries that had fallen earlier that day. No building was higher than two stories, and they all looked like townhouses. The whole complex was surrounded by pines and oaks, just peeking over the tops of the structures.

He parked far away from the entrance, not wanting to take the space of some important executive. He also didn't want to embarrass anyone with his bucket of a car.

He unloaded four of the pies from the car and walked to the entrance. Poking his head out the door was an older, dark-skinned man in a security guard uniform: dark blue vest, red tie, pressed

45

white dress shirt, ID badge clipped to his belt, over which hung a slight paunch. "Ey yo. Pizza?"

Moving swiftly, Richie said, "Yep. Pizza Palace. I'm here."

"Why'd you park so far away, man? Come on, son," he said, waving him inside the front door. "Just put that right on the desk."

There was another guard on the phone behind the desk, about chest-high to him. It lined the left of the room, plastic waiting-room chairs in a half-hexagon shape on the right. The entrance to the main part of the building was a set of French doors, albeit secured with a buzzer. Everything looked freshly painted and regularly cleaned. He put the pies on the desk.

"You got more?" the first guard asked.

"Oh, yeah, and the wings, and drinks and stuff. I'll be right back."

"Hey man, next time you can just park right out front. No one's gonna ticket you here, all right?"

Next time? "Oh, sure," he said. "Will do, thanks."

After he turned toward the car, he heard the guard, say, "Hey, Miller, watch the desk, man."

He started to unload the soda bottles and paper goods when he saw the guard standing over him, waiting.

"Lemme give you a hand with that," he said, arms extended.

"Oh, no, it's no big thing, really. I got it."

"Yeah, but we had somebody slip on some black ice out here the other day. Don't want that happenin' to the pizza guy."

He hated being called that, but it was nice of him to come out and help, so he let it slide. Before he could protest further, the guard took hold of the plastic bags.

When they got to the lobby, the first set of pies were gone. A guard signed him in and gave him a visitor's pass. They were buzzed inside. They passed through another door and stepped into a corridor which reminded him of a hospital, only brighter. There was a small conference room and two doors that seemed to have offices in them, with a telephone affixed to the wall. At the end of the hall was what looked like a solarium – a large, roundish-looking room with many windows.

The guard snapped him out of his wonder. "This must be some good pizza, you came all this way," he said as they walked.

They reached the solarium. The guard opened the door and stood aside. Richie hesitated, then said, "Oh," and darted forward, which got a little chuckle from the guard.

Long folding tables were set up in something of a U-shape, and volunteers, mostly women, were hanging decorations. Some were dressed in jeans and sweatpants, others in business attire, skirts and dress pants. The volume of their voices, already loud, echoed all over the high ceilings and seemingly endless windows.

"Oh, hello," said a tiny, thin woman with jet-black hair and plenty of crow's feet around her eyes. She wore business slacks, a V-neck sweater and flats, making her look shorter than she already was. "Are you the pizza man? I mean, caterer."

"Yes, ma'am, that's me. Richie. Nice to meet you."

She thrust out a small, prim hand. "I'm Frances, the day care director here." *Oh, Frances,* he thought, having been expecting a hulking guy with a potty mouth like Tony. "My son delivered pizza during college. He hated being called that. Sorry."

Before he could respond, she said, "Thanks, Jones. Just set them right on that table…that's it, and could you take them off each other, maybe 3 at a time? Perfect, perfect. And there are plates and cups? Great! We'll take it from here." She turned to Richie. "So nice of you to volunteer for us. Thank you so much."

I did? "Oh, yeah, no problem. Happy to help. Where do you need me? Want me to, uh, set up the food?"

Frances stood arms akimbo, looking around. "Well, that looks fine for now. Maybe the ladies need help with the goody bags?"

"Yes, Ms Frances," said one of the women wearing sweatpants, one leg obviously stained. "The families'll be here any minute. We might need to stuff 'em while arts and crafts is going on."

"Well, I guess that'll have to do," said Frances. "I knew we should have started during nap time. Oh well. So Richie, would you mind helping them?"

Again, he thought: *Wait, why am I here? Did I just get suckered into something?* But what was he going to do? Say "screw this" and storm out? In a homeless shelter? *What kind of a piece of shit does that?* There was no denying it: he'd been trapped.

At the same time, it reminded him of kids parties at the community center. Maybe it wouldn't be that bad.

"OK, sure. Goody bags it is." His enthusiasm was the best play-acting he'd done to date. Frances walked him over to a long folding table with a pile of candy and cheap plastic party toys in the middle. A group of women were stuffing items into plastic baggies, laughing at some private joke.

He said, "Frances sent me here, said you might need some help?"

One of the women, an attractive, petite blonde, maybe his age, too well-dressed in a turtleneck and pencil skirt to be a volunteer, stopped and looked at him, still chuckling a bit. Her straight hair was tied back, and she had eyes that were either blue or green. "Sure. We're just getting goody bags ready. Help yourself."

No instructions, so he just picked up a plastic bag and looked around, trying to decide what he should put inside.

"Well, let me show you what we're doing," she said. She stood up, walked over to his side of the table, picked up a baggie and held it in front of her. "See? Two chocolates, two fruit chews, one lollipop, one Tootsie Roll, then two of any of those toys over there. Maybe mix it up a bit." She counted the items while she talked, and expertly wrapped it with a twisty-tie. "OK?"

"Got it. Forgive me if I mess up."

"Ah, don't worry. They're all getting something, and they're too little to complain. Parents, however…"

Her companion nodded her head. "Mm-hmm."

The blonde shrugged. "It is what it is. Thanks for doing this, by the way."

"No problem," Richie said, and started looking for chocolates.

"Oh," she said, shaking her head. "I'm totally losing it. Long day. I'm Rachel, I'm a caseworker here. That's Dara." She gestured toward her companion, who'd sat back down as she worked.

The word "caseworker" brought negative visions to his mind, like the stuffy person in charge of a person's food stamps. But Rachel didn't seem to fit the bill. "Hi, I'm Richie," he said, shaking her hand.

"Nice to meet you, Richie. Welcome to HSA Greenburgh."

"Thanks," he said, getting to work.

"And hey," Rachel said, "don't rush. We have time. We can do this while the party's starting. They have arts and crafts to do, and a magician, and that'll take a while. They'll get this at the end."

"OK," Richie said. "That's cool."

It was easy work, keeping his hands busy. It reminded him of packing bags of food in Dupont Circle. It always made the time go faster when he started up a conversation with someone, chatting about the weather, the Orioles, politics. He looked at Rachel, smiling and swiftly filling bags. He said, "So, is this really a homeless shelter?"

"Yeah, we get that a lot," she said, looking at him but still stuffing effortlessly. "Place looks like a condo, doesn't it?"

"Makes you wanna move in," Dara said.

"Really," Richie said. "I pulled up and thought I was at a golf course."

The women both smiled. Rachel said, again multitasking: "The place is about four years old. The organization has a ten-year lease on the place. It's only for families, no singles. They get six months to live here and we help them find housing, usually Section 8. We have an educational program, substance abuse counseling, a health clinic, mental health services, and day care, all on site. Oh, and recreation, too," gesturing at Dara.

"That's me," she said.

"We have a little food pantry and a lot of sundries, too, like diapers, some baby clothes. I'll show you around if we have time later. But it's kinda late, so maybe next time."

Again, *next time*. "What are the, uh, apartments like?" he asked.

"The units?" Rachel said. "Like big studios."

"Bigger'n my place," Dara said.

"Well, they kinda have to be," said Rachel. "All one big room, but large, so you can fit multiple cribs and beds just in case."

"How many people?" Richie asked.

"108 families when we're full."

"And everyone gets their own place?"

"Yep."

"So the job is to get them into regular housing, right?"

"Yeah. Like I said, Section 8, maybe they get a job, move in with a family member."

"How successful is that?"

She turned her palms up. "We try. A lot of times they just move, or get discharged or something."

"Discharged?"

"Kicked out, basically. Not a lot, but if they break the rules, or don't go to program, or haven't tried either to get an education, or work, or look for a place to live, then they just get sent to another shelter. But this one's the best, believe me."

"Sure looks like it. I'll bet some folks don't want to leave."

"Yep. That happens, too. After 6 months there's pressure from DSS to move them out. I've had families sabotage Section 8 or relapse with drugs just to stay longer."

He remembered rolling his eyes when he'd heard a Trevor-like kid in his public policy class argue that Section 8, a federal housing voucher program to help low-income people, would kill the free housing market.

"I wonder if there's enough Section 8 out there," he said. "After the whole 'Contract on America' thing, support for Section 8 seems to be drying up."

Rachel paused. "Huh. You know about that?"

"Well, I remember hearing about it in college. And during an internship."

"What kinda internship?"

"Oh, you know... I was an assistant in Senator Moynihan's office."

Dara and Rachel looked at each other.

"Hey, it really wasn't that impressive. Mostly I made copies and answered phones."

Rachel asked, "Where'd you go for college?"

"George Washington." He saw their faces. "Hey, again, not so impressive. Look how bad I'm mangling these goodie bags."

"Ha! Well, you just started. Give it time."

A few bags later, some families started to arrive through the same door he'd used. He had been expecting teen moms, but they were a little older than that. A few young dads were mixed in. For some reason they all seemed to have young kids, none older than maybe six. They were tired-looking, worn-down perhaps, but generally excited to be there. None seemed to take notice of him.

Every so often, a single mom with a newborn in the crook of her arm, a toddler clutching her hand, a full diaper bag, and a double-wide stroller struggled to transmit all her belongings through the double-doors. On the third such occasion, Richie left his post to boost the door. He tried in vain to search for a doorstop. Seven times he became a doorman, springing from the table dexterously to prop the door: all but one said thank you.

They finished prepping the goody bags and set them out across the pink and white tablecloth, lined with pink and red glitter. Dara said to him, "Come with me," and led him to the arts and crafts table. A few parents were chatting loudly while their three-to-five-year old kids were clumsily coloring sheets of coloring books, replete with copier smudges along the right side of every page. He detected a faint odor of stale cigarettes. A boy and a girl had abandoned the crafts and were now running around the room in a pick-up game of tag, causing any adult in their path to swerve wildly. "God damn it, Malik, what the f-", said one very heavy woman, censoring herself at the last minute. He could have sworn he'd seen her glance at him while she did. She snatched him with a chubby hand and commanded him to "sit his ass down." Richie, a little dazed, didn't realize he was staring. When she met his eyes, he quickly diverted his gaze.

A younger woman, eyes drooping, leaned on the table with her chin in her left hand and watched a child, maybe a year and a half old, pick up each crayon from a pile and examine it carefully. He stared at each one with mouth open for about two seconds, then proceeded to scribble wildly on the paper. He had bright, wide eyes and the kind of babyish cheeks that Richie was sure got pinched all the time. He could barely see over the side of the table from his plastic assembly room chair. Sometimes his crayon ran onto the table itself. Soon he saw one of those Crayola boxes of 64, but it was well out of reach. He made a kind of grunting noise, then looked at Richie and seemed to make a pointing sound.

"Oh, you want more crayons?" he said, smiling at the boy. "Well, you better put 'em all back when you're done." He reached over and took the box, but all the crayons fell out of the bottom and rolled across the table. He looked over at the boy with a mock-shocked look and said, "Uh-oh!" Instantly the boy gurgled and burst out laughing, revealing a few white nubs and a whole lot of baby gums.

Richie then made a sound like a bulldozer and pushed them all over to the boy, spilling a few on his lap and onto the floor. "Uh-

54

oh!" he said again, to uproarious laughter and muted applause from the boy's fleshy hands.

"Trying to make a Valentine, huh? Not sure Mom approves of you having a date, mister." Mom had perked up a bit, and was now smiling at her boy.

"Well, let's see if we can help you. Gotta make sure you do this right. We don't want to disappoint your potential girlfriend, do we?"

There wasn't much more coloring after that. The boy seemed to like watching crayons roll onto the floor, and Richie was happy to oblige. The toddler would take a crayon from the pile, put it palm down on the table, look at Richie for his pop-eyed, surprised look, then swipe the crayon from the table with a flourish. They were isolated enough from the rest of the activity that all the errant crayons didn't seem to bother anyone. The finished page was a candy heart with series of Jackson Pollack-like streaks of magenta, blue-violet, yellow-green and burnt umber. "Sorry if he was a handful," said his smiling mother, to which Richie replied that it was no trouble at all.

After arts and crafts there was a magic show. A middle-aged man with terribly obvious illusions performed his tricks with vaudeville jokes. Richie was impressed at how calm he stayed despite children running everywhere. He even let the most energetic child, an enormous kindergartener tall enough to dunk, talk into the microphone, which got him the attention he was seeking and settled him for the rest of the show.

Richie kept an eye on the pizza and wings, but there wasn't much to do. When he saw someone without a slice, he offered to get one. Once he brought back several to a family of five. None of that took very long, however. When he turned around to clean things up, the volunteers and workers had already put the boxes in the trash.

One toddler, a boy, maybe one year old, seemed to make a break from the semi-circle when his mother was busy with his three siblings. He crawled at surprising speed toward a stack of chairs, eagerly pulling himself up onto his feet, looking back happily for mama, who hadn't noticed. The chairs were not terribly stable. So, Richie walked over and said, "Hey, don't you like the magic show? Come on, lemme bring you back."

He extended his hand and the boy took it. He walked the unsteady child back to the circle. The mom eventually swiveled her head in his direction, looking relieved. "Is this yours?" he said.

"Sí, señor, muchísimas gracias!" As he let go, the boy spread both hands and padded three wobbly steps toward his mother, swaying forward into her lap at just the right moment.

"Ah, sus primeras pasos! Estupendo, gracias, señor!"

"Ah, sure, no problem," he said.

"Look at that!" a dapper older man with thick glasses and a slight accent said. "That's his first steps."

"No kidding," Richie said. "Well, happy to be a part of it."

"You a volunteer?"

"Er, sort of. I'm with the, uh, food. Catering, I guess."

"Oh. You seem real good with kids."

"I guess. This is a nice event, such a nice place, too."

"Yeah, nicest place I ever worked." He extended a hand. "My name is Tajo. I'm the family's caseworker."

"Richie. Nice to meet you."

"Thanks for doing this," smiled Tajo, tapping Richie's shoulder. "I hope you come back soon, eh?"

As the exit doors opened, signaling the true end of the party, some parents were negotiating for more goodie bags for additional relatives, or to trade up for different toys. The security guards were chatting amiably with parents and workers.

Twice he had to help a child find the drawing or cut-out valentine left behind. He looked over and saw his crayon-swiping buddy fast asleep on his mother's shoulder, wheezing slightly and drooling on her sweatshirt, which, lucky for her, was black.

"Excuse me, can you help me?" he heard a voice say behind him. He turned and saw a very young, slim woman with a forlorn, weary toddler in her arm.

"Uh, sure. I don't work here, but…"

"My daughter can't find her stuffed animal. She can't sleep without it. I don't know what I'm gonna do if I can't find it!"

He knew it all too well. He still knew where Teddy, his stuffed bear for the first eight years of his life, was in the apartment (bedroom closet, top shelf, to the right).

"Oh, geez, we gotta find that bear."

"Cat."

"Right. What's his name?"

She turned to her daughter. "Shanika? Tell the nice man your cat's name." The girl rubbed her eyes and said something.

"What'd you say?" he asked, peering around her shoulder. "Didn't catch that."

"Kitty," the mother said.

"Well, we gotta find Kitty."

He remembered watching a group of kids play a version of hide-and-seek for a while, and the premium spot, albeit a risky one, was under the folding chairs.

"Come on," he said to the girl. "Can you help me? Maybe if we call his name we can find him."

"Her," the mom said.

"Right. Kitty!" he softly called, leading mom and daughter to the folding chairs. "Kitty, where are you?"

Sure enough, under one of the stacks of chairs was a well-worn stuffed Kitty. The nose, once pink, was completely bald; the whiskers, absent; the color, gone from white to gray.

"Oh, look!" the mom exclaimed. "He found her!"

"There she is!" he said happily.

Shanika, exhausted, with her right thumb in her mouth, reached out for her cat. She snuggled it under her chin and put her head on her mother's shoulder.

"Shanika, now what do you say?"

"Fank-oo," the girl mumbled.

"Thank you," the mom clarified. "I don't know what I was gonna do if she didn't find that damn cat. I thought she was gonna freak. You work here?"

"No, just a volunteer."

"Ah, all right then. Thank you. See you soon. Say bye, Shanika!" The girl waved weakly.

"Bye, Shanika, sleep well. Bye, Kitty, don't get lost again!"

"So," Frances said, waiting until his interaction was over. She clasped her hands together. "How did everything go?"

"Oh, just great," he said, surprised at the enthusiasm in his voice. "What a nice party. Nice kids. Looks like everyone had a good time."

"Oh, sure. We kind of put this together just this week. Thought it would be a good idea to do something for kids. Here," she said, and she handed him a business envelope with a formal-looking check and about forty dollars in small bills inside. "Do you have everything you need?"

He looked over at the table with the pizza. All the boxes were already in the trash. His warming bags were stacked and folded neatly. "Yes, sure looks like it. Someone took care of my stuff. Please thank them for me."

"Oh, I will," she said, waving her hand. "That pizza was excellent. Looks like Anthony still has his touch."

He laughed. How those two were cousins he had no idea. "Yeah, he's a good guy. Too bad about the place closing."

"Yes, he told me. I'm sorry, that's terrible for you."

"It's ok. This was just a stopgap thing until something better rolls around, anyway."

"Oh, I'm sure. Smart young man like you. Anthony said you have a college degree, right? Like my son."

"Yes. George Washington, in DC."

"Ooh, great school. Do you know what you wanna do?"

He sighed. "To be honest, Ms Frances," (he said that because A. she was older than he, and B. he'd heard everyone else that night, including the guards, do that, and C. subconsciously it felt motherly) "I really have no idea."

She smiled at him. "Sure. I know. Be patient. Hang in there. Something'll work out."

He smiled back, looked around. "So, is that everything?"

"Yes, that's it. You know what? Could I have your number? We can always use some help with the kids. You seem to have a real knack for it."

Why not, he thought. *Could be good volunteer experience.* "Uh, yeah, just gotta find a pen."

"Here you go, man." Jones was over his shoulder. He produced a lovely Cross pen and a small spiral notepad, like the ones cops or reporters carry. Richie wrote down his contact information and handed it to Frances.

"Great," she said, looking at it. "I'm sure we'll be in touch." She extended her hand, which he shook. "It was so nice to have you. Take care of yourself."

"Thanks. It was a real pleasure."

"Come on, young man, lemme walk you out," Jones said. He walked Richie back through the solarium doors, again standing aside so he could walk through with his gear.

In the corridor he saw Rachel and Tajo. Rachel looked as perky as the morning sun. She was carrying a huge box of decorations. "Hi!" she said. "How'd everything go?"

"Great, just great. Nothing like spending an evening playing with kids."

"Sure, you were great out there. I saw you with Shanika. That was really cute."

"Hah, I had a teddy bear just like that. Never left my sight. Not sure what I'd have done if I'd lost it. Sweet kid."

"Yep. Do you wanna come back sometime? I'm sure we could use your help again."

"Yeah, Frances mentioned that. I gave her my contact information."

"Great, I'll get it from her."

"Do you need a hand with that?" he asked.

"Oh, no, we've got it. Thanks," she said, touching him on the arm. He hoped he hadn't blushed.

"Nice to meet you, young man," said Tajo, shaking his hand. "Take care."

"Thanks, uh, Mr Tajo, is it?"

"No, no, man. Mr Tajo was my daddy. Just Tajo. *Cuidate*, man. I see you around."

"Bye!" Rachel said over her shoulder. She was already on her way back through the solarium on another task.

Jones walked him back to the front desk and through the security door, standing aside for the last time. "Hey, man, you did all right."

"Yeah, that was fun. Thanks for your help, by the way."

"So, is this your permanent gig?"

"Excuse me?"

"Is this your job," he said, more statement than question.

Richie shrugged. "Not anymore."

"Aw. What happened?"

"Shop's closing. New owners. They already have a delivery guy."

"Too bad. What you gonna do?"

"Not sure. Gotta work on my resume, I guess."

"All right, man. Well, maybe something'll open up for you. I hear Dara's looking for a part-time assistant. Recreation. You should check it out."

For what, 5 bucks an hour?

"Sure, I will. Thanks a lot, Mr Jones."

Jones shook his hand and smiled at him. "Take care, Richard. Watch for the ice out there."

He walked back to his car. It had become colder, and a stiff breeze blew through the darkened lot. The forest around him was whisper quiet. His shoes slipped a little on an icy spot near his car.

He started the car, put his gloveless hands on the steering wheel, feeling the stinging cold. He drove carefully down the dark and windy Saw Mill Parkway, the radio off, the ineffective heater blowing on his face. In his headlights he recalled the children's faces: happy, smiling, laughing. He envisioned the moms, playing with their kids on the lawns, for once out of the dank city, safe from drugs and crime. It seemed impossible: happiness – family happiness – in a homeless shelter?

Maybe, he thought. *In the right place.*

When he got home, Pat and Marilyn were curled up on the couch watching TV. They used to scramble to sit in a more dignified position whenever Richie walked in the room, but those days were gone.

"They're really going through with this crap, man," Pat said.

Richie hung up his coat. "What?"

"Replacement players. Scabs."

Richie looked at the screen and scoffed.

Marilyn said, "Look at that guy. Gotta be 275 pounds."

"Wearing the Yankee pinstripes," Pat said. "Makes a grown man wanna cry."

Richie saw some huge stranger taking ground balls at first base. An errant throw rolled up his arm and into the dugout. "That's sickening right there. That fat crap should be horsewhipped, playing Donnie Baseball's position."

"Fuckin' A, bro."

"How was work, Richie?" Marilyn asked.

Richie laughed. "I was doing catering."

She blinked. "Catering?"

"Sorta. 'Catering' meant I put the food down and that was that."

"I don't get it," Pat said.

"They thought I was a volunteer. Or someone told them I'd volunteer. And it wasn't Tony, unless he's b.s.-ing me."

"Volunteer? What kinda place was this?"

"A homeless shelter."

Pat sat up straight. "Tony made you go to a *homeless shelter*?"

"No, no, it's not like that. They were like condos. The place was spread out like a country club. Everything was so clean and neat. It was tucked away in the woods, so quiet you could hear a pin drop."

"Hmm. What was the party like?"

"Oh, you know, arts and crafts, candy, a magic show, stuff like that."

"What were you doing?"

"I was making goody bags at first, you know, candy and toys and stuff. Then they just invited me to play with the kids."

"Oh."

"Aw, that sounds really nice, Richie," Marilyn said. Pat looked at her.

"Yeah, and they were all little kids for some reason," Richie said. "I don't think I saw a kid older than five or six."

"That's cute."

"Yeah. I don't know, it was a really good time. I spent my time coloring with kids, playing with toddlers... It was so organized, and everyone had fun. Even the workers – the security guards seemed like they were glad to be there. The lady who runs the daycare there took my number down. They might have a part-time job, working in recreation."

"Wait," Pat said. "Working there? At a homeless shelter?"

"I don't know. I guess. I mean, nothing else going on, right?"

"Sounds like you liked it," Marilyn said. "I mean, for once, you come home, I don't know... You look happy."

"Weird, right?" Richie said.

"Nothing weird about it at all, Richie. That's great, I'm happy for you."

Now Pat turned, looked at Marilyn sternly. "What? Don't encourage him, Marilyn."

Marilyn started. "Excuse me? He's a grown man, Pat. Looking for something to do with his life. I think it's great. And it's a hell of a step up from delivering pizza."

"You gotta be kidding me. With all those druggies, crazies and shit? I don't know, I don't think that's such a good idea."

"Why not?"

"'Cause, I don't know. Those people… it's dangerous, Richie could get hurt, or –"

Richie raised his voice slightly: "Would you two PLEASE stop talking like I'm not here?

Pat turned to him. "Come on, Richie. Really? Of all the things you could be doing? A homeless shelter?"

"*Of all the things I could be doing,*" he mocked. "Like I have all these options ahead of me. Come Sunday, I'm on my ass, and I have no way of supporting myself. And I don't even know if they'll call me. And you got it all wrong, this place –"

"I don't like the idea of you hanging out with homeless people all day, Richie."

"It's not what you think, Pat. They're families, moms and dads with kids –"

"Moms and dads with a lot of problems. Drug problems, mental health problems. Criminals. You ready for that?"

Richie shrugged. "I don't know. Maybe?"

"*Maybe?* You can't walk into something like this saying 'maybe.' You gotta be a lot tougher than…" He trailed off.

Richie glared at him. "Tougher than what, Pat?"

Marilyn turned to Pat and said, "You know, Pat, not even a week ago you wanted this kid to go out and conquer the world. Now you're holding him back?"

"Nobody's holding him back, Mar. I'm just saying, does he have what it takes to –"

"Whoa, whoa, whoa," Richie almost shouted. "What the hell do you mean, do I have what it takes?"

Pat matched Richie's volume. "I mean, you go from delivering pizzas to solving the homeless crisis? Someone who's never even worked in an office before? That's a huge step, a step into a dangerous area. I'm just looking out for you, Richie."

"OK, do me a favor, then, OK? Stop looking out for me. Just let me –"

"Hey, don't speak to me like that, I'm just trying to help!"

"I didn't ask for your help, *Dad,*" Richie added sarcastically.

"HEY!" Pat yelled, standing up, fists clenched. "Who the hell you think you're talking to, you little shit?"

"Hey!" Marilyn stood up in front of him, putting her hands on his chest. "Cut it out! Just stop it, OK?"

The two men stared at each other, panting. Marilyn spread out her hands, as if to hold them both back. "Enough!" she said. "That's enough!"

Pat took a deep breath. He looked away, then held up his palms in apology. "You're right. I'm sorry. I'm sorry about what I said. I don't know anything about the place. And they haven't called you yet. And yeah, it's your life. Sorry."

"That's right," Marilyn said. Richie noticed when she stood that she was wearing pajamas. "He hasn't been called yet. But I'm sure it's perfectly safe. And you'd tell us if it wasn't, right, Richie?"

Richie nodded. His heart was racing, his breath short. "I'm sorry, too, Pat. I just... I know you're looking out for me, so... yeah." He extended his hand. Pat shook it.

"Well, uh, anyway," Pat said, sheepishly. He looked at Marilyn. "But, I – uh, Marilyn has some news."

Marilyn paused. "I have an interview. In DC. Justice Department."

Richie swallowed. He could feel his hands, still clenched in fists; his shoulders, slowly softening. "Oh. That's great."

"Yeah, isn't it?" Pat said loudly, a little too enthusiastically. "My gal, Justice Department. Wouldn't that be great?"

Richie put his hands in his pockets. "Yeah, great, great. Congratulations."

Quietly, Marilyn said, "Thanks. Well, I didn't get anything yet, you know. Hey," she said, hands in her pajama pockets, "I guess – I guess we're all waiting on good news, huh?"

The Replacement Player

Richie had a habit of waking up in the middle of the night. So, the night after the party, when he woke at 3:25, he got out of bed, and with a bowl of cereal in front of the TV, he watched SportsCenter until the stories started to repeat themselves. Reporters in suits talked very seriously in front of office buildings, courts or spring training ballparks, offering opinions about what would happen when replacement players showed up. In between there were highlights of NHL games, tennis results and even a rundown of Kentucky Derby hopefuls. He got sleepy again when the sun started to rise, so he went back to bed and drifted off around 7.

He was just about to get out of bed the second time when the phone rang.

"Hello?"

"Good morning. My name is Antonia Petrocelli," said a woman's voice with a slight Brooklyn accent. "I'm the Executive Director at HSA Greenburgh.⁷ Is this Richard McGinn?"

"Yes, that's me."

"The young man at the Valentine's party last night?"

"Right."

"Yeah. Frances told me a little about you. Said you did a nice job with the kids."

"Yeah, it was a lot of fun. That's some place you have there. I was very impressed."

"Yeah, we do the best we can. Anyway, I heard you might be looking for a job. Something about the pizza place you're working at closing up?"

He looked at the clock. It was 9:30. *When did they have time to have this conversation?* "That's right. I work through the weekend and that's it."

"Oh. I was thinking you could come in today to talk. Is that timing no good?"

Again, Richie was startled. "Well, uh, I kinda need to, uh, report to work, you know, the guy kinda needs me…"

"Sure, sure, I get it," she said. "No problem. You have a college degree?"

"Yes. I finished last year. My major was history."

"George Washington, right?

"That's right."

"Good school. What kind of experience do you have?"

He was unprepared for this question, so he started chronologically, beginning with two years in high school as a camp counselor (unpaid, but he didn't tell her that). He moved onto his lifeguard jobs, his Capitol Hill internship, and his volunteer experience, leaving out A&S as he was just embarrassed by it. The more he talked the more pathetic he thought he sounded.

"OK," she said, "not bad, not bad. What about Monday?"

"You mean, come to Greenburgh Monday?"

"Yes. You know, we'll talk. There might be something you can do here. You have a resume?"

He had extra copies in a perfectly neat folder that he'd found at the library. It was outdated, but he didn't see the need to add his delivery job, so he said, "Yes I do."

"No way you can get that to us today, is there? Are you near a fax machine or something?"

"Hmm. No, but maybe I could –"

"Nah, don't worry about it, don't worry about it. You kinda described it all. Just bring it with you Monday, OK?"

"OK, that'll be fine. What time?"

"I get here crazy early. That way I beat the traffic. What time can you get here?"

Jeez, if I wake up at 4 like I've been doing lately I could be there at 5, but that's probably a bit too early. "8:30?"

"Perfect. Things can get hairy around here after that, if you know what I mean. We can talk before all that gets started. OK?"

"Will do, Ms Petrocelli."

"Toni. In front of the clients, Ms Petrocelli. But you can call me Toni, OK?"

Clients? Is this a law firm? "OK, uh, Toni. No problem."

"Remember how to get here?"

"Oh, sure. Nice drive."

"OK. 8:30 on Monday. See you then, Richard."

He said goodbye and hung up. He flicked on SportsCenter; the stories hadn't changed.

He delivered pizzas all weekend long, with the customary patches of inactivity. He stayed for closing on Sunday, Tony locking the door and closing the shutters for the final time. The older man's face curled up on itself, and he sniffled and snorted, holding back tears.

"*Maron*, I'm gonna fuckin' miss you, Richie," he said, grabbing Richie in a crushing hug. Richie felt something crack.

"Oh God – uh, me too!" he croaked into Tony's biker jacket.

"*Dio te benedica, mi amico*," Tony said, squeezing Richie's face, kissing it on both cheeks. "Don't take no shit off no one, capisce?"

Getting into his car, Richie looked at the three hundreds in his hand. They fit far too easily in his vinyl wallet, and gas money alone would eliminate them in no time.

Richie started to regret agreeing to meet Toni so early Monday morning. He wasn't sure what recreation workers wore to an interview, but he could hear Pat's voice, like a conscience, in his ear: "You gotta go conservative, man. If you show up like a bum you're gonna blow it." When he showered and dressed he looked in the mirror: starched white shirt, tie he'd borrowed from his brother, work pants he hadn't worn since high school. *I look like a Catholic school kid.*

Around 8:15 he pulled into the parking lot. He parked a little closer this time, and remembered Jones's warning about black ice, so he padded carefully in his terribly uncomfortable dress shoes, that were too small for him by that point. As he looked around, he saw through the day care windows. He could spy a young woman happily changing a baby's diaper, and another woman soothing a crying infant on her shoulder. He sighed, gripped the door handle, and went inside.

Behind the security desk, two guards – older men whom he didn't recognize – were laughing heartily.

"Ah, man, you got that right," said the lighter-skinned of the two, holding his glasses in his hand, a salt-and-pepper beard lining his amiable face. He turned when he saw Richie, still chuckling. He said, "May I help you, young man?"

"Good morning, I'm here to see Ms Petrocelli?"

"She know you're coming?"

"Yes. I have an interview."

"Oh, yeah, she said somethin' about that. She just got in, herself. Bad traffic on the Grand Central. Where you comin' from?"

"Yonkers. McLean Avenue. Not that far."

"Ah, you probably had no traffic. Go ahead and sign in, man, I'll let her know." He picked up the phone, said a few words. When he hung up he said, "OK, youngblood, you're up. I'll walk you over. Hey, Marcus, buzz him in?"

Richie went inside and made a left, and the guard met him at the door of the security office. He was still smiling. "My name's Wilson. Milton Wilson. It's Richard, right?"

Richie shook his hand. "That's right. Richard McGinn. Nice to meet you, sir."

"Ah, you don't gotta do that 'sir' stuff. Makes me feel old. You can call me Wilson. Come on, I'll take you inside."

They went down the same corridor as the party, but this time they made a sharp left and entered a suite of offices just across from the room with the phone on the wall. Wilson used his key and pushed through the door. There was a secretary's desk and three doors, but only one was open.

"Ms Petrocelli? I got your young man right here."

From the open door came a short, olive-skinned woman with curly hair, wearing a blazer and business skirt. She walked fast, like she was trying to catch a train.

"Morning, gentlemen," she said on the move. She shook Richie's hand. "Toni Petrocelli."

"Uh, Richard McGinn." He almost said "Richie" by mistake. "Nice to meet you, ma'am."

She smiled. "Respectful. Gotta like that."

"Yeah, me too," said Wilson. "Good luck, son."

"Come on in," Toni said, gesturing him to her office. There was a small table on one side of the room along with some file drawers. The executive desk lay on the other side. There were four wide windows, from which you could see the entrance, the parking lot, and the road outside. You could conceivably see anyone coming for quite some distance.

"Coffee?" she said.

He really did want coffee, but erred on the side of courtesy. "No, thank you."

"So, you come from Yonkers?" she said, pouring herself a cup.

"That's right. McLean Avenue, they call it Woodlawn. South end of town. Do you know it?"

"Nah. Only a little since some of our families come from Yonkers. I live in Flushing. So I get here early to beat the traffic, get some work done."

"Yeah, I can understand that."

She moved to her desk, and gestured for him to sit across from her. He noticed a bunch of knick-knacks on the window sill: a number of tchotchkes from past trips to Eastern getaways like Long Beach Island, Cape May and Myrtle Beach. He noticed a plastic cup, a ballpark souvenir, emblazoned with the words "Greensboro Hornets."

"So, Frances talked you up. Said you were a natural with those kids."

"Well, you know. I was just trying to have fun. I tried to treat it like my days at the community center, like I said on the phone. I wasn't sure what to do at first, but Rachel, Frances and Mr Jones – just about everyone – made me feel at ease. It's some place you have here."

"Not what you were expecting, was it?"

"No, not at all. I thought it'd be a converted hotel or something."

"Yeah, most shelters are, but here in Westchester you have some new construction. That's what this place is. Built in '91."

"Yeah, Rachel filled me in."

"OK. So, what do you know about us?"

He shared the bulk of his conversation with Rachel from the previous week.

"All right, so you got the basics. HSA Greenburgh is basically temporary housing for families with children under 5. No school-aged kids. That was the deal made with the county when it was first built." She rolled her eyes. "The idea was that they didn't want the school system to be overwhelmed, or for our kids to have to enroll, register and then have to leave. I think it's something of a cop-out, and maybe they just didn't want homeless kids in their schools." She took a sip of coffee. "But for better or worse, here it is. We're almost always full. 4 buildings with 12 units, 6 with 10. Mostly young mothers and some dads. A number of them go to our own substance abuse program, some on the outside. Some go to mental health programs, some have jobs, some go to school. We have a housing specialist to help them relocate, three guards on station at a shift, and five caseworkers. One of them speaks Spanish."

"Mr Tajo, right?"

She smiled. "Yeah, you met Tajo. Nice old guy, he's got a good heart. Anyway, as you might have known we're part of an organization known as Housing Solutions America. There are a few sites around New York City, mostly Bronx and Brooklyn, one in Buffalo, one in Philly, and one on Long Island. We're the only one in Westchester. We're planning a few more. Here," she said, handing him some glossy brochures. They showed pictures of families talking to caseworkers or security staff, and toddlers playing with toys. "Read this when you get the chance. I've worked in a few shelters, most of them a lot tougher than this. I got my MSW a while back."

"Social work?"

"Yep. For whatever reason, I always wanted to be a social worker. Way back when I was a little girl, growing up on the Island. What about you?"

"Oh, well, like I said, I have a degree in history from GW, and I've bounced around a little. I just came off a job recently –"

"Frances told me the pizza place closed. Sorry about that."

"Oh, that's OK. It was just an in-between thing, anyway."

"So what do you want to do?"

"Well," not wanting to sound too flighty, "I like working with kids. And I liked working at the community center, at least some of the time, when I was working with people. Didn't get to do it all that often, since they always had me lifting and moving stuff. But I liked the idea of making a difference for people."

She sat back a bit. "Tell me more about that." So Richie gave her a copy of his resume, and talked in more detail about his volunteer work, his internship. She asked a lot about his work on Capitol Hill. They talked a bit about his college experience, too.

"OK," Toni said. "So what do you think about this place?"

"Oh, it's great. Clean, organized, and the people seem happy. Or, at least, calm. It's really nice."

"Could you see yourself here?"

"Well, I guess so. I suppose I could help with your recreation program. Mr Jones mentioned something about that."

Toni blinked. "Wait. That's what you wanna do?"

Richie paused. "Uh, yeah?"

Toni softly laughed, shifted in her chair. "Recreation, huh? I was going to ask you about something else."

"What's that?"

"Well, one of our caseworkers, Ellen, just went on maternity leave. It was kinda sudden; she has to go on bedrest. She'll be out for about six months, maybe more. Company policy is kinda lenient on that, that it's our discretion after six months. I thought maybe you could replace her."

"Wait. Caseworker? Like what Rachel does?"

"And Tajo. That's right. I think you'd be good at it."

"Uh," he stammered. "That's kinda out of left field. I thought I was here for recreation or volunteering or something. But casework, like social work? I don't have any experience with that."

"So what?" Toni said, palms up. "You have more experience than most people in those jobs," she added, a thumb towards the door. "Ask anyone. Ask Rachel what she was doing before she came here. Ask Tajo. Hell, I had a security guard fill one of those roles for a while. He did fine. Nobody goes right from a BSW to this job. Or, at least, not many. As long as you have a brain in your head and you can deal with people and their issues, you'll do great."

"Well, what's involved?"

"It's mainly just monitoring their progress, making sure they stick to a program, find something to do. You do an intake assessment, you help them with benefits, you meet once a week, do a service plan once every two weeks. You inspect their units, you work with daycare and New Futures – that's the substance abuse

78

center downstairs – and you send them to Mr Feldman, our housing manager, to help them find a place, probably Section 8. By the way, Rachel told me you were familiar with those programs from school, and your internship. See? You know more than most starting caseworkers."

"Huh. I don't know. It sounds kinda tough."

"Ahh," Toni scoffed. "Not for you. Sounds like you like helping people, and figuring out ways to do that. Right up your alley, if you ask me."

"Huh," Richie said again. He looked out Toni's side window, watching the snow fall from the branches. He had trouble envisioning it: dressing like this every day, looking across at the neediest of the needy. What right did he have, butting into their business? He was just some dumb kid.

"Come on," Toni said, "I'll take you around."

By then much of the office staff had started to arrive. He met Winnie, the administrative assistant who'd arrived when they were talking. He shook hands with Robert Feldman, the Housing Director, an older man with Coke-bottle glasses and long hair not quite long enough for a ponytail. They entered the door with the phone into the "caseworker suite", as she called it, which was divided into six partitions that resembled cubicles and had a waiting room in the front. Rachel remembered him straightaway, smiling with immaculate white teeth, calling out "Richie! Hi!" while on the phone, gesturing that she had to take it. Tajo walked in and patted him on the back. And he waved at Stephanie, who was in a meeting with a family, or a "client", as Toni again put it.

He started to walk away, but did a double-take. Over his shoulder he caught a glimpse of Stephanie's client. She was at least fifteen years older than any other mom he'd seen in the place. She wore drab clothes, sat deeply slouched in her seat, and seemed to sigh into her sentences. Richie caught a familiar, musty scent of whiskey and cigarettes.

Toni gently took his arm. "Everything OK?"

"Oh! Oh, uh, yeah, sorry, thanks."

They went out the back door of the caseworker suite and ran into Jones, the guard that had helped him with the pizzas. "Hey, back so soon? Welcome," and he extended his hand. "Andre Jones, Director of Security here." They shook hands and he went on his way with a thermos of coffee.

They went down the hall and through the Multi-Purpose Room, as Toni called it, where the party had been the week before. They opened a door and went out to where the residences were. The doors all faced the middle of the facility, much like townhouses or a high-end motel. The wood paneling was impeccable, and the stairs barely creaked. Toni used a key and opened a door to a vacant unit.

It was a lot like a hotel room, a big studio, but with something of a corridor leading to a large bedroom in the back. Except for the bathroom, there were no doors. The appliances looked cheap but at least they looked new. Likewise for the beds (really cots) and the crib: not top quality, but clean and sturdy. There was enough light, even on this gray day, to illuminate the place without electricity.

"We can accommodate a family of five," said Toni. "Maybe six, but only if the kids are crib-sized. The County wants to pack 'em in here. We do inspections every two weeks. The caseworker, that is. You'd check up and make sure it's OK. Not hard to do. Most folks are pretty neat, but sometimes you get a bad one."

They walked back and looked into the daycare center, the went downstairs and talked to Lydia, the director of New Futures, the substance abuse facility. Lydia was a heavy-set woman with a long ponytail, a scar on her cheek and a raspy voice. There were a few groups going on behind closed doors and some counselors meeting with clients.

They went back upstairs and sat at Toni's desk. "So that's it," she said. "That's the place. We'd train you as a caseworker for the time that Ellen's out. Then, who knows? If it goes well, maybe we can find you a place with one of our sites in the city. You get health benefits and vacation time after 6 months – if you wanna stay, that is."

"Wow, I see," Richie said, not sure what to say next.

"So, what do you think?"

Richie got a tingling, weak feeling in his hands and feet when he got nervous. He looked at Toni: she wore lots of makeup, stud earrings. It looked like she dyed her hair, as there were gray streaks here and there. There were wrinkles, but her mannerisms didn't seem all that old. He wondered how long she'd been doing this. *She was built for this kind of work,* he thought.

Was he? Not at all. He'd be a replacement player, an inexperienced pretender who was just holding a spot until the big leaguers came back.

On the other hand, Tony's was closed. Pat might be making less money now. What else could he do?

"OK. I'll do it," he said. "Why not," he added, more a statement than a question.

"Great," Toni said, nodding. "Great. You'll do fine. We'll teach you everything you need to know. Welcome to the team," she enthused, extending her hand across the desk.

He shook it. "Thanks," he said. He smiled and added, "Speaking of team, I see your Greensboro Hornets cup back there."

She turned. "Yeah, I went last year. Took a trip with some friends to Myrtle Beach. Greensboro's a minor league affiliate of the Yankees."

"That's right. Gee, I thought maybe you were a Mets fan, being from Queens and all."

"Oh, no," she said, shaking her head gravely. "No, no. I hate the Mets. I grew up a Yankees fan, saw the Mick play. Loved those guys back in the 70s – Munson, Reggie, Willie, Guidry, Chambliss. Remember that '76 ALCS game?"

"The one where everyone rushed the field?"

"Yeah. I was there."

"No way."

"Yeah. I didn't rush the field or anything. Almost got trampled, though. But I didn't want to get arrested. It was a free-for-all. I mean, I was happy and all, but that was crazy. We high-tailed it right out of there. Did you know Chambliss came out after the crowd dispersed, and made sure he touched home plate?"[8]

"Yeah, that's what I heard. Wow! That's something. Ok, you must really be a fan."

"Yeah, I just hope we have a real season. I don't know if I can watch a bunch of clowns puttin' on the pinstripes, know what I mean?"

"Oh, yeah. We can win this year, I just know it. We have the tools, we just gotta follow up on last year. We gotta get Donnie Baseball in the playoffs."

She smiled. "That's your guy, huh?"

"Donnie and me, we've been through a lot. Waited a long time to get to the promised land. Had it taken away last year. But we're gonna do it this time. Get these scabs outta the way, get the real guys on the field, and get Donnie Baseball in the playoffs. Get him closer to the ring he deserves."

"Oh, a real Yankee fan for once. This is gonna be good. Do you go to the games at all?"

"Sure, whenever I can. This'll help pay for tickets."

"Damn right," she said. "What else is money for?"

Richie said he could start "whenever", but he was taken aback when she suggested Thursday. She explained that Thursday and Friday would probably be used for orientation. "No real work," she said. "We'll use those days just to get you used to the place."

He went home and found himself with nothing to do. He looked in his closet and realized he didn't have enough dress shirts to last him one full week, and the dress code was shirt and tie. Using two denim shirts, he thought, would be a last resort. He'd have to borrow ties from his brother, and accept his playful ridicule.

Around six he heard Pat's voice in the foyer. "Hey, *mameluke!*"

"Yeah, you frickin' *foncoul?*"

"Get your coat. Rory's. My treat."

Their apartment was within stumbling distance of many fine Irish pubs, but none classier than Rory Dolan's. The bars and tables seemed to gleam in soft yellow light, the music lively but subdued, the air lightly dusted with their signature fish and chips. There was always a gathering: a work party, a birthday, a christening. The staff was as friendly as any small-town folk, and the clientele always happy.

It had been the scene of Richie's 21st birthday party, just he and Pat and Marilyn. But once Pat made a loud toast, several patrons and staff joined in the celebration, singing him songs, pounding his head and shoulders. It was his first taste of Jameson's, a taste he would not reacquire for decades. By the end of the evening he didn't mind that a group of happy drunken strangers were calling him "Ricky". He didn't remember, anyway.

They sat at the bar this time, at an undisturbed corner. For a Monday night the place buzzed and hummed with conversation and Irish "hurling" matches on TV.

Pat looked tired. He still wore his business suit, tie loosened, a heavier-than-usual five-o'-clock shadow across his cheeks. Richie noticed that he gulped his first Guinness in seconds.

"So," Pat breathed after another healthy sip of his second. "How'd it go today?"

Richie nodded. "You're looking at the newest caseworker at HSA," he said.

"Holy shit, you gotta be kidding me," Pat said, running his fingers through his hair.

Richie scoffed. "Thanks for the encouragement, ass."

Pat sighed. "I thought you were doing recreation."

"Yeah, me too." He explained what happened that day.

Pat drained his second Guinness. "So, casework? Like social work?"

"Well, kinda. Just helping people get on with their lives. Helping them move back into the community. Stuff like that."

"What are the hours?"

"Nine to five. Just like any other job."

"Didn't you go to a recreation party last week? At night?"

"Yeah, I guess sometimes evenings are required."

"That's a hard job, Richie. Tough, thankless. Are you sure this is for you?"

"No. Do I have a choice?"

"Wears on your patience. I wonder if you have enough."

"Me, too."

"Very frustrating."

"Like getting stiffed? Or delivering pies to some douche of a roommate?"

"You know what I mean. People in those situations are needy, in trouble. They'll do anything to get what they want, maybe even take advantage of you. They'll drive you crazy. You gotta watch your ass, like, all the time."

"Well, I didn't get stabbed at the party, and I didn't get mugged on my way out today. This place, it was amazing. Clean, efficient, inviting. And the people are just... people. People who need some help. And I... I think I wanna be a part of that. I saw it, Pat. In DC, at the food pantry, the community center. I see it at this place. These folks... they're not that different from you and me."

Pat just looked at him, so Richie continued,

"Let me ask you this. What if you got hurt, sick, or downsized? What if your company, God forbid, went bankrupt? Do we have enough in savings? Everything's out in student loans, rent, health insurance, right? So... what would happen?"

Pat rolled his eyes. "OK, Rich, I get it. I don't think that's us, but OK."

Richie frowned. "You don't?"

"No, Richie," Pat said, exasperated, clunking his glass on the table. "I don't think so. I've been at this a long time. Taking care of us for a long time. Longer than you know. And... well... I wouldn't let that happen. Not if I could help it."

Richie went quiet. He could feel his heart pumping in his ears.

"Look, when Dad left, Mom fell apart. You saw it, right? Maybe you were too little. But there were times… times I had to walk over to the Kasinskis – remember them? They lived next door? Well, I sometimes had to ask them for bread, or peanut butter, or pasta. 'Cause we didn't have any, 'cause Mom never went to the store. But I did it. And as soon as I could work – remember? Me, working at the deli? Well, sometimes I used that money for us. Notebooks, bookbags, shoes."

Richie shrunk on his stool a little. "Geez, Pat. I… I never knew."

Pat nodded. "Yeah, I wanted it that way. Look, it wasn't all the time, but sometimes. I'm not trying to brag or anything, or make you feel bad, but whenever Mom fucked up, I was there. There were plenty of times that we were in that… scenario you're talking about. But I was there. Doing what I had to do." He took a sip of Guinness. "So, yeah, you have a point. They're just people, they're poor. Maybe a little like we were. But as long as I was old enough, able? I wouldn't have let anything happen to us. And I *won't* let that happen. I'm not that guy. These folks, sure, they need some help, but do me a favor and don't compare me – us – to them. Understand?"

Richie put his shaking hands on the bar and looked at Pat. In so many memories, it wasn't his mom. It was Pat playing catch with him, taking him trick or treating, or teaching him to keep score at the Yankee games. It was Mom cursing at them for making a mess, throwing a lit cigarette at him for getting detention, or dumping them on River Avenue with a pair of subway tokens.

So it was Pat who'd kept them together. And yes, he wouldn't have let anything happen to them. If he could help it.

"OK, Pat. I know. And I'm grateful." He tried his own Pat-like pause. "But I'm just saying. They're people with problems, who need help. Look, I don't know anything about it. I liked what I saw at this place, liked the people. I don't know if I'll be any good at it. But I'm tired of slinging pizzas, Pat. I don't know if this'll be the thing, but I wanna try. To make a difference."

There was a pause. The bartender brought another pair of Guinness. "On the house, boys," he said.

"Thanks, my friend," Pat said. To Richie he said: "What's the salary?"

Richie told him.

"Christ, Richie, that's slave wages!"

"It's a hell of a lot better than pizza. And I get health insurance, vacation time, if I stick around long enough. And they have other sites, once the maternity leave person comes back. And you know what else?" He took Pat's arm. "For once, I get to contribute."

"I told you, you don't – "

"No, Pat. I – you've been doing this too long. I see you, still brown-baggin' it to work. Watching Marilyn sport you at restaurants. Driving a piece of shit car and sitting in the bleachers. OK, forget that last part, I love the bleachers as much as you."

Pat smiled. "Damn straight."

Richie smiled back. "Yeah. Look, I'm saying, it's my turn. OK, I can't take on everything yet, but with a real job, I can kick in. Take the burden off you for a while. Don't you want that?"

Pat took a deep breath. "I just want the best for you, man."

"I don't need the best, Pat. 'Pretty good' will do just fine."

Pat gripped Richie's shoulder. "Know what Marilyn said? 'Let him try. Let him see.'"

"I knew I liked her. 'Try', yeah, 'try'. Let's see how it goes."

They were silent for a while. They didn't even wince when they saw some guy get clobbered with a hurling stick on TV.

"OK, listen," Pat finally said, still watching TV. "So, if this thing goes through. If Marilyn gets the job."

He paused again. Richie could feel the warmth of his pint glass on his fingers. He tried to block out the childish thoughts in his head: *What about me? What about YOU and me? You promised, you promised to go to all the games with me.*

"I think… I think I'm gonna be, you know. Spending some time down there."

Richie looked at him, wide-eyed. "You mean, like, for good?"

"Oh, no!" Pat said, a little too loudly. "No, no, no. Well, I mean, you know. Marilyn and I, well, we talked about it," and he ran his hand across his face. "She, uh… we've been going out a long time and all…"

Richie didn't say anything. He felt his hands and feet go weak for the second time that day. He pushed whatever anger he felt into his stomach.

"Look, look, look," Pat said, perking up a bit. "I don't know what's gonna happen, I don't even know if she'll get the job. But, hey. You would, too, right? I mean, you'd go visit your girlfriend a few times a month, if she lived out of town, right? Stay over her place? Like I do now, except, well, a little further away. Right?"

Richie smiled in spite of himself. Such an idea was purely theoretical to him. Molly from Boston was the longest relationship he'd had; it had lasted one semester.

Pat swirled his Guinness, looking into the glass. "I don't know. I didn't – I didn't think things would, you know... Move so fast. I feel like you just came home from college. Shit, I feel like you just *left* for college. Now Marilyn, me... talking about the future, you know... And you get this... job and stuff." He rubbed his face with both hands. "But look, I promise I'll talk to you about stuff, OK? I won't leave you in the lurch like Mom did. I won't do anything until you're ready. Understand?"

"Sure, Pat. I understand," he said quietly.

"And hey," Pat continued. "If this thing goes well for you, or you, I don't know, find something else just as steady, like a community center or something... you don't mind kicking in a few bucks toward expenses? You said it yourself. Maybe start with the cable bill?"

"Sure, Pat, glad to... Everything OK at work?"

"Yeah, pretty much. Well, you know, start-ups don't make a lot of money to start with. But in, like, a year, I'll be able to sell some of my stock and you and I – and Marilyn, too – are gonna live like this all the time." He spread his arms wide. "Maybe sit in the box seats one day."

"You make us sit in the box seats, I'll kick your ass."

"Oh, grow up, Richie," Pat said, laughing. "But yeah, we can go to the bleachers for as long as you want."

Which might be only two or three games a year, if you're in DC half the time, Richie thought. He considered the cable bill: it was already bare-bones; the only channel they had to have, of course, was MSG Network.

"Just promise me this, OK? No calling Mom."

Richie looked around in confusion. "Why the hell would I wanna do that?"

"Things might get tough. You don't know. You've been in college; paying these bills ain't easy. But we can do this, OK? No calling Mom."

Richie nodded. "OK, Pat. No calling Mom."

They both sipped the dregs of their Guinness.

"By the way," Richie said. "Toni? My boss? BIG Yankee fan."

"Get out. Really?"

"She was at the Chambliss game. '76."

"Ohhhh, I like her already. You're in good hands, my little bro. Good hands."

Welcome to the Show

Wilson was on the phone when Richie arrived at 8:45 that Thursday. He buzzed him in and waved him through the door. The administrative office door was locked, so he knocked. Winnie walked around her desk and let him in.

"An early bird," she said. "Like Toni. Good for you."

He didn't think fifteen minutes was all that early, but was grateful for the compliment. "Good morning. Winnie, right?"

"Yes. Come on in, Toni's waiting for you, Richard. Go on in."

"Hi Richard," Toni said as he walked into her office, just getting off the phone. She got up and walked over to Richie and shook his hand. "What do you prefer? Richie? Richard? Rich?"

It was something he thought about but never really resolved. "Richie," was a childish nickname, which rhymed with "bitchy" as bullies had often noted. He'd introduced himself at the party as Richie, but maybe they all forgot. Nobody called him "Rich," but maybe it was a good young adulthood name. He felt, after all, like a youngster playing grown up.

"Uh, Rich is fine, I guess, but whatever works."

"You got it, Rich," Toni said. "Come on, let me take you to your desk."

They walked through the copy room, a cramped windowless space with room for maybe two people, which emptied into a waiting area, where families would wait to talk to a caseworker. They

93

then entered the caseworker suite. They got to the last row, and Toni showed him into a partition with a window.

"Here you are," she said. "Ellen's office. She cleared her personal stuff out already. Do what you have to do to feel at home. Have a seat."

He dropped into the office chair, so low to the ground he thought he'd bump his chin on the desk. *Ellen must be a Smurf.* He fiddled with the controls while Toni sat across from him in one of two conference-room-style padded seats, the arms of each a bit frayed. There were some crayon streaks on the wall behind her, one of them a sharp, straight line, perhaps an indication of a parent suddenly learning what her child was doing.

"OK," she said, clasping her hands. "A few ground rules. It's all in the handbook," which she had on her lap, "but let me call some out. First, call the clients by last name. 'Ms Smith'. 'Mr Jones'. Et cetera. First names are too familiar, too much chance for fraternization. You can be friendly, but you're not friends.

"Also, the door. Clients should use the phone on the outside, or they should make an appointment to see you. Don't let clients just walk in on you. Pretty soon you'll be inundated. You'll see clients once per week. You have 21 families on your caseload, I think. Let me show you," and she took out a file with the name "Anisha Barkin" on the tab. "See? You do an intake assessment, where you get a sense of the client and what her needs are." There was a stapled bunch of papers indicating name, addresses, family, reasons for homelessness, any mental health or substance abuse issues reported by the client, any education and job history, and the like. Ellen had excellent handwriting, but in some places the entries looked empty, or she'd just written "NA". "Anisha is pretty straightforward. No substance abuse – her drug screen was fine – no mental health, and she has a high school diploma and a little community college. She's bounced around with her son after a few abusive boyfriends. One of them lived here for a while, then we had to involuntarily discharge him because they were fighting all the time. The little boy is three, and see, he acts out in daycare a lot, probably brought on by the abuse in the home. She's been here three months, and her Section 8 is being processed.

"So," she turned the page, "every two weeks you do a Service Plan. This is where you lay out the plan for addressing each of the client's needs. Everything from housing, to education, substance abuse, mental health, child care, et cetera. You set deadlines, and you make notes each time to show what progress they've made. Anisha is doing OK, but really isn't doing much for herself. No job, no school, doesn't come to workshops. So, she goes off and sees this guy of hers, but that hasn't been working out. So, you see in the Service Plan, under 'Goal', there's a lot about Education or Employment, but under 'Action', it just repeats itself, week after week. Not a big deal, but she can't do nothing while she's here. Read through the files and you'll get a sense of things. Ellen's a very good note-taker; she documents everything pretty well. Document, document, document. Take good notes and you'll be OK, trust me."

She went through a few more housekeeping items, like weekly "team" meetings, the conference rooms, where to get coffee. "Well," she said, "I think that's it. Today is reading day. If a client calls you, you can say, 'I'll get back to you'. Don't be afraid to ask questions.

I'll be around here and there, but Rachel or Tajo or one of the other caseworkers can help you, too. Good?"

Wait, Richie thought. *That's it? No video, no classes?*

"Yeah," he said, smiling insincerely. "Sounds good."

She smiled. "Good luck, Rich. I'll check in around lunchtime." She walked down the hall back to her own office.

Rachel was the first of the coworkers to welcome him. "Hey, Richie!" she said cheerfully. He wondered if the name transition would take hold. "Toni doesn't waste time. Hires smart people. Good for you. Hey, I'm right next door, so just holler if you need anything, OK?" The others came and said hello, also offering help. Darlene was the only caseworker he hadn't met. When she came in she shook with her left as her right was full with a huge coffee thermos, a pair of stylish sunglasses, and an elaborate winter hat.

Richie read through the handbook first. It was mostly policy, not a lot of instruction. There was a lot of warning about fraternizing with clients, but not much on, "You fix a client's homelessness by doing *this*". It only took about an hour and a half. Then he tackled the case files. He kept reading and rereading words that made him twitch: "mental health", "sexual abuse", "narcotics".

He was on his fifth case file, looking through the notes written in shorthand ("Cl said unable to reg for classes at WCC, has prior loan issue, wl try again next wk") when the phone rang.

"Hello – ah, Mr McGinn's office?" as he was instructed to say.

"Yeah, uh…" said a young voice. "Is Ms Ellen there?" (Ellen had an unpronounceable last name, hence she was known as Ms Ellen.)

"Uh, no, Ms, er, Ellen, uh, doesn't work – I mean, she's on maternity leave."

"Oh. You a caseworker?"

"Yes. I'm -" he said clearing his throat, "Mr McGinn."

"Oh, yeah, how you doin'? Listen, I was gonna ask Ms Ellen about a weekend pass. I got a birthday party for my kids to go to in Mt. Vernon. Could I get that from you?"

He'd seen something about this in the handbook and in one of the files. Families had to get permission for overnight or weekend visits. But he had no clue how to go about getting one.

"OK, uh, what's your name?"

"Lily."

"OK, Lily, what's your last name?"

"Newsome."

He looked on his list of clients. "B212, right?"

"Yeah, that's right! You got it right, hon!"

You need some acting lessons, Lily, Richie thought. *I can kiss ass better than that.*

"Well, I don't know the particulars, it's my first day and all, so let me get back to you, all right?"

"OK, hon, but I gotta make plans, so you find out and I'll come get it later, OK?"

"OK, I'll get back to you."

"OK, bye! Thanks! Nice talking to you!"

Richie went into the handbook and looked for procedures for asking for a weekend pass and found a blank form in Ellen's desk, but wasn't sure how to start other than getting a signature from Toni. Then he looked in Lily's file: she'd been in residence since just after Christmas, had one son, Treyvon, age 3, and had come from another shelter in Mt. Vernon, transferred for reasons unknown. There were approved weekend pass forms for just about every weekend, but they abruptly stopped three weeks prior. In the notes there was a history of her not coming back until Monday or Tuesday, and she'd been warned that if it kept up, she'd just be discharged since it was clear she had somewhere else to stay. In January she got into a shoving match with another resident right at the entrance over a shared cab from Pathmark. He got that antsy feeling in his hands and feet again.

Then a tallish woman with lots of makeup poked her head into his office. "Hello?" she asked.

"Hi," he said, picking his head up from the file.

"I'm Debbie Thompson. I'm the psychologist here."

"Oh, hello," Richie said, standing up and shaking her hand. "Nice to meet you. I'm Rich McGinn." He had to remember to say "Rich". He motioned for her to sit.

"This is your first day?"

"Yes."

"Oh, good!" she said brightly. "You'll love it here. It's a great place to work."

"Yep. So far, so good."

"Reading files, right? Have you come to Akira Kensington yet?"

"Not yet."

"Well. I work with her once per week, but she's also mandated by Child Protective Services to attend an outpatient mental health clinic in Tarrytown. She has to arrange for transportation but they give her extra cash in her benefits to take a cab. She's very disturbed, almost to the point of removing her son. Nice girl, but very disturbed. Schizophrenia. When she doesn't take her meds she hears voices, and those voices are never telling her anything good."

Richie tried his best poker face. He became aware of his hands on the desk and wondered if they looked like he was nervous about what he was hearing.

She said, "I know. Sounds like a lot. But she's a sweetheart, really. You'll see. Very gentle, soft-spoken. Here's the thing. She hasn't been going to program. Apparently she wakes up late, doesn't answer the phone, just doesn't bother. I talk to her, she's sorry, she promises to do better, but then she does it again." She raised her palms. "So, I thought you might be able to talk to her. Remind her that going to program is part of being at HSA Greenburgh, that it's in her Service Plan. You don't have to threaten to throw her out or anything, but a little, I don't know, push to get her moving. Because nothing else seems to be working. If she keeps this up, like I said, she could lose her son."

Why isn't there a pizza around to deliver when you need one? What have I gotten myself into?

"OK, uh," he stammered, "well, uh, what, uh, what do people, caseworkers do in this case?"

"All you need to do is ask her why she didn't go to program," Debbie said. "Just like you're checking in on any of your cases. Following up on the Service Plan. That's it. So, asking why she's not going to program is part of that. But take a look at her file. She's been here five months, maybe more, I think. She's getting to the end of her time, and Toni's been lenient with her, but it's going to be time to move out soon. But she hasn't made any progress, and her CPS worker is watching her closely. She needs to hear from her caseworker to remind her this is required of her in order to stay here."

It didn't sound like a conversation he wanted to have. Nothing in the handbook about that. "OK, right," he said. "So, I guess I, uh, call her, tell her to come in, go through the Service Plan, that kinda thing?"

"Yes, but try to be delicate about it."

"OK, no problem," he said as confidently as possible.

Debbie smiled. "Not an easy request on your first day, right?"

Richie smiled back. He liked her, even though she could see right through him to the parking lot outside. "It's OK. I'm sure I can handle it. I mean, what's the worst that can happen?"

"Right! All you're doing is checking in. Maybe tomorrow?"

Not next week, or next month? He said, "OK, tomorrow. What time?"

"Probably afternoon. That gives her time to have gone to program that day. You can check in with them during the day. The phone number is in her file. You can talk to anyone there, just tell them you're the caseworker."

"Got it."

"So, it's Rich?"

"Yep. That's me. Debbie, right? And in front of the clients, Dr Thompson?"

"That's right," she said. "A little formal, but formal works around here. Thanks again, Rich. Good luck, and welcome."

"Thanks," he said with a weak smile. Two problems to face before lunch.

Then, Rachel appeared, clipboard in hand. "Knock, knock," she said, rapping on the outside wall of his partition. She was wearing a blue-green ski jacket that matched her eyes and knit gloves. "Hey, how's it going?"

"Hi Rachel. Just fine, just fine, I guess."

"I heard you have a couple of things going on already. It's not even lunchtime."

"Yeah, nothing I can't handle," he lied.

"Whatcha got?" she said.

He explained the situations with Lily and Akira. He talked about what he'd read about Anisha and about some of the files he'd read that morning. Rachel explained what she knew about each of them, which seemed like a lot considering they weren't on her caseload. Each time she seemed to mention that the kids are "so cute, SO cute", She moved a chair alongside his desk and went through a few Service Plans. He felt his stomach flutter.

"You're lucky because Ellen takes good notes and makes good Service Plans," she said. "I inherited Mr Leonard's cases when I first came, and," she shook her head, "uh-uh. I had to go searching around for notes, and I had to kinda start all their Service Plans over from scratch." She showed him how to be as "measurable" as he could be with his Goals, and when she noted his blank look, she explained that they should be things that can be counted, or things that were concrete, not just "Go to program", but maybe "Attend X program five days", so that even the client would know when it was done.

"Don't expect miracles, though, OK? Tough to get people motivated. As great as this place is, you get a lot of hanging around, not doing what they should be doing. It's rare to find someone self-driven, disciplined and such. But hey – I could point out the same from some of my college friends. The difference is, they all had trust funds, so when they pulled straight C's or flunked out altogether, they still had a place to go to."

He thought about Trevor. He'd have as soon seen a unicorn as Trevor in this place. "That's true," he said.

"Hey, I'm going out on some inspections. Wanna come?"

He was dreading this. Who was he to judge people's homes? If it weren't for Marilyn, their place might be crawling with roaches. "Sure," he said.

"OK. Let me just tell Security where we're headed. Grab your coat. Toni'll get you a pass key later, but in the meantime we'll use mine."

RICHIE THE CASEWORKER Christopher Febles

She got on the phone and talked to Wilson. Then they went out the back door of the caseworkers' office and through the Multi-Purpose Room. It was brisk outside, but not quite freezing. They went to the first building on their left, known as "A" building; the rest fell alphabetically. A few doors down on the ground floor, Rachel rapped loudly. "Hello? Alicia?" she said. "Alicia attends New Futures downstairs, so she's probably not here. You should always knock and call out loud, though. Especially as a man." She knocked and called again, and when she got no response, she put her key in the lock and turned it.

"Hello?" she called, waited a bit, and walked in. "It's cold, but whenever possible, leave the door open. And make sure Security knows where you're going. Don't be in a unit with a family by yourself."

The place was near-immaculate. The floors sparkled. There were place settings with plates and silverware on the table. The bathroom had been scrubbed, and the towels were hung or folded. The beds were cornered like a Marine's. Even the toys were arranged neatly against the wall.

"Wow," Richie said. "This looks better than mine. Although that's easy to do."

She grinned. "Yeah, this is always a quick one. Alicia's doing great. She's been here twice, you know. First time she was real messed up, wouldn't stop using. She started going to NA – Narcotics Anonymous – and it really took. Of course, even then she was always neat."

"Well, good for her," Richie said, puzzled by someone who was both an addict and a neat-freak.

"OK, so you see, I just put 'E' for excellent for everything. Believe it or not, most residents are like this. Maybe not this neat, but most are really passable. What you're looking for is anything that would be unhealthy for kids. Dirty floors, spoiled food, unwashed sheets, stuff like that."

They went through five units in total. Only one resident was home, a mom with a newborn and a one-year old toddler. She was boiling milk for the baby and letting the toddler watch Barney on TV. Her eyes drooped and she slouched in her chair.

On the whole, only one apartment had dirty dishes in the sink and an unmade bed, but none reached the 'F' for 'Fail' level.

As they walked back from H building, Rachel said, "So that's pretty much it. Every two weeks, four units. I stagger mine with Service Plans, you know, one, one week, one the next. Put it in your notes, too, even if it's just 'Did home inspection; all excellent'. Use your judgment on the neatness. Like I said, just worry about things that could affect the kids."

"Heeey, Ms Worsham," said a voice belonging to an older mom on an upper balcony, baby in her hands.

"Heeey, Ms Marvin," Rachel said back, just as playfully.

"Who's your friend?"

"This 'friend' is Mr McGinn, our new caseworker. YOUR new caseworker, in fact." She said it in a stern but calm voice that clearly meant business. He thought, *Where's that in the handbook?*

"Oh, OK," Ms Marvin said with a wry grin. He could have sworn he saw her look him up and down, even in his puffy winter coat he'd owned since high school. "How you doin'?"

"Just fine, thanks," he said. "Nice to meet you, Ms Marvin."

"I guess I'll be seein' you soon."

"I guess so," he said with a weak smile.

"OK, Ms Marvin, see you soon," Rachel said.

"OK, bye, y'all! Can't wait to sit down with you!" Ms Marvin said, waving slyly.

"Oh, boy," Rachel said when they were out of earshot. "She's a character, that Eleena Marvin. She's been in the system a long time. She has a sixteen-year old, and that baby you saw right there. In and out of treatment. Does the right thing for a while, but then, well, things happen. I think her Section 8's gonna come through soon. As you can see, she lays it on pretty thick. She's very nice, but don't let her sway you."

"OK," Richie said. "I'll keep my eyes open."

They once again entered the caseworkers' office. "What are you doing for lunch?" she asked him.

"Oh, I don't know. I wasn't sure what, uh, everyone does here, so…"

"Well, as you've seen, there's not much around, so you gotta drive a bit. Frank's Deli is in that strip mall where Staples is. That's pretty good. Pizza and Chinese are up on 100. Pizza is 'eh'. Not as good as the stuff you brought last week."

"Yeah. That seems like a million years ago," he permitted himself to say.

She smiled and touched him on the arm, just as she had at the Valentine's party. "Glad it worked out. And don't worry about those situations with Akira and Lily. You'll handle it just fine."

"Man, I hope so."

She looked around. "I gotta make a few calls. But you should go out for lunch. Try Frank's, unreal sandwiches. See you later!" She walked back to her office.

Richie went back to his desk and fretted some more about what he was reading. Two consecutive women had been clearly beaten by boyfriends. One woman, an infrequent and unwilling participant at New Futures meetings, was a mother for the second time at age 17, and Child Protective Services (CPS) had been called by Ellen for what seemed like neglect, but the case was unfounded. One Service Plan included visits to a parole officer.

Toni stopped in. "Did you go to lunch yet?"

He looked at the clock, showing 1:45. "Oh. I just thought I should get through these files. I guess I lost track of time."

She checked her watch. "Go on and get lunch. When you're done, come on by. I should be ready to talk by then."

He found Frank's, ordered a turkey sandwich and brought it back with him to the lunchroom. Seated there were Jones, Wilson and Dara. They were laughing loudly, drinking coffee when he walked in. He hesitated.

"Hey, don't mind us, come on in – Rich, right?" asked Wilson.

"Oh, snap," said Jones. "You got the caseworker job? Well, hot damn, man, good for you. Welcome to the team."

"Toni don't mess around," Dara said. "She filled that job quick. Good for you. How's it going so far?"

"OK, I guess," he said, unwrapping his sandwich, noticing he was the only one eating. "You don't mind, do you?"

"See, man?" said Jones. "Polite. Nice to see that young people have manners." He looked sideways at Dara.

"Don't start, Jones," Dara said, smiling. "I have manners, too. And see? You're embarrassing Rich here."

He chuckled a bit, something he wasn't sure he'd do on his first day. "No, it's OK. I have manners everywhere except the Yankee game."

"Aww, man!" Wilson said, throwing his hands up. "That's your team? Them front-runners, man?"

"Front-runners?" Richie said. "We got the rug pulled out from under us last year. Shoulda won the whole thing, and poof! Lockout."

"Got a favorite player?"

"Donnie Baseball. Got a good reason, too." And he told them his 1982 encounter with greatness.

"Ha, ha, that's great, that's great," Wilson said. "Yeah, he does it right. Puts his head down, does his job. Had a good year, too, hope he can do it again. Tell you, though. Watch out for Cleveland. Got some lineup. That's a hell of a ballclub."

107

"Yeah, they're not bad, but they don't have the pitching. Yanks are gonna be right there."

"Hey, Rich," Jones said. "You seem like a nice guy. I'm gonna let you in on a little secret. You like basketball?"

Richie died a little every October. No other sport held his attention like baseball. But he said, "Sure."

Wilson rubbed his forehead. Jones said, "New Jersey Nets." He paused, looked Rich in the eye. "1996 NBA Champions."

Richie looked at Wilson, who was shaking his head and smiling. Then he said, "The Nets?"

Jones nodded.

"The *New Jersey* Nets?"

Jones nodded again.

Richie looked around. "They still have a team?"

Wilson and Dara laughed out loud.

"No, really," Richie said, half-serious. "Dr J unretired?"

Amidst Wilson and Dara's laughter, Jones nodded more vigorously. "OK, OK, you all got jokes, right? You laughin' now, wait till next year. That O'Bannon kid has the goods. Kenny Anderson's the best point guard in the NBA. And that frontcourt! Coleman, PJ Brown, and the kid from Africa, Dare? Unstoppable. See what they did to Charlotte last week? More of that next year, you watch," he said, pointing a finger at everyone in the room.

"Ok, Jones," Wilson said. "Keep dreaming. On that note, let's let this man eat his lunch in peace." He tapped Richie on the shoulder and winked. "Have a good day, Richard."

Dara dumped her coffee cup and rinsed it, then excused herself with Jones. Jones shook his finger again. "Remember. Nets. '96."

"I'll tell the Canyon of Heroes to get ready," he said, smiling.

"Ah, see, man," Jones said, laughing and waving his hand in front of him as he closed the door.

He ate fast, went back to his desk for some reason, then went to Toni's office.

"That you, Rich?" she said. "Come on in, have a seat."

"Thanks," he said, and sat down across from her. She was writing a few things down on her blotter. She stopped the moment he sat and smirked a little.

"Long first day?" she asked.

"Oh, you know, just getting the lay of the land. Getting to know the cases I have. I still have a few more to read."

"Talk to anyone yet?"

He described his phone call with Lily, his talk with Debbie, his inspection visits, and the files he'd read. She listened intently, and he was hoping she'd take care of all the issues. Instead, she said, "So, what questions do you have?"

"All of them," he said, not realizing he said it out loud.

Toni laughed. "Yeah, it can feel like that. Look…" She leaned back in her chair. "Casework is really more about coordinating, not treatment. Let the professionals – the therapists and housing staff and benefits people – come up with that. And the clients? Remember:

THEY have to do the actual work. Like Akira: you can't force her to go to program, right?"

He paused. "That's true."

"Right. Here's what you can do: meet with her, ask her what happened. Explain to her that it's part of her service plan, and that that's part of her agreement to stay here and continue to get services. And that that's part of a bigger plan to get her living independently, with her kid, with CPS out of her hair, and more stable mentally. Should she fail on that notion, she could lose it all. You have to strike a balance, though, between being too punitive, too tough, and too lenient. See, you don't want to alienate her, because you need to have a good working relationship to continue helping her. And you have to remind her that she has to own it. That's the nature of casework: getting clients to see that the service plan is really created by them and for them, meant to help themselves in the long term. Sure, there are things we can do to help, like make calls and referrals, and encourage, certainly, but ultimately you're trying to set it up so they can be independent."

He just nodded. *Maybe Pat was right*, he thought. Maybe it was all too much for him, too stressful.

"I know," she said, leaning forward a bit. "Maybe not what you signed up for. Most people come into casework thinking, 'Set up benefits, give people housing, get them food resources and such'. Yeah, there's an element of that. But we're trying to deal with the recidivism. We don't want them having to keep coming back into the system. So, for better or worse, we try to teach them living skills so they can hang onto their homes. Can't say it works all the time, I'll admit. But that's the plan."

"I think I get it," Richie said. *I just wonder what my breaking point will be*, he thought.

"Now," she said, "what else you got today?"

They chatted for a while about his cases. She said absolutely not to Lily's request, given her history, and told him to say a stern "no" with backup from the Executive Director, although in future conversations he shouldn't feel the need to rely on such backup. As for Eleena, she laughed. "Oh, that's just the way she is. She tries to sweet-talk men who come her way. I don't even think it's something she does consciously. Just hold firm and don't talk to them that way. Don't tell clients about where you live, your relationships or such – or if you do, just be careful, and don't fraternize. Kind of like an ump, right?"

"Oh, you mean, umps don't make friends with players, because if they have to make a tough call a friendship could affect their judgment."

"Yeah, like that. You don't want to have to make a tough decision, and someone says, 'Hey, I thought we were cool'. So try to play it straight."

He wished he'd brought his notepad so he could write this down.

"Oh, write notes for everything. Document, document, document. Every encounter with a client."

What the hell, how does she do that?

"You want to know what you've done with a client, what you've promised and such. Ellen was pretty good, although she wrote shorthand. Better if you can spell things out, mainly for you. Like

111

today, write out your encounters with your clients. Even if you have zero success with a client, make sure you document. I'll take a look from time to time."

"Got it," he said. "I'll do my best."

"We'll send you to the next orientation, at our Morris site on…" she looked at her calendar, "March 2nd. But feel free to ask any caseworker for help. You already know Tajo and Rachel pretty well. If I'm not around, just ask one of them."

"Yeah, I already did," he said. "They know their stuff."

She grinned. "Remember when you said, 'I have no experience'? Ask them all what they did before they got here. You'll see what I mean, and why I said it. For now, make that call to Lily, and read the rest of your files today. Any trouble, let me know. Any questions?"

"Yeah," he said. "Are there, like, any books I can read? You know, about being a caseworker."

"Yeah, the handbook. Did you start that?"

"Oh, yeah, great. But, you know, any, you know… are there, like, textbooks? Paperbacks? Something?"

She grinned. "Yeah, there should a caseworker's manual, right? Well, the real manual is up here," she said, pointing to her head. "You need common sense, organizational skill, and nerves of steel. Empathy's great, but empathy's not enough. Knowledge is good, but knowledge doesn't confront, doesn't meet clients where they're at."

Who do I have to kill to get that stuff? he thought.

"Tell you what," she said. "Let me take a look. Maybe I have some old, first-year MSW books. Like, 'Human Behavior in the Social Environment', stuff like that. But I'm telling you: you'll learn by doing." She looked at the clock. "Almost quitting time. So, do a little more reading, maybe talk to Lily. Take notes. Otherwise, have a good night and see you tomorrow."

He went back to his file and read a little about Eleena Marvin. He saw Rachel pass by his office on the way to the back door.

"Oh, excuse me, Rachel?" he said.

She stopped in her tracks, doubled back to poke her head in his office, smiling.

"So, to call a resident, I don't have to dial 9, or the front desk or anything?" he asked, kind of knowing the answer already.

"Yep," she said brightly. "For an outside line it's 9, otherwise, the numbers of the units are right there in the handbook. Calling my friend Ms Marvin?"

"No, Lily, you know, that situation with the weekend pass."

"Talk to Toni about it?"

He described the conversation he'd had earlier.

She leaned on the partition between their offices. "Yeah, that sounds about right. Need me to hang around for it?"

He'd have loved that, but didn't think it would make a good first impression. "No, I think I got it. Just say no, explain about her history, that 'we' think it's not a good idea and not approved. That sound right?"

She nodded. "Yep. I'd do the same thing. If she gives you crap, don't let it get to you. And she will give you crap. Don't take it personally, and don't cave. You can mention Toni but don't make a habit of it."

"OK," he said, glad she couldn't see his sweaty palms.

"Hey," she said, grinning. "Don't sweat it. We're all making this up as we go."

It was the best thing he'd heard all day. He grinned back. "Thanks," he said, making sure it didn't sound sarcastic.

After she left, he picked up the phone and dialed Lily's number. "Who dis?" she answered.

"Hello, it's Mr McGinn, your caseworker," he said, the words sounding strange in his voice.

She brightened in her feigned way. "Oh, hey!" she said. "What's up?"

What are we, drinking buddies? He made a point to sound a bit more distant: "So, about your weekend pass request?"

"Yeah?"

"I think – I think we'll have to deny it for now."

"Huh?"

"Yes," he said, avoiding the word "yeah", "Given your recent history with passes, we –"

"Aw, man, but you new! Can't you give me a slide this time?"

"Sorry, Ms Newsome, but I've been reading in your file that you failed to come back –"

"Yeah, but that ain't gonna happen this time. I got appointments to make, I gotta see a man about housing and stuff, and I gotta do it this weekend else I'm gonna lose the place."

"I thought you said it was a birthday party."

"Yeah, uh, that too."

"OK, well," Richie stammered, "was this in your service plan? Did you let Ms Ellen know about this?"

"No, cuz it just happened."

"Can you give me some detail?"

"No, just, you know, I gotta see this guy who lives with my boyfriend – I mean, like, not with him, not like that, but you know, they in the same building, somethin' like that, and he said he got a place I could look at, you know, and I'm gonna lose it if I don't see."

It could be bogus, or maybe not. He paused for too long. What to do? So, in as professional a voice as he could muster, he said:

"Sorry, but that you'd have to take up with Mr Feldman. If he can verify this chance at housing, maybe we can grant you a pass. But you have a number of incidents in here –"

"Come on, man, why you gotta be like this? I got stuff to do this weekend, I can't be cooped up here."

Then something came to him. *Oooh, I got you now!* "Where's this housing situation?"

"I don't know, Gramatan Avenue or something. Mt. Vernon."

"Buses are running this weekend, right? Can't you just travel down there and come back?"

"Yeah, but, you know, I gotta – ah shit, man, this is some bullshit, man, I got shit to do and shit –" and she hung up.

He took a deep breath, which helped dissipate the fluttering in his hands and feet. He heard Rachel's voice over the partition: "Hey, Rich?" He noted the name; perhaps Toni had spoken to her.

"Yes?"

"Nice one. How'd she react?"

"Lots of curse words."

"'Shit', right? She says 'shit' a lot."

He got startled. He didn't think you could talk like that in here. "Uh, yeah."

"That means you did it right. Don't forget to write it up, OK?"

Follow Through

Richie briefed with Toni the next morning, getting her attention at 9:20. They went through a few more cases and procedures. She said there was a new family on the way, and he would do the intake assessment if she came, and that one of the other caseworkers would help him. "You have Rachel and Stephanie near you; ask one of them if you have a question. But feel free to use your judgment on things," Toni said. Again he thought, *where's the manual on that?*

He came to the file for Maria Vazquez, and saw a note from Ellen indicating a problem with her benefits. Maria had been in the country for twelve years, had graduated high school in the US, but was still undocumented. He called her, and she said: "Yeah, they think my kids are undocumented. They're not, they were born here. Ms Ellen said she was gonna call before they left."

"OK, I'll give a call to DSS," he said, and hung up. He started flipping through Ellen's Rolodex.

"Hey, Rich?" Rachel said from over the partition.

"Yes?" he said, talking to his file cabinet.

"Need a hand with benefits?"

"Sure."

"OK, come on over. Bring her file."

He pulled Maria's file and walked around the corner. He sat in a chair across from her desk, like a client, and handed her the file.

"Hmm, let's see," she said, reading the file. She flipped a few pages and said, "Mmph. She has Ms DeVore. Not good. She's a piece of work." She looked at her watch. "Call her now, she'll be out to lunch." It was 11:00. She handed the file back. "OK. If you call the supervisor, a Mrs Bennett – and make sure you call her 'Mrs Bennett', because the women's lib movement passed her right on by – she can help you. Probably get you right in line with the problem. Don't expect miracles. But hey, you're just looking into things, right? Worth a shot. You can give her my name if you want."

"Wow," he said. "That's great info, thanks a lot."

"Things going OK so far?"

"Yeah, just fine. Some crazy stories here."

"Yeah, you bet. Not for the faint of heart. Just hang in there. Scheduled for orientation yet?"

"Yeah, March 2nd."

She looked around, then bent over her desk. "Total waste of time, if you ask me," she whispered. "I got more out of just what you're doing: trial by fire, getting supervised by Toni."

"Ha! I'll keep that in mind. Lectures have never been my strong point."

"It'll be fine. Eat some donuts, meet some nice people. But believe me, you'll learn by doing. Good luck with that stuff, and don't be afraid to ask for help."

"Thanks," he said, standing up. Before he walked out, he said, "Can I ask you something? A little personal?"

"Sure."

"What'd you do before working here?"

She smiled, showing off her teeth. Must have had braces, he thought. "That's not too personal at all. Bartending. A joint over on the Upper East Side, McMurphy's? Ever been there?"

"Can't say I have."

"Well," she said, again looking around and whispering, "you're not a yuppie douchebag hitting on all the waitresses."

He laughed. He got a little angry at the vision of Trevor hitting on her. "I've never made enough money to be a yuppie or a douchebag."

"I guess that's why you fit in so well here. Anyway, I used to volunteer at Blythedale Children's Hospital in the summers when I was in college. That's where I met Dara, and when she got a job here, she told me about this place. I still can't believe I got the job. Let me guess, Toni tell you to ask?"

"Yep. I think she was trying to make a point."

"Yeah, point being, nobody has experience doing this?"

"Mm-hmm. Unless slinging pizzas is experience."

"You used to deliver pizzas? Musta been a long time ago." She smirked.

He smirked back. "Ages," he said.

"She's right, you know. Ask around. I think Tajo's story is the best."

"I will. Thanks again. Sorry to be a bother."

She scoffed. "Oh, you're not a bother. This is how we all learned. Anytime." And she smiled again.

Ms DeVore was indeed out for lunch. The operator said the lunch period was from 11 to 1. He then asked for Mrs Bennett, who explained that next time he'd really have to go to Ms DeVore, but she looked into Maria's case. There was an error, because Maria's kids were incorrectly listed as undocumented. She told Richie that she'd have Ms DeVore enter the kids in correctly, but she'd have to get fax copies of their birth certificates just to be sure. He almost ran to the fax machine once he saw copies of birth certificates in the file, copied by the ever-prescient Ms Ellen. He called and told Maria the news, who said, "Awesome. Thanks a bunch!" He asked her if she had enough food for the weekend, and she said she did, and that this was as good a time as any to potty train, so extra diapers weren't necessary.

Just before lunch he updated a service plan for a two-person household, Tanya and Alfie Franklin. They were slightly older than him, both high-school grads, the dad trained as a mechanic. They'd been at HSA Greenburgh for about three weeks, so their second service plan was overdue. Tanya was exceptionally pregnant, and Alfie was finding no luck looking for work. Nothing for Tanya to do since she was on bedrest, and Alfie had yet to do his substance abuse and educational screenings. So Richie made the calls right there, Alfie nodding agreeably. Richie wished Tanya good luck with the baby, and she lumbered out of the office, Alfie helping her along.

During whatever down time he had that day, he asked each of the other caseworkers the question he had asked Rachel:

RICHIE THE CASEWORKER Christopher Febles

Darlene: "I was a dancer when I graduated high school. Then, after I blew out my knee, I worked at my church rectory for eleven years. My mom told me to get my college degree, so I did, in social work. Found this job on the bulletin board at Lehman College."

Tajo: "I sold used cars on Boston Post Road in the Bronx. Coulda sworn I sold one to Stephanie. In my free time I worked at the Boys and Girls Club. They told me I could work at Morris, so I sent in my résumé. I moved to Mt. Kisco three years ago, so when a job opened here, I took it."

Stephanie: "You know that Caldor on Fordham Road? The one that used to be Alexander's? Back in the seventies and early eighties I did retail. Got to be a manager before I had three boys. But when my husband lost his job at Ciba-Geigy, I had to go back to work. I threw my résumé up here, saying, 'Hey, I raised three boys, give me some credit'. I guess Toni did, 'cause here I am. By the way, I'm pretty sure Tajo sold me a Chevelle once. Ran great."

Rich was pretty full from the massive tuna sandwich he'd brought for lunch, and a little sleepy. He was making phone calls to families to set up meeting times when Toni walked in. "OK, Rich. Looks like that family just came in. Just a mom and a baby, 4 months old, coming from Peekskill. Angela LeFleur; she'll be in C206. You have a good feel for things, after reading all the files, looking at the intake forms?"

"Yeah, I think so," he said.

"Great. Just keep your eyes and ears open. Observe without looking like you're observing. If you notice anything – mannerisms, language, habits, things like that – write them down in your notes a little afterwards. This should take you... about an hour, maybe a bit more. Rachel?"

She popped her head into his office. "I can listen in, Rich. Don't be afraid to ask questions. Most likely this family needs things like diapers and some weekend food, so come find me at the end and we'll go to the pantry together, OK?"

"Sure, I think I got it," he said. "Where is she?"

"Right in the waiting area, out front," Toni said. He thought he'd have a few moments to compose himself, but that wasn't going to happen. "Come on," she said.

They walked down the hall, Toni with her midtown-Manhattan style of determined walking, Richie in her wake. There, sitting in one of the plastic waiting chairs was a middle-aged woman with a baby sleeping soundly in a second-hand stroller, the bottom stuffed with plastic bags. She wore an old tracksuit with a faded stain on the thighs. Her face seemed permanently set to "scowl". He again caught that familiar scent: cigarettes, spilled drinks... He had to catch his breath, and put his hands in his pockets.

"Ms LeFleur, this is Mr McGinn, your caseworker. He's going to do your intake, ask you a few questions, get you started here."

"Am I gonna get diapers for the baby?" she spat.

"Absolutely," Toni said. "Work with Mr McGinn – he'll take care of it."

"Nice to meet you," Richie said. Angela shook his hand awkwardly, fingers only, like a princess. "Right this way."

She grumbled and stood, pushing the stroller ahead of her so quickly she nearly took out his toes. He stood aside and escorted her into his office, where she sat with a huff.

"OK, so how are you doing today?" He regretted it the moment he said it. Obviously she was not doing so hot.

"Fine," she said. "Except I don't have enough diapers to last the weekend, and they haven't set up my benefits yet. They said I could get some here."

"Yes, we have a pantry. We'll get that set up in no time. Just gotta go through some questions, OK? Get you settled here."

"Fine," she sighed. "Let's get this over with."

He went over a brief intro to HSA Greenburgh, trying not to read directly from the rules and regs. He felt like a dumb teenager giving safety instructions on a roller coaster. Angela just looked annoyed.

The intake form itself was pretty easy. Name, last address, family members, extended family. She kept her arms tightly folded and gave terse answers to questions that needed more nuance. He had a hard time believing, for example, that she'd never worked before, owing to the care she gave her mother. She didn't want to talk about why she'd become homeless, insisting it wasn't anyone's business.

"Why do you need to know how far I went in school?" she demanded.

"Uh, it's part of the intake," he stammered. "See, you know, we're going to come up with a program to help –"

"Look, I'm here just temporarily. I just need a place to live. I need some time to find my own place. I don't need any programs. I don't need any of the stuff you do here."

123

"Well, it's, uh, part of what we do here, part of living here. It's the rules, you know, right here, where you'll need to sign," and he showed her the Resident Agreement. "See, by living here you agree to get assessed for each of our programs: health, substance abuse, education –"

"So I have to do a drug screen? Meet with one of those counselors, hang around with a bunch of addicts?" she barked.

"No, no – you know, you only go to program if your screen comes back with something, if they feel like you –"

"I ain't going near no druggies, no way. No way am I doing that. Why do I have to do all this, just to get Section 8?"

"Well, like I said, it's part of living here. Part of the rules. If you don't, uh, comply, it's, uh, hard to, uh, get you to stay here."

"I don't want no one taking my blood. I don't want no one asking me a bunch of questions. I'm not a druggie, I'm not crazy, and I don't wanna be around all these... these ghetto people, mugging each other and stuff, playing their rap music all hours. My baby, Jonathan..." She paused, then started to cry. She folded her arms, and her lip quivered.

Very carefully, Richie checked the drawers of his desk. In the last one he found two napkins emblazoned with the McDonald's logo, and he silently thanked Ms Ellen for her pregnancy cravings. Without a word he handed Angela the napkins. She dabbed her eyes in a futile battle against the tears. *She must have been holding this in all week,* he thought. He heard a soft coo from the stroller, and she rushed to pick up the baby and cradle him.

"Well, someone's up from his nap," Richie said, feeling grateful to the baby.

"Yeah," Angela said. "He had his formula just before coming here. He always falls asleep after that."

Jonathan had the biggest eyes he'd ever seen, shining in cobalt blue. He was a little on the skinny side but very alert, staring intently at Richie.

"Wow, look at those eyes," Richie said.

"Yeah," Angela said. "He's a beautiful boy. He's the only thing I've got now. Everything else sucks."

Rachel appeared at his office entrance, a welcome sight. "Mr McGinn? I need to make a pantry run. Do you need anything?"

"Oh, yes. Ms Worsham, this is Ms LeFleur. I think she's in need of diapers, right? Size...?"

"Three," she said.

"You got it," Rachel said. "What about food? Got enough for the weekend?"

"I got nothin'. I got one can of formula, that's it. I don't care about me, I'll eat bread and water. It's formula I need, Similac with Iron."

"I'll see what we have. Allergic to anything? Canned goods ok?"

"I'll eat anything. I'm gonna miss not havin' a McDonald's around, but what're you gonna do. I haven't been eating that much anyway."

"OK. I'll pick a few things. Be right back."

125

"Oh, Ms Worsham?" Richie called. Rachel stopped short, looking back into the office. "Is there any need to, you know, finish the intake today? I mean, we can take care of all the appointments and stuff Monday, right?" To Angela he said, "I'm kinda new here, still getting to know the rules myself."

"Sure!" Rachel said brightly. "You won't get any appointments with anyone today, anyway. You can do it Monday. This mom must be tired. Give her a break. You need to do all the signatures and an initial service plan, but other than that, you're good."

"OK, sounds like a plan. Sound good to you?" he asked Angela, who just nodded as she held her baby.

"Great, I'll be right back," Rachel said, and she left out the back door.

"OK," Richie said. "This won't take long. Few forms to sign and off you go."

Angela signed things a little less hurriedly than before.

She asked, "Can I call my caseworker at DSS? I wanna know when my benefits and my food stamps will kick in. And when do I get to meet the housing guy?"

Richie explained that Mr Feldman would be in touch with her Monday. "You can give it the old try at DSS," he said, "but 3:30 on Friday? I don't know."

"You got that right, mister," she said, rolling her eyes. "Those jerks probably went home already. So lazy." He turned his phone in her direction, and she dialed. "Is Ms DeVore there?... No?... She coming back?... Figures. Can you look into my case? My name is

Angela LeFleur... L-E-F-L... No, not 's', 'f'... 'LEFLEUR'. Uh-huh." She waited and sighed. "Oh, screw that," she said after a moment, and just hung up.

Mom used to say that, Richie thought.

"No luck?"

"Whaddya expect?" she said. "They're not working."

Rachel came back with a large pack of size 3 Huggies. "That ought to hold him until about Monday," she said. "Mr McGinn, could you give me a hand with the food?"

"Yeah, sure. Excuse me," he said to Angela, grateful for the break.

He held the door for Rachel on their way outside. The cold air felt wonderfully refreshing. He took a long, deep breath. It seemed to cool off his lungs and settle his arms.

Rachel said, "How you doing there, Rich?"

"Man," he said, running his fingers through his hair, "this is something else."

"You know," she said, slowing a bit as they walked up the path, "one of my first weeks here, I met this client. Diane. She looked exactly like a babysitter I had when I was a kid, one that turned out to be crazy, you know, like hospitalized. Diane, well... boy, did she have problems. Alcohol, anger issues – coulda sworn she beat those kids. I got so wrapped up, spent more time with her than all my other clients. Toni? She told me to stop. I don't know. Couldn't do it. Too personal. I was almost glad when she just disappeared. It was hurting too much."

127

Richie just listened, nodding. He was a little surprised at hearing such a personal story. "Gee, I'm sorry about that."

"Well, you know. I guess the moral to the story is, you're gonna hear a lot of stories like that. Lots of people you think you know, ones you really wanna help. But you can't save 'em all."

He nodded some more. "Thanks. I'll do my best."

Rachel opened a storeroom door in "A" building, revealing shelves with non-perishables and a whole trove of diapers. "Here's where you come when you need food and sundries for a new family. Don't use it for regular families unless there's an emergency. They'll use up the supplies in no time, and these are all donations. So just be careful."

They filled a few plastic shopping bags with canned vegetables, boxes of pasta and jars of sauce, and plenty of oatmeal. They found two cans of Similac; Rachel imagined that would hold her for a while. They threw in a package of Oreos.

As they walked back, Rachel said, "Not bad, by the way. Normally you'd try to get all those appointments scheduled today, not Monday. But she needs some time to soften up, so I get it. Do it Monday. Also, don't be afraid to probe a bit. Ask more questions, take your time. Don't be afraid of silences. She's a tough cookie, but maybe along the line she'll give you a little more. Be ready."

She went down the hall to use the bathroom. Richie shimmied through the back door with bags in hand, found his office, placed the bags on the floor near Angela, and said, "OK, here we are. Will you be able to carry all this?"

She had Jonathan nestled comfortably on her shoulder. "Yeah," she said, and loaded everything in the spot where the baby would have rested. "Now we'll try and sleep in that freezing cold place up there. Hope it's not too noisy." She started moving down the hallway.

"All right, so before you go," he said, moving behind his desk, "let's plan on meeting at, uh, 11:00 am on Monday. OK? Just come downstairs and use the phone out front, and I'll come get you."

"Can you call me at 10:30? Jonathan is all over the place with sleeping these days. Not sure I'll be awake."

"Sure," he said, then checked himself. "Well, I have a few appointments. Do you have an alarm clock?"

"Do I have an alarm clock," she said derisively. "No."

"All right, well, let me see what I can do," he said, a little testily.

"Great. See you Monday," she grumbled with her back to him, already moving down the hall.

"OK," Richie said to her back. He hadn't sat for long before Jones called.

"Hey, Ri– uh, Mr McGinn," he said, "I have Ms Kensington here, and I remember you said you wanted to see her, right?"

He'd forgotten all about the conversation he was supposed to have, the one where he was supposed to admonish a person he'd yet to meet. It was 3:45 PM.

"That's right," he said, trying to keep his voice from cracking. "Thanks for remembering, Jones. Please send her in."

He walked to the suite door so she wouldn't have to use the phone. There he met a dark-skinned, heavyset woman with unkempt hair, a man's coat and a wrinkled T-shirt. Any mother would have urged her to button her coat. Her jeans looked very much unwashed.

"Ms Kensington? Come on in," he said, mustering a crooked smile.

"Hi…" she said with a dreamy, low voice.

They went back to his office. She sat very much on the edge of her seat.

"So," he said, "I'm Mr McGinn – Rich McGinn – your new caseworker. I'm taking over for Ms Ellen until she comes back from maternity leave, OK?"

"OK, nice to meet you," she said softly, with a smile.

"So, how have you been?" he asked.

"OK. How are you?"

No client had asked him that yet. "Oh, just fine. Getting to know the place. You have a son, right? Two years old?"

"Yes."

"What's his name again? I forget."

"Giuseppe."

"Oh, good. He likes day care?"

"Mm-hmm."

He knew he was skirting the issue. So he just went ahead and asked.

"So, how was program today?"

"Huh?"

"How was program? You know, the one you attend every day? What's it called again?"

"Oh. Well, I had things to do. I had to, uh, meet with DSS. Stuff for my benefits."

"Couldn't you have called them instead?"

"Well, no. It had to be in person." She folded her arms like a pre-teen.

"Did you go to program Wednesday?"

"Wednesday?"

"Right, Wednesday."

"I don't remember."

"Well, I talked to Dr Thompson. She said you hadn't been to program Wednesday, and that you've not been going regularly. Is that true?"

"Look, I don't like the place, OK?" Now she really sounded like a pre-teen. "Bunch of stupid meetings and whatever. They're always just checking my meds, making sure I'm taking them. It's just stupid. Why should I?"

"Because it's in your service plan," he said. He hated the tone of his voice: directive, sharp. He really needed practice at this. "Which means it's required of you in order to stay here. And because it's required by your CPS worker. You need to do it if you want to maintain custody over your son."

Again, it was a mistake the moment he said it. She snapped. "Nobody gonna take my son! I'm doing my best! Why is everyone all over my case?"

"OK, Akira," he said, "just calm down…"

"'Calm down?'" she yelled. Tears were forming in her eyes. "Why can't I get a break? Why do I have to do all these things? Why me? Why?" and she slapped the wall next to her.

"OK," he said in a low voice, in an attempt to be soothing, "sorry –"

"I just been doin' my best. I just get tired sometimes. Sometimes I don't wanna go."

"Yeah, I understand," he said. It was a new record: he made'd two people cry in the same day. "Is there something you wanna do instead?"

She scoffed, not looking at him. Then she just walked out.

He took a deep breath. He reclined in his chair a bit and rubbed his eyes.

"Hey," said Rachel, now standing at his office opening. "You OK?"

"Oh, yeah," he said, sitting up straight, wondering if she'd seen him. "She was just upset about, you know, going to program."

"She'll be fine," she said. "She doesn't mean anything by it, if that makes any sense. She's been through a lot, and she has lots of issues. Talk to Debbie about it, a little more in depth."

"Sure," he said. "I mean, she seems nice. I'm sure it's just her, uh, issues coming through. I hope she's taking her meds."

132

"Ehh," Rachel said. "You never know. I've had clients like her. They can't work, can't concentrate long enough to stay in school, and don't want to go to program. Tough. The good thing is that, yeah, Akira's very sweet. Doesn't make it easier, though."

Richie exhaled. "I got a lot to learn here."

She shrugged. "Like I said, we're all making it up as we go. You'll get it."

"What did I do wrong?"

"Not a thing. Well, pretty soon you'll learn about tone, about how to confront a client. That was fine, though, you being here for what, 24 hours? You did what you had to do. It's OK. One thing: next time you should talk to her about storming off like that."

"Hmm," Richie said.

"Well," Rachel said, "you've had an interesting start to things. Just make sure you do your case notes before you leave, OK?"

It was 4:25 PM, and he still had to debrief with Toni at the end of the day, as she'd requested. "I gotta go see Toni," he said, rising.

"Cool," Rachel said. "She'll give you some good advice. Good luck."

"Oh, and Rachel? Thanks for your help. I have no idea what I'm doing. But you – and everyone, you know – you've been real helpful."

She smiled. "No problem, Rich." And she walked back to her office.

He remembered to bring a note pad this time, and went through the copy room to the admin office. He waved to Winnie, who was on the phone. She smiled and waved her hand, motioning to go on in to Toni's office.

"Hey, Rich," she said, walking over to the conference table. "How'd it go today? I heard you had a busy one."

"You could say that," he said, "but it was no big deal."

"It's OK, Rich," she said, smiling. "You've had some initiation, buddy. Though, all in a day's work, as they say. Let's talk."

He recounted the reading he'd done in the morning, the encounter with Maria, the intake with Angela, and the run-in with Akira.

"She's a disturbed lady, that Akira," Toni said. "We took her in as a favor to the court, or really to her psychologist – not Debbie, but the one at her program. See, they don't really want to separate her from her kids. No court really wants to do that unless the kid is really being abused, and I mean like being beaten right in front of a cop. We'll talk about CPS at some point, when to call in a report, and you'll go to a training. But everyone wants to see her get straight and just take care of her kid. Don't expect her to work, go to school, any of that. Her job is to stay in program."

"Is she really that bad?"

"I know. She's sweet, a very nice person. When she's on. When she's off… well, there's no telling. She's not the violent sort, but those voices… they never say anything good. All negative, all, 'you're no good,' stuff like that. Makes a person like her want to just stay inside, or just wander off, seeing friends, looking for a boyfriend or

RICHIE THE CASEWORKER Christopher Febles

something. Not sure that's for her, but we know she avoids program because they make her confront things she doesn't want to confront. The meds make the voices go away, but it also makes the person feel, I don't know, less complete."

"Hmm," he murmured.

"'Hmm?'" she said. "What's that mean, 'hmm'?"

He scoffed. "Man, people around here sure are direct."

"Get used to it, pal," she said, pointing a pen at him. "I got no time for BS. So, 'hmm'?"

"I don't know. Sure seems like a lot."

She looked at him. "How'd it go with Angela?"

"Fine, I guess. Did the intake, though she didn't wanna say much. Pretty defiant, like she's too good for the place. Softened a little when we got her diapers and stuff. She'll be kinda tough."

She nodded. "You know, Rich, a little advice? Keep track of your feelings, OK?"

"What do you mean?"

"I mean, these folks, these stories, they're gonna trigger things in you. They'll do things that seem cruel, self-destructive, stuff like that. I know they say, 'don't take it personal,' but I don't know about that. Just... well, find someone to talk to about this stuff."

"Yeah, OK. I will."

She paused and sat back. "Hell of a day, huh?"

"Yeah, you could say that. Always like this?"

"Uh-huh. What, you were expecting a country club?"

"Well, kinda looks like it, right?"

"OK, well," she said. "Then, why stick around?"

"Geez, Toni."

"What?"

"Direct."

"Works better that way, kid, so like I said, get used to it," she said, grinning. "Well?"

He paused. "How direct can I be?"

"Oh, I love it. So polite. Shoot."

He cleared his throat. "Well, for one thing, I need a job, I need the money. I don't ever wanna be a pizza guy again, so this is a step-up. Also, the setting is beautiful. And I like the people I work with here."

"Nothing wrong with any of that. And the work?"

He paused. "It scares me."

She nodded. "Mm-hmm. Tough choice, Rich. Work with cool people in a cool place where you make a salary, but the work is rough. Challenging. What do you wanna do?"

"Do I have to make that decision now?"

"No!" she said, sitting forward. "No, not at all! You have a built-in trial period! I mean, you don't wanna quit now, do you?"

"No."

"OK, then," she said, cycling her hands. "You got six months. Let's see how it goes. If it doesn't work out, we'll shake hands when

Ellen comes back. In the meantime, learn. Ask. Maybe you actually end up liking this business, find it's not so scary. OK?"

"OK, Toni. I'll do my best."

"Listen," Toni said, "you're one of the smart ones. You don't have to come up with any magic solutions. Keep your eyes and ears open, watch your coworkers. And don't let those tough days, tough clients, get you down. After a while you'll get some confidence. OK?"

"Thanks," he said. "This helps a lot," although he wasn't sure it did. He was awfully tired. It was 4:50.

"OK, good first week. Or good 48 hours, I should say. You fit in nicely here. The guards and the caseworkers seem to like you. Just don't let Wilson know you're a Yankee fan."

"Too late for that."

She laughed. "He's an old Brooklyn Dodgers fan. He's a retired cop, just like most of our guards, grew up in Brownsville. Saw Jackie Robinson a few times. So he hung onto the Mets when they came to town in '62. But mostly, he just loves the game. Jones is more of a basketball guy."

"Yeah, he told me about his prediction."

"Ha! You don't believe that, do you?"

"The Nets have about as much chance as Mr Ed winning the Triple Crown."

She laughed out loud. "That's good. You should tell him that."

"Mmm, I think I want those guys on my side a little more often."

"OK," she said, gathering some papers. "Listen, why don't you just jot some notes down for yourself, and finish the formal case notes on Monday? It's late on a Friday, time to go home."

"Ah, well, I think I'll try to write something now. By Monday I'll forget."

"Ok, but not too late, understand? Don't need you burning out this early."

"Thanks, Toni. And thanks again for the opportunity." He extended his hand.

"My pleasure," she said, shaking his hand. "Have a good weekend."

Richie went back to his desk. He made some copies of a blank case notes sheet and sat down to work. He looked at the clock and decided to leave at 5:30. Staying late on a Friday might be good for visuals. Everyone came by to say goodbye.

"Trial by fire, young man," said Tajo. "That's how it goes. Keep up the good work."

"Don't forget to document," said Darlene. "So important. Don't stay too late, but make sure you write things down, especially about that new lady."

"Good to have you aboard, Rich," said Stephanie. "Hope you like it here."

"Hey, neighbor," said Rachel. "Plans for the weekend?" asked Rachel, again wrapped in her ski jacket.

"Sleep 'til noon and make a huge omelette, read a book or something. But mainly, sleep."

She laughed. "Sounds good."

"How about you?"

"Meeting up for drinks with some friends."

"McMurphy's? Get some nostalgia?"

She laughed. "Only if I'm nostalgic for getting my ass pinched."

"Men are such pigs," he said.

"I know, right? No, a place in Tarrytown. Kinda close to home."

"Where's that?"

"Ossining. You?"

"Yonkers, Woodlawn."

"Rory Dolan's is near there, right?"

"Yeah, you know it?"

"Geez, who doesn't know Rory Dolan's? Hey, lucky you. Well, enjoy that omelette."

"Have a nice weekend. Oh, and thanks again for your help. I don't feel so lost anymore."

She smiled again, full teeth. "Good to have you here, Rich," she said. "See you Monday." And she left, leaving the entire office to him.

He was writing for Akira but got distracted by Ellen's prior notes. There was a copy of a CPS report submitted earlier in the year. It indicated potential neglect after not showing up to pick up her son from day care until 8 PM. At that point he'd been left with a shelter resident willing to babysit him. A CPS worker was "monitoring" her. He rubbed his forehead again.

It was 5:30. He had more to do, but not enough energy to do it, and the forest started to go dark, making the place seem a little more daunting. He put the files back, made a note on his blotter to finish notes for Angela and Maria, and got his coat.

"You all set, young man?" said Jones as he exited. "Had a good day?"

"Yeah. Busy, but good."

"Ain't nothing like the precinct, but yeah, always something goin' on here. You do OK?"

"I don't know. I guess. I'm still learning."

"You'll get it, youngblood. Hey - Nets playin' the Cavs, man. You watch, they're gonna put up triple-digits on those fools."

"So that means they'll have 500, 600 people in the stands?"

He laughed out loud. "Oh, you got jokes. You got jokes, young man. Just wait for the Yankee season, man. You may have to get out there and pitch."

"I wouldn't do that to my team," Richie said. "Hope the Nets get one this weekend."

Jones winked. "Take care, youngblood."

He got to his car and let out a huge sigh. The steam fogged up his windshield. His lower back felt tight, his shoulders weak. He thought about Toni's advice to check his feelings. He'd have loved to talk to Pat about them. But he was going out for drinks with Marilyn.

Spring Training

The orientation on March 2 really was a waste of time.

Richie drove to the site, located just off Claremont Park in the Bronx. Had there been a game that night, he'd have been able to walk to the Stadium, though that wasn't advised. It really did look like a homeless shelter: six stories, the balconies already chipping paint, and there were bars on the windows to the outside. There was playground equipment on the inside, but it looked worn and uninviting. At least he got out at 3:30, and when he called to ask Toni if she wanted him to come into work, she said, "What are you, nuts? Go home. We'll be fine without you."

He thought he was ready to hear all the stories during his first few weeks. But he felt his hands and feet tingle several times a day. A woman described sleeping with her kids under the Triboro Bridge for a week. A man said he'd been in prison three times for armed robbery and he was only twenty-nine. A mom who had diligently attended college classes suddenly quit the whole thing and moved to Pittsburgh with the same man who'd broken her jaw.

He did another intake with an older white couple and their two small, mousy, girls. The father was thin as a rail and hollow-eyed, and when Richie spoke to him his knee bobbed frantically. In the first week he was AWOL four times. He missed two appointments with New Futures, and when Toni called the man into her own office with Richie present, she insisted he walk him downstairs to Lydia. Later, Lydia called Richie and said, "This guy's an active user. I don't even have to look at the screen, he's strung out. Won't be surprised if he left today to go score." Sure enough, the man disappeared that night and never returned. The mother lasted a week before she, too, never returned from an overnight visit, with nothing left in the unit except the same garbage bag of clothing with which they'd arrived.

He wrote down items on a Service Plan, clients signed it, and he wrote about it in his notes. Then they never did any of it. He told the same woman to go to New Futures for three weeks straight, when she finally said, "I don't know why you even asking. I ain't doin' that shit."

He reported this in a "team meeting", a weekly meeting where everyone, from across departments, talked about different situations with clients. Toni said, "Just keep at it, Rich, and document it. She doesn't do it, we kick her out."

One of his clients got into a loud shouting match with another woman right in the caseworker suite, standing up and walking into the hall just as he was writing up her service plan, pointing in her face and explaining that she would be happy to kick her ass in Tarrytown. Richie was taller than either of them, so he stood between them, arms outstretched. He almost took a troll doll in the eye before Wilson arrived to settle things down.

He watched Rachel, half his size, confront clients about their inactivity, their behavior, even their drug use, and elicit real progress. He sat in on a meeting in which Tajo was able to convince a client to check himself into a 28-day rehab program. None of his clients did that. He was always on the lookout for some book, some manual to tell him what to do. But Toni, who'd occasionally plop herself down in his office, assured him: "This is how it goes, Rich. Clients are gonna screw up. Just make sure you write it down."

He'd drive home from work, envisioning his college roommates, golfing with Congressmen or traveling to Paris on business. *What am I doing here?* he'd ask himself.

But a modest success was Akira Kensington. She'd apologized for her outburst and looked better: more rested, cleaner clothes. During her first service plan meeting, Richie played trucks with Giuseppe for twenty minutes. In the weeks that followed, he just stopped talking about program, but he did call to check her attendance, and it was perfect. When he heard that, he told her and said he was proud of her. That made her blush. Then, she asked a question that permanently got her on his good side:

"I see all your Yankee stuff in your office. What's the big deal with this team? Why does everyone love them?"

The answer took half an hour. He went all the way back to the Highlanders, then went through the Murderer's Row era, the DiMaggio years, the Mantle years, the "Bronx Zoo" years and, of course, the life and times of Donnie Baseball. Akira was rapt.

"Oh, so that's why!" she said. He let her keep a number of scorecard pencils she noticed on his desk, looking reverently at the words "New York Yankees" emblazoned on the side.

"Hey, Rich," he heard Rachel say across the partition when Akira had left. "What are you, George Steinbrenner or something?"

"Hey, now," he said. "That ain't cool."

"No, I mean, you know everything there is to know about the Yankees."

"It's kinda my thing," he said. "I've been going to the Stadium since I was a little kid."

"Oh, so *that's* why you got the job," she said. "Toni. Favoritism. That's messed up." He could hear her giggle.

Despite the hard knocks, it was a great atmosphere. He looked forward to cramming into a small spot in the lunchroom, where he was always welcome, always included. He listened to a long story from Tajo about how he played ball with a milk carton for a glove in his home country. He playfully told Stephanie and Darlene that he didn't need – or want – to hear the plot of "Steel Magnolias". And all voices went silent when Wilson asked him to share his Donnie Baseball encounter.

He had an embarrassing moment when he wanted to ask a question about benefits, and Rachel wasn't in her office. He went by Tajo's office, poked his head in and saw not Tajo, but a mother with a preschool kid at her breast.

"Oh, shit!" he said, not realizing he'd cursed.

"Oh, disculplame, senor!" the woman said in Spanish.

"Oh, hey, Rich. What you need?"

"Uh, well, I, uh, just had a question," he said, eyes darting to his office.

Tajo followed his eyes. He pulled Richie aside. "Hey, man. It's OK. A lot of moms, especially a lot of moms from Latino households I know, they breast-feed the kids much later than American moms. And Hector there? He looks big, but he's not even three yet."

"Oh. OK. New thing for me," he said.

Tajo smiled. "No problem, man. Now, what you need?" And he answered his question in the aisle.

But it was always Rachel who was the most helpful. They developed a habit of just talking across the partition. He'd say, "Rachel? Where do I find referral forms for Debbie?" And she'd say, "Page 210, handbook." Or, "Rachel? Can I just send someone to the health clinic here?" And she'd say, "Sure, but remember the schedule. Only here Monday, Wednesday, Thursday." Or sometimes she'd say, "Hang on, I'll be right there," and she'd appear in his office, pulling up a chair alongside him.

"Sorry to keep bothering you," he'd say.

She'd touch his forearm and say, "Hey, you're learning. It's OK," and smile at him. She never refused any of his requests.

Inspections went better than he expected. Some were neater than any hotel he ever visited, and almost all were passable, no reproach required. But the unit belonging to Maritza Martinez, an obese woman with two very dirty toddlers, however, was deemed a hazard. He'd met her during a service plan meeting, and though she fell behind on most items, including a plan to take the GED exam and two appointments for Section 8, she was polite and agreeable. He'd done the inspection the same day, and she was far less compliant, yelling at him that he should have called first, that it wasn't fair, and that she was going to get him fired. Richie felt his stomach churn at being berated, and did his best to ignore the abuse, going about his task robotically. Dirty dishes were piled in the sink, the garbage was overflowing with dirty diapers, there was an overturned bowl of cereal in the bed, and his shoes stuck to the floor. There were cardboard boxes containing hoarded clothing, DJ equipment and a stripper pole obstructing the path to the bedroom. The stench of spoiled milk stung his nose. After as strong a warning as Richie could muster to a person who had at least eighty pounds on him, two weeks later nothing had improved, and there appeared to be stacks of sequined clothing to go with the pole.

"This lady needs to be discharged," Jones said in a team meeting where she was discussed.

Instantly the thought of packing up a resident's belongings, of maybe getting punched in the face for delivering the news, entered his mind.

"Rich," Toni said. "What do you got?"

"Uh, well… She, uh, there's a long history there… I saw the unit and, well, like Jones said, it's pretty bad."

"How long she been here?"

"Eight months."

"Eight months? She done Section 8?"

"Uh, sorta. She kinda missed the meetings."

Toni leaned forward a bit. She looked annoyed. "Wait. Eight months and she missed Section 8 meetings?" She paused.

"Uh, right," Richie said.

"She followed through on anything?"

"Well, uh, she, uh… did her assessments. Got her benefits together." He went silent. The eyes on the room just looked at him.

Toni spread her hands in impatience. "And?"

He scrambled to look at his notes. The ruffling was the only sound in the room. "Uh, well. I guess, she hasn't, uh, followed through."

She nodded, staring at him. "Yeah, it's time. Rich, let's meet to talk about the papers. This'd be your first, right?"

During his supervision time Toni suspected Maritza was sabotaging efforts to get her moved out. "You looked at this?" she asked him, again with a surprising air of impatience. "Look at Ellen's notes. Eight months she's been warned about that unit. Look, there's a letter here, she got a formal warning from me, four months ago. We agreed, another set of poor inspections could lead to discharge. She's had a ton of bad inspections since then. She shoulda been out of here months ago."

She looked through the file. "Hey, Rich. Where are your case notes?"

Richie's heart went into his throat. He'd been so overwhelmed that he hadn't written anything for Maritza yet.

Toni slapped the file on the desk when he admitted it. She sighed. "OK. You're new, so it's OK. But this isn't acceptable, Rich. You gotta keep good notes. You gotta document. There's gotta be a trail, a story, of what's been happening. Otherwise, we have nothing to stand on. Maritza could say none of that happened, and it might be true. Take your notes, Rich. It's more important than you think."

Richie gulped. He felt his hands unclasp. "Sorry, Toni. I'll, uh, I'll be better about that."

She sighed. "S' OK, Rich. You're learning. Now let's show you how to fill out these discharge papers."

She told him to have a draft by day's end, and to ask Rachel for help if he needed it.

"Ooh," Rachel said when he asked her. "Tough task. And you've only been here a month." She told him to write it up and she'd review. He brought it to her later and she said, "Good. Specific. Hey, you write pretty well, like Ellen."

"Thanks," he said, breathing it more than saying it.

"You OK?"

"Yeah, yeah. You know. Tough day."

"She was kinda rough on you back there, right?"

He just nodded.

"Mm," she murmured. "Yeah, I don't know. I love Toni, but hell. When a client messes up, it's like it's *your* fault. She hammers you like YOU did something wrong. We've had our shouting matches, lemme tell you. Try not to take it personal. She kinda, well... doesn't like, I don't know... Delays? Not following protocol? I don't know. But you know, she's good, really good. Try to be on point in all those meetings. Then you can kinda stick it in her face, like, 'See? I know what I'm doing, so up yours.'"

"I probably shouldn't say that."

"You? You're a Yankee fan. You could probably stab her and get away with it."

He grinned. "Thanks again, Rachel."

She winked. "No problem, neighbor."

The actual discharge, a day later, was a nerve-wracking affair. He read out the discharge papers word for word, not making eye contact. There was a voice in his head he couldn't shake: *I can't believe you're gonna kick someone out of a homeless shelter. Don't you feel like a scumbag?*

Maritza was non-plussed. "Whatever," she said, storming out after the evidence was provided.

"Not bad," Toni said in supervision. "Although you probably feel pretty low right now."

"Bulls-eye," he said.

"But what's the alternative?"

"You're right. She hasn't done anything here, she sabotaged her Section 8 appointment, and the unit's been filthy for eight months. Having a lousy attitude doesn't help."

She nodded. "Yup. You got it. Hey, Rich, we did the right thing. This happens once in a while. Just remember that we're here to help, but when someone doesn't want the help, well, this is not the place for them. Doesn't feel good, but we gotta do it. Right?"

She was always right, but it didn't make him feel better. When it was over he sat in the lunchroom, staring at the wall, hardly touching his lukewarm lasagna.

On a Friday afternoon in late March, Richie called Lydia at New Futures. Angela LeFleur's substance abuse screen had come back: negative. He remembered how she smelled when she arrived and was surprised by the result.

"Nope, she was clean, Rich," Lydia said. "Yeah, she drinks on the weekend, but I don't know. I didn't get the sense it was ever out of control. Never, like, passed out drunk. Mighta been that her mom was the drunk. And man, is she protective of that kid. Can't imagine she'd do anything to hurt that kid."

He hung up, mulling it over. Angela, in her meetings with him, was still kind of resentful, but she was at least compliant. She took her educational assessment, which showed her reading at an 8th grade level. She eagerly met with Rob, appearing at his office thirty minutes early. She called Richie often, sometimes just to see if he could help with her benefits or if he'd heard about any secondhand clothes for Jonathan. "Probably just needs someone to talk to," Toni observed.

He was scrambling to finish case notes for this and six other encounters, one a domestic dispute that resulted in a frying pan stuck in the drywall, when the phone rang. "Rich McGinn," he answered.

"Yes," said a theatrically serious voice. "I'd like to speak to Mr Jass, first name, Hugh, please?"

"I'm sorry, who?" he said. He heard snickering on the line.

"Jass. Hugh."

"Uh, what? Who is this?"

The person on the line burst out laughing. "Hey, man, how's it going?"

"Jesus, you're immature," Richie said to his brother. "That what you do in your fancy office all day?"

"Only to my little brother. Oh, I mean, Caseworker or something."

"That's Mister Caseworker to you, damn it. What's up?"

"How are all your crazy-ass clients?"

"Don't be a dick – ah, jerk."

"What are you doing later? Wanna go to Rory's?"

Marilyn was at a conference, so Pat was free for the first Friday in several months. "Sure. I'm there."

"Great. I got a few things to do here to finish up. Meet at home? Will you have to stay late?"

"Yeah, but it's OK. I got a lot of writing to catch up on."

"*I got a lot of writing to catch up on*," Pat mocked. "OK, social worker, see you later."

"I'm just a caseworker. The social work thing, that's a little more complicated."

"Sure, sure, I get it. See you later."

He worked through some case notes, watching the clock. Rachel dropped by, holding a SUNY New Paltz sweatshirt in her hand, just after 5.

"Hey, you're still here," she said. "Great. We're all gonna head out for some drinks at a place in Elmsford. Cactus Jack's, kind of a Tex-Mex place. Like 6, 6:30. Wanna come?"

He froze. How did social work-types socialize? What did they drink? Did they get wild, totally smashed? Then he remembered: "Well, I was meeting up with my brother later. We were gonna go to Rory's."

"Oh, you have a brother? What's he do?"

"He's a CEO at some Internet company. Not a yuppie douche, exactly."

RICHIE THE CASEWORKER Christopher Febles

"Ha! If he's related to you, that's impossible. Hey, maybe you could bring him! We're going to a bar, too."

"Huh. OK, lemme see. I'll try to get him on the phone, if he hasn't left yet."

"Cool. We'll have a good time. Know where it is?"

He did, as there was a taco joint nearby that he'd visited a few times. He felt good having made no promises.

"OK," she said. "I gotta run home first, so I'll see you there, I hope. Talk your brother into it, OK?"

He waited until the suite door closed, so as not to seem so eager. Then he called Pat's job.

"What's up, man, you OK?"

"Oh, yeah, yeah, just great. Hey, listen. My, uh, coworkers, well, they're getting together at this Tex-Mex place near work –"

"Holy crap, meet your coworkers? Hell yeah!"

"Seriously?"

"Yeah, would I pass up on a chance to learn from other people what a psycho you are? No way."

"Really?"

"Yeah, really. Sounds great."

"Don't make fun of 'em, though."

"What? Why would I do that?"

"You know, social work-types."

"I hang out with you, don't I?"

152

Richie picked up Pat at a nearby Metro-North station. They pulled into the dark parking lot of Cactus Jack's, a dangerous left on a busy Route 9A, which still had a few tractor trailers pulling through. The place was like a rip-off Chili's with a few ounces more class. It was clean enough and lacked the corporately-produced decorations of the chain restaurants popping up all over America. It promoted heavy drinks involving "bombs", "bowls", or even "snooters" of various alcohol. There were plenty of dinner tables free, but most patrons were enjoying the remainder of Happy Hour around the bar. Countless varieties of tequila lined the walls. ESPN and various sports networks were on all the TVs.

"You're driving, right?" Pat asked, looking at a menu.

"Sure," Richie replied. "Just don't puke in the Escort."

"What are you talking about? With you driving it, now it smells like dogshit."

There was no mistaking his coworkers. He could see the six-foot three Jones from across the restaurant, laughing loudly as Toni held court. Wilson was cradling a whiskey sour at one of the raised tables, smiling as usual. Darlene, Rachel and Stephanie were chatting as the tall Rob, holding a stein of amber beer, looked on. Sipping what looked like a white wine was Frances.

Before he could wave, someone grabbed him by the shoulder and shook him violently. "My man, Richie!" yelled Tajo. By hearing himself called "Richie," he felt like his cover had been blown. "How you doin'?"

"Hey, Tajo."

"You made it! We sitting right over there."

"Doesn't look like anybody's sitting over there."

Tajo laughed loudly. "Ah, you got a sense of humor, man. You gotta have a sense of humor for this job. Good for you. Who this?" he asked, pointing to Pat.

"I'm his big brother, Pat," said Pat, giving him a handshake.

"Oh, snap! Look at that. You got a brother! Now I see who got the good looks."

"And the brains," Pat interjected.

Tajo laughed again. "Come on, young bros. Have a drink."

They followed Tajo over to the tables. "Hey, look who I found!" he said. A loud cheer went up as if he'd been away for months, not minutes.

Richie looked around playfully. "Did the mayor just walk in here?" he said.

"Glad you made it," Toni said, toasting him with what looked like a rum and Coke. "Hey, get this man a drink," she gestured toward the bar.

"Oh, just a Coke for me. I'm driving."

"Good man," Jones said. "Remind to think of you when we have the Christmas party."

"Who's this, Rich?" Toni said, pointing with her drink.

"Pat McGinn, the smart brother," Pat said, shaking hands.

She looked back at them both. "Huh, I see the resemblance. What're you drinking, Pat? Driving, like him?"

"He lost Rock, Paper, Scissors again, so I'm drinking for two. What you got there? Rum and Coke? I'll have that."

"Good man," she said. To Richie she said, "He's a Yankee fan, too?"

"He better be, or I'll kick his ass," Richie said.

"You dream of kicking my ass, you better wake up and apologize, kid bro."

There were laughs all around. He heard Tajo say, "Sounds like my brother."

"Ah, I'm just playing with him," Pat said, putting his arm around him. "I couldn't pass up the opportunity to meet the people he works with. I keep thinking he's faking this whole casework thing. How's he doing, screwing up?"

"Doing great," Toni said. "We kinda threw him in the deep end and he just started swimming. Got some tough cases right off the bat. Stays calm. Writes well, but," and she pointed at Richie for emphasis, "falls behind on those notes too often."

"Yeah, sounds like him," Pat said. "Can I buy a round for you nice social-work types?"

"Oh, I like this kid already," Toni said. "Got any more brothers?"

Richie introduced Pat around as they made their way to the bar. Pat blanched at the cost of drinks. "Holy shit. This is happy hour? What's with the discounts?" He haggled a bit and left a miniscule tip.

They distributed drinks to all the staff. Richie hoped they wouldn't spit in the burritos they'd just ordered, Pat again noting the prices. "Eleven-fifty for a burrito, in this joint?" he said, too loudly. But he scoffed and sweetly said, "My treat," when Toni offered some money for the drinks.

Rachel flung her arm around Richie and pulled him in for a half-hug. Her scent was lightly sweet, a flowery aroma he couldn't quite place after a month of proximity. "Love your little brother," she said to Pat. "He's my office neighbor. Works hard. Good guy."

"You know, it's kinda dark in here," Pat said. "You sure you're talking about Richie?"

She laughed. "Oh, I'm sure. Good with kids, too. I like it when he plays trucks with the little boys."

"That's 'cause he never grew up."

"Rachel's been super-helpful," Richie said. "I ask stupid questions, she gives me smart answers."

"Oh, you're doing fine, Rich," she said. "Even with that discharge the other day. That wasn't easy, but Toni said you handled it well, like a pro."

"I wish I could say I knew what I was doing."

"We're all making this up as we go, right?" She turned to Pat. "Oh, and your brother's like a Yankee encyclopedia, right? Oh my God, he knows everything!"

"Yeah, cool party trick. Watch this," Pat said, putting a hand on his forehead as if in thought. "Richie. What'd Donnie Baseball hit in '86?"

Richie scoffed. "Gimmie a hard one. .352. Lost the batting title to Wade Boggs. 238 hits, that's the most by a Yankee."

Pat just smirked and pointed at his brother. Rachel gaped.

"Oh my God! How do you do that?" she exclaimed.

"He has no life," said Pat.

Richie started to argue, but caught himself and said, "Yeah. He's right. I suck."

Toni came over and said: "Last Yankee to win 20."

"Too easy. Guidry, '85. 22-6. He always seemed to pitch well for Billy."

"Last guy to hit 50."

"For the Yankees? Maris, of course."

"No, for anybody."

"Uh…Cecil Fielder, right? 1990."

Toni turned to the group. "How's he do that?"

"Man knows his stuff," Jones said.

"Yeah, but he can't find his keys in the morning," Pat said.

They all laughed, including Richie.

Rachel touched Richie on the arm. "Good to have you, Rich." Then she went to the ladies' room with Stephanie.

The waitress brought burritos over for Pat and Richie. Everyone else had already eaten, so they stood at a raised table a little off the group.

"Not a bad place," Pat said. "Good choice. I like your coworkers, man. Looks like you picked a good crowd."

"Yeah, they're all right," Richie said. "Very down to earth. Everybody's been real helpful."

"Good to hear. How's the work?"

Richie swallowed. "You were right, Pat. A lot of hard stories. Hard to hear sometimes. Drug users, abused women, dropping out of school, mental illness. I have one woman who's really mentally ill. Schizophrenia. But she's a nice lady, you know?" He paused. "And I always have to, you know, confront people."

"Confront?"

"Toni talks to me about it. Says I have to learn how to confront people without taking it personal. You can't be too permissive and let people do whatever they want. But I feel so caught in the middle. Telling people they can't, you know, go away for the weekend, or that they have to do things on their service plan or they might get kicked out."

"Well, that's true no matter where you go. You always have to confront people. Doesn't mean it has to be angry. It just means you give it to people straight. Guess you're getting a crash course."

"Yeah. I guess good news is on the way."

"Sure, sure. So, what do these people do all day?"

"Maybe go to drug programs, mental health programs, school. I don't know, though. Hard to make people do that stuff."

"I told you. Needy people will drive you nuts."

"Yeah, you keep saying that. What, you know lots of needy people?"

"Sure I do. So do you."

"What, Mom?"

"Yeah, Mom. She shoulda gone for help a bunch of times. We argued about it sometimes. I wanted her to, I don't know. Go to AA, or spend more time with you, or…just not be so…shitty all the time. She told me to mind my fucking business." He huffed. "Huh. She was something else. People like that… I don't know. Can't be helped, I think."

Richie looked at the TV. He didn't want to argue the point with his coworkers nearby, so he stayed quiet.

Pat shrugged. "Ah, what do I know? Just watch yourself, man. Take care of yourself first. OK?" Richie nodded.

"By the way," Pat said, looking over his shoulder. "What's up with Rachel?"

"What do you mean?"

"Geez, are you clueless. Are you kidding? She's into you, man."

Now he was grateful it was so dark, as it hid his blushing face. "Oh, come on, really."

"Hey, maybe it's not a good idea to date your coworkers or anything, but, hey. She's all right."

"Smart, too," Richie said.

Pat grinned. "So you *are* into her."

"Oh, shit, Pat. I have enough to worry about on the job without thinking about picking up chicks."

Pat waved his hands. "OK, OK, I get it." He looked over to where Rachel was talking, and nodded. "No worries." He took a bite of his burrito. "Shit. Not bad, but eleven-fifty is out-friggin'-rageous."

"Hey, what's up with that?"

"With what?"

"You're so concerned about prices today. Are we tight?"

"No, no," Pat said, waving him away. "We're fine. Well, maybe a little tight. Con Ed was up this month, no clue why. And remember: I'm cash-poor. Stock-rich, cash-poor. Oh, don't get me wrong. I got the rent, I got the bills. And hey, you have a legit job, so you're gonna be set up. Plus, you said you wanted to contribute, right? OK, so go ahead. Wanna take the Con Ed for a while?"

Richie toasted him with his Coke. "Done."

Pat smiled. "Wow. Look at that. My bro, payin' his own way."

"Yeah, slave wages, like you said."

"And like you said, every little bit helps. But really, man, don't worry about it, we'll be fine," Pat said, going back to his burrito. In between bites he said, "Hey, I got some good news. Well, sorta good news."

"What?"

"Marilyn got the job at the Justice Department."

Richie had forgotten about that. "Oh," he said.

"Yeah, I know what you're thinking. What about you, what about our place?"

Richie said nothing.

"Like I said before. I told her we needed to wait until you were permanent, settled, stuff like that. She was totally cool with it. Mostly."

"Mostly?"

Pat sighed. "You know. She wants me to... be there. Someday. I think."

"Oh."

Pat shrugged. "I don't know, Rich. I love Marilyn. I think she's gonna be the one. But, you know, me in DC? That's... that's a big step."

Richie huffed, stood back from the table. "Shit, Pat, I don't wanna get in the way –"

"No, no, you're not, you're not," Pat said. He put his hands on his chest. "This is all me. All me, don't worry about it."

"Yeah, but –"

"I told you, Richie. Don't worry about it." He paused, looked Richie in the eye. "OK?"

Richie nodded. "Well, what are you gonna do?"

"Go down like every other weekend, holidays, stuff like that. She'll come up once in a while, too. We'll work something out."

Richie looked at a hockey game on TV. He calculated six months from his start: August. The month when Ellen came back.

He thought about working at the Morris site. *Nope.* So, what then? Where would he be living, what would he be doing, where would Pat be, where would Marilyn be?

Toni snapped him out of his daydream, nearly tackling him, and slapped Pat on the arm. "Hey, hey! Look! Look at that!"

She was pointing at one of the TVs. A news channel was on, muted. Across the bottom of the screen were the works, "BASEBALL WORK STOPPAGE ENDS."

"Holy shit!" yelled Pat. "Yeah, yeah, yeah!"

Richie squinted, trying to read the captions. "Players going back to spring training in two weeks. Something about an injunction. Who the hell is Sonia Sotomayor?"

"Who cares?" Pat said. "Yankee baseball! Let's go!" He started high fiving other patrons. After a few moments, he got a "Let's Go Yankees" chant going.

"Hey, how about that?" said Wilson, clapping his hands. "Let's get a little baseball goin'. Real ballplayers."

"We're going to the Series, damn it!" said Pat. He got Richie in a headlock. "Donnie Baseball, in the Series! Let's go!"

"Hey, hey!" Toni yelled. She raised a glass. "To the Yankees!"

"To baseball," said Wilson.

"To Michael Jordan not playing baseball and droppin' a double nickel on the Knicks," said Jones.[9]

More laughter, more cheers. The female caseworkers thought it was a general toast, so they came over and toasted everyone, too. Pat bantered with Toni, Jones and Wilson about the Knicks, even though Richie didn't think Pat followed them. He thought he heard a nearby patron say, "They party like lawyers." He felt a little outside the reverie, as the designated driver.

"Hey, Richie!" Pat pulled Richie aside. "Good news, huh?"

"Yeah, baseball's back. Awesome."

"How many games we going to this year?"

"How you gonna swing that? You gonna be around?"

"Come on!" Pat said, straightening himself. "You kidding? Yankee baseball, man. Priorities. Hey, my office is still in New York, right? And plenty of night games? We're there, dude. We gotta be there when they make their playoff run. And if – I mean, when – they go, we're going. We'll camp out in front of the Stadium for tickets."

"OK, Pat," Richie said. "We'll see."

Pat wiped his mouth and approached the bar. He opened his wallet as he looked at the bill. "Hey, I think I'm gonna come up short. Got any cash?"

Pat had never asked Richie to pay when they'd been out to eat. So he excused himself, went to the car, drove to the Chase Bank up 9A, and took out $80 – really, $83.00 with the ATM fee.

Budding Prospect

Lily Newsome, "a problem case", according to Toni, came down to do her Service Plan on an April afternoon. Richie noted that in her file, "Education" was listed as a goal for weeks and weeks, with zero progress. She didn't need substance abuse or mental health counseling. She'd already earned a GED through a Mt. Vernon community program, but never went any further. Toni, Ellen, and a visiting teacher from Westchester Community College all encouraged her to get an associate's degree, and the positive attention helped for a little while. But she dropped out the moment her son got sick. She didn't want to "work in no fuckin' McDonald's and shit" (he felt keen irony at telling someone to watch their language), so there was nothing left for her to do, and her Section 8 wasn't coming through. Richie was frustrated by the whole thing, and so, in the midst of the Service Plan, he just stopped what he was doing. "I kinda don't see the point, here, Lily. What's going on with you?"

"OK, well, you see, Mr McGinn, it's like this," Lily answered.

"OK, Lily," Richie said, leaning back, arms folded. "Tell me about it."

"I hated school. But I had one teacher, Ms Hernandez? Eighth grade? She gave me stuff to read, you know? About Rosa Parks, MLK, Jackie Robinson, people like me, you know? So I really liked to read, and I figured out that gangs and stuff don't go in the library, so I was, like, safe, you know? But school, man, that just got worse and worse. They was like forty people in a class, nobody listenin'. You gotta start some... stuff to get attention. Hell, by tenth grade it was boring as hell and I got a job at the bowling alley, so I was like, later for that school shit – ooh, sorry. Then I fu– I mean, I messed up and got with Harold, and next thing you know –" and she pointed at Treyvon.

Richie nodded. "OK, so what do you wanna do?"

She scoffed. "I don't know. Go to school, I guess. I could go back to that dude at WCC. I'll get on it, Mr McGinn, don't you worry."

He called and made an appointment for her. A day later he called and learned she'd made it there, and since classes didn't start for a while, she was going to get some vocational testing.

Talking the case over with Toni, he told her about stopping in the middle of Lily's Service Plan. She stopped writing notes and looked at him sternly. "Who told you to do that?"

He froze. *Oh, shit*, he thought. *What did I do now?* "Uh, nobody, nobody. Sorry about that."

She waved him off. "Rachel? Darlene, Tajo? 'Cause it wasn't me."

He went wide-eyed. He could feel the sweat in the middle of his back. "Uh, really, I just, uh, you know. She, uh, wasn't following her Service Plan, and stuff. So, I, kinda… got frustrated, stopped what I was doing, and… asked her to, I don't know… explain?"

Toni nodded. A smirk crawled across her lavender lips. "Son of a gun. Not bad, kid. Not bad."

"OK," Richie said, looking around the room. "Uh, thanks, but… what'd I do?"

She shook a finger at him. "See, I knew you had good instincts. When things aren't working, you just stop. If you're doing more work for the client than she is – and believe me, that's one of your problems; too often you run to the pantry when you need to do some listening – if you're working harder than she is, something's wrong. So you just stop. You took it another step, asked her about it. How'd you ask?"

"Uh, I think I said, 'Tell me about it.'"

She pumped a fist. "Nice! Very good! See, you heard her, met her where she was at. Who knows if it'll stick – my guess is it won't, given her history. But, good, Rich, real good."

Despite this, by April Richie still felt adrift. His supervision meetings with Toni seemed just like a review of Service Plans and notes, on which he was still delinquent. He just recited what he did, and she criticized and analyzed it. "Why'd you do that," "What's your next step," and "What's your plan," were her favorite comments. He stuttered and stammered his way through those meetings, unsure what he was doing right, if anything. Any compliments he got, like the one on Lily, he felt he'd earned by accident. He'd get in the car after a day's work and say out loud, "I still don't know what the hell I'm doing."

He went through the motions, filling out lots of Service Plans and doing his inspections on time. But just doing the paperwork was boring, so he called around, visited programs. He liked Lydia at New Futures, who just told it like it is ("He's an asshole and he's using," she'd say about a non-compliant guy), and he got to know that Dr Farnsworth at Akira's program was a Yankee fan ("Steinbrenner? Classic narcissist"). Toni said, "Hey! Good follow-up! See, you're learning!" He thought, *Well, if you just told me to do that in the first place...*

He didn't like feeling like a moron in team meetings, babbling that he didn't know why a client did something, eliciting harsh looks from Toni. So he spent five minutes each week talking to Debbie about his clients. He went scrambling to the dictionary, and on weekends, the library, to figure out just what the hell she was talking about. So at the next meeting, when Debbie mentioned a client's "passive-aggressive" behavior, Richie said he'd observed his client arriving later and later to Day Care, and thus confirmed what she said. He felt a zing of pride at Toni's grin in his direction.

One day, a family that had mainly worked with Ms Ellen secured a Section 8 apartment in Mt. Vernon and moved out. The mom hugged him saying, "I couldn't have done it without you." His only contribution to her situation was to let her use the phone.

He found writing case notes difficult and tedious. He wasn't sure what to say, and Toni criticized it to no end. "You gotta write your impressions, Rich. You gotta keep an eye out and show us what you observed. This," she said, holding up his pages, "doesn't tell me anything. Work on it." But with everything else going on, he left it for the last part of the day. Before he knew it he was behind by weeks, not days.

The good thing was he asked for less and less help from the other caseworkers. He did supervision weekly with Toni, whereas the others were bi-weekly, but she said soon bi-weekly would be OK for him, too.

Rachel, his next-partition neighbor, shared some of her trade secrets. After a particularly bad client meeting, she suggested that he to go to Day Care, on the pretense of monitoring his clients' kids' progress. Frances let him build Legos with a four year old and showed him how to change a diaper. He felt guilty for shirking his work, but was more relaxed.

Secretly he listened in on Rachel's client meetings. She was painfully direct: "Are you using, or what?" "Well, you go to college or you pack up." "Sorry, saying 'I can't' when it comes to Section 8 doesn't fly." Richie felt disgusted and ashamed whenever he had to look someone in the eye and tell them what to do. So he avoided it, leaving his Service Plans vague.

He also developed a reputation as a pushover. Rather than have a client call DSS, or help them budget their money better, he'd just run to the pantry and get them what they needed. He was on the path to the pantry one afternoon when he saw Rachel.

"Hey, Rich, where do you think you're going?"

He was stunned. It sounded threatening. "Uh, the, uh, pantry."

"No way, buddy. We're running out of diapers up there. That's really just for emergencies, Rich, or when clients first come in. What's the deal, anyway?"

"Well, Angela said she was short –"

"Yeah, right. She's just doing that because she's too lazy to go to the store. Her benefits are active, right?"

Richie said they were.

"OK, then," and she spread her hands. "She can do it herself. Just tell her."

He didn't like confronting to begin with, and certainly didn't like confronting angry Angela. Her eyes got narrow, she hunched her shoulders, and talked like she was growling. He also didn't like being talked to this way by Rachel. She'd been helpful and upbeat the whole time. This felt like a betrayal, like he was a little boy and she the disciplinarian mom. He thought, *Talk to me like that? Who the hell put YOU in charge?*

But he just nodded, and quietly said, "Yeah, you're right. I'll do that." He turned, didn't say "thanks."

Sure enough, Angela said, "Ah, see, you're just like those goddamn stuffed shirts at DSS, thanks for nothing," and stormed out.

On a Tuesday morning in early May, he got a call from one of Rachel's clients, Shaniqua Rivers. Ronnie Teneille, one of Richie's newer clients, had left her four-year-old daughter Taisha with Shaniqua for almost three days straight with no word at all.

"So, Mr McGinn, I don't wanna get no one in trouble," she said.

"No, no, it's OK," Richie said. "You can't be expected to do this forever. Let me see if we can reach her again. In the meantime, do you need anything?"

"Imma need a break pretty soon," she said.

Ronnie was an indifferent woman who attended an outpatient alcohol treatment program. It wasn't going well. Her attendance was sporadic, and she went out almost every weekend, leaving her daughter Taisha with just about anyone. She also had a habit of arriving from her program late and failing to pick up her daughter from the bus.

And Taisha was a weird kid. He took several calls from the Head Start program she attended in White Plains about her behavior, including a frantic one that she was missing. (An hour later they called back: she was hiding in the folds of a curtain in the infant room.) He had to watch Taisha more than once in his office when Ronnie didn't show up on time. He was no match for her. Crayons and toys didn't last her three minutes, and she was never hungry for snacks, or even candy. She would run down the hall, opening file cabinets and interrupting other clients' meetings. She once stole another child's toy and managed to open the door to the hallway and run out to the playground. And she always had the wide-eyed, tooth-filled grin of someone who'd just dropped a handful of mushrooms.

Richie called Ronnie's emergency contact, her program, her DSS worker. No one had heard from her. He told Toni, who said it was probably time to call CPS.

He'd attended a training on reporting to Child Protective Services in mid-April and actually learned things, things he wished he hadn't. He was a "mandated reporter", which meant that if he witnessed child abuse he would have to report it according to New York State law. He was disgusted with learning the different ways young children could be abused or neglected, and silently hoped he'd never have to use the information.

"Can I see what's in her file?" He did so knowing what she'd say.

Toni hung her head. "So, just one note? From the intake? Come on, Rich, you're better than this. Didn't you babysit the kid, multiple times? Where's that note?"

"Sorry. I know. I gotta work on it."

"Again, if this thing gets worse, how will you know what to do? What track record do you have? Let's do better on this, OK?"

He agreed. After reviewing for a few moments, she said, "Yeah, I think it's time. We need to call it in."

"What if she shows up?" he asked.

"Doesn't matter. It's a situation where she left her kid in someone else's custody with no contact whatsoever. There's no communication, right? And there's a track record, too, right? This is a kid who's clearly being neglected."

He exhaled. "Really? We gotta call?"

"Rich. Let me ask you. What's the cost of doing nothing?"

He didn't have an answer.

She rolled her eyes. "Try," she said.

"Well," he stammered, "if a kid really is being abused, and he gets hurt, or, uh, worse… we could be in a lot of trouble."

"We're liable for it. *You're* liable for it. And you could have an abused or even a dead kid on your hands."

He inhaled as deeply through his nose as he could.

"Look," Toni said, leaning over her desk a bit, "I know you don't wanna do this. This is what you're dealing with, though. Sometimes these situations are going to pop up. This one's pretty mild, if you ask me. I don't think the kid's in any real danger, but what happens if nobody shows? Trust me, this is the right thing to do. Sometimes you have to do it, even if it doesn't feel good. I know you know this."

She walked him through the procedure, gave him the phone number and one of the forms to fill out after the call was over. She told him to make sure to take down the name of the person who took the call and the case ID number. She said it was his option to give his name, since the call would be anonymous, but the client always figured it out anyway, and giving his information would make follow-up communication easier.

"And push," she said. "Make sure they take it. If you leave it open, they won't set her up with a CPS worker. That's what you want. That'll give us leverage to work with her."

He called as soon as he got to his desk, hoping to get it done quickly. Toni was right: they asked why he was calling if someone was watching the child. For two or three agonizing minutes he just repeated the facts of the case. Then the voice paused and said, "Hold, please. We'll have a determination for you shortly."

He realized he was pressing the receiver so hard to his ear that it had turned red-hot and was sweating, as was his palm. He relaxed his grip and again inhaled heavily through his nose. Rachel had showed up in his entry way to ask a question, saw his face, and made an elegant U-turn.

"Sir?" the voice shook him awake.

"Yes?"

"The case has been accepted. Do you have something to write with? I need to give you my name and the case ID number."

He took the information down, writing it down on the corner of his notepad, hardly recognizing his own handwriting.

"Please verify the address," said the voice, and Richie confirmed. He was told the investigator would be in touch in the next two hours, and the call was over.

He took a deep breath, stood up and walked to Toni's office.

"Good," she said. "You made them take it. Doesn't always work out that way. Now, you have to fill out that form and fax it to the number on the top. Did you let security know an investigator is on the way?"

"No, you were my first stop."

"OK, take a walk and let the guys know. Hey, after the worker gets here, take a long lunch. You need time to clear your head."

He nodded back, and walked out to the front desk.

"Hey guys," he said. Jones was leaning on the desk; Wilson was sitting behind it. "Just wanted you to know. A CPS investigator is gonna be in touch with us soon."

"Oh," Wilson said somberly. "Damn. OK."

"Not for Ronnie Tenielle," said Jones.

Richie was surprised. "Yeah, that's her."

Jones and Wilson looked at each other. Jones said, "We just let her in."

"What?"

"Yeah, she got here," he looked at his watch, "fifteen minutes ago? Tried to brush right by, asked us if Shaniqua had left. That's who has the kid, right?"

"Fuck!" Richie said, surprising himself with his language.

"Hey, man, don't get mad at us," Jones said. "Nobody told us."

"No, no, not your fault," he said, "Just… uh… shit! I…"

Wilson stood up. "CPS on the way?"

"I think so. They usually quick on this sort of thing?"

"Depends. How quick is the investigator, how severe the case, is there already a case open, stuff like that."

Richie put his hands on his hips and looked around.

"What you wanna do, man," Jones said.

I'd like to go back to delivering pizzas. He just frowned.

"Hey," Wilson said. "If she comes back, I can tell her you – maybe even Ms Petrocelli – needs to see her. That way we can stop her from leaving. She bolts, we can call the cops. But that's never happened. That sound good?"

Richie wished he'd thought of that. He sighed and reluctantly nodded.

"All right," Wilson said. "Can you give us the worker's name and number?"

"I'm gonna take a walk by the building, see if I notice anything," Jones said, reaching for his blazer behind the desk as Richie gave Wilson the information.

Shit, shit, shit, he thought. He walked back to Toni's office. She said, "What's up?"

"She's back."

"Who?"

Who the hell do you think? "Ronnie Tenielle."

"Wilson let her through?"

"She beat me to it. She must have come in while I was making the call. He said she got here about fifteen – I guess now twenty – minutes ago, asking for Shaniqua."

"Damn," she said, shaking her head. "And you told them to hold her if she tries to leave?"

"Well, Wilson said he'd hold her up, saying you or I" (*preferably you*, he thought) "needed to see her."

"OK, that's good. You might want to beat her to it. Try calling her at her unit. Let me know if you need me, and don't forget to get in touch with the CPS worker."

"OK, I got it," he said, and walked back to his office. There was a phone ringing in the caseworker suite, and he correctly assumed it was his. He jogged down the row to answer it.

"Mr McGinn? This is Ms Langone, the CPS worker assigned to Taisha Tenielle."

Richie rehashed the situation, said that Ronnie was in the building. She asked him questions about her background, and he gave her some basics.

"I tried her at the unit but didn't get her," she said. "Can you patch me through?" He did. The phone rang about five minutes later, as he was filling out the form.

"OK, I got a hold of her. Sounds like she has custody again, like you said. Things sound stable, though I'm sure she has a lot to do here. As you probably know, the investigation is open for 60 days, but I doubt the case will be anything but unfounded. I'll try to get out there soon."

"Can you give me an idea when?"

"Maybe tomorrow. Definitely end of the week."

"End of the week?" he repeated testily.

"Yeah, it's not urgent, is it? You said the mom has custody again, right? There's no outstanding reports on her. It was a bad idea to leave her child with someone else for so long, but there's no imminent abuse, and whatever abandonment is over now. Ronnie shared with me that she attends a treatment program, but that's not a reason to do a removal. It can wait until later."

He rolled his eyes. "Well," he said, "what should we do now?"

"Get the report in as soon as you can. Call me if this happens again or if something happens that makes you concerned, like if she stops going to program. If there's another case of abuse, though, call it in."

"OK," he said, rubbing his face. "Uh, I, uh, guess that's it."

"Good. Have a nice day," she said.

He hung up and started to walk back to Toni's office when the phone rang again.

"What the fuck? You called CPS on me?" yelled a voice.

Richie coughed, put his hand on his chest. "We had to," Richie said quietly, "you hadn't showed up, and Shaniqua couldn't watch Taisha anymore –"

"I ain't lettin' that bitch watch Taisha no more. She ain't have to call y'all, and y'all dint have to call CPS. Now I got some fuckin' worker coming after me? Wantin' to take my kid? Uh-uh. That some bullshit right there."

"Listen," he said. He almost said, "calm down", but remembered how pissed off Akira got when he did. He gathered himself and continued: "We didn't have an option. Shaniqua was running out of food, Taisha was asking for her mom," (not true but a reasonable assumption, Richie thought) "we didn't hear from you. What else could we do?"

"You ain't have to call no CPS."

"Yeah, we did. And remember, we've had a few times when you didn't get here in time to pick her up."

"The bus was late, I told you! It ain't my fault!"

"Program ends at 2, pick-up is at 4:15. I don't think it takes 2 hours, even if a bus is late."

"I been tryin' to do the right thing, goddammit! What the fuck I'm gonna do now? CPS worker all in my business. Why you have to do that?"

"We had to call CPS," he said, trying not to burst, "because a child was here without her mom for forty-eight hours. Sure, there were plans made, but not for that long."

There was a silence. "Shit," she said.

"Did you talk to the worker?"

"Yeah, I talked to her. Askin' a bunch of questions and shit. Told me that can't happen again, gotta follow the program here, my program in Tarrytown, bladi blah, whatever. She said she comin' out to see me and Taisha."

"She said something about 60 days, right?"

"Yeah."

"Anything else?"

"She said not to worry about it as long as I'm doin' the right thing here."

"OK, she said the same thing to me. She said she didn't think this would go anywhere. I agree. You just can't let that happen again. And you gotta make program more oft- no, all the time. No more misses, no more weekend hangouts."

"Fine, I get it. I'll do it or whatever. Fuckin' CPS and shit."

"Sorry it had to come to this, Ms Tenielle, but I hope you understand. Let's give you the day to cool off, then we'll meet tomorrow after program. Let's say 4:30, right after you pick up Taisha, OK?"

He heard a deep sigh. "Whatever. Bye."

"Good-bye, Ms Tenielle. See you tomorrow." He hung up, and rubbed his eyes. The phone rang again, jolting him.

"Ah, hell," he said a little too loudly. "What now?" he mumbled, before answering.

"FREE TICKETS!" Pat yelled.

"Jesus Christ!" Richie gasped. "You nearly gave me a heart attack, a-hole!"

"The – friggin' bleachers are free today, damn it! FREE!"

"Whoa, slow down. Tonight's game?"

Rachel appeared in his doorway, squinting and mouthing the words, "Everything OK?" He nodded and gave her a thumbs-up.

"Yeah! I heard it on The Fan just now. The bleachers are free, dude, FREE!"

"They're only $6 anyway. You're that excited about this?"

"You think I'm gonna pass up an opportunity for free shit? Especially when free shit includes Yankee baseball?"

"OK, sounds good. I'm there," he said.

"What the hell, man? Why aren't you jumping through the roof?"

"Kinda rough day."

"Oh," Pat said. "What happened?"

"I had to call CPS. You know, child abuse hotline."

"Oh, shit. Yeesh. Friggin' people. You OK?"

"Yeah, yeah, just fine. I, uh, just gotta fill out some forms and see some clients. I'll meet you there. Section 41. Probably 6, 6:30."

"Sure, sure, I understand. But hey, we're making history: free baseball."

"Sounds good. Looking forward to it."

After hanging up, he completed the CPS form and sent it through the fax machine, then called to make sure it was received. Rachel was making copies when he was at the fax. "Make sure you confirm. Those guys lose stuff all the time," she said. Then he had three back-to-back service plan meetings and a team meeting. He didn't eat lunch.

Around 4:00 he was working on case notes when Toni stopped by.

"How you doing?" she asked, hands in her suit pockets.

"I'm beat," he said.

"How'd it go with Ronnie?" He explained her reaction.

"Yeah, that happens," she said, taking a seat in his office. "Something like this has an effect on your relationship with your client. You lose a little of their trust when something like this happens, when you have to make a tough call for a greater good, maybe for the kid's sake. They trust you, they like you, so when they learn you called CPS on them, they feel betrayed. Just remember: it's a professional relationship, not a personal one. I've said things like, 'This might hurt our relationship, and I understand if you're mad at me.' She might not be able to hear that now, but maybe she'll come around to that. Give her a day."

"You were spot-on," he said. "The investigator didn't think much of it. She's coming out later in the week."

"I'll be shocked if this goes through. But let her follow-up with Ronnie. It might be the thing she needs. Because right now, you can see: she's falling apart. When you meet with her tomorrow, say that maybe this'll be the thing that turns things around for her. She might, you know, push it off or something, but let that sink in."

He nodded, tiredly. She looked at him. "You doing OK?"

He sighed, slouched down in his chair. "This place is something else."

"Yeah. That's what we deal with around here. That's the population." She shrugged.

"Well," Richie said. "I get it. Thanks, by the way. For the help."

"No problem, Rich. By the way, I asked people not to call you 'Richie'. Said you prefer 'Rich'."

Since the night at Cactus Jack's, Tajo had taken to it. "Oh, it's OK," he said to Toni.

"No, you said you wanted to be called 'Rich,' so we call you 'Rich.' No big deal. Hey, did you hear about the Yankees tonight? Free bleachers?"

He laughed. "Yeah. Pat and I are going."

"Great, great. Can't turn down free baseball, right?"

"That's just what he said."

"Isn't he a CEO or something?" Richie shrugged. "Anyway, have a good time. Donnie Baseball playing?"

"If he's not, I'm going home."

She smiled. "Have a good time," she said, and left.

"Hey, neighbor," he heard Rachel say.

"Yes?"

"Tough day."

"Yeah. All in a day's work, I guess."

"Mmm. Who called just now? If you don't mind my asking."

"Nah, it's OK. It was Pat. We're going to the game tonight."

"Oh!" she said. He heard her get out of her chair. She came over and appeared in his entryway. "Oh, how fun. Who they playing?"

"Red Sox."

"Ooh, the rivalry. Are they good this year?"

"Well, there've only been four games. Yankees are 3-1."

"I bet you know everyone's batting average."

"Donnie Baseball is at .263. He went 3 for 5 the other day. But early batting averages are useless."

"I haven't been to a ballgame since I was a little kid. None of my friends are into it."

He looked gravely at her. "Rachel? I gotta ask you something. Very important."

She paused. "God. What is it?"

He cleared his throat. "Are you a Yankee fan?"

She smirked; even her smirk was pretty. "My dad sold peanuts at the old, OLD Stadium. What do you think?" She winked. "Say hi to Pat. Have fun, neighbor."

Richie left at five on the dot. He decided to stop at home and change his clothes before going to the Stadium. As soon as he opened the door he heard the phone ring. He dropped his keys and made a run for it, picking it up just before the answering machine clicked on.

"Hello?" he said breathlessly.

There was a click, and the sounds of a call center in the background. "Good afternoon, this is Amber from the Sallie Mae Student Loan Corporation. May I please speak to… Patrick McGinn, please?"

"Oh, uh," Richie stammered. Sounded like a telemarketing call, so he made to hang up quickly. "He's not here. We're good for now, thank you."

"Is this a relative? His brother, Richard, perhaps?"

Holy shit, he thought. *Are they watching us or something? I knew that van outside was suspicious.*

"Wha – uh, yes, uh, that's me."

"Do you know how we can get in touch with him? Do you know his whereabouts?"

Whereabouts? What the hell's going on?

"Uh, well, I think he's at work."

"Mr McGinn, I'm not authorized to disclose the details of the situation, but I can tell you that it's extremely important that your brother contact us immediately. Calls like this indicate the possibility of default on a student loan, and we will continue to call until we have arrived at some resolution, some plan to repay these loans. We have sent several notices, we have tried to reach him both at home and at work, and have not received a response. This is not the first missed payment, by the way. We do not want to pursue legal action, but we may have no other recourse if he continues to evade us. Now, you're in residence at this address as well?"

His feet felt glued to the floor. He thought the FBI had tracked him down and had the house surrounded. *Come out quietly and tell us where your brother is.* "Uh, yes."

"Very good. I'm going to relay some contact information for you. Please take it down." He got a pencil and wrote carefully. "Our department can give him forty-eight hours to respond. After that, we may have to take more serious measures, including but not limited to garnishing of wages. Will you communicate that to Mr McGinn?"

The fear of Amber put a lump in his throat, but he managed to croak, "Uh-huh."

Richie actually found a space on 164th Street overlooking the north end of the track at Macombs Dam Park. He thought about stopping for a sandwich, but didn't want to be late, and he was gun-shy about spending even that little bit, so he scarfed down a frozen burrito before leaving. The traffic and the crowds headed down River Avenue were surprisingly light.

Twilight had just set in. There was a chill in the air. He walked up a few rows, looking around for Pat. It wasn't easy since the bleachers were, by far, the most crowded section in the massive Stadium.

He heard a familiar voice yell, "HEY, THAT GUY'S A MET FAN, HE SUCKS!"

Instantly, a few dozen fans started booing him, serenading him with the "Ass-Hole" song (to the tune of "Air Ball"). As if showing his credentials, he opened his jacket to reveal his Don Mattingly T-shirt. The boos turned to cheers, and some fans high-fived him.

"Hey, Mr Social Worker! Over here!" yelled his brother, waving wildly from a seat about twenty rows from the field, just a stone's throw from Ali's cowbell. He high-fived Richie and started chanting, "FREE STUFF! FREE STUFF!" and a handful of fans chanted along. Some chanted "Mets Suck!" instead.

Richie just clapped his hands and took it all in.

"OK, I'm driving," Pat said. "You need a beer. Doesn't this guy look like he needs a beer?"

"I look like I need a beer," a loner in a Thurman Munson shirt turned and said.

"You got it, Thurm," Pat said.

"Actually, I'm good," Richie said.

"You sure, man? You driving?"

"Yeah, sure, I'll drive again," Richie said flatly.

Pat paused, then shrugged and said, "I guess it's just you and me, Thurm," and he ordered two from the beer man, handing one to Thurman and refusing to be paid back. Before he sipped his, he glanced at Richie, offering it to him.

"It's OK. Let's just watch the game. BOSTON SUCKS!" he yelled to cheer himself up.

Richie was comforted by Ali's cowbell, but he didn't clap along. When a Red Sox player meandered to first after a weak groundout, someone near them yelled, "You look like 200 pounds of chewed bubble gum, you fat fuck!" Pat guffawed while Richie just grinned.

"That's funny, man," Pat said, elbowing Richie's ribs. "You OK?"

"Huh? Oh, yeah, yeah, you know, just, rough day."

"So, what happened?" after Mattingly grounded out to end the second.

Richie recounted the CPS call, doing his best to speak over the trivia question on the PA.

"Holy shit," Pat said. "That's some heavy stuff. Makes sense, though."

"What makes sense?"

"Well, like I said. Tough characters with hard lives. I guess it was just a matter of time before something like that happened."

"Yeah. It was no fun, though, let me tell you. I felt like shit trying to explain to the lady why I did it. Got cursed out for my trouble. And you know it's gonna happen again."

"Yep. Probably worse."

He slouched a bit. "I don't know, man. I don't know if I can handle it. And this whole thing, dealing with abused kids, abused families, drug addicts, crazy people, getting cursed out..."

They didn't say anything for a bit.

"Ahhhh, don't walk this guy, he sucks!" Pat yelled a few batters later. Then he said, "You know what Toni said at Cactus Jack's? You were talking to that guard – Jones, was it? She said to me: 'This kid has it.'"

"She said that?"

"Oh, shit, NO!"

A Red Sox player launched a towering grand slam home run into the left field seats. The fans erupted in boos until someone threw the ball back on the field.

"That's more like it," Pat said. "Yeah. Toni thinks you walk on water."

"She's all over my ass, Pat."

"The good ones usually are. You should be worried if she stops. That means she doesn't give a shit and you're probably on your way out."

"I thought you hated my job."

"I don't hate it, Richie. I don't have a whole lot of faith that, you know, people get better. Marilyn and I, we – disagreed on this, this job of yours. Argued, really."

"Oh." He drew back, furrowed his brow. "Sorry. Everything OK?"

"Oh, sure, sure. Kinda getting used to the 'sleep over on weekends thing'. But anyway, she's some attorney, though. She fought for you, man, fought for you on this job. She told it to me like this. Hard to argue." He took a big sip of his Jumbo. He counted on his fingers. "One. You have an office."

"I have a desk."

"OK, a desk. Share an office?"

"Well, it's kind of like... partitions?"

"OK, well, you have a desk. Two. You have a team. Nice team, man. The way they reacted when you walked in, the way they talked about you. And you'd only been there a month. Love those folks."

"Yeah, I think that's the best part."

"Mm, I can tell. Three. You have a salary."

"It is nice, getting a steady paycheck. Instead of nickels and stuff."

"Right? And benefits. Like a grown up. And finally – Aw, what the FUCK!"

As Pat talked, they heard a massive crack, and a fly ball soared above their heads and into the upper deck for another Red Sox grand slam, making it 8-0.

"Je-SUS!" Pat yelled. "Come on!"

"What was the last thing?" asked Richie.

A chant of "Box Seats Suck" drowned out their conversation. "Oh, yeah," Pat said. "Pluff-ass."

"What?"

"Pupp-up-us."

"I can't hear you. What?"

"PURPOSE!" Pat yelled. "Purpose, purpose, goddammit." The noise died down. "I don't know, you have these great stories when you come home. You helped someone with a GED, got them housing, got them food, stuff like that. Tough stories, too, and you gotta watch yourself, don't get bogged down or anything. But it's a hell of a lot better than pizza delivery. And I hope maybe you, I don't know, work somewhere safer, like a school or a hospital or a foundation or something. But wow. My brother, the social worker. Helping families. Cool."

"I'm not a —"

"Yeah, I know, I know. But… hey. It works, I guess." He smiled.

Someone tapped Richie on the shoulder. A bearded older man with a beer belly protruding through a severely old t-shirt with the round Yankees logo leaned a little too closely to him, revealing his bad body odor. "You're doing the right thing, son," he said. "You're doing the world some good. God knows we need it. God bless you, son," and he shook his hand much too hard, and slapped him on the shoulder again.

"Besides," Pat said, "There's that cutie you work with. That's the reason to hang around, right?"

Richie blushed again. "Geez, lay off, huh?"

A group of fans had started a "You! Are! Fat!" chant as Mo Vaughn stepped to the plate. Pat sang along with the dirty "Take Me Out to the Ballgame" parody. But Richie didn't. After a while, Pat turned to Richie and said, "Hey, man, something else bothering you?"

Richie exhaled shakily. "You're not gonna like it," he said.

Pat squared his shoulders toward him. "It's OK, you can tell me."

Richie took a very, very deep breath and said, "OK… Well… So… I get home —"

"What'd you go home for? Shoulda just come straight here."

"I get home," Richie continued, "and I pick up the phone. It's this lady, Amber or something, from Sallie Mae, you know, the student loan thing."

Pat covered his face with his hands. "Oh, fuck me, FUCK ME!" he said loudly.

"Jesus, Pat. They made me feel like a criminal or something. They knew who I was! This lady, she meant business, talking about 'garnishing wages' and stuff. What the hell is going on?"

"God damn it," Pat said. "Damn student loan people, I thought I straightened this out."

"Are we gonna default? Whose loan is this, anyway?"

"Mine, mine," Pat said quickly. "All mine. You're good, you're good, don't worry about it. It's just – well, remember what I said about being paid in stock?"

"Yeah."

"Well, you know, the market, it's volatile. All over the place. Up, down, up, down… you know how it is. Well, uh, we took a hit."

"Yeah, but she said this wasn't the first time."

"Right. You know, there were months where the car went dead, or something was wrong with the house, or I got a parking ticket. So I… worked out a payment plan, consolidated. Stuff like that. I thought I'd worked it out this time, but now I have less cash flow than when I was in banking. Ugh, sorry you had to hear that. It's not as bad as it sounds. I'll take care of it, don't worry."

"OK, well," Richie said, nodding, "what do we do now? Can we still pay bills and stuff?"

"Well, yeah, you know, everyday stuff. Maybe we'll put off that new TV a little while longer. But hey. You got a job now, you can contribute. Can you kick in for rent? Like, four hundred or so?"

"Yeah, sure. But what are you gonna do about those student loan people? Never thought someone named 'Amber' could scare the shit outta me like that."

Pat laughed. "Yeah, I'll call Killer Amber first thing in the morning. Gotta be some miscommunication or something. Sorry, Richie."

"It's OK," Richie found himself saying. He hadn't paid much attention to the game, so he looked up and saw that some guy named Joe Ausanio was pitching, down by 8 runs.

"What the hell is an Ausanio?!" he yelled.

Pat laughed loudly, slapping him on the back. "That's the spirit!" he said.

Hot Streak

The week before Memorial Day, Richie was sitting in Toni's office for bi-weekly supervision when she said, "So listen. I want you to teach Independent Living Skills. It's a workshop the caseworkers do twice per week, for about a six-week session. Budgeting, setting up electric, shopping, stuff like that. Getting them so they can have the skills when they get to their apartments. It's a retention thing. Ellen and Darlene used to run it, we haven't done in a while, Darlene's gonna run it, and you can help her. Perfect."

"Huh," Richie said.

"What is it?"

"Well... I don't know if I'm an expert on those things. My place is a wreck."

"You and me, both, Rich. Ah, the trainer can teach you that stuff. You go to the training, pick up the knowledge, bring it back here to the residents. You went to college, you lived at school, right? You must've learnt how to cook, pay a phone bill. So you can do this."

He imagined how hard Pat would be laughing hearing this. He might as well have taught Donnie Baseball how to hit. But, in his three months he learned that refusing Toni something was a bad idea.

He arrived for the training at Morris a week later. As he was walking through the barbed-wire-protected parking lot, he heard, "Hey, neighbor!"

It was Rachel. She was carrying a huge water bottle and wearing a shorter skirt than he was used to, since it was a pretty hot day. He forced himself to look up, not down.

"Toni wanted me to take the training, too," she said. "Glad I'll have someone to goof off with."

The training was quasi-useful at best. He realized that yes, he knew how to do most of this stuff. He could easily teach someone how to cut coupons and call Con Ed for service problems. But the trainer, a middle-aged woman who claimed to be a professor of public speaking, had a droning, boring voice. After an hour Rachel started making notes on her pad close enough for him to see, like "WTF?" and "Please kill me." For lunch, they went to a Peruvian chicken place at his suggestion, since he'd eaten it regularly in Adams-Morgan, and brought it back to the Multipurpose Room at Morris.

"Wow, this is delicious. And it was so cheap!" she said.

"I must have eaten a coopful of chicken in college," he said. "I'm such a cheapskate, I like cheap food so much, I knew these guys by first name. I even picked up some Spanish."

"So what was going to college in DC like?" she asked.

He told her about his roommates, the food pantry and community center, and about changing majors four times. He told her about the time he visited all 435 offices of the House with a policy brief from Senator Moynihan in one day. She asked him about Pat, Marilyn, and her job at the Justice Department. She asked him to tell her again why Mattingly was his favorite player. She looked him right in the eye as he spoke, smiling and asking questions about it all.

He laughed when she told him about getting hit in the head with a fly ball in her first, and last, game of high school softball. They laughed about the horrible pick-up lines she'd get every night while waitressing (the winner: "If you were a burger at McDonald's, you'd be named the McGorgeous!"). She told him about how she walked out of a sorority in her junior year at New Paltz because she refused to participate in their hazing rituals. She was shocked when he said he'd seen and loved the film *My Own Private Idaho*. "None of my friends have even heard of it," she said.

The trainer was late after lunch, on the phone to another site. There was still time to kill. So he said to Rachel, "Hey, let me show you a game we used to play on the Hill when things got slow."

He got a sheet of paper and folded it several times into a triangle. She knew the basic football rules, but he had to show her the right way to flick it. "By the way," he said as she set up for a field goal, "you might want to –" And he got hit square in the forehead.

"Oh my God!" she said, laughing. "You could've lost an eye! Are you OK?" And she touched his face, examining him.

"It's a rough game, paper football," he said, smiling. "Not for the weak."

After lunch, during the lectures, Richie drew up a game of hangman and showed her, pretending he was conferring on something important. They went through two games, getting her "hung" on his second word: "zabaione." They barely paid attention to the rest of the training.

"What the hell is a zabaione?" she said as they left, punching him playfully.

"You never had one? It's an Italian dessert."

"Oh, bullshit, Richie. You made it up."

"No! Swear to God! The pizza guy I worked for, Tony, he told me about it. Next time you go to an Italian restaurant, ask. If I'm wrong, I'll give you fifty bucks."

She shook her head. "Zabaione. Pretty slick, McGinn. See you tomorrow, partner." He noted that she'd switched to the word "partner", and spent the next few hours wondering why. She hugged him around the neck and left.

He drove home trying to get her out of his thoughts. It didn't help that her subtle fragrance – lotion or perfume, he couldn't tell – was on his clothes. *Not a good idea,* he kept thinking, sometimes out loud. But images of having a long conversation over pints at Rory's, or even holding her hand at the Yankees game, wouldn't leave his head. Pat was away, so he had no one with whom to talk it over.

When sessions started the very next week, Darlene took the lead. He and Rachel pretty much just helped. Darlene taught them icebreakers and set a good example for tone and enunciation. After three weeks, he and Rachel took over the training together, with Darlene observing. They picked up on each other's cues and added fun games, including Hangman (Richie took it easy on everyone), and the numbers started to grow. Lily Newsome came to every session, although she derailed the group often with conversation or off-color jokes. Angela and Tanya Franklin also came, nodding and contributing.

"You know what would make this easier?" Lily said at the end of the food shopping lesson, with a week left to go. "A J-O-B. Lord knows Food Stamps and welfare don't last. I'm tired of peanut butter and ramen noodles." There were a number of mm-hmms and yeses.

"Yeah, that's true," Richie agreed.

"How you go about getting a job around here?" asked another woman, a client of Stephanie's.

"Well," he said. "You know, you can pick up the paper, search the want ads. Maybe when you're out shopping, check out if they're hiring."

"Yeah, but we ain't got the papers," Lily said. "And man, I done retail, supermarkets. They don't pay sh– uh, nothin'.."

"Yeah, that's kinda true," he said. He wanted to say, "If you work hard enough you can work your way up," but thought better of it, thinking the cliché would ring hollow. He got a flash, an elevator pitch, so he said, "You know, what if we did a job workshop? You know, looking at want ads and stuff. Maybe interviews, resumes and stuff. Interested?"

"Yeah, I'd be down for that," Lily said. "Friend of mine? She got a resume, it looks nice. I got skills just like her. I need one of those." Others nodded their head and mm-hmmed.

"OK, great. Let me talk to Ms Petrocelli. See if we can get this thing off the ground."

"Huh," Rachel said after the clients had left. "Job Skills, huh?"

"Hey," he said. "I just came off a job search myself, so the info is totally fresh. Nobody's a jobs expert like a guy who's job searching. Maybe someone here can get a job, supplement the income a little."

Toni was enthusiastic about the idea. "OK, you're in charge. Let Darlene help you structure it, and it's all yours," she said.

"There's a computer and a printer in the back office, I noticed. Anyone using it?"

"It was a donation from one of the banks near us. I have no idea who's using it. Have at it."

It was actually a decent computer, loaded with Windows 3.1 and MS Word. The printer was a joke, however; a dox matrix deal that screed back and forth with painful slowness. When he wanted to print his own resume he walked away, got a cup of coffee, and it was still printing. He had to remember to use simpler font.

"Hey, partner," he heard across the suite.

"Yes?"

"Stop strangling cats over there. I'm trying to work."

It was a smaller crowd for his group which started mid-June, with two dads this time. One of them was Alfie Franklin, and Angela actually showed up. "Nothing else to do in this crummy place," she groaned. There was also a middle-aged, West Indian man actually named Don Johnson. Mr Johnson was a former bank teller, so on the side Richie asked if he would mind using his resume as an example. He was happy to oblige, and at the next session there were oohs and aahs, and funny questions from his star pupil Lily, like "What the f– uh, hell does that mean?"

The resume session was akin to a summer camp arts and crafts workshop, everyone working on a blank sheet. Their spelling and grammar, on the whole, was atrocious, but Angela's penmanship was brilliant. There were only eight of them, so he told them to make an appointment and he'd help them type it up on the computer. As predicted, the younger ones were much better than the older ones. Angela was a total wreck, barely able to point the mouse. But Lily was a spitfire, typing away faster than any intern he ever met. "I kicked a– uh, butt in typing in school," she said.

One day he just picked up the phone and started calling local banks, knowing that he had a real star on his hands in Don Johnson. He wrote out a sales pitch and put it in front of him, trying not to make it sound like he was reading from a script. On the second call, to a Citibank near the strip mall on Tarrytown Road, he got a positive response. "Sure, send him in," the woman had said. He immediately called Don and gave him the information. A week later, he saw Don waiting at the bus stop, looking like an English gentleman, replete with overcoat and umbrella. When Richie stopped his car to ask him if he got the job, Don said, "Yes, of course. They didn't tell you?"

"Hey, partner," Rachel said one day in the hallway. "Clients are talking about your jobs workshop. They love it. You're awesome, you know that? Keep it up." She winked and touched his arm.

"All in a day's work," he said, and winked back. Her smile this time seemed different; fewer teeth, brighter eyes. Or maybe he was imagining it. After she passed by, he went in the lunchroom and took a long drink of water.

Richie started to see progress among his clients. Angela had actually gotten involved in a lot. She came to all the recreational activities and attended a parenting workshop with Debbie. She even babysat for a family. Ronnie Tenielle found a distant family member willing to take Taisha and she went to a twenty-eight-day treatment program.

Lily Newsome's story, however, defied belief. Richie sent her on an interview with a temp agency. They offered her a receptionist job with a White Plains law firm on the spot. Two weeks after that, she disappeared from the shelter, gathering her things and leaving in the middle of a Thursday night. A week after that, she called him and said, "The firm hired me for good after a week. Then, they found out where I was living and hooked me up with a place owned by one of the partners. I pay less rent than these fools get from Section 8. Bladow!" At a team meeting, he said he considered it a result of Lily's latent ambition, along with a dose of dumb luck.

"Ah, take some credit," Toni had said. He saw Rachel lean back and wink at him.

In next week's meeting, Debbie said, "Akira's doing great. Comes to program all the time. Better attitude. Smiles a lot more, gets involved in more stuff, parenting workshops and stuff. I don't know if it's the meds or just a good time of year, but you keep encouraging her, pushing her gently. You made a difference."

Again, he didn't really see how. All he really did was fill out her service plan and check on her progress. He gave her little Post-It notes for important appointments, such as his own, and learned that orange was her favorite, so he gave her a whole pack. He was just being friendly, but it was true that they had a rapport. It seemed that every meeting she asked a question, like a curious sixth grader, like, "What does 'condensation' mean?" or "Why is the Gettysburg address such a big deal?" He was happy to oblige, and she nodded through his explanations.

"Uh, Rachel?" he asked over the partition at the end of a meeting with Akira.

"Yeah?"

"Do you have any Post-It notes? I gave Akira my last set."

She didn't say anything for a moment. He heard some rummaging. A moment later, a pack of orange Post-Its landed on his desk with a sudden thud.

"Jesus!" he yelled in surprise. Rachel burst out laughing. "By the way, 56 games in a row?" He'd just told Akira the story of DiMaggio's record streak in 1941.

"Yeah. They say it's statistically impossible. Then you know what? He hit in 15 more after that. Insane."

They had full-on conversations like this over the partition several times per day. Once in a while Darlene or Stephanie would ask them to keep their voices down.

One day, Richie said, "Hey Rachel. Want coffee?"

"Oh. Sure."

He knew where she sat and where things were on her desk, so he timed his toss perfectly. The bag of gourmet coffee beans landed on the right corner of her desk with a loud thud. She shrieked, then laughed.

"You nut job!" she said. "You almost killed me!"

"Sorry about that," he said, snickering. "Cream and sugar?"

"NO!" she yelled, and Stephanie asked them to keep it down.

Then they got into a playful habit of tossing things at one another over the partition: Post-Its, stuffed animals, paper wads. He brought an old Nerf basketball from home, and after hours one day they played "Blind Basketball": taking shots over the partition, guessing where the wastebasket is. Rachel had him shut out one Friday afternoon, so as he said, "Here it comes," he sneaked over to her office opening and saw her moving the basket.

"Cheater!" he yelled as he caught her. She shrieked with laughter. No one else was in the office, so no one told them to be quiet.

When one of the security guards went home sick, he offered to drive the residents on their daily ride to the Pathmark in White Plains. They needed a representative for a DSS meeting, so he volunteered and spent the day taking copious notes and writing a report on one of the most boring things he'd ever attended. When a family arrived late on a Friday, he offered to stay and do the intake, arranging all the sundries by himself and even helping them move their meager belongings into their unit, leaving just shy of eight o' clock.

"Hey, here's my spot starter," Toni said playfully, when he went into her office to ask something. She was finishing a meeting with the department heads. "I ask him to do something, he just says, 'no

202

problem', and does it. Gotta love that. Takes the ball every time. What do you need, Rich?" It was a much better internship than he'd ever had, if it could be treated that way. He was learning a lot, and Toni was an apt mentor, better than any professor. She never lost that slightly impatient way of probing him, never letting him go with "I don't know" or "I guess". She scrutinized his notes and service plans with painful meticulousness ("What do you mean by 'go to program'? How often, for how long, and what kind of interaction, and how are you gonna check?"). On the drive home, after stewing all afternoon, he'd realize that the advice made sense.

But one day he heard Rachel talking to Ellen on the phone. "How *are* you, partner, we *miss* you!" At lunch or in meetings sometimes the other caseworkers would talk about Ellen and the things she'd done, how she'd taught ILS or other workshops. They mentioned how she handled past difficult clients, how she'd intervened with substance abusers, put herself in harm's way when there was an argument between residents. Sometimes they'd talk about her baby, her husband, how generous she was.

He also still needed to work on confronting clients. He felt like a little kid again, like the time he told his mom he broke a vase. He recalled her screams, her outbursts, and spankings. So he stumbled and stuttered every time he had to tell a client something they didn't like. He sneaked up to the pantry when no one, especially Rachel, was watching.

The subject matter, the clientele, still made him nervous, uneasy. When some people didn't get what they wanted or were pushed even slightly to do the right thing, they went ballistic. Sometimes he thought he made progress with someone, and they'd get kicked out

RICHIE THE CASEWORKER Christopher Febles

for fighting over something stupid, like the way someone looked at another's boyfriend.

And more often than not, there were client failures. He'd send someone to New Futures, and they'd relapse. He'd refer a smart young man to WCC, and he'd get arrested. He had a client lined up for a job at a meatpacking plant, and he showed up intoxicated. "What the hell kinda people you sending me? Dirtbag," said the owner, who hung up in his face. And at least once a week, a parent would show up late to pick up their child from day care or the bus, and he'd have to babysit on top of his regular duties.

"This is so fucking frustrating," he once breathed to himself at his desk.

"What's that, Rich?" Rachel said from the other side of the partition.

"Oh, uh, nothing, nothing," he said.

Meanwhile, Richie had been to no other Yankee games that season. Every weekend the Yankees were in town, Pat was away. Or, when he was home, he spent time with Marilyn.

"Ah, you know how it is," Pat would say. "Marilyn wants me to go to dinner. Parents' house. You know." He'd shrug and apologize.

Richie said it was fine. The team was mediocre, anyway, less fun to watch.

One day, when he walked in, Wilson asked, "Hey, how's your boy doing?"

"Donnie Baseball? Eh, he's always been a slow starter. He'll come around. Good glove, though. Always scoops those infield throws."

"Oh, yeah, that's worth its weight in gold, ain't it? He's a great ballplayer, man, don't let no one tell you different."

"Oh, I don't. Just ask that guy in college who said, 'Wally Joyner's better.'" He'd had to be separated from that California surfer kid at a frat party.

Wilson laughed. "Hey, are you comin' to Johnny's Reef tonight?"

"Where?"

"Johnny's Reef. It's a seafood joint on City Island. Get some shrimp, have a few beers. Everyone gets there around 7. Same crew that goes to Cactus Jack's. Right on the water. We'll have a good time."

He'd never been to City Island, so he had no idea what to expect. Pat was on a date with Marilyn, again. He'd planned to relax at home with a pizza and the Yankee game. This sounded better.

"OK, sure. I'm there."

"It's BYOB, so bring something if you want."

"What?"

"BYOB. Bring your own beverage."

"I went to enough BYOB parties in college to know what that means." Truth be told, the number was two. "Really? What kinda place is this?"

"Outdoor joint. We get some shrimp, hang out in the parking lot. Real-laid back."

"They let you drink out in the open like that?"

He chuckled. "Don't worry about that. Remember you partyin' with two ex-cops. Just don't get hammered or nothin'."

He was skeptical, but on the way there he stopped at a deli and picked up a six pack of Sam Adams, hearing Pat's voice in his head: "Don't bring the cheap stuff! What's wrong with you?" He badly underestimated the traffic: only a narrow one-lane road over a dinky drawbridge connects City Island to the mainland. He didn't see many buildings more than one story. The town from "Jaws" came to mind.

He'd been on the road an hour when he got there at 7:30. To call it a restaurant was a stretch; Wilson was right to refer to it as a "joint". The parking lot was so huge and so packed, and the view of the Sound so spectacular, the restaurant itself was something of an afterthought. The Throggs Neck Bridge, not to mention Queens, never looked better, the placid waters glistening bronze and gold in the twilight. Parking was like a mall on Black Friday. But as he tooled around for a while, he spotted Rachel waving at him. She was standing in a space, holding it for him, holding a Coors Light in a bottle cosy in her hand, smiling with all her white teeth.

"Hey, partner, you made it!" she said, hugging him around the neck again.

"Thanks a bunch," he said. "What are they giving away in this place, anyway?"

"Free views, great fried shrimp, and work buddies," she said. "Jones has the radio on. Figured you and Toni'd wanna hear the game." She pointed at a big Ford pick-up truck, its tailgate open with a huge red cooler and a boom box in the back. He walked over and made his offering.

"Oh, he brought the good stuff," Jones said, accepting the six-pack and putting it in the cooler.

"Yeah, 'cause he has taste," Toni said.

"What's wrong with Bud Light? I got two cases for twenty-five dollars at Costco."

"That's what's wrong, right there," Wilson chimed in. "Can I have one of those, Rich?"

"Sure," he said. He looked around and looked for something other than the textbook definition of what he saw: a bunch of people hanging out in the parking lot drinking beer. Four years ago he could have been arrested for what he was doing now. If someone asked what he did this weekend, he'd say, "I enjoyed cocktails at a waterfront bistro with my colleagues." But no one ever did.

He excused himself to get his dinner. It was packed to the gills, nowhere to sit, much less stand. Fans blared overhead, orders shouted from across the worn steel counter. In line in front of him was a man wearing a polo and a pink sweater tied around his neck who asked what the cashier recommended. "Let's go!" said a huge guy behind him. Richie knew better than to dawdle, so he ordered the shrimp basket. It was greasy and salty, and complemented his beer perfectly.

His work friends were holding court on their health plan and retirement options, both paling in comparison to what the NYPD offered. Though the conversation was heated at times, the glory of the city's underrated waterfront soothed him. The game played on the radio, but he allowed himself a talk with Stephanie, who told a lovely story about one of her clients.

During a break in the baseball action, he went to take in more of the view. He leaned over the railing and took a deep breath, filling his lungs with a surprising and refreshing scent of the sea. Not at all what he expected.

After a few moments, Rachel came up alongside him. "No bleachers tonight?" she asked.

"Nah," he said, smiling. "Pat's on a date with Marilyn."

She had her hair down around her shoulders. The breeze forced her to brush it away from her face often. "You like her?"

"Oh, sure, sure. She's great, very funny lady, keeps us boys in check. She's practically family. But you know, she lives in DC now. I don't see her that often."

"Oh. Is Pat moving there?"

Richie shook his head. "Not – not exactly. They kinda split time every weekend or so. He goes there, she comes here. They're, uh, trying to make it work long-distance."

"Oh. You think… You think they'll, you know…"

He nodded again, looked straight ahead. "Yeah. Yeah, I think so. I don't know, it's…"

"What?"

He inhaled, a little startled. If he could tell anyone, he could tell Rachel.

"It's just… I think he's kinda… in between? You know, to get married and live together, start a family and stuff, but he's kinda… keeping an eye on me, sorta. And, well… sometimes I feel like I'm standing in the way. He's been… supporting me since I went to college. So…"

"You'd miss him."

"Yep, that's about right. Me and Pat? We're kinda the only family we have."

She looked at him. "Really? What about your parents?"

Again he thought: *this is probably as safe as it's gonna get.*

"Well… my dad was never really around. He cheated on my mom, got fired from his job, and took off when I was nine; never heard from him again, not really. And my mom… well, we had kind of a… falling out five years ago. She moved to New Hampshire with her new husband. She was… kinda messed up. She had a way of, I don't know… making us feel bad about ourselves. So, Pat and I, we kinda said, you know, a few years ago that we… wouldn't talk to her anymore."

"Oh. Oh, Rich. I – I'm sorry, I didn't mean to pry –"

"No, no, it's fine, really, it's fine. We've been, you know, surviving for all these years, me in college and him at work, and it's been really fun. He's the only guy I'll see games with. We'll…see what happens with Marilyn, you know?"

She tapped his arm. "I hope it's not for a while. You guys seem to love each other."

"Yeah. He's a good guy. I guess I'm putting it out of my mind for a while. What about you? Brothers and sisters?"

"Nope," she said with a sigh. "Just me and my mom."

"Oh?"

"Yeah. Well, my dad died about ten years ago."

"Oh, God. Now it's my turn. Sorry, I didn't –"

She shook her head, and touched his arm again. "It's OK, it was a long time ago. Lung cancer. He smoked a lot. He was always working, too. Construction. Didn't see him a lot when I was a kid. He went pretty quickly. So, my mom and I got to be real close. Like roommates."

"OK. That sounds nice."

"Yeah. Funny lady. Reminds me of Toni sometimes."

"Cool. Sorry about your dad, though."

"Oh," she said, waving her hand. "That's OK. Thanks. You know, I think it forced me to find family wherever I could. Like college, like volunteering, and definitely like HSA. Right?"

"Yeah. Best thing about this place is the coworkers. Great people."

She looked out onto the Sound with him. "We should do that. All go to a Yankees game."

"I'd like that. It'd be fun. When was the last time you went?"

"Oh, man. I don't remember. I think my dad took me when I was a little kid, and..." she pretended to cringe, "I think I fell asleep."

Richie gasped in jest: "How dare you!"

She laughed. "I know, I suck. I'm not a diehard like you. But it's always fun."

She was looking out on the water, again brushing her hair from her face. She had a petite nose, and he just noticed a few light freckles just beneath her eyes. He looked at her hands, the shiny red nail polish that had to have been done just hours ago. His own hands were clammy and twitchy, so it was a good thing he didn't follow his instinct and clasp hers in his. The sea breeze, the view, the comfort in talking, all prompted him to say:

"Uh, Rachel? I was wondering, uh... maybe, uh... you'd like to... you know. Go to a ballgame? Uh, just- just... us?"

He knew the answer in a second.

She started, stood up a bit straighter. Her pretty smile darted away.

"Oh," she said. "Oh. Rich. Oh, geez. I'm really flattered –"

I could probably swim to Queens from here, he thought. *Maybe I'll get lucky and get hit by a tugboat.*

"Oh, OK, uh, OK, OK," he stammered, looking at the ground.

"No, no," she said, touching his forearm. "No, it's OK, really. It's a lovely offer. I'm sure it'd be fun, but, you know, uh..." and she squinted a little when she looked at him. "Well, don't take this the wrong way, but, uh… I don't think it's such a good idea to date someone you work with."

It was on the list of rejections he thought he'd get. But far below "I have a boyfriend" or "I like you as a friend".

"Oh," he said, nodding furiously. "Yeah, yeah, yeah. That's right, you know, true. Sorry I assumed –"

"Oh, no, no," she said, touching his arm again. "No, you didn't do anything wrong. Really, I'm touched you think of me that way. It's been really great getting to know you, Rich, being your partner, your office neighbor. You're smart, you're funny, you work hard, and you care. Those are all great things. I'm sure someday you're gonna make some girl very happy."

"Thanks," he said, mustering a smile. "That's real nice of you. Sorry, again."

"Nothing to be sorry for," she said, smiling with those shiny white teeth, a once-thrilling sight that now hurt him. "You, uh, wanna go back to the group?"

Actually, I gotta go for a swim, so peace out.

"Sure," he said, not looking at her, walking a little behind.

Jones had just finished an anecdote, and everyone was laughing. They hadn't noticed he'd returned. He knew that just storming off immediately would give something away. So he opened a Sam Adams that he didn't intend to drink, and stood there, smiling stupidly.

After another inning came to a close, Toni came over to him and said, "Hey, Rich, got a minute? I'm taking off. Walk me to my car?"

He walked alongside her in the buzzing parking lot, relieved to have an excuse. "What's up?"

"So, listen," she said. "You might have heard. Ellen had the baby premature. June 7. She was due in July."

He'd forgotten about Ellen, about her return, scheduled for August. What did this mean for him? "Oh, geez. That's awful. How's the baby?"

"Still in the hospital. He's OK, surviving, but not home yet. Might be a while, and even when he does come home he's gonna be in and out of the doctor's office. Rough."

"That's terrible. Is Ellen OK?"

"I talked to her on the phone this morning. She's OK, but stressed out and very busy. She's a steady lady, though. I'm sure she'll be OK in the long term. But she's gonna need more time. She asked me about you, wanted to know what your situation was."

"Situation?"

"Yeah. Whether you liked it here, if you thought you'd want to stay longer."

"Oh." His eyes were steady, but his mind scrambled for a suitable reaction. No dice.

"So I know six months comes up in August, but what do you think?"

"You mean, stay on? Casework?"

Toni nodded.

"How much longer?"

"I don't know, Rich. Could be a while. She told me maybe October. Company policy is iffy on that one, but Central told me I could use my discretion."

He looked at her. She'd changed into jeans, and had put on a SUNY Stony Brook sweatshirt. She had her hands on her hips and wore that same, expectant look on her face, one that asked him to come up with a good answer fast. His mind went to the smell of fish, cigarettes and car exhaust.

"I know," Toni said, guessing his thoughts again. "It's a weird situation. You're still learning the job, still feeling out if this is the thing for you. But you're a vested employee once you hit six months, OK? You'll get vacation time, personal days, health care, the works. Maybe that's a little incentive. And when Ellen comes back, we can offer you a spot at one of the other sites. Maybe Morris – they're always looking, and you've been there."

And I'll pass, he thought. He also noticed she said "when" and not "if". He was feeling antsy, nervous, angry after his conversation with Rachel. He felt a powerful urge, an energy in his legs and feet to run, get in the Escort and drive out west until the wheels fell off.

He said: "Could I have some time to think about it?"

Toni started. "Well, sure, Rich. Of course you can. I just thought you'd have jumped at it."

"Oh, no, no. It's a great offer, don't get me wrong. I'm just… thinking about a few things. Thinking things over. Is that OK?"

"Of course, of course. Sooner rather than later, though. I'd like to know if I need to go out looking. Early next week?"

"That'd be great. Thanks."

She paused. There was that look again. "None of my business, but you OK? Anything happen recently?"

Damn it, stop doing that!

"No. I'm good. Why?"

She looked at him, shook her head. "No reason. Let's talk soon, OK?"

"Sure, Toni. And thanks."

"No problem," she said. She looked back at Jones' pick-up. "Hope the Yanks can pull this off."

He almost choked on his most evil thought of the decade: *Who cares about the Yankees?*

"Well, they're not looking too good lately," Richie said, folding his arms. "But with this Wild Card thing, anything can happen."

"That's right. Playoffs. Ever been?"

"Nope. Me and Donnie Baseball. Never been."

She snapped her fingers. "That's right. You're too young to have seen the 70's guys in action. Oooh, boy, we gotta get you to the playoffs."

He just smiled weakly. "Sure. And, and uh… thanks again for the opportunity."

"Wish I could do more," she said, getting into her car, giving the thumbs up to an SUV that wanted her space.

When he opened the door to the apartment, he heard Marilyn's voice. It was sharp, louder than usual.

"OK, Pat. But now you know how I feel. I just think –"

He heard Pat interrupt her. "Richie? That you?"

He approached on tip toes. Marilyn was standing with her arms tightly folded. On seeing Richie, she dropped them to her sides, one hand clasping the other wrist. Pat sat on the couch, leaning forward, head drooping.

"Hey," he said softly.

"Hi Richie," Marilyn said, forcing a smile. "You – did you have a good night?"

"Yeah, it was good. What's going on?"

Marilyn slowly sat in the easy chair. Pat put his hands on his head.

"God," Richie said. "What? What is it?"

Pat finally raised his head and let out a huge sigh. "You're looking at an ex-CEO, Richie."

Richie felt his arms go weak. *More good news*, he thought. *Maybe there'll be another baseball strike.*

"Oh, shit. Really?"

"It was too good to be true, Richie. Always be careful of that. This really looked like a cool thing to do, like I could be someone. Nope. We were getting hammered by AOL and Mindspring and

Earthlink and every other monster ISP from here to Silicon Valley. Then, both of our web developers quit, half of our board quit, and I was answering the goddamn phones, sweeping up the office. Now our stock is worthless. My stock, the stock I'd hoped to cash in on someday, is worth shit. We made the decision today to close up shop."

Richie took a deep breath. He put his hands in his pockets. "Oh, shit. I'm – I'm sorry, Pat. I know this meant a lot to you."

He straightened a bit, threw up his hands. "Hey, I tried, right? I tried. I guess… whatever."

There was a long silence. "So… it's over?"

Pat just nodded. He clasped his hands in front of his face.

"Oh, man. I'm really sorry. What… What're you… gonna do now?"

Pat threw up his hands. "Look for a new job, I guess."

"And, uh," Marilyn said, her hands clasped. "Richie? Pat and I were talking and, um…" She sighed, and restarted. "OK. Cards on the table. I want Pat with me. In DC."

Richie's breath got short. "OK," he said softly.

There was a pause. Marilyn brushed her hair out of her face. She looked at Pat, then Richie. "So… I don't know. This…"

"You want him to look for a job in DC," Riche said softly.

She nodded. "Mmmhmm. But I know. That splits you guys up. That splits up your family. And I feel like shit just asking, just telling you that. But it's true. And I don't know what to do about it."

He furrowed his brow, stretched out his fingers to prevent them from becoming a fist.

Marilyn looked down. "Guys. I'd never do anything, anything, to come between you, to split you up. I love you guys, both of you. I just – I just want you both to know that… I – Richie, I love Pat. He's the one. I hate to be selfish, but… I just don't know what the solution is."

Richie said nothing. He noticed a stain on the rug from one of the pizza nights.

"I guess I can stick it out a little longer," she said. "I mean, we see each other enough. But one of these days… I just want to be part of this, too."

Richie picked his head up and looked at her. Her legs were crossed and her hands were in her lap.

"Can you guys do me a favor, and just talk about it? Think about it? I know, it's a tough situation. And I don't want to do anything until you're ready. OK? I'd never want to split you up. I just wanted you – really, you, Richie – to know how I felt." She got her purse. "I'm sorry, guys. Please talk." She kissed Pat. She touched Richie on the shoulder. Then she let herself out.

Richie drifted over to the easy chair. He took the same spot Marilyn had just occupied. He exhaled in relief at finally sitting down.

Pat shook his head. "I'm sorry, Richie. I failed. I failed you. I'm sorry."

"No, Pat. Not your fault about the company."

Pat threw up his hands. "Well, actually..." Then he put his hand on his forehead. "Sorry about Marilyn. She was a little forward."

Richie swallowed. "Well. She expressed how she felt. She loves you and wants you with her. I get it."

Pat nodded.

Richie swallowed, stretched out his hands. He noticed his lip shaking, so he rubbed his face. He took a deep breath and said, "Pat? I meant what I said. I'd never, ever, get in the way of anything you want to do. You did so much –"

"It's OK, Richie, it's OK. No, she – she kinda talked out of turn. This distance thing, it's been tougher than we thought. Really, we get, like, Saturdays to be together, that's it. She wants more, I want more. I don't know. We're... working on it."

"What are you gonna do?"

Pat shook his head. "Look. For jobs. But I don't know, Richie. She wants me to look in DC. I... don't know yet. I guess I'll see what works out."

A fire engine went by. Richie's urge to run away had evaporated, replaced with a desire to hide in the closet. He considered lying, saying he got fired or the place was closing. But instead he put one hand on the arm of the chair, as if to steady himself, and said: "Uh... Toni asked me to stay on until October."

"Oh," Pat said, picking up his head. "Oh. That's good, that's good. Right?"

Quietly, Richie said, "Yeah. Good."

"I mean, you like it there. Tough job, tough place. But, hey. That – that means you're permanent, right?"

Richie nodded. "When Ellen comes back, I probably have to work at, you know... Morris, or Brooklyn or something. But, yeah. I have a regular job now."

"OK," Pat said, looking away. "Good, Richie. Congrats."

"So, look," Richie said, hands and feet tingling, "if, uh, if this means, you can, you know, look for jobs in DC –"

"No, Richie," Pat said, "I – this isn't all about you." He shook his head. "That came out wrong. I mean, this is my home, Richie. I mean, I don't know. Am I ready to leave New York? Be apart from you, from everything here? I don't know. So, yeah, thanks for letting me know about your job. I'm happy for you. But... we'll see. OK?"

Richie nodded. He smiled, doing his best to hide the shivers and his closing throat.

"Well, here's one thing," Pat said, running his hand through his hair. "I think you're gonna have to take the bills for a while, man."

"Right," Richie said, hands on his lap. He thought about Monday morning: having to slink past Rachel's office, hearing her voice over the partition, smelling her lotion or perfume, getting ready for a day of being screamed at. He wondered how he'd fake enthusiasm in answering Toni's offer.

"Sure, Pat," he said. "No problem."

Pat nodded. "OK. Good. And, um, I'm sorry, but… we're a little short on last month's rent."

Richie tried to hold his gaze, tried not to react. "Oh."

"But it's OK. I told Charlie I'd send him the balance of the rent in a check. I'll get you the address. You know what? I'm tired of this 'leaving cash in the basement' thing. Just not secure. I'll ask if we can just send a check a little ahead of the first of the month. Transition over, you know? I'll take care of that."

Great way to start this whole independence thing. Thanks for the head start.

"OK," Richie said. "I already know how to do the rest of the bills. I'm pretty sure I have enough to cover it. But, uh, no big purchases for a while, right?"

Pat smiled. "Thanks, man. You're a lifesaver. My bro. World-saver, brother-saver."

"Nah," he said. "I'm just a caseworker."

He took the remote to see the game highlights. The screen flashed and cut out, and all that remained on the fifteen-inch screen was a tiny white dot.

"Damn," Richie said.

Richie came in at 8:30 that Monday and told Toni he'd stay the extra two months.

221

"Great," she said. "Talk to Winnie about setting up your benefits and stuff. I'll keep my eye out for jobs at Morris or maybe one of the Brooklyn sites. They always need people."

"OK," he said. "Thanks."

"You're welcome, Rich. It's been good to have you," she said, moving on to other paperwork. He excused himself.

"Hi, Rachel," he said, more softly than usual, passing her office.

She looked up. She smiled with all her teeth again. "Hi, Rich!" she said in her perky voice, and went back to what she was doing.

A few moments later, the phone rang.

"Richard McGinn," he answered.

"Hello, Richard," said a flat, annoyed voice.

"Oh, uh, hi," he said, not wanting to say the word, 'Mom' in the office.

"Hi. What do you want?"

"Uh, yeah…" he said, taken aback and frightened. He almost forgot he'd called. "Um, how are you?"

He heard a sigh. "What do you need, Richard?"

Everything he planned to say, to ask, went out the window. "Oh, uh, you know, just wanted to, I don't know, say hello?"

She scoffed. "Right. You probably need money or something. Well, you two cut me out. Anyway, we're not doing so hot here, either. So I can't do anything for you."

There was a silence. His throat closed. The receiver got damp. "Um, uh, OK. I, uh… I guess, I'm sorry to have bothered you."

"Right. Bye, Richard." She hung up.

He talked to the dial tone, so anyone listening wouldn't know the difference. "OK, thanks, bye."

He sighed. What was he thinking? He didn't have money for too many pints, so he couldn't have been drunk. He looked out the window for a while. It was a scorching summer day outside, and he could see waves coming off the parking lot asphalt. He wondered if she would call home and tell Pat that he'd called.

He doubted it.

The Slump

After that day at Johnny's Reef, Richie started coming in at 8:55. Then 9:05. Then 9:15.

He never did case notes. He stopped following up with programs. Instead, he just reacted with annoyance anytime someone called to consult on a client. A few times he had clients sign blank service plans, filling in the details later. He cut his conversations with Akira short, claiming he had things to do, and tried not to notice as she sadly slinked away. He discovered that the computer in the back had Tetris, and he made a point of looking serious, like he was working on something important. As an excuse to get out of the office, he volunteered to drive the van to Pathmark whenever he could. He took all his lunches outside, stretching the limits of the hour he was allotted.

At least the Yankees had revived themselves. They'd become competitive again, so when a doubleheader with the powerful Cleveland Indians was scheduled for a Thursday afternoon in August, he asked Toni if he could leave early. Seeing two games for the price of one was a bargain, and Pat readily agreed to go, even as he was in the middle of a job search.

"You're lucky you're a Yankee fan," Toni said. "Anyone asks, you're going to a meeting off-site, which is technically true. Just remember the visuals of leaving at 4. Some people might get the wrong idea."

The plan was to come in at 8 and leave at 4; he arrived at 8:15. Toni dropped by at 8:30 and did an impromptu supervision, which devolved into a preview of the big doubleheader that night. As the meeting ended, she whispered, "I'm the only one who knows you're going to the game, right?"

"Yeah, no doubt about it," he said.

She called him as the clock ticked toward 4. "Get outta here," she said. "Finish up what you have and go. Make sure you drink your water. It's hot out there."

"Yes, Mother," he said playfully.

"Do it, smart-ass," she said, chuckling.

When he hung up, he realized there was someone waiting outside his office. It was Angela, pushing ahead Jonathan in the stroller.

"I hope I'm not interrupting," she said, as she pushed the stroller into his office and plopped down into a seat.

He got flustered. "Actually, I have a meeting I need to go to, right now," he said, gathering up things, hoping she'd get the hint. But hints were not Angela's strong point.

"Actually," she said sarcastically, "I need diapers."

"You don't have any?"

"Nope."

"What happened?"

"I left a big package behind when I went to Peekskill," she said. "And I'm fresh out."

He looked at his watch. "And you can't get to the store."

"Nope."

"You don't have taxi money."

"Nope."

"Our diaper supply is running low, you know. It's really just for new families and emergencies."

"This isn't an emergency? I don't have any. He'll just poop his pants."

"Nobody has any you can borrow until you get to the store tomorrow?"

"Nope."

He frowned, unable to hide his annoyance. "Just a sec," he said, sighing. He stomped out of the office and speed walked to the pantry. On the way, Alfie Franklin spotted him and called to him. "Hey Mr McGinn, can I talk to you?"

"Mmm, I got something to do, then I got a meeting to go to."

"It'll only take a sec."

He had his back to Alfie, so he rolled his eyes and clenched his fists. He turned and said, "OK. Give me a moment to collect this stuff. Then you can walk me back to the casework suite."

He gathered some loose diapers and put them in a plastic bag. He came back out and said to Alfie: "What's up?"

"I need a reference for a job."

"That's great! A mechanic's job?"

"No, it's a CVS in Mt. Vernon. But it's somethin'."

"Good to hear, good to hear. Happy to do it. Come on down and leave me the info. I'll call them first thing in the morning."

"Actually, can you call right now?"

"No, I can't. I gotta go somewhere."

"Ain't the office open until 5?"

"Yeah, but I have somewhere to be."

"Leaving early?" Alfie said, hopefulness in his voice.

"No. I have a meeting off-site. Can't this wait until tomorrow?"

"Yeah, but I wanna get the job now."

"It's not like you'll start tomorrow."

"Come on, man. Help me out?"

He saw the doleful look in Aflie's eyes. He huffed and said, "Come on."

He walked Alfie back to the caseworker suite. Rachel saw him in the hall and said, "Don't you have a meeting?"

"Yeah, just gotta take care of some stuff," he said.

"Are those emergency diapers?"

"Yeah, Rachel, they are," he said tersely. "I don't have time to argue with Angela right now. I know they're only for emergencies. Can you give me a break?"

"OK, geez!" she said, frowning at him. "Don't get all testy, Rich." She scoffed and kept walking.

He entered his cubicle and all but plopped the bag of diapers in Angela's lap. "Here," he said. "That's got to be the last time. You have to learn to hang on to things and budget."

"Yes, sir!" Angela said, saluting. "Just kidding. Thanks. Hey, can I talk to you about something else?"

"Ms LeFleur, I have another client with an urgent matter, and I'm late for my meeting. It's going to have to wait."

"Oh, excuuuse me," she said, standing and wheeling her stroller out and around Alfie. "Just kidding. Thanks again!" she added cheerfully.

"OK, Mr Franklin, give me the info."

He wrote it down, picked up the phone and called. The manager was not available. He told Alfie this.

"Can you try later today?" he asked.

"No, I can't," Richie said sternly. "You just heard: I have somewhere to be, and I'm already late." He gathered himself, as he knew he was getting upset. "Look. I'm really glad to hear about this job, but it's going to have to wait. First thing in the morning, OK? I have the info. I'll call you before 11 and let you know what's going on. Deal?"

"OK, thanks," Alfie mumbled, and skulked away.

Richie grabbed his keys and wallet, and did his best to sneak out. "Bye, Rachel," he said, walking past her office. She didn't respond. He saw one of his clients in the quad by the playground, and moved faster through the front door, saying a quick good-bye to Wilson at the desk.

"Big doubleheader today," Wilson said. "Cleveland looks unstoppable."

"You watch," Richie said. "They're gonna show something today." He instantly regretted saying it.

"All right, my friend. Good luck at your meeting. Go Yankees," he said, which made Richie wonder.

He had to park way up the hill on Ogden Avenue, so high up that he was above the lights of the Stadium. He had changed into his Don Mattingly shirt in the car, pausing to let a group of neighborhood women walk by before he did so. By the time he reached Pat he was covered in sweat.

"Holy crap. You look like shit, dude," Pat said, who was drinking from a water bottle. "Finish this. Cleveland just scored."

"Shit," Richie said, finishing the water in one gulp. He was surrounded on all sides by similarly sweaty fans. The place was as packed as he'd ever seen it.

"This is fucking nutso," Pat said. "Watch your ass. Let's try not to get our asses kicked tonight."

"Deal," Richie said. "I didn't blow off work to watch some suck-job game or get beat up."

Pat looked at him. "You're not in trouble, are you?"

Richie waved him off. "Don't worry about it. Toni's my boss. I'm golden."

"Hey, did you get benefits yet?"

The question pulled his attention back from the field. "Huh? Oh, yeah. I'm all set. Health insurance, sick time, whatever."

Pat smiled and patted his shoulder. "Wow. A real working man. I'm proud of you, man. Good for you. Oh, of course. OF COURSE! YOU SUCK, KELLY!" Light-hitting infielder Pat Kelly had just struck out. "That guy's a menace. Teach Jeter to play second and GET THIS ASSHOLE OUT OF HERE!"

Richie laughed out loud. "Hey, how's your job search?"

"YOU'RE WORSE THAN STEVE SAX, YOU TURD!" Pat yelled at the field. "Eh, still looking. Rough out there. Eh, but who gives a shit. This is Yankee baseball! Let's beat these shitbags!" And he let out a loud whoop, other fans joining in.

It was so hot they opted against beer, knowing it would dehydrate them. The bleachers were extra rowdy. They had to sit way up in Section 41, underneath the Diamondvision, across from a group of fans who had in their possession a number of percussion instruments, including a guira. They were ready to cheer on Cleveland's Dominican phenom, born in the DR and raised in Washington Heights: Manny Ramirez. Queen Tina had to be restrained from taking them all on a once.

The first game was a great one. Everyone seemed to know, as he did, that beating the Indians would mean a lot toward making the playoffs. Donnie Baseball got a hit to give the Yankees the lead; Pat nearly tore his shirt shaking him. And when the Yankee catcher, Mike Stanley, hit his third home run of the day, Richie thought the place would explode. He'd never seen the feat accomplished, and neither had the other fifty thousand or so fans. A tornado of water bottles, beer cups, stale hot dogs and underwear went soaring onto the field.

"Holy shit!" Pat yelled, shouting over the din. "Have you ever seen anything like this?"

Richie started a "Cleveland Sucks" chant, then gained momentum. Then he yelled, "We're going to the fucking Series!"

As he said it, he got nervous. Was he superstitious? No. Not really. Yes?

Then, the Yankees slowly, tortuously surrendered their four-run lead. An error here, a bloop single there, a line drive double driving in two. Manny joined in the parade of hits with a ball that caromed off the right field wall. By the time Donnie Baseball came up in the ninth, they were losing. Then Richie's hero hit into a double play to end the game. Richie heard somebody echo his sentiment by yelling a petulant, "Fuck you guys!" as the Indians trotted off the field. Manny, playing right field, pounded his glove in triumph, pointing to his cheering section in the back.

"Are you fucking serious?" Pat hollered at the field. "I sweated through my favorite T-shirt, for this?"

That made the second game something of an anticlimax. The Yankees blew a lead, and Richie was too tired and crusty with sweat to rally his team. Sure enough, they wilted and lost that one, too. The bleacher crew was mostly silent, only cursing when fans started to leave in the fourth. Manny's fan club serenaded them out of the building.

Richie and Pat trudged up the long incline of Ogden Avenue to reach the Escort. Their feet got heavier and heavier as they approached, and by the time they got to the car they were once again drenched in sweat.

"Ugh," Pat groaned. "I wasted all afternoon with this shit when I coulda been getting a job."

"I should've been at work, doing notes or something," Richie whined. "Maybe mopping the floor. Anything but this shit. Goddamn it."

Pat sighed. "Hey. I think it's gonna be a while. Until the next game, I mean."

Richie waited in the queue on 164th Street to get to the Concourse. He didn't look at Pat. "Yeah. I figured."

"I mean, you know. We gotta save money, and I gotta look for a job. And spend time with Marilyn. You know what I mean."

Richie turned onto Jerome to escape the traffic. Still not looking at Pat, he said, "Yeah, Pat. I get it. Don't worry about it."

"Hey, what's your problem?"

"What?"

"I said I was sorry."

"Fine, Pat, I said I get it. Fine. OK."

Pat shook his head and gently threw up his hands. They drove the rest of the way in silence.

Richie thought about the next day: half of his inspections, a team meeting, and someone from the Board of Education was coming to review cases, none of which were his but he was required to sit in. He had four Service Plans, one with Angela.

Had he known they'd blow both games, he'd have stayed home and listened to it on the radio. They still hadn't bought a TV.

The next day, Pat told Richie that he was going to take a break from job searching and spend a week in DC with Marilyn.

"Hey, you have vacation time now," Pat said. "Why don't you come down?"

"Oh, I have client meetings I can't miss," he lied. "Besides I have to give more notice."

Late that morning, Toni pulled all the caseworkers into her office. She told them that Tajo was going in for surgery on his foot and would be out for two weeks. Everyone would take a few cases, and Darlene would take all the Spanish-speaking clients, with Hector from Maintenance to help her translate during meetings.

"Rich," she said, "you have the smallest caseload, so if we have families come in, you'll do the intakes, OK?"

"Sure, no problem," he said, groaning inside.

But the extra work was a problem. That same day, Ronnie Teneille didn't pick up Taisha. Wilson brought her into his office by the hand, saying, "She's all yours, Rich." He was able to distract her with crayons for about three minutes, when she got up and ran down the hall. He had to play hide-and-seek to find her, rolling up his sleeves to cool himself off. When she tried to bolt for the back door of the suite, he grabbed her by the arm, and she slipped and fell, and started crying.

Stephanie came by, "Aw, are you OK?"

For a second, Rich thought she was talking to him. He felt awful for having hurt the little kid. "Uh, yeah, she just fell as she was trying to, you know, leave."

For forty-five minutes he got nothing done. She opened all his drawers and started taking out files. She drew on the walls with crayons and markers. She spat out the candy he offered her because it was mint, right into his cupped hands. Stephanie finally came by with a resident willing to take Taisha, whose mother showed up five minutes later. The episode caused him to miss an intake with a family.

The next day, he stayed until 6:00 with a family intake. As soon as he walked out the caseworker suite, however, Tanya Franklin was there with her baby.

"Yo, Mr McGinn, you got diapers?"

Yeah, I got some in my wallet, he thought. "What happened?" he asked.

She explained that she set them down when she was transferring buses, and someone must have run off with them. "I don't have no money, and I got like three diapers left."

He sucked his teeth and asked her to wait in the lobby. But when he got to the pantry, his key didn't work. He trudged back to the security desk. A new guard on the late shift didn't seem to understand that he was a caseworker and was entitled to a pass key. He tried to call Jones but he was gone for the day. Instead, he radioed for one of the other guards, who took twenty minutes to get there. Then he walked Richie up to the pantry and watched him as he took diapers. When he got back to the lobby, Tanya was gone.

"Sorry, but Harris was fussin'," she said when he called. "Could you bring them up here?" He huffed his way to "F" Building and dropped them off. "Oh, could I ask you a question?" she said.

"Let's do it tomorrow," Richie said, walking away.

Later in the week there was an organization-wide training on sexual harassment. The trainer banged on the table like a second-grade teacher to get their attention. It was all lecture-based, without a video in sight. At each of the breaks he saw Rachel chatting and laughing with coworkers from other HSA sites. So he went back to his desk, where there always seemed to be messages: from Lydia about a client that hadn't showed, from DSS about a discrepancy, from employers telling him there were no openings, from Eleena Marvin asking for something. Around 4, Wilson got his attention through the Multi-purpose Room windows, and when he excused himself to see what he wanted, he saw Taisha holding his hand. He was almost grateful for the distraction until Taisha started another impromptu game of hide-and-seek. He found someone to watch her around 4:55, and was so worked up he left immediately at 5. He saw Ronnie getting off the bus on the way to his car.

"Pick up your friggin' kid," he said angrily.

He was exhausted, so tired in fact that he accidentally turned off his alarm instead of snoozing on Thursday morning. He arrived at 10:05. Angela LeFleur and Eleena Marvin were waiting for him outside the casework office.

"Yo, Mr McGinn, I gotta talk to you," Eleena said.

"I was here first!" Angela said indignantly.

"No, I got somethin' important."

236

"Nuh-uh. I got housing stuff to do, and I was waiting here since 8:30."

"No way you was here that long, sweetie."

"Well, whatever, I was here first. Listen, Mr McGinn –"

"Back off, bitch –"

"No, no, no," Richie intervened, just in time. "Slow your roll, back up, both of you. Can't have that here."

"Yo, Mr McGinn, why you didn't call Gramatan Housing Services yesterday?"

"Hey!" Angela yelled. "I was here –"

"Yes, I know, Angela, just give me a second. Please?"

He'd earned just enough street cred to earn this one favor. "OK," she said. "Can I wait inside?"

"Yes," he said, opening the door. He turned to Eleena. "Now, what do you need?"

"What I need? I needed that furniture, that cookware! Now they went and gave it away! You dint call them, and now they gave that shit away! What the hell you gonna do?"

"Wait a second, wait a second," he said. "What furniture?"

"Ah, shit," she said, throwing her hands up. "You forgot, dint you?"

He thought for a second. Around 2 PM the day before, Eleena had left a message, saying that a Gramatan Housing Services had some furniture and other items that were donated. They needed to verify that she was an HSA Greenburgh resident. But he'd been so

237

shaken by Taisha that he'd completely forgot to call. Though she was delinquent on most service plan items and really didn't do anything all day, losing this furniture meant she'd have to spend money she didn't have to furnish her place.

She stood there, hands on hips, stroller to the side, eyes boring through him.

"Oh my God," he said. "I just forgot."

"FUCK!" she yelled. "Goddamnit! You fuckin' forgot? What you mean, you forgot?"

"I'm sorry, Ms Marvin, uh, I just had –"

"Uh, uh," she mocked. "You just had – you dint have shit! Man, you fuckin' stupid! How the fuck you gonna forget? Shit!"

"Look," he stammered, his voice shaking in a conciliatory tone, "maybe I can call –"

"It's too late to call! I called this morning, they said they dint hear from anyone so they gave it away to someone else! I was gonna move out this week, now it's gonna be even longer! I been in this motherfuckin' place so long, now I gotta be here longer, thanks to your dumb ass!"

Jones came by, hearing the noise. "What's going on here?" he said.

Eleena ignored him. Richie was speechless. His insides started to turn on themselves.

"You got nothin' to say? Just gonna stand there all stupid and shit?"

"Hey, now, Ms Marvin," Jones said, moving to where he was to the side of her, but not touching her.

"This ain't your business, Mr Jones," she said without looking at him. "Your stupid-ass caseworker done fucked something up for me, that's what!"

"Yo, Ms Marvin, you can't be talking to people like that, you been here long enough, you know that."

"I got someone waitin' for me outside, gonna take me to Mt. Vernon, I ain't got time for this! Fuck this!" She huffed and pulled her stroller right out the door. Jones followed her out.

Richie felt ridiculous, backpack on his shoulder, keys still in hand. He was still shaking as he put the key in the lock. Angela was sitting there, looking alert. He really needed a moment to calm down, and he'd hoped Angela would say, "You know, I'll come back later."

Instead, she asked sheepishly, "Uh, can I call my DSS worker?"

He didn't want to argue any longer. "Yes, let's go," he said. Rachel popped out of her office with a look of concern. Richie waved her off, marching down the hall. Angela quietly made her call as he readied things on his desks and listened to his messages.

She finished and then asked, "Can I talk to you about something else?"

He took a deep breath and said, "What."

"Well, uh, I uh, could you help me type something up? A letter?"

He sighed, sitting back in his chair. "Sure, Ms LeFleur. No problem. Not right now, but yes. I'll let you know when I'm free."

"OK," Angela said. Her eyes were wide, her voice softer than he'd ever heard it. "When's a good time?"

"Can you give me a few? I don't know yet."

"OK. Uh, I'll call you?"

"Sure. Anything else?" he snapped.

"No, thanks," Angela said, already moving out the door. "Uh, thanks," she said again, maneuvering the stroller down the hall.

He took a deep breath, and found it wavering. He got up, went out the back door of the caseworker suite, looked around to see if anyone was looking, and sat in the lunchroom. He slouched down into what was usually his lunch chair. He felt the back of his throat get tight, and the sting of tears came into his eyes. Knowing this was happening just made it worse. He put his elbows on the table and his head in his hands, simulating a headache. His breaths were short and his muscles tightened all over.

Suddenly, he heard the doorknob turn. He heard some conversation in the hallway, then Jones walked in.

"Hey, Rich. You doin' alright, man?"

"Yeah. Headache," he said, not taking his face from his hands.

Jones went to the fridge and put something inside. Then he poured himself a cup of coffee.

The doorknob turned again, and Wilson poked his head in. "Hey, Jones, you got today's log?" he called out loudly. "Oh, hey, Rich, what's happening?"

Before Richie could answer, Jones said, "Uh, yeah, I gotta enter an incident report, but yeah, I got it. I'll take care of it."

Richie was doing his best not to make eye contact with anyone. There was the slightest pause in the conversation.

"Oh, no problem, no problem," Wilson said. "You doing rounds now?"

"Did 'em. Just getting coffee."

"Got it. Gotta use the men's room, then I'll relieve Deandre at the desk."

Wilson didn't say good-bye as he closed to the door. Richie could hear Jones stirring his coffee. He didn't have the eye strain anymore, and his breathing was shaky, but back to normal. Jones patted him on the shoulder, surprising him a bit. Then Jones, too, walked out without a word.

He was in dread of someone else walking in on him, so he did his best to compose himself, smoothing out his tie and running his fingers through his hair. He stood, took a deep breath, and walked out.

Just as he plopped into his chair, he got a call from Angela.

"So, is now a good time?"

"No, now's not a good time!" he huffed. "Give me a break, OK? I'll call you when I'm ready." And he hung up.

Rachel appeared, brow furrowed. "Hey, what just happened?"

He shouted, "Angela's driving me crazy, that's what happened! I can't sit for two seconds without her asking me for crap!"

"OK, OK, Rich!" she said, hands up. "Yeah, she's a handful. But listen, be careful how you talk to the clients. It's –"

"Are you kidding me? The way I get talked to?"

She moved in further to his office, cocking her head to the side. "Yeah, Rich, you need to be the bigger person here. You can't freak out on them like that."

"Oh, great," he said, snatching up some blank case notes. "On top of all the other shit around here, I gotta be a saint. Thanks for the advice."

"Hey! Don't snap at me, Rich. I'm just trying to help."

"Come on, Rachel. Really? Bigger person? Please."

Rachel looked around. She sat on the edge of one of his office chairs and leaned in. She whispered, "Hey, what's going on with you lately? Did something happen?"

He started writing notes. "No, nothing happened, Rachel," he said sharply, not looking at her.

He could feel her gaze, but still didn't look at her.

"This isn't you, Rich," she said again quietly. "Is this because of… what I said back at –"

He looked up. He sucked his teeth. "No, Rachel, it's not about you. Don't worry about it, OK?"

She sat up straighter, and folded her arms. "Hey, I'm not worried about it, OK?" she said, louder than before. "You don't have to talk if you don't want to, but I'm just letting you know –"

"Good, more advice. More people telling me what to do. Thanks a bunch, Rachel."

"Oh, Jesus, just forget it," she said, huffing and turning sharply from his office. He heard her quick steps down the hall.

A little later he stood up to go to lunch. As he went down the hall he caught her fragrance. He walked a little faster to get away. He went to a pizza place on Route 100 and sat in a booth for about seventy-five minutes, trying to read the box scores from games around the league.

On the way home, he felt a rumbling on the left side of the Escort. He pulled over and saw that the driver's side rear tire was completely flat. "Fuckin' A!" he yelled, the sound completely drowned out by the traffic. Though he had to whale on the tire with the spare several times, he managed to get it off in about half an hour, though he was a sweaty mess.

He brought it to the garage around the corner from the apartment. "Be with you in a minute, boss," the mechanic said. Half an hour later, he was told the shop was closing and he could bring it by in the morning.

"You need four tires, boss," the mechanic said that morning.

"Huh?" Richie said. "I only had one flat."

"Yeah, but you need four. You can't pass inspection like that."

Richie looked at the window. "Inspection's due in November."

The mechanic shrugged. "Whatever you want, boss. Gonna be... $135."

"$135?" That was almost a third of his bank account, and would make paying utilities and food just about impossible. "For one tire? How long would this take?"

"I got jobs up the yin-yang today," the mechanic said. "Maybe getcha outta here at lunchtime."

Richie threw up his hands and spun around. "Forget it," he said.

"Whatever you want, boss," said the mechanic to his back.

He pulled in at 10. "Toni wants to see you," Wilson said at the desk. He rolled his eyes and went to her office.

She shut the door, looked at him and said, "So, talk to me. What happened yesterday with Eleena?"

He explained.

"OK," she said. "You need to talk to her," she said.

"Isn't she moving out soon?"

"Confront," she said. "Confrontation. Doesn't have to be angry. But yeah, this is the kind of thing, you have to have a conversation. What if something falls through, and she's here longer? What about our other clients? Keep it simple: 'I'm sorry about the error, but you can't talk to a caseworker like that.' She knows what she did, flew off the handle. Hey, I bet you she apologizes on her own. But, you gotta do it."

"Yeah, I know, I know. This whole confrontation thing. I'm working on it."

"Work on it," she said. "I'm sorry this happened."

"Sure," he said with a sigh.

"Hey," she said, squinting at him a little. "What's going on?"

"What?"

244

"You get all short, distant, when you're in a bad mood. It's not often, but it's noticeable. More, lately."

And I hate it when people notice it, he thought. "Sorry," he said insincerely. "Car trouble. Flat tire."

"Ooh, sorry. Guy probably said you needed four tires."

"Exactly. Screw that."

"Mmm. Sorry about that." She paused, examining him. "Are you sure nothing else is bothering you? Something you wanna talk about?"

He sighed again. "Unless you wanna talk about a new tire and a new TV, I'm fine. Really."

She looked him in the eye. "OK. Have a good day, Rich."

He had three intakes, two of which were overdue since Monday. He didn't bother contacting Eleena. He left at 5 on the dot without doing any notes at all.

When he got home, Charlie was waiting for him at the door, arms folded and looking pissed. He was a big guy, as big as a doorway, and cut his hair in Marine fashion. His huge frame blocked the walkway. "Hey, Richie," he said. "Where's the rent?"

"What do you mean?"

"I came outta my way two weeks straight to get the money out of the safe, and it ain't there."

"Yeah, but I sent you a check. You said that was OK, right?"

Charlie shook his head. "That was July's rent, Richie. What about August?"

Richie stammered, "I thought, Pat, uh, called and asked if we could send checks from now on."

"No, but I never got a check anyway!" Charlie said, spreading out his hands. "I can't do checks. Not good for taxes. What, you been here five years, you don't know that? Come on, I wasn't born yesterday."

"Well, uh, what do you want me to do?"

"I want my rent money, that's what I want."

So, Richie drove to the bank around the corner, with Charlie following him in his pick-up truck. He took $340 out, which left him with $48.37 until next paycheck. He handed it to Charlie, who grumbled and said, "I'm gonna be nice and just add the rest of what's due onto September. You guys better be sure to have the whole thing." And he left the parking lot without saying good-bye.

Richie came back home, shaking with anger. When he thought of what was in his bank account, he took the packet of ramen noodles in his hand and smashed it on the floor, then stomped on what was remaining. He swept it up, grumbling. He dumped himself on the couch, waiting for the Yankee game to start, thinking about how much gas he had and how much food there was in the house. He even contemplated 'borrowing' things from HSA's pantry. When he turned on the radio he realized the Yankee game was in California and wouldn't start until 10:30. "Fuckin' California," he grumbled to no one in particular.

Around 9, the key in the door turned. Pat and Marilyn came in, laughing. Richie thought they were in DC.

"Richie!" Pat said, smiling broadly. "Surprise! Hey man, how you doing?"

"Oh, just fantastic. Fucking fantastic," he said sarcastically.

Pat started. "Something wrong?"

"Yeah, you could say that."

Marilyn stopped smiling. She looked at both of them.

Pat said, "What? What happened?"

"When I got home, Charlie was here."

"What did he want?"

"What did he want?!?" Richie stood and yelled. "What do you think he wanted? He wanted the rent money! It wasn't there, he didn't get a check, and I had to drive to the damn bank and give him $340 of my own money! It's like he held me up! I have like forty bucks in there now! What the hell, Pat?"

"Whoa, whoa, calm down," Pat said, "Back up. He didn't get your check?"

"He didn't have any idea about it, Pat. None. He said it was for July, but he wanted cash for August. Now I'm fucked. I got no money, and my whole next paycheck is gonna go to him. God damn it, Pat!"

"No, no, no," Pat pleaded. "I took care of this! I talked to him, I said, 'Is a check ok,' and he said, 'OK, this time, but September we gotta go back to cash.' I remember, it was right after you sent him a check last month!"

"Well, now it's all fucked up, Pat. Now I don't have a pot to piss in. What am I gonna do?"

Marilyn stared at him, her smile completely erased. Pat took up the phone and dialed a number. "He's not there," he said as he hung up. "I'll try him in the morning. OK? It'll be fine."

"Hey, Richie," Marilyn said. "I – I'm sorry about that. Can I give you some money?" She reached into her purse.

"Wait," Richie said. "Wait one second. What's that?"

Marilyn looked up. Richie pointed at her hand.

Pat said, "Richie, what are –"

"THAT?" he said, pointing closer now. "What is THAT? On her hand?"

Marilyn slowly took her hand away from her purse.

Pat sighed. "Well, not exactly the way we wanted to… tell you this, but… yeah. We're engaged." He took Marilyn's hand, displaying a tasteful diamond on a golden band.

Richie could feel his breath, hot and deep, through his nostrils. He tugged at his pant leg, hard.

"Yeah, so," Pat said. "We, uh, I proposed right at the Mall, you know? Right under the Lincoln Memorial. Romantic, right, Mar?" Marilyn looked sadly at Richie. "Anyway, um. I thought – things were looking good for you, you know, you got benefits, they have a place for you there, you're pretty much… permanent…" He looked at Marilyn, then back at Richie. "Well, you know, I was talking to my old job, the bank, right? They said I could probably get a job at the DC office. But, look," and he held his hand up. "It's not gonna happen for a few weeks. Maybe even a month. So look, I'll fix this situation with the rent –"

"Yeah, Richie," Marilyn cut in. "I can – I can kick in some money. You know, to cover some... expenses and all. Happy to do it. Really. Anything you need."

"Yeah! Anything you need, Richie. OK?"

Richie's shins tingled. He felt his neck go stiff, and he held his breath.

"I know, I'm sorry, Richie," Pat said. "I'm sorry. I – I didn't know it was gonna be such a bad day for you, but –"

"Are you fucking serious?" he spat.

Pat stopped in his tracks. Marilyn covered her mouth.

"What'd you say?" Pat said.

"I said, goddamn it, are... you... FUCKING... SERIOUS!" He was yelling now.

Marilyn said, "Richie, listen –"

"You stay out of this, OK, Eastchester?"

"HEY!" Pat yelled. "Don't talk to her like that!"

"No, you listen, Pat! Who do you think you are, anyway, sneaking off, leaving me with all these fucking bills, and you come back with a goddamn diamond ring?"

Marilyn stomped her foot. "Now, wait just a second, Richie –"

"I said, stay out of it!"

"Richie, Richie," Pat implored. "Please, just stop! Stop! I'm sorry about the rent and stuff, but –"

"But what, Pat? What? 'Fuck you, you're on your own now'?"

"Richie, just stop it! I would never do that to you – WE would never do that to you –"

"Wait, wait, what is this 'WE' shit all of a sudden?"

"Because we want to help, Richie," Marilyn implored. "Please, listen to me, we – me and Pat, we'd never leave you alone, not without –"

"Really? What am I supposed to do now, huh, Miss Perfect? Mr Genius CEO over there left me in a giant fucking hole –"

"You need money?" Pat said. "Let's go to the bank right now, we'll get you money. That make you happy?"

"Then what about next month, Pat? You gonna make some deals, talk to people? For that matter, how do I know you didn't take the rent money and blow it on something, like that fucking ring?"

"OK, now I know you're insane. Stop talking to us like this, understand? There's nothing to worry about!"

"Nothing to worry about, are you fucking nuts? I don't have shit to my name, and now you're gonna go off to DC and leave me here with a stack of fucking bills!"

"You're not gonna be stuck with bills, Richie! You have a regular job now, and I wouldn't leave you like that. This job is good for you, Rich, I'm so proud of you, and it's a regular thing, more than enough to cover expenses here. You'll be fine, I swear. As for all the bills stuff, I got things under control!"

"Oh, cut the bullshit, Pat. You were right, OK? You're right: I'm stuck taking shit from junkies, bums and assholes all day long. I don't have what it takes, isn't that what you said? But now, Mr and Mrs Perfect over here are taking off, so now I have no choice but to stay chained to that fucking place! Thanks a lot, asshole, and have a nice time at the fucking country club sipping your fucking champagne!"

"Hey, stop the shit, all right? Just remember who you're talking to, OK? I covered your ass for five years. Five years! When you needed books, who got them for you? When you wanted clothes? Or spending cash? It was me, god damn it. Me! I took care of you! ME!"

"Yeah, you really know how to take care of things. Now I'm fucking flat broke, working some shitty job that now I'm stuck in, so now you can just fuck off to your little perfect life with your little perfect wife and let me rot in this shithole. I'm no better than I was five years ago! Thanks, Pat, thanks a lot for setting me up. You did an awesome job, fuckface. Just as good as Mom! Bravo!"

Pat grabbed a lamp and smashed it on the floor.

"PATRICK!" Marilyn screamed. She stepped in front of him, hands on his chest.

Pat roared, over Marilyn's head, "NOBODY can talk to me like that, goddamn it! I sacrificed five years of my life, man, five years! I'm twenty-eight, I paid my dues, and now I have a chance at a life of my own! I worked my ass off, day in day out, kissing ass up and down the ladder, working my hands to the bone! I coulda gone on vacations, I coulda had box seats, coulda taken Marilyn to fancy places, but instead, I had to pay your loans, your expenses, and all but wipe your ass for five years! And you know what? I did it all for YOU, you little shit! And now you're set up with a good job, with good benefits, you cry like a little bitch? 'I don't like it'? That's how life is, Richie! You work a shit job to take care of yourself, to take care of your family! I know because I did it for FIVE YEARS! What more do you want from me?"

"You know what? Just go off with your fucking wife and live your perfect little fantasy life, OK? I don't give a shit. Just run, run away and leave, go to fucking New Hampshire for all I fucking care!"

"I can't believe you right now. I can't fucking believe you. You talk that way to me? Your own brother, who took care of you all those years?"

"I don't give a shit. You fucked me over, you're leaving me in the lurch, just like Mom. Get out!"

Pat just stared at him. Richie stared back. Marilyn stood between them, hands at her face, crying softly.

"Goddamn it, Richie. You're a spoiled little bastard." He took Marilyn's hand and they left.

Richie got a broom and started cleaning up the lamp. Faintly, he heard the pregame show on 770. He switched it off.

Richie knew driving around on a donut was a bad idea. But driving used to calm him down. So he took a reasonable Saturday drive up to the train station in Port Chester. There wasn't much to see. He might have walked around Rye Playland but he didn't have any money for parking or amusements. So he sat watching the trains arrive and depart for a while. Sunday, he went to Rory's and nursed a Coors Light, the cheapest beer on the menu, and five glasses of water while he watched the Yankee game. No one made him leave.

"This team must be just fucking with me," he said, completely alone, in the apartment as he listened to the team lose its third in a row, slipping further and further from the playoffs.

It seemed that every time he tuned into the game, they stunk. Monday night he flicked on 770 on the drive home, and they were already losing, 10-1.

He had a static-y clock radio at work and tried to hear a day game in his office the next day. Toni passed by at one point and said, "What's the score?" He just shook his head.

"Damn it," she said. "Don't tell me next time. Not if it's bad."

She was back thirty minutes later. Again he shook his head.

"I told you not to tell me," she said. She threw her hands up and walked away. They lost that one, too.

She did the same check-in ritual the following day when they gave up seven runs in the first two innings. "What a nightmare," she said.

"What's wrong with this team, Rich?" Wilson asked as he left.

"They suck, that's what's wrong," he said, and kept walking.

Pat began leaving messages for him. "Richie. I'm so sorry about what happened. I – I should have never talked to you like that.

Please, I would never leave you all alone. Never. I'm your brother, I love you. I'd never do anything to hurt you, OK? I'm sorry. Please… call me," he said.

The next morning, at work: "Hey, Richie. Guess I missed you. Did you get my last message? Listen, let's talk. Please. Please just call, OK? Thanks."

The next afternoon: "Richie. Come on. Please don't ignore me. I'm your brother. I know you're mad, but… Come on. Please. Call me."

The morning after that: "OK, now I'm worried. Are you OK? Are you still there? At work? This isn't funny, man. It's not right to leave me in the dark like this, even if you're upset. Come on. Call me."

That evening he heard two more messages from Pat on the answering machine. He erased them both. There was a third message:

"Hey guys, it's Charlie. Holy shit, guys, I'm so sorry, my wife says she got the check and deposited it already, like on July 31. She didn't tell me, goddamn it. Ah, I feel like shit now, perp-walking you to the bank like that; it was a shitty thing to do. I'm gonna run up there over the weekend and give it back, OK? If you're not there I'll put it in the safe. And tell you what, I'll knock $100 off next month's rent, OK? Geez, I feel like shit now. Anyway, be good, see you soon."

When Richie went to bed Thursday night, he learned that Don Mattingly would be "day-to-day" with a strained back. The team lost their sixth in a row.

He was watching the clock as early as 9:30 AM that Friday. At 11 he agreed to drive to Pathmark again. He pulled the van in front of the building. There was a swarm of residents ready to go, escorted by Rachel, who was chatting pleasantly with one of the moms. He looked at his clipboard showing the list of residents who'd signed up. He counted and thought there were perhaps more on the curb than there were on his sheet.

Sure enough, a tiny mother was not on the list, but stood smiling at him. "I'm sorry, ma'am, but you're not on the list."

"*¿Que?*" she said. "*¿Puedo pasar?*"

It was obvious she didn't understand. "Christ," he said out loud. "Come on." He waved her on board, asking a few residents to make room.

As he looked back into the van, he noticed one mother holding an infant on her lap. This was strictly against the rules, according to Jones, as a cop pulling him over would issue a major ticket, which he'd have to pay.

"Excuse me, ma'am," he said to her wearily. "You can't carry the baby like that. You need a car seat, and there's no room left."

She sucked her teeth. "Well, that's too bad, 'cause I gotta go to Pathmark. You just drive."

He took a deep breath. "Don't you get it? If we get seen with a kid not in a car seat, we're gonna get a ticket."

"You mean YOU gonna get a ticket," she said. "That don't confront me. Maybe you shouldn't a let that Spanish lady on."

255

"No, no," he said louder. "Either we get a car seat, or we're not going anywhere. Got it?"

"Yo, that's not my problem, yo. You shouldn't a fucked up that list, man. Not my problem."

Other residents began to grumble and yell. "Yo, I ain't got time for this. We gotta figure this shit out."

"Come on, man, don't be so stupid, yo!"

"Just do yo' fuckin' job, driver!" someone said derisively. The entire bus started laughing.

"Uh-huh, that's what I'm talkin' about!" someone said, high-fiving another client.

"GODDAMN IT!" Richie yelled. He'd never been louder in his whole life. "I DON'T HAVE TIME FOR THIS SHIT! YOU CAN GET YOUR OWN FUCKING ASSES TO THE GODDAMN SUPERMARKET!"

"Richie!" yelled Rachel. He'd forgotten she was there on the curb. He turned and saw her shocked look.

The van went completely silent. All the clients were looking at him, stunned.

He stepped down off the van's sideboard. "Fuck this," he said, walking back to the building. He spiked the clipboard on the pavement with a loud crack. Behind his back he heard, "Yo, he's an asshole."

"Rich, wait –" said Rachel. She went to touch his arm and he jerked it away. He got to the door, passing by Wilson, who was standing by with a concerned look. It was locked.

"Hey, Rich, what just –"

256

"Could you just open the goddamn door, please?" he yelled. "Is that too much?"

Looking at him cautiously, Wilson reached over and pressed the buzzer. Richie flung the door open, and it clanged against the desk. He did the same for the door to the hallway. He made a beeline for the men's room. He opened a stall and sat on top of the handicapped toilet, putting his head in his hands. He tried to hold it back, but before long he was outright sobbing. He tried gripping his hair as hard as he could and digging his fingernails into his palm, but nothing worked. At least he was able to control the sound, stifling a whine by just breathing deeply.

It took him a few minutes to stop. Thankfully, no one came in. But once he got himself a little composed, he realized he was trapped. He was an emotional wreck, surely red in the eyes and puffy-cheeked. His outburst had been witnessed. He didn't have his car keys, so he'd have to go back to his desk. He formulated a plan to run through the back door of the caseworker suite, grab his keys, use the back door again, and sprint from there to the car as quickly as possible. He'd go for a drive, go home, and leave a message that night that he'd quit. He stood in front of the mirror, ashamed of how he looked. He took off his tie, one which A&S had let him keep, and threw it in the trash. He took a deep breath, gripped the doorknob, and turned it.

Right outside the door was Toni. She immediately turned, arms folded, when he opened the door. "Rich," she said, "What –"

"No, no, no," Richie said, bolting for the back door. "No, I can't do this. Sorry, I –"

"Hey, hey, Rich, just wait –"

"No, Toni, sorry, I'm done. I –"

"No, you're not done," she said. She somehow maneuvered in front of him, blocking his way. "That's not how this works. You can't scream at people and then just walk away. Not how that works."

He felt the tears come on again. He avoided her glance, looking at the ceiling, hands on hips. He took a deep, shaky breath.

"Richie," she said. "Come. Please. Just talk to me." She gestured to the lunchroom door.

He took a moment to breathe. Then he nodded.

"Come on," she said again, opening the door. She put a hand on his back. She pulled out a chair for him, so that his back was to the door. She got him a drink of water, placed it in front of him. "Just take a few minutes."

He gulped the water in one swallow. He put his face in his hands, took deep, wavering breaths. He heard Toni pour a cup of coffee.

After a few moments, he took his hands away from his face. He never thought there'd be a more humiliating feeling than being turned down by Rachel. But Toni's subtle smile brought him back a little.

"OK?" she said. "Feeling a little better?"

He just nodded. She took her eyes off him for a second to wave off someone who wanted to come into the lunchroom.

She leaned forward. "Come on. Talk to me. Please," she said softly.

He said nothing. He was slumped in his chair.

"Come on, now, Rich. This isn't gonna work. You can't go on like this. We're here to help you. All you have to do is talk. I'd never judge you, OK? Even if you really do wanna quit. But I'm invested in you, Rich. Please. Just tell me what's going on."

He took another deep breath. He couldn't make eye contact.

"It's just..." he whispered. "It's just... too much. Too much."

"Yeah, I know," Toni said softly. "Tell me."

He poured out his heart. Estranged from both parents, the shame of working a pizza delivery job, Pat's CEO job going bust, his guilt over Pat's sacrifices. He told her the frustrations of taking over the bills, and his fears about casework and being left alone when Pat got married. He even told her about his feelings for Rachel.

Toni looked at him gently, quietly. She nodded, kept her eyes fixed on him. Slowly, Rich felt his muscles unclench the more he talked.

"Mmm," she said when he'd paused. "Yeah, you've been through a lot. That's what I thought."

"It's stupid," he said.

"Are you kidding?" she said. "Rich. The guy who basically raised you, was there when you needed someone the most – he's leaving. I

259

mean, when your mom left, I'm sure you were scared. But Pat was there to take care of you. But when Pat leaves, what then, right?"

"It's wrong," he said. "It's wrong. Pat gave me everything, gave away five years of his life. I'd never stand in the way of his happiness, never. It just feels… terrible."

"That's very noble, Rich. Doesn't make it hurt any less."

"That's true."

"Hey," she said, leaning forward. "I know. You feel lonely, like you have no one. You put your heart out to some girl, she says no. And, you work in a place with sad, sad family stories. And your family story, well. That was no picnic either."

He sighed. "It all just hit me. All at once."

"Mmm, yeah. Maybe screaming at everyone wasn't such a great idea. Maybe that's something you'll work on. When all this is over, I think you owe a few apologies out there. But listen," and she put his hand over his, "we want you here. Everyone loves you. The clients love you, despite what happened out there. You're too valuable, too talented to just walk away from all this. I knew it the day I met you. A little rough around the edges, but you've been here, what, six months? You still got a lot to learn. Stay and learn it here. Where people care about you, where you can grow and thrive."

He looked at her. "Pat hated the job at first."

"Really?"

"Yeah. Didn't like the idea of me working with a bunch of druggies or something, maybe getting stabbed."

She laughed. "Yeah, people who don't know think that sometimes."

"But then, back in May? He turned around. Maybe not all the way. But he liked you guys, liked the stories I'd tell. And he liked that it was a steady job. I mean, he's right, after all. I have a real job now, not slinging pizzas." He sighed. "I just feel terrible. Ungrateful."

"Well, there's that, too," she said, leaning back in her chair. "Sorry about your fight. Bad timing. Good news can sound like tragedy in some circumstances. How do you feel about Marilyn?"

"Oh, great! She's lovely, funny, generous. So good to Pat. And I'm thrilled, really. You know? For the first time, I can help make him happy. But I stood in the way." He felt the tears well up again, took a few breaths, and composed himself. "But I can make it right. It's gonna be hard. Taking care of myself, living on my own. But I owe it to him, I really do."

She smiled. "Yeah, it's gonna hurt. But you can absolutely do this. You won't be that far apart, you know? You're smart, you're tough, you can do it. And when it comes to the job, you have a place here, in this organization, OK? You're one of us now. You're never gonna be wealthy or anything, sorry to tell you. But you can do it, Rich. You can have it all: your own place, a career, a family of your own one day. Maybe even season tickets."

He laughed out loud at that. "Season ticket holders get automatic dibs on playoff tickets."

"See? You did the research already. If you do that, give me a call. Maybe I'll split it with you."

RICHIE THE CASEWORKER Christopher Febles

He smiled. "Deal."

She smiled back. "Better?"

"Yeah, still got stuff to work on. I'm not fired, am I?"

"Eh, like I said, I think you need to mend some fences. But I've seen workers do worse things and keep their jobs. Next time you feel like that, just walk away and find one of us. OK?"

He nodded again.

"Now," she said. "Why don't you collect some things and take the rest of the day off?"

"Oh, geez. I have a lot of work, and I wanted to apolo –"

"Ah, there's time for that. I think you need to collect yourself first. Don't you think?"

He thought for a second. An afternoon might afford him a chance to get something done, something personal. "Yeah. That would be OK?"

Richie looked at the map he'd bought at a rest stop. It was hard to see the numbers on all the townhouses; they all looked so similar. He finally figured out the groupings of the houses in the cul-de-sac, and pinpointed the address. He parked the Escort, walked up the brand-new walkway and rang the doorbell. It took a moment for someone to open the door.

"Richie!" Pat exclaimed. He threw the door open and wrapped Richie in a tight embrace. "My God! I was so worried about you, man. So worried. I'm so glad you're here."

The tears flowed again, staining Pat's dress shirt. He could smell Pat's familiar detergent, could feel the bones in his shoulders. "I'm sorry, Pat. I'm so sorry. I'm so sorry."

"Shh," Pat soothed, stroking his head. "It's OK, man, it's OK. I'm the one who should be sorry. It's OK. I'm just glad you're OK. I was so worried I'd never hear from you again." He patted Richie on the back, breaking the embrace. "Come in, come in."

Richie came in and sat on the sofa. Pat got him a glass of water. "Unless you want a beer? Decent beer for once, not the cat piss you drink."

Red-eyed, Richie laughed and coughed at the same time. "Maybe later," he said.

Pat smiled, took a seat in a recliner across from him. "Man, I thought I lost you."

Richie just listened. The idea of "losing" Pat had never occurred to him.

"You know," Pat said, leaning forward a bit, "Marilyn and I were talking about the wedding this week. Where it'd be, what day, who we'd invite. You know, her family is pretty big. So, we got to talking, and I realized something." He paused, took a deep breath, ran his hand over his mouth. "You're all I have. We don't talk to anybody, right? Mom? Huh. Whatever. Dad? Who knows. Dead in a ditch somewhere. No aunts or cousins or grandparents or whatever. The last five years? It's been you and me. That's it. You're the only one who'd sit on my side, Richie. The only one. And I don't think I wanna go to a wedding where I don't have any family on my side, without you there."

Pat's mouth trembled. He leaned over, put his head in his hands. Richie could hear him softly sobbing. He got up and sat next to Pat, putting his hands on his shoulders.

"I'm sorry, Richie, I –"

"No, Pat. No more apologizing. You gave me everything –"

"And I'd do it all again, Richie. I'd give five hundred years for you. I'd never change a thing."

"I know, man. I know. But look." Pat turned his head. "I decided. I'm not gonna stand in your way anymore. I'm sorry I was so mad at you. You're right, you deserve this, deserve to be happy. I was just scared because, like you said, we're all we have. So I felt like I'd be all alone. But I'll be OK. I'll find a way. You... you deserve to be with Marilyn. She loves you, makes you happy. I'd never, ever deny you that."

Pat put his hand on Richie's. "Thanks, Richie. And look. I really am proud of you. I saw how your coworkers feel about you, I heard your stories, and I said, 'Wow, he's really gonna be OK. He's all grown-up.'" He took a deep breath, composed himself. "And I thought, 'He can handle things on his own. He can do it.' I still believe that. Shit, I'm sorry about what happened with Charlie –"

Richie explained what happened.

"Oh, whew. Good news. But really, I meant well. I saw you working, paying bills, being responsible, and I thought, 'OK, now's the time.' Maybe a little early, though. Maybe I was just... excited, excited about my chance to be with Marilyn. So, I'm sorry."

Richie smiled. It was the first time he'd ever consoled Pat. "I forgive you, Pat."

Pat sat back. "I saw somebody from my old company, the DC office, today."

"Oh," Richie said. "How'd it go?"

"Pretty good, I think, same thing I was doing before. I don't know, though. I still have the feelers out in New York. She knows. Yeah, eventually we'll live together, maybe here, maybe there."

"What? Pat, no. No, no, no. Don't change your life for me."

"It's OK, Rich. We know we wanna be together, but we're being... flexible. Yeah, makes more sense to be here. But let's see how things go. OK?"

Richie smiled. "I asked Rachel out. Back in July."

Pat blinked. "You did?"

"She doesn't wanna date a coworker."

"Aw, shit, man, I'm sorry."

"Ah. It's OK. You know, that's one reason, I think, why I've just been... not myself lately. I've just been... checked out. I really like her, she's funny, and kind, and smart, but I was... rude to her, too. I've really been a piece of crap lately, and maybe that's one of the reasons. It's been rough. But I'll be OK."

"Want me to get you fired? So you can date her?"

Richie burst out laughing.

"Hey, I'm your big bro," Pat said. "I'd do anything for you. Like call in a bomb threat or send them photos of you with farm animals."

"Jesus. You screw one sheep for beer money, you're paying for it forever."

They were both laughing now.

"By the way," Pat said, "what the hell did you do to the Yankees? It's a fucking nightmare."

"And Donnie Baseball's out. Yeah, it's a mess."

"Christ. What a disaster."

Just then, the door opened.

"Richie!" yelled Marilyn. She dropped her briefcase and her keys, and ran up to him and hugged him. "Oh my God! We were so worried about you! Are you OK?"

"I'm an ass, but I'm OK, thanks for asking. I'm sorry I talked like that in front of you."

"Oh, hell," she said. "You never heard my dad watch the Giants games."

"I like him already."

"Oh, Richie," she said, caressing his cheek. "I didn't mean to put myself between you guys. I felt like your mom, trying to split you up..." And she started crying. Pat came over and put his arms around her. "I'm so sorry, so sorry. I'd never seen Pat so upset. When he thought you wouldn't talk to him... I just felt so awful, like I... put myself ahead of your family. God, I'm so sorry, Richie." She reached out and hugged him again tightly.

"Marilyn," Richie said. "You've been so good to me. Patient, and kind. You... you're a part of our family now. For better or worse," and he hooked a thumb at Pat.

She smiled her way through the tears.

"I'm sorry, both of you," he said. "I won't shut you out like that again. And I'm so happy for you. I like watching you two be happy."

Pat came over and wrapped an arm around Marilyn. She said, "You know, we have an extra bedroom. You could live here with us."

"I love you guys, but I don't wanna be a third wheel the rest of my life. But if you'll let me stay the weekend, I'd like that very much."

"OK," Pat said, clapping his hands. "Since bachelors outnumber bachelorettes here, let's order some pizza and shitty beer. Whaddya say, fiancée?"

"We have a garage," she said. "Feel free to tuck in there, fiancée."

The Push

When Pat saw the Escort, he said to Richie, "You drove that far on a donut? Are you nuts?" Marilyn took him to a tire shop and got him four new tires. He and Pat drove back on Sunday.

Richie felt heavy walking through the casework suite that Monday. The words inside his head and heart weighed a ton. He'd have preferred to crawl, but instead he just hunched over as he poked his head into Rachel's office.

"Um, Rachel?"

She looked up.

"You got a sec?"

"Sure, Rich," she said, gesturing to the chair.

He slinked in the passageway and sat down gently. He looked at the carpet, took a deep breath, then raised his head.

"I'm so sorry, Rachel. You've been my best friend here. You've been patient, and kind, and understanding. You taught me so much, and I'm amazed by you. I shouldn't have lost my temper with you. I'm sorry for the way I've treated you lately. I'm sorry I stormed away from you like I did. I can't tell you how embarrassed I am. Please forgive me."

She looked at him. Her hands were on the table, intertwined, like a high school principal. There was no smile. She paused, took him in a little.

"You know, Rich, you've really been a… different person lately. Irritable. Nasty. Sharp. It hurt. It hurt to be around you. I like working with you, Rich, hanging out with you. What happened?"

He sighed. "I've been going through some… stuff lately. Stuff outside here. Both good and bad. Things are gonna be changing for me, for Pat. I… just haven't handled it well. I took it out on lots of people, but I took it out on you most of all. I'm totally ashamed. Please accept my apology."

She nodded. She leaned across the desk, speaking softly. "Of course, Richie. I know you better than that. I know, this is a stressful job, stressful place. It can get to you sometimes. Me, too. But, you know – just… I'm your friend here, OK? This… thing doesn't change that, at all. I… you can come talk to me. Anytime." She looked over his shoulder. A client was ready to walk in. She stood and smiled at Richie. "Have a good day, partner."

He wrote an apology to all the residents on the van on Friday, made copies and put them in each of their mailboxes. Angela saw him as he was doing it, and pushed her stroller over to him. "Hey, I heard you were upset. Are you OK?"

"Good news travels fast," he said, smiling. "Thanks, Ms LeFleur, I'm fine. How about you?"

"Got my Section 8," she said, a little despondently. "I'm out looking for apartments now."

"That's great! Best news I've heard in a while." He looked at her. "Then why the long face?"

She inhaled. "I don't have any friends in Peekskill. No classes or community stuff. It'll just be me and Jonathan."

He looked at her face. Her shoulders drooped, her eyes looked down. It was a surprise, seeing her sad, lonely. He knew she wouldn't react well to an "I told you so" conversation, so he said, "Come on by later. Let's talk about where you're moving and try to connect you with some people, some services wherever you're going. I'm sure Peekskill has a community center, like a Y or something, or some free classes somewhere. OK?"

She smiled. "OK," she said, and made her way to the door.

He found Wilson and Jones in the lunchroom. "Ancient history, man," Wilson said when he apologized. "I forgot all about it."

"S'ok, youngblood," Jones said. "We all know you good. Sometimes you gotta get your money's worth."

"Hey, Rachel," he said over the partition when he got back to his desk.

"Yeah, partner?" she said.

"I'm going out for pizza. Need anything?"

There was a pause. "The one on 100?"

"Yeah."

Another pause. "Can I ride up with you? I gotta run an errand up that way."

"Uh, sure," he said.

"OK, just gotta do something, then I'll be right with you." He heard her walk down the hall. She came back a moment later with her pocketbook, and said, "OK, partner. Let's go."

"I apologize in advance for the condition of my car," he said as he held the door for her. "If you hate it, I blame Pat."

She laughed. "My car's not much better, partner."

They arrived at the pizza joint and placed their order. "Oh, shoot," she said. "I forgot my glasses in the car. Would you get them for me?"

"Oh, sure," he said, walking out to the car. He searched for thirty seconds until he realized something. He came back to find Rachel seated in a booth with their orders, a smug grin on her face.

"You don't wear glasses, *partner*," he said.

"Oh, so *that's* why I couldn't find them," she said slyly.

They ate, chatting about work for a while, and he thanked her for lunch.

"Hey, I thought you said you had an errand," he said when they'd finished.

"Yep," she said, looking right at him.

He paused. "Do you need me to take you somewhere? Where is it?"

She just looked at him, grinning.

"Oh," he said, sitting back.

She sighed, and the smile crept away slightly. "You know, Rich, you hurt my feelings. Like you said, we're like best friends in this place. I felt terrible when you shut me out. We don't talk over the partition anymore, we don't throw things anymore. I miss that."

"I know," Richie said. "I'm sorry. I've been a real piece of crap lately, mean and nasty, like you said. And I lost my cool, left you in the lurch that day at the van. I just... I don't know. But I shouldn't have trashed our friendship like that. I'm really sorry, Rachel. I won't do it again. And I'd be happy to go back to kicking your butt in Blind Basketball."

She laughed. "Yeah, right. What was the score last time?"

"I don't remember. I just remember you cheated."

"Wha– me? Never," she said, and they laughed.

"Thanks, Rachel. Forgive me?"

"Well, of course," she said, touching his hand. "But, is that all that's bothering you?"

"Oh, no, of course not."

"Then what is it?"

He paused, looked at his watch. "Gee, Rachel. I'd love to talk, but do we have time?"

"I told Toni we had a conference about ILS training. Might be the afternoon. She said fine."

He looked at her askance. "You are some kinda sneaky, you know that?"

She smirked. "OK, then let's start our conference. You first."

He told her everything. The same as what he told Toni, but with no tears. He felt a lightness, a comfort he hadn't experienced in many, many years, watching her watch him. Her eyes gently looked into his; her hands were flat on the table; her posture was erect, but her shoulders were relaxed. She never interjected, never interrupted; just nodded and took it all in.

"Geez, Rich," she said. "I'm so sorry about that. Thanks for trusting me with it. Want me to go to New Hampshire and kick some ass?"

He laughed. "Nah. Pat's my family now. And Marilyn. Who needs a derelict mom when you've got them, right?"

"They seem great. You're lucky to have them."

"Yeah." He cradled his chin in his hand, rubbed his face. "But, you know... ah, never mind. You'll think it's childish."

She shook her head. "Uh-uh. I'd never do that to you, Rich. Please, tell me."

He sighed. "I don't know if I'm ready. To be on my own, for Pat to leave."

She nodded. "Yeah. Yeah, I get that."

"Silly, I know."

"Eh, I don't know, Rich," she said, shaking her head. "Me and mom, we're like bachelorette sisters. That's why I'm still there; we have a lot of fun together, just the two of us. I think you're gonna miss that with Pat. And this year, you've hardly been to any ballgames, right?"

"Only the free one and the doubleheader. When I was home from college, we'd go to dozens, just in the summer months alone. And once he leaves, I got no one else. I don't know if I'll bother going anymore. Kind of pathetic going by yourself, right?"

She looked out the window. "Don Mattingly. He's a... What do you call it? Free agent, at the end of the year, right?"

He paused. "Yeah. What's that got –"

"Means his contract with the Yankees is over. Right?"

He was confused. "Well... sure, I guess."

"They gonna re-sign him?"

"Hell, he's the captain. Of course they will."

She looked at him, suspiciously. "Really?"

"What?"

"He's what, thirty-four? Back injury, right? He doesn't hit home runs anymore, you told me they shoved him down in the lineup. You said they have a bunch of superstars on the team already. That the kid, Jeter? He's on his way up. What's that mean for Donnie Baseball?"

He got his back up. "OK, so you're saying, what? They'll let him go at the end of the year?"

She shrugged. "Is he gonna get better, or worse?"

He said nothing.

"Look at it this way. If you were the Yankees' owner, and not Rich McGinn, Don Mattingly's best friend, and you knew some superstar first baseman, under thirty, with 40 home runs a year is available, what would you do? Honestly."

"OK, so you're crushing my dreams here. What's the point?"

"My point is, this is it for him. I'm sure he knows the writing's on the wall; he's not stupid. The Yankees aren't gonna keep paying him that salary when they can give it to someone better, younger. That can't be a good feeling, when you can see the end. When all those years go for naught. And if he never reaches the playoffs? He's gonna feel like shit. And people like you are gonna be very upset. Crushed."

He nodded. "Well, thanks for the good news report, Rach. I think they have some sharp knives here if you wanna keep going with this."

"And this is it for you and Pat, too."

He stopped. "What?"

"Last season for you two. You know Pat's going away. You can see the end. You're hoping that it won't be, but that's not reality. You know it in your head, but your heart denies it. You're clinging onto that last season. That last chance to be in-the-flesh brothers."

He exhaled, shook his head. "This is some baseball analogy. Maybe the best I've ever heard. But, Rach... What am I supposed to do?"

"What would Donnie Baseball do? What's he doing right now?"

He looked away for a second, then back at her. "Probably taking BP, extra ground balls."

"Working hard. Working like he can see the end. Trying to bust his ass so he doesn't have to live with that regret. You know that, right?"

"Again, awesome analogy, partner. I just don't see how it's relevant to me and Pat."

276

She grasped his hand. "Go. Go to all of 'em, Richie. Go until they make it."

"What? What are you talking about?"

"When's Pat moving?"

He scoffed. "I don't know. Soon?"

"Season ends in October? And the further they go in the playoffs, the deeper into the year, right?"

"Yep."

Now she grabbed his arm. "Get him to stay. Tell him to stick it out until Donnie Baseball makes the playoffs. Tell him you should go to as many games as you can. It'll be the one last thing you can do together before he goes off to DC."

"But he might have a job there. Starting soon."

She nodded. "Yeah, that might be a complication. But hey, he's in demand, right? Could probably work anywhere, write his own ticket. Maybe he'll hear you out and put that job off, tell them he has a 'family emergency' or something. Or find something else. Mattingly made sacrifices for his team, right? Pat – he loves you, he'd do anything for you. If you pitch this to him, I'll bet you anything he agrees. He loves the Yankees as much as you. What's the worst that can happen? He says no?"

"He can always just come up for the playoff game."

"Yeah, and if they don't make it?"

Richie said nothing.

"And what about the playoff *push*?" Rachel continued. "If he leaves tomorrow, are you gonna go to any of those games? You said

277

RICHIE THE CASEWORKER Christopher Febles

it yourself, that's kinda sad. You might not go to another game again. Hey, you could throw that guilt at him. Works for me," she said, winking.

"But they suck. They're not gonna make it."

"Oh, don't be such a downer! They're still in it, right? Mathematically?"

He nodded.

"OK," she said, leaning forward. "And if they make a run? Win, like, six, seven in a row? Make it close for that Wild Card or whatever? And you didn't go to any of them? What are you gonna tell your grandkids? How are you gonna feel? How are you gonna feel about Pat? 'You abandoned me when they made a playoff run', that's how you're gonna feel. Resentful. You really want that? You wanna end on that?"

He shook his head some more. "This is nuts. I'm gonna ask my brother to stay until the Yankees make the playoffs. Until Donnie Baseball makes the playoffs. To put off a new life with his fiancée. For a stupid dream."

She put up her palms. "He loves you. He'll do it. If I'm wrong, I'll eat this plastic tray."

He smiled at her. "You're a good friend, Rach. A great listener. But I don't want you to get sick from eating all this plastic."

He practiced what he'd say in the car ride home. When he walked in the door, he said, "We need to talk, man," as serious as he'd ever been. Pat sat attentively, facing him on the couch.

278

He didn't get three sentences in. "Done," Pat said.

"What? You're not gonna argue?"

"Argue what? That I don't wanna go to the games with my little bro? Before I leave for good? To see Donnie Baseball make the playoffs? To watch *you* watch *him* in the playoffs? Nothing's more important, man. No way. I wanna be there for that. I have to be there for that."

"What about your DC job?"

"Oh, that? Yeah, I got the job. They called me today."

"Holy shit. That's great. Congratulations."

"And I'm gonna tell them I can't take it until mid-October. That I have a family member that needs to get settled before I relocate."

"What?! Christ, don't do that. They might fire you."

He scoffed. "Well, if so, screw them. I'm in demand; I can get a job anywhere."

"Holy shit," he said, looking away. "That's just what Rachel said."

"You talked to Rachel about this?"

"Yeah. Everything she said is coming to pass. Eerie."

"Think she talked to Marilyn?"

He squinted. "They don't even know each other."

"'Cause this was her idea, too. She says, 'Take Richie to as many games as you can. The last season together. Spend one last playoff push together. You'll regret it if you don't.'"

Richie sat, thunderstruck. "Jesus. I guess women are smarter."

They heard a car honk in the driveway. "Speak of the devil! Come on," he said, waving him outside.

Marilyn was at the trunk, hands on hips. "Hey, guys. Give me a hand with this, OK? It's heavy."

In the trunk was a brand-new, 28-inch TV. "OK," she said. "Game starts in half an hour. Can you two geniuses figure out how to hook it up by then?"

Pat's half-truth worked like a charm, and his company gave him all the time he needed. They went to the game the next night, and the Yankees crushed the California Angels. "It's a good omen," Pat said.

The next day, Pat asked to use the car to pick up some things for the engagement party, scheduled for October 1 at Marilyn's family's house in Scarsdale. There was a 1 PM game that day, and Toni told Richie he could take half a personal day to attend. ("Community research," she called it.) So Pat said he'd drop Richie off early, and come back around 11 to go to the game.

As they pulled up the access road, Pat drove right past the entrance. "Hey, dumb-ass, you passed it!"

Pat looked around. "What, that place?"

He made an awkward u-turn and pulled in front of the building. "Holy shit," Pat said. His eyes widened. "You work here?"

"Yep. Wanna come see?"

"Well, uh…"

"Come on."

As they walked through the parking lot, they heard someone yell, "Mr McGinn!"

They turned. Running up to them was Alfie Franklin. He had on a shirt and tie, an ID badge dangling from his belt.

"Hey, Mr Franklin, looking good," Richie said.

"Yeah, yeah, thanks. Hey, I gotta catch the bus, but I meant to tell you. I got that security guard job. Today's my training. See?" And he showed off his spanking new uniform.

"Hey! That's great, that's great. Ooh, you better hurry. Bus'll be here any minute."

"Yeah, yeah, thanks again, man! Thanks!" And he jogged toward the bus stop.

Pat looked confused. "What was that about?"

"Alfie's been looking for a steady job for a while, bouncing around and stuff. I found this security company willing to give him a look. Not much salary but it's got benefits down the road. Nice guy; he's a new dad, he can use the money, the health insurance."

"Oh," Pat said quietly.

Richie opened the door for Pat. "Hey, Wilson. I have a guest."

"Hey, look who it is!" Wilson said brightly, tightly grasping Pat's hand. "Welcome to HSA Greenburgh, big brother! Come on in."

Richie pointed Pat to the desk and said, "OK, just sign the book –"

"Aw, no, man," Wilson said, waving them away. "It's your bro. We can trust him, right?"

"This guy? He'll steal all the office supplies." He and Richie laughed.

"Good game last night, man. They can pull this off. Just gotta keep winning, right?"

Pat just grinned.

"That's the plan, Wilson," Richie said. "Thanks again. This way, Pat."

He took Pat through the caseworker suite. It was early, so it was mostly empty. He took him to his desk and showed him around. He explained about intakes, Service Plans and the like. He saw Pat looking at a pile of toys in the corner.

"You can play with those if you want. They're really for the kids, though."

Just then, Rachel came in. "Hey, Pat! Good to see you!" She shook his hand. "Come to check on your brother? Trust me, he's doing great."

"Thanks, partner," Richie said. "Actually, he's coming with me to a community meeting later. Research."

"Yeah, I heard about that," she said, looking sideways at them. That glance, showing off her rosy cheek with her eyes half shut, made his hands sweat. "Bring back notes, OK?"

From there, Richie took Pat out to the quad. He explained the size of the place, the logistics, the history. He saw Jones, who took them to an empty unit. Debbie was in her office, so she described to Pat what she did. He showed him the day care center, where Frances gave Pat the full description of the services. A toddler offered Pat a blue plastic block. Richie told Pat it probably wasn't a good idea to visit New Futures, as everything there was confidential, but he explained what they did. Throughout all this, Pat was mute, straight-faced, nodding at what he heard.

Just as Richie was about to walk him out, they saw Toni in the lobby. "Hey, look, it's the smart one!"

Pat smiled and shook her hand. "Nice to see you, Toni."

"Sorry, buddy, but we don't need any more caseworkers." She and Richie laughed. "Richie show you around?"

"Oh, yes. Wow, this is some place you have here; you should be proud."

"Well, you should be proud. Your little brother is turning into a good caseworker. Got over his little... thing, and he's doing better, improving. Gotta do those notes, though."

Pat put his hands in his pockets. "Yeah."

"Nice game last night. They keep playing like that, we'll be in the playoffs."

"Yeah, there's a 1 PM game today," Richie said. "Too bad I'll miss it."

"Oh, yeah," she said, winking. "Too bad. Well, see you soon, Pat. Good luck with that 'research' at 1, OK? Let me know how it goes."

"Will do," Richie said. "I'm gonna just walk Pat to the car."

In the parking lot, he noticed Pat lagging behind, hands still in his pockets, looking at the ground.

"You OK, Pat?"

Pat stopped and looked up. "You work here?"

"Uh, I think that's been established, Pat," Richie said, chuckling.

"You do all those things, those services? All those people?"

"Yep. Well, not everything. But yeah, that's what we do."

"That guy. You got him a job?"

"Well, I just referred him, helped him with a resume. Gave him a reference. He did the rest."

Pat looked back at the building. "Wow," he said. "You... It's..." Richie watched him run a hand over his face, letting out a deep, quivering breath. "Good job, good job," he finally said.

"Thanks," Richie replied. "See you at 11. I don't wanna miss BP."

At 1, they saw the Yankees pummel the Angels yet again.

On Thursday, Toni got his attention in the hall as he made his way to the caseworker suite. Someone had given her eight box seats for the game that night, and she'd asked if he and Pat were interested.

"Definitely," he said. "Although it'll break our bleachers streak."

"Oh geez," she said, rolling her eyes. "Grow up, you two, and sit with the civilized people."

It was another of Rachel's wishes come to pass. She and four of their coworkers went along: Jones, Tajo, Stephanie, and Wilson. The seats were once again on the first base side. Richie started by sitting next to Wilson, who proved to be a font of great baseball information. He watched the game like a manager, chomping peanuts and commenting on the field alignment. Sometimes he'd peek over at Richie's program to see how he'd score something. He also told him stories about playing semi-pro ball as a youngster, a career cut short when he joined the army, then the NYPD. "I almost hit for the cycle one day," he said. "Needed a triple. I'd have had it, too, 'cept they called me out even after I slid under the tag. Terrible call." From his seat he could hear Pat and Toni commiserating about him.

"How's the streak coming, partner?" Rachel asked, sitting next to him in the sixth.

"So far, so good," he said. "You were spot-on, by the way. Pat didn't even flinch."

She smiled. "I knew it. He –"

Just then, Paul O'Neill hit his third home run of the night. This one was in the lower deck, near the foul pole. They were close. So he bolted from his aisle seat, running to beat a group of pre-teens to the loose ball. The entire HSA section cheered him on, but he came up empty-handed and damp from sweat. His workmates gave him a mock round of applause, and he bowed. Rachel was doubled over laughing.

"I'd have paid money to see you hip-check some ten-year-old," she said.

"Little bastards," he mumbled through a smile. "Hey, I need to use the bathroom. Need anything?"

"Water?"

"I don't think they sell them in the missile silos you like to drink from, but I'll do my best. Hold this?" and he gave her the scorecard.

When he returned, he gave her a water bottle, and she gave the scorecard back. It was filled in with the at-bats he'd missed.

"You keep score?" he asked her.

She looked at him. "After I got bonked on the head, it was either stay on the team or go to PE. So I learned to keep the book and sit on the bench. I stand by my decision. Oh, Donnie Baseball hit a rocket, caught by the second baseman. You missed it."

He looked away, breathing deep and trying not to look at her. They sat together for the rest of the game, talking about sucking at high school sports, working crappy jobs, and the best sandwich places near work.

They barely watched the action. The Yankees had it well in hand.

As September rolled on, so did Richie's team. Something woke them up.

They beat the Mariners and Athletics when they came to town. They stole two out of three from mighty Cleveland and they beat the "ever-loving holy shit" (according to Pat) out of the hated Boston Red Sox in three straight. Toni loved it.

"Ahhh, I love it when they beat the damn Red Sox," Toni said, leaning back in her chair, hands behind her head, for an early morning "supervision" meeting with Richie and Wilson in her office, which involved supervising the Yankees. "All's right with the world."

Don Mattingly had returned to form. Not 80s form, but back in the middle of the lineup. His sharp singles were a key contribution. Richie cited stats to anyone in the office who'd listen.

He and Pat had a fabulous time at the games. Richie was a whirlwind at work, taking his notes to the lunchroom to avoid distraction. When the clock struck 5 he burst out of the office and reported right to the bleachers, in time to see a few batting practice reps from Donnie Baseball. To save money, they brought their own sandwiches and limited the Jumbos they drank, and they used an old high school notebook to keep score. They sat close to Queen Tina and her entourage, staying to the ninth for every game. They smiled and sang, and booed every opposing fan right out of the ballpark. After smacking around the lowly Blue Jays, Richie taunted the losing club: "Go back to Canada, you hosers!" Tina smiled in approval.

And the team rolled on and on. Closer and closer to that playoff spot.

One Wednesday, when he came back from lunch, he had a call from Debbie. "I think we need to talk about Akira," the message said.

He found Debbie in her office. She invited him to sit.

"I got a call from Giuseppe's day care program," she said. Giuseppe attended an off-site day care center called Little Tykes that was close to her program. "They called CPS."

"What?"

"They've been noticing some odd behavior from him."

"Like what?"

She took a deep breath. "Sexual behaviors."

Richie blinked. "Really? Isn't he two years old?"

"Yes. Touching the grown-ups in... inappropriate places."

"Wow. From a two year old? Does he even know what he's doing?"

"That's just it. Giuseppe barely has a hundred words. Sweet boy, but this is troubling. Troubling because he had to have learned it from someone."

"Wait. You're saying it was Akira?"

She nodded gravely. "There's no one else. No family, unless there's a friend or a boyfriend I don't know about."

"She already has a CPS worker because of a previous incident," Richie said. "It was a while ago, and it wasn't related to sexual abuse, but this is bad."

"That's right. You have the contact info?"

"Yes, I do. I'll get it to you. Should I talk to Toni?"

"Yes, fill her in."

He rose to leave. He turned and said, "So, what do you think will happen?"

"There's a good chance she could get her child taken away," Debbie said, a pale look on her face, the first time he'd seen her so shaken. "I mean, anyone will tell you it takes a lot for a child to be removed, but with a track record and her mental illness, I don't know."

He nodded and left. As he got back to the caseworker suite, he exhaled hard. He gave Debbie the contact info for the CPS worker, then went to Toni's office.

"May I shut the door?" he asked.

"Sure," she said, looking concerned. "What's up?"

He explained what Debbie had told him.

"Oh, boy," she said. "This could be bad. When's the CPS worker getting here?"

"I don't know. Debbie's gonna call. Apparently they've been in contact before. I've never had the need."

"OK," she said. She looked at her watch. "My guess is they'll come tomorrow. You should be part of those conversations, too."

"Oh, great."

"Hey," she said, changing her posture a bit. "I know it's uncomfortable. But think for a sec. If there's abuse, if they find something... It'll have to be done."

He sighed. "Damn," he said. "She was doing so well. Going to program, looked happier, looking toward the future. Her Section 8 was gonna come through."

She frowned and shook her head. "I really wanted this to work. I really did. I – we – really thought maybe if she could be mentally stable, if the meds and the program worked out, that she could live on her own with her kid. A different kind of life, you know, though.

I can't see Akira living that American dream, you know, white picket fence. But taking her kid to school? Staying in an apartment, surviving? I thought it could happen. Doesn't look like it will."

Richie said, "So, we're giving up."

"Nobody's giving up. But she is a disturbed lady, with a kid exhibiting sexual behaviors."

"Alleged sexual behaviors."

Tony looked at him. "Yeah, alleged. What are you getting at?"

"Ah, forget it."

"No, don't do that. You got something to say, say it."

He exhaled. "She's been doing great, Toni. Going to program. She looks better, happier. She's got hope now. But if the kid gets taken away…"

"Yes. We'd have to discharge her. It's a family shelter. She'd be single. Probably we'd give her time, maybe a week. Then she'd go into the single system."

"Which is not an improvement, as I've heard."

She shrugged. "We can make a recommendation for her for one of the better shelters, more suited to clients with mental health issues. But, since when do they follow our recommendations?"

He paused, tapping a pen on the table. "I think this is bullshit."

"What?"

"I don't think this is abuse. I think it's a two, three year old doing bad things without really knowing what he's doing. And I think it's ludicrous that anyone thinks Akira is showing him. He's not verbal. How are they gonna prove he was sexually abused?"

"Jesus, Rich," she said, folding her arms. "Are you serious? This is a really disturbed young lady. She might be a sexual abuser."

"'Might'. Or she might not be. I don't think this is so slam-dunk that it warrants a removal."

"Rich. Come on. This is Akira we're talking about – we're talking about CPS. Serious stuff. What do you wanna do, question the case or something?"

"I wanna talk to this CPS worker. I wanna find out what these allegations are. I've heard – I've seen – plenty of kids show sexual behavior like touching and grabbing. Doesn't mean their families are abusing them."

"Yeah, but Akira has a track record."

"Of sexual abuse? Or even abuse at all? She left Gio with a babysitter too long."

"A few hours too long."

"Ronnie Teneille went three days. Twice. CPS closed her case in 60 days on the dot."

"Rich, come on! I've seen it happen, OK? They got her dead to rights. Just let them do the investigation. Leave it alone."

"Well, can't hurt to look into it. I wanna know what these allegations are, what these behaviors are. 'Cause I don't see her as a sexual abuser."

Toni nodded slowly, and exhaled. "This is nuts. Fine, look into it. But don't embarrass me, OK? And you be careful. I don't want this to hurt you down the road if it ends up Akira really did this."

"You always give good advice, Toni." He paused. "That wasn't sarcastic, by the way."

"Well, I'm glad you got that out of your system, smart-ass. Let me know the details when you get them."

The CPS worker, a Ms Arnold, called him and got some more information about Akira. Toni told him to be as factual as possible, to give an idea of her program attendance, sessions with Debbie, child care, and her inspections. He liked the picture he painted for her: good attendance, stable moods, Gio in good health. He asked if she could provide some detail, but she said she'd be by first thing in the morning and do it then.

Richie told Pat the story during batting practice that night.

"Holy shit, dude," Pat said. "Sexual abuse? A three year old?"

"Sexual behaviors. That's just one out of like eighteen indications of abuse. Me, I think Akira is just easy-pickins. A very disturbed person who's too fearful of the world to defend herself."

"And you're gonna defend her?"

"Well, not like a lawyer or anything. I just wanna know if there's more to it. I'm not willing to sell Akira up the river if it's just the kid acting out. She's worked too hard for that."

"*You've* worked too hard for that."

"I could give a shit about myself. I'm not the one homeless, mentally ill, afraid. I don't want her to lose her kid – to get kicked out – for the wrong reasons. It's not right."

Pat looked at the field. "You've been at this job, what, seven months? Still learning? Now, you're ready to charge in there and fight The Man, the system?"

Richie shrugged. "Whatever, man. I just wanna do what's right."

"This is some heavy shit, man. Wouldn't wanna be in your shoes."

"Me neither. Too late to go back to slinging pizzas?"

Pat just smiled at him. "Good luck tomorrow, man. I'll be thinking about you."

The Yankees won a close one that night. But they didn't cheer as loudly as they had been.

Toni had asked Richie to come in at 8:30 on Thursday if he could, and he was there at 8:25. He brought an extra-large Dunkin Donuts coffee, splitting the contents with her and Jones as they conferred in her office. Debbie was there, as well. Richie put off all his appointments for the day. Jones was asked to quietly spread the word to the other guards to let them know, just in case there was a reaction from Akira. Richie would greet Ms Arnold and bring her into the conference room. Then, Debbie would meet Akira in her unit and bring her down for a meeting. She'd been contacted the day before and was asked to stay home from program.

The phone rang as they were talking. Ms Arnold had arrived. Richie was dispatched to retrieve her. At the front desk he found a plump, middle-aged woman with hair dyed an unnatural reddish-brown. She smiled brightly at him, not at all the greeting he expected. He escorted her to the conference room and offered her coffee, which she accepted. Then he got Debbie and Toni and brought them back as well, introducing them to the sprightly Ms Arnold. Jones joined them as well.

"Well," she said, putting on her reading glasses. "I've visited the day care center, and talked to Debbie, and Rich. The allegation is sexual abuse, based on the child's behavior and the mother's mental state. It might not be safe for him to be with her. What's left to do is interview the child. I'll need some time alone with him, preferably in the unit."

When she said she spoke to the day care center, he got an idea. While he was formulating it, Toni asked a few questions. Then Debbie went to get Akira. Richie excused himself and went to talk to Rachel. She was with a client.

"Rachel," he said, "can I talk to you for a second? In private?"

"Uh, sure," she said, excusing herself with her client. They stepped into the back of the casework suite by the file cabinets.

"Remember a while back?" he said. "Over the partition, you were telling me about some day care teacher? Told you about a kid who, well, touched a teacher... inappropriately?"

"Well, you sure know how to sweet-talk a girl. Yeah, I remember."

"What's the place?"

"Little Tykes Day Care in White Plains."

"Did they call CPS?"

"No. Kinda filed it under 'bad behavior' and told the parent. Coulda sworn it happened more than once. Why, what's going on?"

"Do you think you could come into a meeting? With Akira's CPS worker?"

"Whoa. What? What's going on?"

He explained as quickly as he could. "They're talking about a removal. I think these allegations are overblown. If it comes down to a removal, I need all the help I can get to defend her."

She looked at him, arms folded. "Rich. Are you sure you wanna do that? What if she is an abuser?"

"No," he said, forcefully. "No way, Rachel. Can't be."

She paused, put her hands on her hips. "You're sure?"

He sighed, rubbed his forehead. "I'm like 80% sure. Maybe it's just a stupid idea. But I can't live with myself if they take away Akira's kid, and she falls apart, all on shaky evidence."

She said nothing.

"OK. Maybe you don't agree. Or don't wanna get involved. But all I need is your word. I know I ask a lot of you, Rach. But I don't wanna see Gio get removed if he doesn't have to be."

She nodded slowly. "OK, Rich. Call me when you need me. I'll tell them what I know about the place."

"You're the best, partner," he said, and went back to the conference room.

Just after he returned, Akira arrived. She seemed her usual self when she arrived, soft-spoken and smiling. She wore a T-shirt and jeans, clean and neatly pressed. Giuseppe was in a stroller, which was also clean and neat, if a bit worn.

"Hi, Ms Kensington," Ms Arnold said, smiling but monotone. Akira sat and put her hands in her lap, like a child in the principal's office.

Ms Arnold got right to the point. Her voice never wavered. "Ms Kensington, we've had a report of mistreatment on Giuseppe. The allegation is sexual abuse. He's showing behaviors at day care that indicated that he may have been sexually abused."

Akira said nothing. He thought maybe her eyes widened, but this was probably in his imagination. There was no reaction yet.

"Now," Ms Arnold continued, "these are very serious allegations. We have to take them seriously, and we have to investigate. Do you understand what's happening here?"

Akira took a moment to respond. She looked at Richie and Debbie. "Uh, I think so," she said, hands still in her lap.

"Now, Akira, I'm going to have to see Giuseppe alone, in your apartment. Mr Jones here, along with Ms Petrocelli, are going to escort us there. You can wait here with your caseworker and Dr Thompson. Do you understand?"

Akira nodded. Her lips tightened.

Ms Arnold greeted Giuseppe brightly, like a grandmother seeing her grandson on Christmas Day. He brightened to her greeting, and eagerly put out his hands to be picked up. "We'll be back in a little while," she said, and left with Toni and Jones.

"Could I have a few moments with Akira, Mr McGinn?" Debbie said. He excused himself and went to Rachel's desk. She was on the phone, so he went to his desk. A few moments later, over the partition, he heard Rachel say, "OK, partner. What's up?"

"When I go back in there, can you come with me?"

"Oh, you bet your ass I can."

He looked at the file cabinet. "What does that mean?"

"It means I take good case notes. Can I come over?"

"By all means."

She arrived with that playful smirk that he knew meant, *I've got a secret.* When he heard her talk about what she'd learned from her notes, he said, "OK, that helps. Not sure that'll be the main thing, but it helps. I hate to put you in this position –"

"Oh, forget it, Richie – ooh, I meant, 'Rich'."

"If this comes through, you can call me whatever you want."

He had lots of case notes to do, but didn't touch them at all. He mostly looked out the window. Finally, around 11:30, Toni called him. "She's ready," she said. "Meet in the conference room."

"OK, be right there," he said, and hung up.

"That our call, partner?" Rachel said over the partition.

"If you're ready." Richie held the door for her into the conference room.

The same group as before, without Akira, was seated around the table. Ms Arnold was writing something on a form.

When they walked in, Toni looked at them both with concern.

"Ms Arnold, this is Rachel Worsham, another caseworker here. She's not involved with this case, but she's also been in touch with Little Tykes, and that teacher in particular. Is it OK if she sits in?"

Ms Arnold looked at the both of them. "Well, I don't see how it's pertinent, but OK."

He and Rachel sat. Toni shot them a look.

"OK," Ms Arnold said. "We are going to have to remove the child."

Richie shuddered.

"He's a sweet little boy, just like you've all said," she continued, folding her arms on the table. "But even in the time I had him, even just playing with him, he exhibited sexual behaviors. Grabbing my... chest. It's clear that there's been inappropriate touching. I also interviewed Akira. She was tearful, she was sorry. It clearly has something to do with her mental condition. I called into the office, and they agreed. A removal will take place. Today."

Richie felt his heart drop to his shoes. For a moment he froze. But he could feel Toni's and Rachel's eyes on him.

"Just a minute, Ms Arnold," he said, trying to keep his voice from shaking. "Uh, could you go into some detail here? About the allegations?"

Ms Arnold raised her head from her paperwork. "Well, it's as I've said. I witnessed sexual behaviors myself. So has his day care center. The mother admitted what happened. She was tearful, sorry, said it was her fault. She also has a prior CPS case. Clearly, this boy is in danger."

"What about from the day care center? What was in the report?"

"The boy grabbed the teacher's breasts on numerous occasions."

"What was the teacher's name?"

She paused and looked at him. She checked her paperwork. "Ms... Varsegian."

Without even being prompted, Rachel said, "Ms Arnold, I think there's something you should know."

"What is this?" Ms Arnold said.

"Well, at the same day care, I had a call on April 4 about a two-year-old boy and inappropriate touching. Different teacher, a Ms Elkins. She corrected the behavior and called the parent, but didn't call CPS. Also, another teacher in the four-year-old class, Ms Gentry, called me February 1, same thing: inappropriate touching. Didn't call CPS."

"So," Richie said, "what makes this case so severe that it warrants a removal? Why did Ms Varsegian call when the others didn't? Because it doesn't sound like it's more severe than the others."

Ms Arnold took off her glasses. "Look, that may very well be, but the fact is he exhibited those exact behaviors as I was observing him. And, this mother has a prior open case, and a history of mental illness. This child is in danger."

"But the prior case had to do with babysitting, right? Not sexual abuse."

"But there is a history."

"I had a parent not show up for three straight days. They closed her case exactly at 60 days."

"Well, that's not my case."

"May I ask what her mental health has to do with this?"

She threw up her hands. "What do you mean? She's unstable."

"Unstable?" he said, hearing his voice get louder. "Have you spoken to her program?"

She went silent for a moment. "I have reports that her attendance has been sporadic."

"Recently?"

Ms Arnold looked at Toni, who didn't move. She looked back at Rich. "She's missed program on several occasions."

"OK, let's do this," he said, opening her file. "You give me a date, and I'll tell you what happened. Tell me when you're ready."

Ms Arnold huffed and threw open her file. "March 10," she said.

Rich shook his head. "Kind of a while ago. But, here, in my notes... It snowed. Bus got stuck. She was stranded. She didn't have a quarter for the phone, so she hoofed it all the way back here."

"April 28 to 30."

"Gio had a fever. Little Tykes doesn't let you take the kid back for 24 hours after they discover one. She went to the clinic on the 29th and he still had one. Didn't go back until May 1."

"August 15."

"That's the Assumption of Mary. Catholic holiday. Akira's Catholic, according to her file."

Sarcastically, she said, "Oh, so now she's a churchgoer?"

"So now you have to be a churchgoer to observe a holy day? Should we check her church attendance, see if she brought home a Mass card?"

"Look, Akira Kensington is very disturbed – you know this, and you know she shouldn't have children! She is a danger, and you all know it! And, she all but admitted it!"

"Did she admit it, or did she apologize? You said she was tearful. She's afraid, and she doesn't speak up for herself. Dr Thompson can corroborate that. You took that as an admission of guilt?"

"Rich!" Toni exclaimed.

"Besides that," Richie continued, "in the CPS manual, there are eighteen indications of sexual abuse. How many does Gio meet? One?"

"OK, Mr Expert," Ms Arnold said snidely. "How do you explain this behavior?"

He was stumped. Saying 'boys will be boys' would be a bad answer. "It's just bad behavior. Not a sign of abuse."

"Well. I've been at CPS ten years, and I think it's clear this boy was abused, that someone showed him these behaviors, and that Ms Kensington is not fit to have children in her care, for the moment. I intend to file for a removal."

Richie sat back in his chair, his right knee bobbing up and down. There was a silence.

"This may take a while," she said, not looking up from her paperwork. "I need to write this up, and then I'll need to use someone's phone. May I have a moment, please?"

"Of course," Toni said, gesturing everyone to clear the room.

Richie slowly got out of his chair. Toni made sure she left after he did. When they got into the hall, she gestured him and Rachel into the caseworker suite. Debbie walked to her office, Jones to the front desk. A mother was sitting on the waiting area chairs with a fussy toddler, trying to soothe him in Spanish.

"That was a valiant effort, Rich. Made some good points," Toni said.

"Yeah, Rich," Rachel said. "You had something there, I thought."

"Damn," he said. "Something's not right. I just know it."

Out of the corner of his eye he could see the child tugging at his mother's t-shirt.

"Might be right," Toni said. "But I think these folks are determined to remove her kid. She'll get a chance to get him back."

The mom looked around, turned her back to them, and pulled up her t-shirt. The boy reached underneath with his head.

Toni looked at him and Rachel, "So, when –"

"Holy shit!" he suddenly exclaimed, startling everyone. "That's it! That's it!" Then he ran out of the suite and burst back into the conference suite, causing Ms Arnold to jump.

"She breastfeeds!" he yelled.

"Oh my God," Ms Arnold said, "you scared the –"

"Akira, she breastfeeds Gio!"

"Are you kidding? That boy is almost three years old."

Toni and Rachel entered, looking shocked.

"Rich, Jesus –" Toni said.

"Yeah, I know, it looks weird, right? I thought so first time I saw it. Walked into Tajo's office, and this lady's, well, exposed, and this really big kid is, you know, uh, suckling, right? So he says, 'Yeah, some moms in Latino households do that until the kid is, like, three.' And look!" He put her file and rifled through the papers. He found the intake sheet and pointed a finger. "Look! Mom: Xiomara Hernandez. Dad: Winston Kensington. And the dad left Akira at age two."

"She doesn't speak Spanish," Ms Arnold said.

"I knew a guy in high school named Pedro Angeles," Rachel said. "Not a word of Spanish. Family wanted him to speak only English."

"There you go!" Richie said excitedly. "So my theory is –"

"Theory?" Ms Arnold hissed. "I'm –"

"– that Gio, who's a really outgoing kid, when he feels comfortable with a woman, with a mom, that's what he does. Look, he probably really likes his teacher – he did great with you, nearly threw himself into your arms –"

"Oh, just stop it!" she screeched. "Stop this nonsense right now! You're questioning my judgment? She's a mental case, a –"

"Damn it, her mental health has nothing to do with it!" He was yelling now. "She's on her meds, she's doing so much better, she'd never do this!"

Toni put a hand on his shoulder, gripped it lightly. He took a deep breath and calmed himself. "Sorry, sorry. Sorry for coming on so strong. But please, can't we look into this? Do we really want to do this to this woman, this family? Isn't there an inkling of doubt here? And if so, can't we investigate? Please, give her one more chance. I'll stake my reputation – my job – on it. Please."

Ms Arnold eyed him suspiciously. She looked at Toni, who had no expression. She tapped her glasses on the table.

"Ms Petrocelli?" she finally said. "Could we visit Ms Kensington again?"

"Of course," Toni said. "Rachel, would you go get a guard, please?"

She left, and came back with Wilson. Everyone rose and made their way to "C" building. Toni knocked at her door. A friend answered and let them in. "Akira?" Toni said.

"Just a minute," they heard Akira say from the back. Gio bounded from the back, into the arms of Akira's friend. After a moment, she appeared, adjusting her t-shirt.

"Ms Kensington," Ms Arnold said. "This is very important. I need you to answer honestly."

Akira just looked at her.

"Do you breastfeed your son?"

She looked down and away, embarrassed. "Yes. I'm sorry. My mom told me to. Until Gio's three or so. I won't do it anymore."

Richie tried to stifle his smile.

"Has he done that with anyone else?" Ms Arnold asked.

"Well, I have a friend. Yeah, he did it to her. I didn't tell anyone. I thought it was bad."

Richie nearly jumped through the ceiling. Ms Arnold glared at him through the side of her eye. He was grinning like an idiot.

"Thank you, Ms Kensington," Ms Arnold said. "We'll be back in a few."

They left the unit. "Ms Petrocelli, may I use your phone?" asked Ms Arnold.

"Sure," Toni said. "Follow me." They walked back to the office. Toni let Ms Arnold into the admin office. She gave Richie a stern look. He held the door for Rachel, stifling a smile. Then, she silently waved him to his own office. She gestured for him to sit.

"Oh my God, Rich," she said. "What was that?"

"Christ, I'm exhausted," he said, looking skyward. "This place. This place is nuts."

Just then, Toni came by. "What the hell was that, Rich?"

"I just didn't wanna see Akira get sold out on flimsy evidence. She's doing so much better. That's all."

"Well, the worker's on the phone now. She told me she's going to ask for an extra day. Wants to talk to her supervisor, and he's not in until tomorrow. So we'll know then."

"Damn it. I hate waiting," he said.

She curled her lip. "That was some performance in there, buddy. I hope you're right about this woman."

"Me, too. It's a risk, I'm aware of it. But that's just how I felt."

Toni sighed. "Good luck, Rich." She walked out.

Rachel was still sitting there, grinning.

"Hey," he finally said. "Thanks for coming in on that. Sorry if it, well, made you uncomfortable. And sorry if it took too much time."

She didn't move, or stop smiling. After a moment, she said, quietly, "Nice job, partner." And she went to her desk.

--

"Geez," Pat said in the bleachers that night, when Richie told him what happened at work. "You stood up for someone. You put yourself on the line for someone." He let out a deep breath. Looking at the field, he whispered: "Christ. Good job, little bro. I hope it works out."

Richie had read the paper that day, knew that every game counted. But that night the Yankees seemed to drag through the first few innings. With each out he got angrier and angrier, kicking a soda cup across the aisle when Kelly bobbled an easy grounder, letting in a cheap Blue Jays run. Sitting nearby was a chubby fan about his age, with a scrawny beard and a visible butt crack above his dirty jeans, like a plumber. He was muttering to himself like a subway wanderer. "God durgins fuckin guy, dusbbly farghen furve," he mumbled.

In the fifth, chin in hand, Pat said, "This sucks."

"Sucks ass," Richie added.

"Fuckin' shlubbin papa looby," said the mumbling fan.

The Yankees did nothing in the sixth and seventh. Richie stood and yelled at the field. "Come on! What are you guys doing? This is too important!"

"Schurffen mother fuzzer lappa dong," said the mutterer.

In the eighth, down 4-1, Bernie singled. "Big deal, flurben," he heard the mutterer say.

Then O'Neill singled. Ruben Sierra came to the plate as the tying run. Pat stood and yelled, "Come on, get up! Get your asses up!" The fans stood as well, not clapping as vigorously as Pat, but excited nonetheless. Even the mutterer stood, hands in pockets. "Let's go!" Richie yelled at the fans around him, urging them with his hands.

And then, on the first pitch, he heard that sound. That wonderful, violent sound.

How he could hear it above the din of the crowd was anybody's guess. But it could only mean one thing.

Then he came to realize that this towering shot was on a trajectory directly toward them.

The ball lifted higher and higher, then it looked like it would land just behind them. Sitting to Pat's left, he shoved him out of the way and started running on the rows of seats behind him, slipping twice and bashing his shins. Fans at the front of the bleachers ran toward the back like the field had caught fire. The ball clanged on a bench almost twenty rows back and caused another scramble for the ball closer to center field. Richie came up empty handed, but high-fived everyone on the way back, arm-in-arm with the muttering guy.

"You shoved me, you jackass!" yelled Pat.

"Huh? Oh, sorry, man," Richie said. The game was tied.

Then Richie's team rolled again.

Donnie Baseball doubled and the team scored two runs to take the lead. Richie bear-hugged the mutterer. Wetteland came in to pitch and wiped away the Blue Jays. They paraded out of the ballpark, chanting, "Let's Go Yankees" louder than they'd ever done before.

They all but collapsed into the Escort. "Christ, this is exhausting," Pat said hoarsely. "I wish they'd hurry up and clinch, or I'm gonna have a stroke."

"If you have a stroke, I'll wheel your crippled ass into the bleachers," Richie said.

"Aw," Pat said. "That's the nicest thing I've ever heard."

Toni called him at 9:10 the next morning. "OK, big guy. I have Ms Arnold on the line for you. Good luck."

He paused. The red light on his phone blinked. He steadied his hand. Clearing his mind, letting go of his hopes, he picked up the phone. "Ms Arnold?"

"Mr McGinn," she said, as pissed as the day before. Richie listened for the content underneath her patronizing tone. "So, I reviewed the case with my supervisor. The allegations are very serious. Sexual abuse is very serious. You need to understand that. I know you're new there – what, seven months? A leave replacement?"

It was an insult, but he heard Rachel's words: *be the bigger person.* "That's right."

"Well. We have decided to issue a warning to Ms Kensington in lieu of a removal."

He stood up, phone still at his ear. He threw a notepad into Rachel's office in a spot where it wouldn't hit her, but would at least get her attention.

"I think you should understand what's happened here, Mr McGinn. We still have a suspicion of abuse in this house. We still think Ms Kensington should not have children in her home, that she's too disturbed. It's only a matter of time before she breaks down again."

You're full of shit, that's your opinion, he thought, but didn't dare say. He was actively pumping his fist now, as Rachel and Stephanie stood outside his office, watching him.

"You did a good job defending your client, bringing issues to our attention. Clearly you believe in this young lady. Clearly you're passionate, too. But be careful. I wonder how you'll feel if this client hurts a child someday."

The phone was burning his ear; he was desperate to get off. "Yes. That's good advice. Thank you very much."

"Well," Ms Arnold said. "We'll be watching this young lady, don't you forget it. I'll be out to visit her early next week. Good day, Mr McGinn." And she hung up.

"Well?" Rachel said, eyes wide. Tajo and Darlene had joined them.

Richie smiled. "Warning, not removal."

They exploded in cheers. Rachel threw her arms around his neck. Darlene and Stephanie did the same, just not as strongly. Tajo bro-hugged him.

"Damn, son," he said. "That was legend back there, young man. Everyone's talking about it."

"Yeah!" Stephanie said. "What'd you do in there, threaten her?"

"No, really," Darlene said. "This is a good case study. Can we talk about it sometime?"

Toni came by. Without a word, she also hugged Richie.

"Well," she said. "That was something. Maybe I wouldn't have yelled at her and everything, but you got the job done. You should be very proud. I sure am. Darlene, I thought you said, 'case study', right? Well, yeah, let's do a lunch meeting. Everybody give their orders to Winnie, and we'll talk at 12:30. That work for everyone?"

Just then, the phone rang. It was Pat.

"Ooh, let's let Richie take the call," Toni said, and they all dispersed.

"Bro, I just got the word," Pat said. "Tickets for the playoffs are on sale after Sunday's game. Did you hear that? Tickets. On sale. Sunday. We can ACTUALLY BUY THEM," slowly pronouncing the last three words.

"Wow. Good news all day," he said.

"Oh, shit. Your client?"

"Warning, not removal."

"Oh my God. You did it. Wow. Congratulations, man. I'm so proud of you."

"Thanks, Pat. Hey, I gotta write this up. Talk tonight?"

"Sure, man," he said, and hung up.

Rachel was still there, hovering. "More good news?"

"Playoff tickets go on sale Sunday. After the game."

She put her hand to her mouth. "They did it?"

"No, not yet. They still have to win to get in. And the other teams are still chasing them. They just need to sell these in advance."

He got to see all those lovely teeth again, and she was wearing that same skirt from the ILS training. The rational part of him fought back bravely. She said, "Good for you, partner."

Toward the end of the day, a paper wad hit him in the head. He was about to throw it back when he noticed it had some handwriting, so he opened it. It said:

Hey partner,

Wow. That was the best thing I've ever seen here. I've never seen anyone stand up for a client like that. And you say you don't like this job. Could have fooled me.

- Rachel

P.S. Go Yankees!

There were only seven games left in the season. All they had to do was win. And keep winning. It couldn't hurt if the Mariners and Angels lost. But Richie couldn't do anything about that.

They looked unstoppable. The Tigers were a bad team, and Mattingly led the way with two big hits as they won both games of a doubleheader with ease. Richie had never seen Queen Tina smile so much.

The next day, a Sunday, was the last time the Yankees would be home – if they didn't make the playoffs. Tickets would go on sale at the ticket booths right after the game. They had too much energy for sleep, so instead of watching Saturday Night Live, they planned the next day's strategy.

Richie had just enough money in his account to pay for one playoff game, given the postseason markup. Since the world might end at any moment between Games 1 and 2, they agreed to go to Game 1. He might have borrowed some money and afforded better seats, but when he asked Pat where they should sit, he said, "You're kidding right? Didn't you learn anything? As Oscar Wilde once said, 'Box Seats Suck.'"

Sunday's game would start at 1:35 PM. They'd get there at 11:30 or so and scope out the place. If the line was long, one of them would wait while the other attended the game. They settled it the only way brothers would: Rock, Paper, Scissors. Richie got cut as Paper, but Pat chose to be the 'waiter'. But hopefully, the line would be short and they could just go at the end of the game.

"I can't believe this is happening," Richie said as Pat went to his own room. "We can actually buy playoff tickets."

"Yup," Pat said, smiling. "No matter what happens, it's a milestone. We get to wait in line like any other shmoe. Nobody can take that away from us."

Pat was on the phone with Marilyn most of the morning, planning for their engagement party. Richie paced past him several times, bouncing a tennis ball. Finally, at 11, Pat was ready. They packed him a sandwich, some granola bars, a crossword puzzle book, and a big water bottle, along with a transistor radio and an earphone. He also had *Beloved* by Toni Morrison in a paper bag.

"That any good?" Richie asked as they got in the car.

"Marilyn turned me onto it, said it was the best thing she ever read," Pat said. "It must be amazing, because I can't understand a word of it. The paper bag is so I don't get my ass kicked."

Getting in line, however, was a tough call. There were about twenty or thirty people waiting along the River Avenue wall, but far from a Rolling Stones-style campout. One guy had a lawn chair and was reading the Daily News. But would it get longer throughout the day? And how would they keep an eye on it? They stood in front of Stan's until it opened, nursing beers in view of the box office, stakeout style. Not many more people were added to it by 1.

"OK," Pat said, polishing off his beer. "Let's do this thing."

"What do you wanna do?" Richie asked.

"Just what we planned. You get in there, I'll wait." He got in line behind a guy who looked a lot like the mutterer from the Blue Jays game, smiled, and furtively opened *Beloved*.

Richie bought a ticket for the current game, but before going to the gate he asked the ticket seller, "Hey, think the line's gonna be much bigger than that?"

The man, old enough to have seen the first Yankees playoff game, turned and looked out the porthole window behind him. "You know, that's not so bad right now. You might watch part of the game, leave maybe in the 6th. We're not doing anything until half-hour after the game ends anyway."

He thanked the man and went inside. It was a much bigger crowd than the day before. Queen Tina's entourage had grown. They jeered Cecil Fielder when he struck out, chanting, "YOU ARE FAT!" He watched Mattingly ground out to second. Neither team scored.

But he couldn't concentrate on the game. His neck ached, his knees bobbed, and he dribbled a large sip of his Jumbo onto his shirt. Finally, he decided he could wait no longer. He polished off his beer in terribly unhealthy gulps, belching loudly. Then, he committed an act of bleacher blasphemy by not only leaving early, but in the second inning.

He spotted Pat quickly in line; a few people had joined it behind him.

"Ah, shit," he said when he saw Richie.

A fan behind him said, "Pay up, dude." Pat rolled off a fiver to the man.

Richie looked at him. "What was that?"

"You couldn't have made it to the fifth? Really? I bet that guy you'd stay until at least the fifth."

They listened to the game on their giveaway radio, which ended in a heart-breaking loss. It was a setback that added to Richie's growing anxiety, causing him to gnaw on his thumbnail. But now, all he wanted was to get to the ticket booth. As the crowd let out of the game, hordes of people now made for the back of the line. There were scrums here and there, and a shouting match behind him that summoned a pair of police officers. "Check your pockets," Pat said as everyone craned to watch.

The crowd got antsy. Someone yelled, "Let's GO, what the FUCK!" A huge "Ass-hole" chant rang out when a guy wearing a Red Sox t-shirt walked by across River Avenue, flipping them off. Finally, after an eternity of chanting, groaning and cursing on all sides, the line shuffled ahead like the Cross Bronx Expressway. A cheer rang out.

When they were three spots away, Richie took out his wallet and removed the bills he'd brought. He started to put them in Pat's hand. But Pat shook his head, and closed Richie's fingers around them. "You do it," he said.

"You sure?"

Pat took a deep breath. He kept an eye on the person in front of him. Then he turned to Richie, looked him in the eye, and said, "You waited a lifetime for this. You and Donnie Baseball. It's not fair to him, and it's not fair that you had to wait your whole childhood, your whole life, for this little bit of happiness. It's your turn. You do it."

"Come on! Step up!" growled the ticket seller.

Richie took a deep breath. He stepped up to the window. "Two bleacher seats for Game 1," he said confidently.

The man, not looking at him at all, typed a few things into a keyboard, printed the tickets, counted them. He quoted the price. Richie already had the cash ready. The man gave him his change, put the tickets into an envelope advertising Modell's Sporting Goods, and slid them through the window.

"Enjoy the game. NEXT! LET'S GO!"

He walked carefully away from the window, stunned, clutching the envelope in his fingers. He opened it and slipped the tickets out. They were glossy, just as he expected. They had a Yankees logo, a Division Series insignia, and the term "GAME A" on them. They felt heavier than other tickets. He had the same sensation as the night he met Donnie Baseball, worried they'd fly away or get stolen. He wasn't sure if he should hold them in his hand, or keep them in his pocket, or let Pat hold them, or take his and give Pat the other. He nearly tripped on the sidewalk. So he clutched the envelope even harder.

Pat was standing on the curb, smiling widely, hands in his pockets. "Congratulations, man. We did it. We got playoff tickets."

He held the envelope out to Pat. "I just hope we can actually use them," he breathed.

"Well, that crapstorm of a loss in there didn't help," Pat said. He looked at the envelope. "You hang onto them. Put them in your sock drawer. In fact, let's get 'em home before someone steals them or something happens to them."

"Just a sec," he said, eyeing Stan's Sporting Goods. "I need to buy something."

The Yankees went on the road. Only five games remained. Two in Milwaukee, three in Toronto.

Sunday night, he had a nightmare that Mattingly was traded to Cincinnati for Ben Affleck and Matt Damon, then they lost five in a row and missed the playoffs.

Driving to work on Monday, he wondered if he'd been to his last game with Pat. He thought about the tickets, unsure if he'd locked the front door.

He was a wreck. His nails were bitten raw. At a noon team meeting on Tuesday, Wilson signaled that he'd left his barn door open. He wrote a Service Plan with his own name as "Client". "It's gonna be OK, partner," Rachel said as she helped him clean up a spilled bowl of sugar in the lunchroom. "Breathe. Go hang out in Day Care."

He was doing great there, playing with the toddlers, until Alfie Franklin came to pick up the baby and said, "Hey, how about those Yanks?" Then he knocked over a set of Legos.

Pat was in DC, so he had to watch Tuesday night's game against the Brewers alone. They won in a nail-biter. He listened to the ninth inning on the toilet.

Wednesday was a day game, but he was in a Crisis Intervention training at the Morris site. He retained none of it. Lunch was at noon, thus too early to hear or see it. He tried to sneak out during the breaks to hear the score, but the security guards didn't seem to be listening to the game, and there wasn't a TV to be found. All throughout the exercises, Richie dug his fingernails into his palms and squirmed in his seat. The trainer took it all the way to 5:00 PM on the dot. By that point he figured the game was over. He rushed to the car, and flipped on the radio to 770. They were back on news programming. So he flipped to 660, where they were talking about the NFL Draft, not taking place for another seven months.

"What the hell are you talking about THAT for, assholes?!?" he yelled, not realizing his window was open. The driver next to him gave him a blank stare. He flipped back to 770, which was in the midst of an insurance ad.

He made sure to roll up the window this time. "What that hell, you dipshits?! Tell me the FUCKING SCORE!"

Finally, he was obliged. They announced the score: the Yankees had won, 6-3. He hollered and honked the horn.

On Friday he showed up at Toni's office with another extra-large Dunkin' Donuts coffee for another "supervision" meeting.

"Three games left," Wilson said. "The way the Mariners and Angels are playing, there ain't no room for mistakes. They gotta win 'em all."

"This is gonna give me a friggin' heart attack," Toni said, leaning back and covering her face with her hands. "Why can't they just make it easy on me?"

Late in the day, he heard, "Hey, partner," over the partition.

"Yes?"

"Give me a status report. Yankees."

"Grab your Zantac, partner."

"Huh?"

"Three games left. In Toronto. They lose one game, they're screwed."

"Excited?"

"Scared shitless."

"Got your tickets?"

"Yes, ma'am."

"Where do you keep 'em?"

"Wouldn't you like to know."

"Huh?"

"I don't know. You could be some maniac, kill me and Pat and take 'em for yourself. Sell 'em to pay off your Mafia debts."

There was a pause. Then he was hit squarely in the crown with a large paper wad, a perfect hit.

"Oh! That reminds me. I kept forgetting to bring this in." He threw something back at her.

"OW!" she yelled.

Alarmed, he ran over to her desk. She was rubbing her head, wincing a little.

"Oh, geez! I'm so sorry! Are you OK?"

"You jerk! What the hell, huh? What was that, anyway?" She leaned over to pick it up. It was a Mattingly t-shirt wrapped in a

Yankees cap, the brim of which must have hit her on the head. It took her a moment to figure out what it was.

"God, I'm sorry about that. I, uh, just wanted to thank you for helping with Akira. And for helping me with ILS, and, you know. Just thanks."

"Aw. That's nice of you, Rich. Thanks." She stood up, hugged him around the neck, and kissed him lightly on the cheek. He thought he was going to choke.

"How's your head?" he asked her. "Good thing I didn't get the coffee mug, huh?"

She laughed. "I'm fine. You gonna watch the game tonight?"

"Not sure I have a choice. But yeah, Marilyn's coming over. And my psychiatrist, in case I need a double-shot of valium."

"Well. I'll be thinking of you," she said.

He'd be thinking of that statement for the next three hours, and after the game, and the three hours after that.

The engagement party was Sunday, so Marilyn was in town for the weekend. She'd come over to watch the game with them. She looked different: an old pair of jeans, worn tennis shoes, and a Yankees softball-style shirt. She wore no makeup, and her black hair was done up in a bun. At the start of the game she nestled next to Pat on the couch. They'd ordered pizza from the new place down the street.

"This tastes like fucking Domino's," Pat said.

"What a disgrace," Richie said. "Tony should come back and kick their asses."

Marilyn sipped a Sam Adams. "So, they pretty much gotta win 'em all, right?"

"Uggh," Pat groaned.

"And the Blue Jays, they suck, right?" Marilyn asked.

"Yes, in a general sense they do," Richie said. "They've been phoning it in for weeks. But they'd love to stick it to the Yankees. This whole thing makes me nervous."

"We can do this, boys," she said, clapping her hands.

It was a rough night. The Yankees sputtered and failed to score. A bunch of no-name players scored three runs for the Jays. Those runs held up all the way to the ninth, when the Yankees were down to their last three outs. Richie sat forward on the couch, arms folded, muttering like the guy from the previous week. Pat had moved to the kitchen, watching from as far away as he could, shaking his head and tapping a fork on the table. Marilyn was on the easy chair, staring at the TV like a concerned doctor.

Then, Donnie Baseball singled. Leyritz walked. Everyone in the room stood. A Blue Jays player made an error, and Mattingly scored: 3-1. Then they scored again on a sac fly: 3-2. One run down, one on base.

Up to the plate came Pat's nemesis, second baseman Pat Kelly.

"Well, at least they'll pinch-hit for this ding-a-ling," Pat said. "He sucks. Bring up Strawberry."

But on the screen, Kelly took his practice swings, then calmly strode to the plate.

"Wait. What the hell? They're letting him hit?"

"Don't they have a pinch-hitter?" Marilyn said.

"Yeah, Darryl Fucking Strawberry," Richie said. "What is this?"

"Aw, you gotta be SHITTING ME!" Pat bellowed at the screen. "WHAT THE HELL ARE YOU DOING? GET THIS ASSHOLE OUTTA THERE!"

"They have Darryl Strawberry!" Marilyn implored. "He hits home runs for a living! What are you guys doing?"

Kelly drew two strikes. "Christ, here we go again," Pat said, who turned toward the kitchen.

Then, Kelly hit a fly ball to left. Richie saw him fling his bat away in disgust.

But the ball kept going. The left fielder tracked it. His head slowly swiveled – ahead, up, up, up, behind him. His eyes followed the ball just as it barely cleared the ten-foot blue wall in left. 4-3 Yankees.

Richie exploded from his seat on the couch, spilling beer everywhere. Marilyn screamed, and Pat threw a Sicilian slice onto the ceiling. They gathered in the middle of the room, hugging and cheering.

"HOLY SHIT!" screamed Pat. "Pat Kelly! You stupid bastard! I can't believe it! I can't believe it!"

Wetteland came in to pitch and again blew the Jays off the field. Two games to go.

"Oh, we're almost there," Marilyn said as she held both men's hands. "I'd give my ring to see them win these next two."

Richie was losing it. This time he dreamed that every Yankee showed up to the next game with full, wet diapers and couldn't run. He saw the Blue Jays parading around the Stadium with a trophy made of ham. Joe Carter took a big bite and spat it out in triumph.

Pat was busy with engagement party details, so he walked over to a basketball court nearby and shot hoops for a while. Then he went to Rory's.

"Coors Light, right? Glass of water?" the bartender asked him.

He hung his head. "Uh, yes, please. Sorry."

"I get it. Here to watch the game." And he changed the channel for him. "Enjoy."

This was far less stressful than the previous night. Donnie Baseball doubled and they cruised to an easy 6-1 win. One game left. He heard an announcer say about tomorrow's game: "They win, they're in." He had to take a long, deep breath when he heard that.

When he got home, there was a message to call Pat at Marilyn's parents' house.

"Shit yeah!" Pat whispered into the phone. "One more, one more win! One more, and we're in the playoffs! Donnie Baseball, in the playoffs!"

"I can't even think about it. I'm not gonna sleep tonight. I might sleep with the tickets in my hand, Pat."

"You go ahead, Richie. Oh, man. We're so close, so close!"

He'd felt that way before. Fourteen years earlier.

That night, Richie dreamt about Pat. They were getting off the 4 train, on their way to the playoff game, laughing. Pat was wearing a tuxedo for some reason. They stepped off the train, but when they looked up, they were in Coney Island. Richie ran back to the train, but couldn't find it. He ran outside to call a cab, but realized he didn't have his wallet. Pat was sitting on a beach chair in the sand, saying, "Ah, don't worry about it. Mazeltov." Then he woke up, sweating.

He made pancakes that morning but didn't eat them. For the engagement party, he wore his work uniform without the tie, with one of Pat's jackets. Pat had gone early with Marilyn. Richie drove the Escort to the Harringtons', parking two blocks away due to the crowd.

"Hey, you're here!" Pat said on his arrival. He introduced him to Marilyn's many aunts, uncles, and cousins.

"He's a social – I mean, caseworker at a homeless shelter," Pat proudly said.

"Oh, isn't that nice for you!" Richie heard more than once.

He looked at his watch: game time was approaching. He barely touched his beer, and ate not a thing. He kept his hands in his pockets.

"Hey, Richie!" Marilyn said, working her way through the expansive living room. She looked radiant: her hair perfectly arranged in a bun, wearing a light green sun dress with a cardigan. She made every gesture with her left hand, so as to show off the ring. Her head was held high, and her smile lit up the room.

"Today's the day, right?" she said.

"Uh, you mean… your engagement, right?" he said.

"Pfft. No, the Yankees. They win, they're in, right?"

"Yeah, that's right. One more win."

"Well, come with me," she said, taking his hand. "It's on at 1:30, right? Let's put it on TV."

"What?"

"MSG Network, right? What is that, channel 36?"

"Wait, wait, wait," he said, looking around. "This is your engagement party."

"That's right. It's our engagement party," she said. "You, me, Pat? We're family now. The Yankees are our family. Let's watch them clinch." She pulled him by the hand through the crowd of people, took him by the shoulders and pushed him down into a recliner. She looked at the remote, keyed in the numbers, and put it in his hand. "Good? I'm sure Pat and other folks'll wanna see."

He looked up at her. "You sure this is OK?"

"I'll make it ok," she said, hands on her hips. "I'll try to stay in view. Find me if anything big happens. PAT! TIME FOR THE GAME!" She touched his shoulder, smiled, and went off.

"OK, here we go," Pat said, rubbing his hands together, a balding adult in his wake. "Richie, this is Uncle Danny. BIG Yankees fan."

"I knew I liked this family," Richie said, standing up and shaking hands.

"Hey, I heard you guys have tickets," Uncle Danny said. "I went to the last time they were in the playoffs. '81 Series. Too bad they lost." Richie and Pat looked at each other.

As the game got underway, Richie sat, glued to the couch. Pat wafted in and out, greeting guests and schmoozing with new relatives. Once in a while Marilyn would drift in and ask about the score.

During the fifth, a booming voice filled the room. "Whoa, whoa, whoa. What is this?" It was Marilyn's father, a tall, gray-haired linebacker of a man with a slight limp and a salesman personality. He was carrying a large bag of ice on his shoulder.

Richie stood. "Oh, Mr Harrington," he said. "Sorry about this. Marilyn said it was OK for us to watch baseball. But we'll turn it off if it's distracting."

"I don't care if the TV's on. But you're watching the Yankees?"

"Uh, well, you know, they're one game away from the playoffs. Kind of a big game, you know. It's –"

"Uggh!" he groaned. "Watching the Yankees! In MY house!" He rolled his eyes.

"Come on, Bill," Uncle Danny said, lying back on the couch, smirking. A couple of nephews had come to his side. "Come and watch a REAL baseball team. One that's actually still in it?" The nephews giggled.

"Oh," Richie said to Mr Harrington. "You're a Mets fan?"

"Damn right!" he said. "Saw them at the Polo grounds way back when. Went to the '73 Series. My dad would be spinning in his grave if he saw what was going on here." He shrugged and sucked his teeth. But then a broad smile ran across his face. "Hey, have fun, kiddo. I'm rooting for you and Pat, not those guys. Just try not to cry too loud when they lose, OK?"

"Sure thing, Mr Harrington."

Suddenly, he heard Marilyn scream, "RICHIE! RICHIE!" She grabbed his shoulder, spilling champagne on him. She pointed frantically at the TV.

A high line drive rose on the screen. The ball hit the yellow foul screen for a home run.

The next scene showed Donnie Baseball rounding the bases.

Richie shouted and leaped in triumph. Marilyn screeched, and Pat and Uncle Danny hugged. Richie started a "Donnie Baseball" chant. A crowd of cousins, aunts, uncles and grandparents started to build around the TV.

The ninth inning came on. The Yankees got two quick outs. Richie stood. His hands were clasped, his breath running hot between them.

The Blue Jays batter dribbled a ball weakly into the shortstop's glove. Richie raised one arm.

The shortstop threw it to second. Richie raised the other.

He saw Kelly step on the base. The announcer said, "The ballgame is over, and the Yankees are in the playoffs!"

Richie whooped and cheered. Pat threw a bowl of peanuts in the air. Uncle Danny and a group of cousins surrounded Pat and Richie, jumping up and down. A rugby-like scrum developed, bouncing around the room, knocking over a coffee table. Mr Harrington explained to a curious group of partygoers what just happened. They applauded politely, smiling.

Richie finally found Pat. Pat embraced him, squeezing him tightly, rocking a little back and forth. The salty liquid came to Richie's eyes as he whispered, "I can't believe it. I can't believe it." Over Pat's shoulder he could see the TV. On the screen, a long receiving line of Yankees formed, taking their turns hugging and shaking hands with Donnie Baseball.

Running into the room when she heard the commotion, Marilyn said, "They did it?" She looked as fresh as the first thing in the morning, not a hair out of place. She threw her hands in front of her mouth. "Oh my God, I can't believe it! Dad, did you see?"

Mr Harrington smirked, rolled his eyes, and tied a garbage bag. He said with a chuckle, "Yeah, I saw it. What time's the Giants game?"

"Oh, Dad," Marilyn said.

Mr Harrington stopped what he was doing. He straightened and shook Pat's hand, then Richie's. "Congratulations, boys. I know you waited a long time for this. Have a great time."

"Thanks, Mr Harrington," Richie said. "I'm sorry about the mess."

"It was worth it." He winked and went back to the kitchen.

"Fourteen years, man," Pat said. "We waited fourteen years for this! How many horseshit games did we go to, how many terrible teams did we have to watch?"

"Who cares?" Richie said. "Who cares. Nobody cares about the past. Let's focus on the future, on where we'll be in forty-eight hours. In the Stadium, watching Donnie Baseball finally in the playoffs!"[10]

"I guess those tickets finally mean something, huh?" Pat said.

"I'm in shock. I can't believe this is happening. I might not go to work this week. I might not leave my bed. What if I get in an accident or get eaten by a tiger or something?"

Pat stood on a chair and got the room's attention. "Hey! Hey, everybody! Me and my brother, we're going to the playoffs! First time in fourteen years! First time in our lives! A toast to the Yankees!" The group smiled and raised their drinks.

In a rare display of gregariousness, Richie stood on the chair next to him. "Hey, and a toast to the Harringtons for hosting, especially to Mr Harrington for letting us watch the Yankees on his TV, eh?"

He got a lot of smiles and a number of here-here's. Then he said, "But, if it's OK, one more toast to my big brother and his wife-to-be. Marilyn? You treated me like family from day one, always looking out for me. You told me I could do things even I didn't believe I could. And Pat, well. You took care of me, supported me, kept our family together. You put me on your broad shoulders no matter what. I can never repay you for what you've done. Watching you two, watching you get engaged, it's an inspiration. When I fall in love, I'll know how to do it from watching you. May you have fourteen thousand years of happiness."

"Aw," the guests said. Marilyn smiled and wept, dabbing her eyes with a napkin.

Pat held the back of his neck. "We're going, man. We're there."

The Wildest of Cards

Wilson stood the moment Richie walked in the door, clapping his hands. "There he is! The most faithful Yankee fan I know! Congratulations, young man!" he said, and he shook his hand with a crushing grip. "Ha! You gonna have a good time tomorrow night! Who they gonna pitch?" And they chatted at the desk about the potential lineup, about the starting pitchers. It took him nearly ten minutes just to get through the door, when Jones saw him as well.

"All right," he said. "You in. Road to the 'ship! You got tickets, right?"

"Oh, yes. Got mine right here, and it's not leaving my side. Oh, and I might be out with the flu tomorrow."

"Oh yeah, we call that playoff fever," he said, chuckling. "Congratulations, man. Good for you."

As Richie walked away, Jones said, "Oh and hey! Nice job last week, man. That was somethin'."

He made a detour to Toni's office before going to his own. "Yes! We did it!" She came from around her desk and hugged him tightly around the neck. She was so much shorter that she was on her toes. "Unbelievable. And he hit a home run in the clincher. Classic."

"I still can't believe it. Finally, the playoffs. Gonna be great."

"You want the day off Tuesday?"

"Seriously?"

"Yeah. You have the vacation time, you know."

"Huh. Don't I need to let you know in advance?"

"Come on. 'Community research', remember?"

He thought for a second. "You know, if I stay home I'll just be a mess, puttering around and such. I'll come in. It'll be a good distraction."

"Good man. But maybe leave early so you can go home and change."

"OK, I'll take that."

"Done." And they chatted about the lineup just as he'd done with Wilson.

Rachel came by his desk. "So. Can you use those tickets?"

"I told you, I'm not telling you squat. You and those gambling debts."

"Ooh, you," she said, looking around, shaking her fist at him. "If only I had something to throw at you."

He chuckled. "I'm just kidding, partner. Here, check it out." He took it out of his pocket and put it in her hand.

"Ohhhh," she said. "So fancy." She started to slowly walk away.

"Hey, hey, HEY!" he said, rising from his chair, laughing. "Come back here!"

"What?" she said playfully. "I gotta pay off Frankie the Nose." She laughed, and put it back in his hand.

"Thanks," he said, putting the ticket in his desk. "Tomorrow night. 8 PM start. I'll probably get there at 3."

"Who're they playing?"

"Seattle Mariners. They're good."

She shook her head and smiled. "God, Richie. You and Pat are finally going. And Donnie Baseball. That's great. I'm so happy for you."

He smiled. He felt himself getting a little choked up. "You know, that was a nice errand you ran a few weeks ago."

"Oh, that? Ah, it was nothing. It made me feel good. If it helped my friend, great. I'd do it again and again."

He was speechless. He took her in: green sweater, black dress pants, comfortable flats. And that smile, the smile that made his shins go weak and his palms damp. But she was a coworker, after all. The voice in his head said, *Quit. Quit your job right now.*

"Anyhow," she said, "I'm gonna be out tomorrow. Doc's appointment for Mom."

"Oh," he said. "Hope everything's OK."

"Yeah, routine. Anyway, you'll have a great time. Talk to you later, partner."

His day on Tuesday was productive, but not so meticulous. He got some service plans done, inspected everyone's unit, ran Independent Living Skills with gusto. But he was distracted any time he wasn't busy with his hands or talking to people. Forget case notes, he thought. Toni called him at four on the dot.

"Get outta here," she said. "You know how it is. You dawdle, you're gonna get stuck here. Move."

He thought maybe she said something to Wilson on the way out, because as he walked confidently but briskly through the front door, he seemed to look for something under the desk, not even saying goodbye. He got home, changed into his Mattingly shirt and jeans, wolfed down a microwave burrito, but it was still just 4:45. He did some push-ups in front of ESPN, which had some kind of college football analysis. The apartment seemed eerily quiet. He could take it no longer, so he left at 5:15. He started the Escort, then slapped his forehead. He forgot the ticket.

He went back in the house. It wasn't on the nightstand. His heart stopped. He looked at the fridge. Not there. The bathroom? The couch cushions? No. Nothing.

As he was rifling through all his work pants, he remembered: "Ohh, fancy," Rachel had said. He had taken the ticket back and put it in his desk.

"Shit!" he yelled. But the game didn't start until 8, so he had plenty of time. He called Pat to tell him he'd be late, as they planned to be there the moment gates opened at 6. But he'd left for the day.

He pushed the speed limit, hoping that no cop would pull him over on the Sprain. There was a little backup on 287. He honked and hollered at the cars ahead. He sped up 100, and parked right in front of HSA, where he should have when delivering pizzas eight months earlier.

Wilson was still at the desk. When he saw Richie, he went pale.

"Rich!" he said, shocked. "What are you doing here?"

"I'm an idiot," he said. "I forgot my ticket. Buzz me in?"

Wilson hesitated. "Rich. I don't think you should go back there."

"What? Why not?"

Wilson said nothing.

Richie turned to him. "Whoa. What happened? What's going on?"

Wilson kept staring at him. "Lemme call one of the other guards. He'll watch the desk and I can get your ticket."

"What? What are you talking about? I'm late already. Just let me in, OK?"

Just then, Jones came through the door. He started when he saw Richie.

"Rich! What you doing here?"

"I told Wilson, I forgot my ticket," he said, passing through the door.

Jones grabbed his arm, but said nothing.

Rich took his arm away. "OK, what the hell is going on? Why are you two acting like this?"

Jones looked at Wilson, then back at Richie. "Come with me."

Richie stared at him. "What happened?"

Jones took him to the conference room. There, he saw Lily Newsome in a sharp business suit, holding her arms, red-eyed and looking terribly frightened. Angela was there as well, playing with Lily's son.

The moment Lily saw Richie, she shouted, "Mr McGinn!" She jumped out of her chair and threw her arms around his neck, sobbing and shaking.

"Whoa," Richie said. "Easy, Lily, easy." It took a moment or two for her to extract herself from Richie. He helped her sit down. "My God, Lily, what happened? What are you doing here?"

She sobbed a bit more. "Here," Angela said, handing him a handful of tissues. "I saw her in the lobby when I was coming in. I asked her what happened. Mr Jones let us use this room. It's bad, Mr McGinn. Really bad."

Richie thought. By now the traffic on the Deegan would be building. Time was running out to get to the Stadium on time. "OK," he said. "Angela, can you take Treyvon out on the playground? Maybe watch him for a little while?"

"Sure thing, Mr McGinn. Come on, Trey!" she said with a smile, holding his hand.

"OK, Lily," he said, putting his hand on her shoulder. "Tell me what happened."

She took three long breaths. "One of the partners. Dylan." She started crying again. After a minute or so, she said, "He gave me a ride home. Nice guy, that motherfucker. Said he used to own the building I was livin' in. Aksed if he could come up and check the place out. So I let him in, right? And I gave Treyvon a snack, and he's watchin' TV, right? And this motherfucker, he pushes me into

336

the bedroom, puts his hand over my mouth…" She started shaking and sobbing. She slapped the table, hard. "An' when he was done, he says, if I tell anyone, he's gonna get me kicked out, fired and shit. I dint know what to do, so I took a cab over here, thought I could stay here a night. I know I gotta go through DSS and shit, but I'm so scared. Please, please don't kick me out. I'm so scared, Mr McGinn!" And she threw herself into his arms again, crying and shuddering.

Richie shook with murderous rage. His hands, patting Lily's back, were like concrete. He tried to calm himself with deep breaths. In so doing, he could feel Lily's tears slowly subside. He rubbed her back. When she was a little calmer, he asked Jones, "Have the police been called?"

"NO!" she yelled. "I don't wanna do that. I could lose my job, my place."

"Lily, it's not safe. You can't go back to those places, not with a rapist running around." He shocked himself with his own language. "I won't let you go back, not with a guy who thinks he can get away with this. You can stay here, I'll make sure of it. But you can't stay here without getting taken care of, and only the cops and the health people can do that. Not me. So we're calling the cops."

He thought carefully about what he'd say next. His stomach fluttered. He felt like something was slowly slipping away from him, like he was drifting into danger. *Be brave,* he thought. *You can do it.*

"Lily," he croaked. "I'll stay with you the whole time. No matter what happens. I'll go to the station with you if I have to. No one's gonna hurt you again. Got it?"

She looked at him, her eyes completely bloodshot. She just nodded. He looked at Jones, who also nodded, and left the room.

Richie talked a bit more to Lily. She loved her job, loved her coworkers, even Dylan. She was making an excellent salary, and everyone talked about her rags-to-riches story with pride. This act was completely out of the blue. "I'm sorry, Mr McGinn," she said, "I shoulda said goodbye. In person. But it happened so fast."

Jones came back. "OK. County police are on the way. Toni's on the line; she wanna talk to you."

They switched places. He went behind the desk, where Wilson and a night shift guard he didn't recognize were. He picked up the phone. "Toni?"

"What are you doing there?" she barked. "Don't you know what time it is? Go!"

"No," he said. He tried to be firm, but his voice cracked like a teenager. "Not doing it. I told Lily I'd stay. That's what I'm doing."

"Richie," she said slowly. "These guys can handle it. I'm coming in. Get out of there. Pat's waiting for you. Go!"

"Nope. I won't do it. I'm staying, I don't care what anyone says." He released the breath he'd held for the last few seconds.

There was a pause. "Fine," Toni said. "Stubborn... When I get there, though, you're going to the game."

"We'll see," he said. He saw flashing lights coming up the drive. "Cops are here. I gotta go."

"OK. Go. I'll be there in an hour."

Two uniformed cops came and talked to Lily by herself, despite her protests that she wanted him to stay. Richie stayed behind the desk. The clock said 7:35. Wilson got his coat. "Hang on," said Richie. He walked back to the caseworker suite, cloaked in darkness, went to his desk, and found his ticket. He came back to the desk.

"Wilson," he said as he was walking out the door. "Take this." And he held out the envelope. Wilson looked at it in horror. "Rich," he said. "You waited your whole life for this. Fourteen years, man. I can't."

"Somebody has to," he said. "Might as well be you. I don't want it to go to waste. I want it to go to a real fan. Just tell Pat what happened, OK?"

Wilson looked at the ticket for a moment. Then he took it from Richie's hand. "I'm sorry, man. I'll tell Pat. Thanks." He walked into the dark parking lot to his car.

The police had called an ambulance, which arrived at 8:30. They allowed Richie to climb in and accompany her to Valhalla. As they drove away, he saw Toni's car out the rear window, speeding in the other direction.

Richie sat in the ER waiting room for twenty minutes before he realized the game was probably in the second or third inning. Frantically, he looked at the TV. There were reruns of Jerry Springer running. It took twenty additional minutes to get the attention of the receptionist, who said, "We lost the remote. Let me see if someone else has it." But half an hour later, nothing had changed and the receptionist was gone. The security guard had no idea how to change the channel.

Lily was released at 9:45. The police were still there. They asked to take her to the station for her statement. Once again, she asked that he accompany her, which he did. He was, however, getting antsy about the score.

"Hey, guys," he said from the back of the police car. "I hate to ask, but can you guys flip on 770?"

"Sure," said the cop in the passenger seat. "News?"

"Yankee game."

"Oh, yeah!" and he flipped it on. Once again, it took forever to get the score. He heard Sterling yell about a sharp line drive from Boggs, but Vince Coleman made a terrific running catch. Then he heard, "No runs, no hits, one left. At the end of five it's 2-1, Yanks."

"YES!" he said, pumping his fist.

"Big Yankee fan?" the cop said.

"I had tickets for this," Richie said.

Everyone in the car, including the driver, looked at him. Lily said, "You did?"

"Yeah. I gave it to Mr Wilson."

"Mr McGinn," Lily said, "I dint –"

"Not another word," Richie said, as calmly as he could. "No way. I said I'd stay, and I'm staying. There are more important things than baseball."

He could see the cops smirking at one another.

They got to the station in White Plains. They took Lily inside, and he again had to stay in the waiting room. He could see the cop he'd been talking to in the car talking to a desk cop. The desk cop opened the station door and said to Richie, "Come with me."

He led Richie to the break room. There were two cops standing, hands on their belts, watching TV.

"Hey," the desk cop said. "This guy's the caseworker for that girl with the rape case. Can he watch with you guys?"

"Sure," one of them said, not taking his eyes off the screen.

"Go ahead, boss," the desk cop said.

"Thanks," Richie said. "Score?"

"2-2," one of the cops said. "Cone walked in a batter. Donnie Baseball's up."

Just then, Mattingly stroked a single into right. Bernie Williams raced around third and scored.

Richie yelled and hollered, startling the cops. He high-fived them both.

"Man, you're some fan," one of them said.

"I had tickets for this," Richie said. "But, you know," and he gestured out the door. The cops just looked at each other.

He lost track of time. It was a see-saw game, but Ruben Sierra hit a monster home run right where he'd have been sitting. For good measure, Mattingly hit a sharp double for his second hit of the night. By the eighth it looked like they'd cruise to victory. Finally, one of the original cops he met poked his head in the room and said, "OK, she's ready, boss."

They got back in the car. 770 was already on the radio. The Mariners just wouldn't go away quietly. But finally, Wetteland got a strikeout to end the game.

"YEAH!" Richie yelled. He high-fived Lily, who smiled for the first time that night. He high-fived both cops through the mesh.

When they got back to HSA, Jones wasn't there. Toni was standing behind the desk. She threw up her palms when she saw him. She addressed Lily and sent her to one of the units with one of the guards.

Richie stood in the lobby for a moment. There was nothing he needed from his desk. So he said, "OK. I guess I'll see you tomorrow."

Toni came around the desk and put a hand on his arm. "Damn. You poor guy. Hey, at least they won."

He sighed. "Duty calls, I guess."

"You wanna take tomorrow off?"

"No, I wanna check on Lily. Maybe I'll come in a little late, yeah?"

"Come in whenever you want. God, I'm sorry about this."

He shrugged. "Well, Donnie Baseball got two hits and an RBI. At least one of us got to go. See you tomorrow." And he walked to his car and went home.

Pat was inconsolable.

"It's not fucking fair!" he yelled, a little too loudly for that time of night. "You waited so long, worked your ass off, so patient. I'm so sorry, Richie, I'm so sorry." He put his head on the kitchen table and sobbed. Richie consoled him, waited a few minutes, and asked him to recall the evening.

"Yeah, it was great," Pat said glumly. "Watching Donnie Baseball run on the field was the greatest thing I ever saw, the loudest I ever heard the Stadium. Oh, shit, Richie," and he held his head in his hands.

Richie had heard enough. He watched ESPN until they finally showed the highlights from the game. The weariness finally caught up to him around 1 AM. But he still rolled around for about an hour before he fell asleep.

He came in the next day at 8:45. Wilson shot straight up when he came in. "Rich," he said. He put out a hand as if to stop him. He took out his wallet.

"No, no," Richie said, holding up his hands. "No way. Not happening."

They argued for a bit. Richie finally said, "Tell you what. If they make the next round, you buy 'em. OK?"

Wilson smiled. "You all right, Rich." He buzzed him in. Richie dragged himself up the caseworker aisle, hoping no one would talk to him. But Rachel was there.

"Hey, partner!" she said, shooting out of her chair. "Oh my God! They won! How was it?"

He dropped into his chair and grunted. "I wish I knew," he said.

Rachel looked puzzled. "What? What happened?"

He explained as Rachel sat in a chair across from him. As he talked, she put her hand to her mouth.

"Oh, Richie," she said, her lip trembling. "Oh, no. I'm so sorry. You missed it. I'm so, so, so sorry. It's just not fair." She put both hands over her face and started to cry.

He came around the desk and sat in the chair next to her. He gave her a tissue and patted her back. "Hey. It's OK. Really. There was no way I was gonna leave Lily. You know that."

She sniffled. "Yeah, I know. Damn. Bad timing. Worst timing of all time."

"Hey, at least they won. If this goes well, there's the ALCS and the World Series. Maybe I'll go to that."

She looked at him. Her eyes were red and puffy. He smiled, and she smiled back.

"Poor Rich," she said, touching his face. "I sure hope they make it."

He had to explain it a few more times to all the other caseworkers, Frances, Rob and Winnie. Lily came down and they talked. She looked a lot better but still spooked. She thanked him profusely, and said, "You gonna get me a new job?" Toni straightened out the paperwork with DSS.

At day's end, he heard over the partition: "Hey, partner."

"Yes?"

"I gotta run an errand."

"Now?"

"Yeah."

"Same place?"

"Nah, somewhere else."

"Um, OK. How long, uh, do you think?"

She came over this time. She looked serious. "I really need your help on this errand, Rich. I don't know how long it'll take. But I could use a favor."

He looked at her. He did, indeed, owe her a favor. "You got it," he said, getting his jacket.

He started toward his car. "No, let's take mine," she said. He shrugged.

She drove out the exit, but made a left instead of a right on 100.

"Where are we going?" he said.

"Richie," she said. "This is a big favor to ask. And one part of the favor is, no questions. At least for a while. Is that OK?" She looked at him, again, with a serious look.

"Geez," he said. "Are we gonna kill someone?"

"I said, 'no questions'."

"OK, so that means yes. OK, Rach, for you, I'll murder the shit outta someone."

She laughed. "Thanks, partner." Then she locked the doors. Richie started to ask a question, but decided not to.

She went west on 287, then south on the Deegan. They kept going and going, past Yonkers Raceway, past Woodlawn, past Van Cortlandt Park.

"So, no questions," he said, looking out the windows.

"Right."

"So I can't ask where the hell we're going."

"You can look in the glove compartment for my lipstick if you can't sit still, Mr Question."

He shrugged. He opened the glove compartment. He saw a red lipstick, but underneath he saw an envelope that said, "For Richie."

"What's this?" he said.

"What part of 'no questions' don't you get?" she said. "Just open it."

Inside were two reddish, glossy tickets with the same Yankees logo and the same Division Series insignia. In computer print were the words: "GAME B" and "BLEACHERS SECTION 41 ROW 23". One said "SEAT 3" and another said "SEAT 4".

"WHAT IN THE NAME OF HOLY SHIT IS THIS?" he yelled.

"Man," she said, "you just don't understand the whole 'no questions' thing, do you? Where do we park?"

"Rachel! What is this?"

"What do you think? It's an errand. For a friend."

"Jesus, Rachel!" he exclaimed. "Where did you get these?"

"They fell off a truck. Don't worry about it; Johnny Two Times owed me a favor."

"No, really, Rach. What is this? How'd you get these?"

She sucked her teeth. "I could tell you, but… then I'd have to kill you."

He paused. "You're not gonna tell me, are you?"

She said nothing. She wore a goofy grin, like the cat that ate the canary. She looked straight ahead.

"Rachel, I –"

"Where should we park?"

"Get off at the Macombs exit," he said. "It's early enough that we can park on the street."

"Oh, no, Mr Cheapskate," she said. "We're not parking my baby where some lunatic can scratch it. Find me a good lot and you can spring for that, deal?"

"I'd pay to park behind third base after what you just did. Can I please give you some money for this?"

She just stuck out her tongue at him. It was a lovely tongue, he thought.

They parked in the 164th street lot. It was barely 6 PM, so they got a spot right by the exit.

"Perfect," she said. She took off her SUNY New Paltz sweatshirt, revealing the t-shirt he'd bought her. "I didn't have time to take you home to pick up your stuff, so here," and she tossed a brand-new Yankees cap at him. She breezily popped out of the car and jogged toward the bleacher gate. She waved him along. "Come on, partner. We can catch batting practice."

The gate was open. There was no line at all. They came out of the tunnel and saw the Yankees taking their swings. Richie turned around and looked at the video screen. It read, "WELCOME TO GAME 2 OF THE 1995 DIVISION SERIES." The Mariners' and Yankees' logos gleamed. Red, white and blue bunting graced the walls. He put his hand on his chest, catching his breath.

"Never sat here before," Rachel said. "You'll have to show me around."

Richie looked at her. "Never?"

"Uh-uh."

"Uh-oh," he said.

"What?"

"Ooh. It's a rough crowd."

"I was a bartender. Remember?"

"At a yuppie bar. This is way different."

She shrugged. "Ah, we'll see. Anyway, this is some view."

Richie looked at their tickets. "Yeah, but we're up there." He pointed to a spot just under the video screen.

"Holy shit," she said. "Might as well watch from my house. I'm gonna kill that Johnny Two Times – OH! Oh, Richie! There he is! There he is!"

He looked, and he saw Donnie Baseball walking into the batting cage. "YEAH!" he yelled, clapping. "All right, Donnie Baseball!"

Rachel put two fingers in her mouth. She whistled. Loudly. "YEAH!" she yelled. Richie cracked up laughing.

"Hey, don't shove me out of the way if he hits one out here, OK?" she said.

He watched her as she looked at the field. "Hey," he said, getting her attention. "This is just about the nicest thing anyone's ever done for me. And I have Pat for a brother. So that's saying a lot. I don't know what to say. Thanks, partner."

She smiled, paused a second, patted his knee. "You earned this. Buy a girl a drink?"

"You bet."

"I'll have a lemon drop martini, no sugar."

"I'll see what I can do." He came back with two Jumbos and a bottle of water. "They were out of triple sec," he said.

Eventually they had to sit in their assigned seats. Richie had trouble finding them.

"I thought you sat here all the time," Rachel said.

"There's never been assigned seating before. I don't even know – oh, there it is," he said as he found the seat numbers, small metallic decals stuck to the front of the bench.

Rachel wrote the lineups in the scorecard in her bubbly handwriting. "How the hell are you supposed to write in these things? They're tiny."

"I know, right?" Richie said. He paused, then said, "Rachel?"

"Yeah?"

"What does this mean?"

"What do you mean?"

"Well. You know. We're coworkers."

She smiled. "It means I didn't want to miss the chance to see you at your first playoff game. It was kinda my idea anyway, right? That's what it means, partner. Let's just enjoy the game, OK?" She smiled, and went back to entering the lineups.

"By the way. These things are really stressful."

"Yeah, you said that. We'll see."

"And if this thing goes south," and he paused, "...I don't want you to see me lose my shit."

"I already saw you lose your shit, remember? I get it, you were going through a lot. You were stressed. At least this time I'll be expecting it."

"OK, partner. You've been warned."

"Duly noted."

The Yankees ran on the field. They joined in when Ali rang his cowbell, Rachel enthusiastically clapping and cheering. When they finished with the "everybody sucks except the Yankees" chant, she spit out a mouthful of beer.

"Holy crap, are you OK?" Richie asked, giving her a napkin.

She was choked with laughter. "OH MY GOD!" she breathed as she cracked up. "'Box seats suck.' 'Everybody sucks except the Yankees.' Priceless."

In the bottom of the inning, they sang a filthy song to Jay Buhner involving his wife and sister. Once again, she was doubled over laughing. Richie put his hands out to make sure she didn't fall.

"Holy shit," she said. "I can't believe it. These people are crazy. I love it."

Just then, the crowd started chanting "Jump!" at someone in the upper deck. Once more, Rachel couldn't breathe from laughing. Richie was smiling ear to ear.

"Jesus, this is awesome," she said. "I'll never sit anywhere else."

"Wait'll we get to the seventh inning stretch," he said. "They –"

"HEY BUHNER!" shouted a nearby fan. "I HEARD YOU'RE GREAT ON THE PIANO BUT YOU SUCK ON THE ORGAN!"

Rachel stumbled with laughter, grabbing Richie's arm for support. "Oh my God, I'm gonna pee my pants," she said, wiping her eyes.

Mattingly singled in the second. "Hey, your guy!" Rachel said, grabbing his arm. She joined the crowd in arguing balls and strikes from five hundred and fifty feet away. "Ah, you suck, ump!" she yelled when a Yankee struck out. He looked at her and started laughing. "Yeah, you tell 'em, Rach!" he said.

The Mariners scored in the third. "Ah, they'll get it back," she said, and then said, "See?" when Bernie Williams doubled in a run to tie. And when Tino Martinez homered to give the Mariners the lead in the sixth, silencing the crowd, she yelled, "What the hell kind of stupid-ass name is 'Tino', anyway?" A few people turned and laughed.

Then, in the sixth Sierra did it again, hitting a towering home run into the bleachers. Rachel was now jumping up and down, screaming, banging on his shoulder. The game was tied again.

And then everything went black for Richie for about ten minutes.

Old Ruben. Tugging at the jersey, shuffling to first, soaking it in a leisurely jog around the bases. Well, not that old. What is he, 29? All that God-given talent. Good for him, good for us, who cares if he's the Village Idiot.

God, this girl's gorgeous. Why is she torturing me? Why can't I get her out of my head? Why is she having such a good time? Why can't it be easy, why can't she leave me in peace?

OK, focus. Game tied, Donnie Baseball's up. He'll take a strike. That's good hitting discipline, just like the 80s, just like when he hit in the .350s. Oh, little outside. Yeah, good eye. Advantage, 1-0 count. Just get on, the guys behind you'll do the rest. They're gonna need a rally, a few more runs, Wetteland's shaky –

Oh shit. Oh shit! A line drive! Rising, maybe a double – no, NO! It's getting higher! Did he get it? YES! YES! OVER THE WALL! THOSE LUCKY BASTARDS IN THE FRONT! THEY CAUGHT IT! HE DID IT! HE DID IT! IN THE PLAYOFFS! DONNIE BASEBALL DID IT! IN THE PLAYOFFS! HE GOT US A LEAD! WHAT'S IT

BEEN, THIRTEEN YEARS, A MILLION GAMES? HOW MANY SHITTY TEAMS DID HE PLAY FOR? HOW BAD DID HIS BACK HURT? IT'S ALL BEHIND US, ALL BACK IN THE ON-DECK CIRCLE! JESUS CHRIST, A PLAYOFF HOME RUN!

Where'd that liquid come from, is it raining? Probably beer. What's this on my head, somebody's jacket? Yes! I'll wave it - no, only Midwestern hicks do that. Ah, fuck it - Whooooooo! Whooooo! Hey, Rachel! Oh, no, she's getting crushed by the crowd, she's falling, get her! Got her! Oh God, are you ok, are you hurt? She's laughing, her cap's pulled over her face, oh thank God she's ok. Hey, another one of her choking hugs! Oh, God, don't let this end. Oh, wait, she's high-fiving strangers, OK! Someone just opened an umbrella, why? Who cares? Crowdsurfing time! High-fives, you total strangers! Holy shit, that guy is crying! Go ahead, throw bottles, throw t-shirts, throw hot dogs on the field! Hey, stuff's raining from the upper decks! I hope it's not people – no, just beer, peanuts, newspapers. 57,000 people going apeshit! I can't hear anything, I think I'm deaf, my voice is running out, I almost slipped on this shitty plastic seat and broke my neck! Come out, Donnie, come out and get your curtain call – oh, but he won't, he's too classy, the game's not over – but why not, why not, we love you, this one's for you, my friend, my distant friend, you've got my pen, I've got your ball, come out and get your praise, you waited forever, suffered, worked hard, why not get your reward –

Uh-oh. Where are the Mariners going? Buhner's jogging in, Piniella, he's waving, he's waving – oh, come on! BOOOOO! Hey, Rachel just said, "Fuck you guys!" She's awesome, please stop being so attractive. That's right, don't be such candy-asses, get back out here, just let us have this moment and play the game, you're a former Yankee, you're gonna lose anyway, the umps don't know shit, I know they're acting like animals, but let us – oh, ok. The Voice of God says to stop it, he might take the game away from us, and that homer will never count, we'll never make it to the Series. Hey, shut up, you assholes! Stop, stop! Stop throwing shit on the field! Stop or they're gonna cancel it! OK? OK? Understand? Can't act like that. Can't be a bunch of animals. Next time, if there is a next time, go nuts but don't throw things, don't jeopardize the game, I'd hate to see things get cancelled. OK, those candy-asses are getting back on the field – YOU SUCK! YOU'RE GOIN' DOWN! FUCK "REFUSE TO LOSE"! REFUSE THIS! WE WANT KEN PHELPS![11] BOOO! BOOOO! LET'S GO YANKEES! LET'S GO YANKEES! YEAH! YEAH! WE'RE GOIN' TO THE SERIES! BRING ON CLEVELAND, THEY SUCK TOO! LET'S GO YANKEES! Cowbell, cowbell! Let's keep the rally going! Let's go, LET'S GO!

Another explosion of mayhem almost occurred when a Mariners pitcher hit catcher Jim Leyritz two batters later. Richie joined everyone in cursing the Mariners, and Piniella along with them. "Your Yankee privileges are revoked!" he yelled. But as the debris rained down again, he worried that the Yankees would have to forfeit the game. Sensing this, Rachel stood on her seat.

"Hey, cut the shit!" she shouted to those around them. "Don't give the game away to those douchebags!" Richie joined the throng in dutifully doing as a pretty woman in the bleachers commanded.

There seemed to be fumes emanating from the bleachers. Every batter, every out, every pitch was contested, greeted with either loud cheers or vicious boos. Items were thrown, hair was pulled, and curses in thirty languages, not all of them modern, rained down on the field. Everything the Mariners did was a slap in the face. It seemed the Yankees could not get Ken Griffey, Jr. out (but then, no one could).

Later, there was a controversial call which allowed the Mariners to score. There was on-field discussion among the umpires, and Richie thought there was a replay on the Diamond vision, but they couldn't see it. They were so far back in the bleachers that the fifty-foot screen was too steep to read. Then the Yankees trotted on the field, and the Mariners' run still counted. More boos and more trash flew, and once again Bob Sheppard gently admonished the crowd. Rachel threatened to kick someone's ass.

"Jesus, Richie," she said, holding his arm and bending over to catch her breath. "You weren't kidding. This is so stressful. I don't know how you do it."

"You're strong, partner," he said, patting her hand. "You can do it."

She looked up and smiled at him.

More chaos ensued when Paul O'Neill hit a massive home run to tie the game. A thrown newspaper covered Richie and Rachel's head. She crumpled it and tossed it forward.

"What the hell? This is insane," Rachel yelled at Richie. She was getting hoarse, which he found both sexy and concerning. He didn't want her throat to hurt, but he was trying to stop thinking of her that way.

"Hang in there, partner," he said.

The ninth inning came and went with the score tied. The night that had started off balmy had turned breezy and damp. Richie and Rachel finally sat. The teams themselves seemed to lose energy, making easy outs. The action turned to inaction. That didn't, of course, prevent the bleacher fans from telling right fielder Jay Buhner how bad he sucked. Rachel leapt from her seat along with Queen Tina's crew when a Yankee struck out looking.

"All right, forget the umps," declared a fan nearby. "We're gonna win this game without 'em!"

"Yeah, fuck those guys!" yelled Rachel, and cheers ensued. Queen Tina applauded her.

In the twelfth, Rachel turned to Richie and said, "Hey, is that the same pitcher? Wetteland?"

Richie bit his nails. "Yep."

"Isn't he getting tired? This is like his fourth inning."

"Uh-huh. Shit. Makes me nervous."

Just then, he heard that familiar sound. Now he hated it.

Junior Griffey destroyed a Wetteland fastball, deep into right. Fifty-seven thousand people sat on their hands and shut up.

It was whisper quiet. It was also getting on midnight. Richie looked at the clock and realized he and Rachel would have to be at work in a few hours. He felt the pins and needles in his legs and a droopy feeling in his eyelids. He thought about crawling into his warm bed and falling asleep. He saw Rachel massaging her neck and yawning, her face in a frown.

The Yankees came to bat. The bleachers ebbed and flowed with the action. They moaned with the first out. A modest cheer broke out with a walk. Then got louder with another, but dropped again with an out. This was their last chance.

As Sierra came up, as the buzz in the bleachers grew and grew, Richie felt Rachel slip her hand into his. It was damp and cool, but soft and petite. She wound it through his fingers and squeezed gently. Since he was so focused on the field, it took him a few beats to realize what had happened. He turned to her. She was fully focused on the field, eyes wide, biting her lip. Her cheeks were glistening, and a few strands of hair peeked out of the brim of her cap.

He started to say something when he heard a vicious crack of the bat and a deafening roar. Sierra hit a screaming line drive to left. Rachel let go his hand; now both hands were over her mouth, and she was bouncing up and down. He'd hit it hard, but it was low. Diaz turned his back, a good sign. Was it gone? No, but it bounced off the top of the wall, right back to him. Lucky. Posada, running on contact, scored. Bernie, track star that he was, was sure to score – right? Game over? They pulled it off, stole it?

No. Out. Richie had to admit: a perfect relay throw, textbook. A shame, but at least the game was tied. They would have to keep going.

Rachel collapsed into his chest, her arms around his neck. She felt slightly limp, like she would fall.

"Rachel? Are you OK?"

"Oh my God, Richie. What the hell is going on? Why is this happening?"

"Hey, sit down, sit down," and he helped her into a seat, taking her hand. "Breathe, partner. Easy."

She was panting, and her skin was wet from either mist or sweat. She had one hand over her face. "Oh, man. This is awful. I can't. I can't do this."

"OK, just hang on, OK?" He ran to the water fountain and filled up her water bottle.

She guzzled half the bottle in one swallow, and wiped her brow. "Oh. OK. I feel better. I was a little too excited there."

"Hey," he said. "This is nuts. Want me to take you home?"

She shot straight up. "I should slap you right now, Rich. How dare you? Game's not over!"

"Yeah, Rich!" a fan in front of them said. "The hell's the matter with you? The lady's staying, got it?"

"All right, all right, Jesus!" he said.

Rachel smiled at him. "Thanks, I'm OK. I'm having a great time."

He smiled back. "I hate this. But yeah, me too."

The marathon went on. The thirteenth: nothing. In the fourteenth they came close but didn't score. Richie grunted as he sat down. His feet were sore and his back ached.

Rachel put her hand on his shoulder and said, "You OK, partner?"

"Ugh. Hanging in there. When is this gonna end?"

"Look at it this way. We're making history."

"Another inning and we'll *be* history."

She looked at the field. "Wow, that guy's pitching awesome. Who is he?"

"Mariano Rivera," Richie said. "He's OK. Kinda shaky. But looks good tonight, right?"[12]

At that point, it started to mist. Rachel leaned forward, holding her arms. Richie found a jacket on the seat next to him and placed it around her shoulders. After a moment, she sat up, looked at what she had on, and said, "Is this yours?"

Sheepishly, he said, "Uh, no."

She examined it for a few seconds. Then she said, "Thanks."

The clock passed 1 AM. Rivera blew away the Mariners in the 15th. When the Yankees came up, Pat Kelly walked. Richie thought, *Let's not get too excited, we've seen this all night.* Then Leyritz brought the count to 3-1. They stood, clapping weakly.

Then, he heard the sound.

Or did he? Muffled by the rain? It carried. Deeper, deeper into the night. He saw Buhner drift back, slowly shuffling to the wall. Rachel gripped Richie's arm. Hard, hard enough to bruise. Their seats were so far back, they couldn't tell where it would land. The box seats would have the best view, so once it got to the field... good news if there were cheers, bad news if there were 'aws'. Just before impact, the bleachers went silent.

Then they heard the box seats cheer.

The bleachers erupted just a beat late. Water bottles, magazines, umbrellas, raincoats, pants, and socks went flying. Richie jumped one and a half inches off his seat on shattered legs. Rachel squealed and shouted, waving her hands in the air.

No one had gone home. Only a few diehards ran on the field, and were summarily pummeled. They saw the dogpile at the plate envelop Leyritz, then teeter and fall a few feet behind. Rachel waved the jacket he put around her, then let it fly. Someone jumped on Richie's back and pounded his head, yelling, "Holy shit! We're going to the fucking Series!" Damp from the mist, soaked to the bone, Richie saw fans running up and down the aisle, high-fiving everyone. They watched the Mariners walk silently off the field, the outfielders jogging, some fans yelling, "Get the fuck outta here!"

Then, low and soft beneath the cheers still lingering, a voice rang out over the PA. It was Frankie, thank goodness, not Liza. Fifty-seven thousand hoarse throats, weary from five hours of active yelling, screaming, crying, arguing, and cursing, joined in, horribly off-key, but happily singing about spreading news, shoes longing to stray, and of course, being a part of it.

They'd taken one another's arms, swaying back and forth. Richie had one arm draped around Rachel, the other around a stranger who smelled like peanuts. When they sang about the blues of some other little town, he looked at Rachel. She was looking up at him, under the cap he'd bought her, her sea-green eyes gazing at his, smiling sweetly. He took her face in for just a second or two. Then, suddenly, she reached up, took his face in her hand, and kissed him.

Her cheeks were slick with the falling mist, warm and flushed with excitement; her lips cool and soft. She took her other hand and wrapped it around the back of his neck, her fingers gently pressing.

She took off his cap and ran her fingers through his hair. He took his other hand away from the stranger and pulled her closer. As he did he felt her take in a deep breath. He heard only her slightly labored breathing, blocking out everything: Frankie's voice, the off-key fans, the cheers, the falling rain. His mind was nowhere near the South Bronx.

She pulled away slightly and opened her eyes. She leaned into him, embracing him tightly, and he stumbled a bit on the bench. She gasped, then laughed. She bore those eyes deep into his own. He'd never been closer to the lovely sight of her smile.

"What does this mean?" he said to her in a whisper.

"It means we won," she said.

When the song ended, fans began jogging toward the exits. Richie took Rachel's hand and they descended the steps. Cops stationed in the tunnel were high-fiving fans, smiling and waving them out of the building. Echoes of "Let's Go Yankees" serenaded them in the tunnels, in the corridors, and out onto River Avenue. The #4 train blew its horn, but the crowd's elation drowned it out. They high-fived anyone coming their way, jogging up the avenue. They made a run for the parking garage, soaking wet.

"My God, Richie," she said once they got to her car. "That was amazing! I mean, it sucked, but it was awesome, incredible. What a game!"

"Best game I've ever seen, hands down," he said.

"Really? I mean, you've been to a lot."

"Yeah, but this had everything. Comebacks, drama, mayhem, laughter. A certain something else. Everything."

"And Donnie Baseball, your hero. His home run."

He blinked. "Oh. Oh, yeah."

She laughed. "That was amazing! But oh my God, I slipped, and thought I was gonna get trampled. Thanks for pulling me out of there."

Again he blinked.

She drew back a bit. "Richie? You OK?"

He looked away. "I think so."

"What? What... what happened?"

"Well, I remember the sound, the ball going up. Then…" He closed his eyes. "Nope, got nothing."

"What about waving the jacket over your head?"

"What jacket?"

"The one you gave me at the end. When I was cold."

"I was waving that? Nah, don't remember that."

"The guy opening the umbrella?"

"He did?"

She glared. "The guy who was crying."

"Who, me? Or someone else?"

She gasped. "Oh my God, Richie! You blacked out!"

"Huh. Yeah, I guess I did."

"Oh, no," she said, caressing his cheek. "That's awful. Such a wonderful moment, and you won't remember."

"Oh, no," he said. "No. I'll never forget this night. Never."

She smiled, with all her teeth. Then she wrapped her arms again around his neck and kissed him again.

"Rachel?" Richie asked. "I meant what I asked in there. What does this mean?"

Her grin grew slowly into a smile, then a laugh.

"What?" he said in mock frustration. "What is it, every time I ask that?"

"Richie," she said, "You're so sweet. I'll never forget seeing you like this, so fulfilled. So generous, taking care of me when I fell, getting me water when I didn't feel good. Making sure I didn't lose my shit in there. Laughing and cheering and cursing. It was a thing of beauty. It was wonderful, everything I could have wanted."

"Biggest and most wonderful surprise of my life," Richie said. "So... is that it? We work together, so this can't be?"

She brushed his hair back, looking into his eyes. Her face was still stuck in a grin.

"Remember that doctor's appointment today?"

"Yeah. Everything OK with your mom?"

"God, you're cute. I'm sorry to have done that, but I wanted to wait until I knew."

"Knew what?"

"I should probably tell you the truth," she said with a glint in her eye. "I'm leaving."

"What?!" Richie exclaimed. "Leaving?!"

"No, no," Rachel said, holding his hand. "Not leaving New York. Leaving HSA."

"Oh, Jesus," he said, clutching his chest. "God, you scared me half to death."

"Sorry, bad choice of words. I'm sorry," she said, stroking his cheek. "Yeah. I got a new job. You remember Blythedale Children's Hospital? Where I used to volunteer? Well, they hired me as a social worker in training there. They have this great tuition reimbursement program, way better than ours. I'm taking an MSW class at Fordham, in Tarrytown, non-matric. Next semester, I'll be enrolled in their degree program. When I graduate, I'll be pretty much debt-free. And I can get my practical work done at Blythedale."

Richie blinked.

"So you're gonna take my job, Richie. Well, I mean… you don't have to leave, go to another site. You'll be permanent. Ellen comes back, but I leave, so… little switcheroo. You like that?" She spread her palms in a 'ta-da!' motion.

He was speechless.

"You OK, Richie?" she asked.

"Oh, I'm a lot better than OK," he said. "That's amazing, you're a genius! So, when did you…"

"Well, I've been planning this for a while," she said. "You might be iffy about social work as a career, but not me. This is what I wanna do. And I wanna work directly with kids. So I heard about this, what, late August? And really, this had nothing to do with you. Well, almost nothing. When it looked like I was gonna get the job is right around the same time you defended Akira. God, I fell hard for you that day. You really cared. It was a major turn-on, I gotta admit. So that made it a little more urgent. I said to myself, 'If I get this job, I'm gonna totally ask him out.' I'd have knee-capped some other chick to get that job.

"So Tuesday I went for my third interview. Jesus, they really put you through the ringer, right? Anyway, I got the job right then and there. I almost called you that night, but I thought you were at the game.

"Richie, my heart broke when I saw you this morning. Wait, I guess that's yesterday morning, right? Anyway, ugh," and she clutched her chest. "You poor thing. I was so sad. I sat outside and sulked for a while. And then I got this great idea. I went out to lunch and – well, I'm still not telling you how I came across those tickets – and I got this idea about, well, you know… kidnapping you and taking you to the game. I love a good surprise, don't you?

"Anyway, I brought you here, and I was thinking, I don't wanna take this moment over by, you know, saying I wanna date you or anything. I just wanted to have fun. But, oh my God, what a great time I had. I had no idea how awesome the bleachers are – I'll never sit anywhere else. I was right there with you, you at your happiest, your big moment. Your hero hit a home run in the greatest game ever played. And I was there with you, holding your hand, kissing you. I'll never forget it, as long as I live." She pulled him close and kissed him, hard, on the lips, his face in her hands.

Richie looked like he'd been hit with a crowbar. Finally, he managed to say, "Wow. That's like the mother of all first dates."

"I know, right? Good way to start this off."

When Richie turned the key to the apartment, it was 3:25 AM. He took off his shoes and opened the door slowly so it wouldn't creak. He tiptoed into the living room. He was a few steps in when Pat walked out, holding a cup of water, rubbing his eyes. When he saw Richie, he froze. He stared at him for a beat, stunned, and simply said:

"No."

"Ohhh, yes," Richie said, grinning.

They spent a few seconds staring at one another.

Pat looked at him sideways. "Stop. Get out of here. No way. Did you…?"

Richie kept grinning. He nodded and turned up his palms.

"Holy shit!" Pat shouted, putting his hands on his head. "YOU JUST WENT TO –"

"Shhhhhhhhh, you maniac!" hissed Richie. "People are trying to sleep!"

Pat whispered, "You just went to the greatest fucking game I've ever seen in my whole life!"

"Yes, I did, bro," Richie giggled. "And yes it was, the greatest game I ever saw."

Pat pumped his fists. He ran in place, then around in a circle. He grabbed Richie ina crushing bear hug, lifting him off his feet, hopping up and down. "Yes, yes, yes! Oh my GOD! Unbelievable! Fifteen innings! Back and forth, the kid Rivera, Sierra's double, Jimmy Leyritz!"

"Yep. All that. The bleachers were on fire. I thought the place was gonna explode. I've never heard anything so loud in my whole life. It was just... magic. Just... well, whatever I could have dreamed of or imagined... it was better. Unforgettable. Wish you coulda been there."

"Oh, there is a God," Pat said, looking at the ceiling. "Oh, thank you, thank you! And Donnie Baseball, the homer, you were in the bleachers, right? Right there? Was it close?"

"Oh, well, that's kind of a different story."

"What? Why? What, you were in the crapper or something?"

"No, I just kinda... blacked out."

"What? You *blacked out*?"

"Yeah. I know I saw it, saw it going up. But then, nothing. Rachel had to give me the description later."

Pat's blinked. "*Rachel*? Rachel was there?"

"Yeah. Oh, and she had to drive me to my car, otherwise I'd have been back earlier. See, we left from HSA. Well, sorta… she… kinda… Well."

Pat squinted. Then he shook his head and waved his hands in front of him. "Wait, wait. Back up. You blacked out. And Rachel. She was there. What the hell's going on?"

Richie, still smiling, exhaled. "OK, Pat. It's… early or late, I can't tell. But if you're not too tired, I'll tell you all about it."

Somehow Richie woke up at 8:30 the next day. He thought about not showering but he smelled like the bottom of the bleachers. He ate nothing, drank no coffee, and just jumped in the car. He hit no traffic. He made it to work at 9:15.

Wilson was talking to a day care worker at the desk, but abruptly stopped his conversation when he saw Richie. "YES!" he yelled, pumping his fist. "Hot damn, what a game! Jimmy Leyritz, who'd a thunk it!" He reached across the desk for a tight handshake, pulling him in for an awkward half bro-hug due to the distance. "That game? That was a classic, man. One for the ages. Did you watch the whole thing?"

He thought about what Rachel asked him on the ride back from the Stadium. "Can you fake it until Friday?"

He realized he might be hoarse. He covered his mouth as though coughing. "Sure did," he said, more whisper than spoken word. But it was audible, at least.

Wilson laughed heartily. "And your man! What a shot! Can you imagine what that was like? I mean, I saw him get a big hit on Tuesday, but, man! Whoo!"

Richie just smiled and pumped his fist.

"Ha! Yep, up 2-0 on a hot team. That's how it's done. They got a shot to go all the way, man, that's what momentum does for you."

He nodded. "Yeah," he mumbled.

Then, Jones burst in. "Ahh, yeah! Yankees, baby! Yankees!" He didn't bother with the handshake, and just pulled Richie in with a monster dad-hug. "You must be tired, watching a game that late. You OK?"

He nodded again. Covering his mouth, he coughed and said, "Nah, I'm fine."

"All right, youngblood. Run to the 'ship. Good for you."

"And, hey," Wilson said, "You did a great job the other night. That was a good thing you did. And thanks for the ticket. We had a good time. I got the next round, you hear?"

He smiled and nodded.

He walked through the caseworker suite. He looked in Rachel's office. "Hi, Rich," she said, going back to writing.

"Hi, Rachel," he said.

He got lucky in that Toni was at a meeting off-site. He had a pretty uneventful day and was grateful for it. He talked to Lily on the phone; she was doing better. He looked up some community resources for Angela. He did some inspections. He was careful, though. He made sure to say to anyone who asked that he went to bed just after 1 AM, when the broadcast ended.

"Hey, partner," he heard over the partition, just after lunch.

"Yeah?"

"How's that thing going?"

"What, the thing? The thing we talked about?"

"Yeah. Where I asked you to do me a favor?"

"Oh, yeah. Just fine, just fine."

"No problems with anybody?"

"Oh, no. Not at all. Everybody's fine."

He heard a pause. "That's good, partner. Thanks."

"No problem. So, Friday?"

"Yeah. Friday."

He was diligent about staying until 5:15, putting in an eight-hour day. He drove carefully, knowing he was a little drowsy.

He fell asleep at 8:30.

On Friday, Toni called a general staff meeting for 4:30 PM. She assembled everyone in the Multipurpose Room. She announced precisely what Rachel had said in the parking lot: Ellen was coming back. Rachel was taking a job at Blythedale Children's Hospital, going for an MSW. Richie, who'd been Ellen's replacement, would now replace Rachel and be permanent. There was a little cake and coffee, and some kind words exchanged. Toward the end, Toni spread the word that there'd be a gathering at Cactus Jack's after work.

The bar was packed, overloaded with HSA staff. There were day care and maintenance people he didn't know at all or had only met once. They pretty much crowded out everyone else. Game 3 of the ALDS was about to start on TV.

"Hey, I didn't even know you were temporary, Rich," Wilson said at a table overlooking the TV.

"Ah, I just tried to play my way onto the team," Richie said. "You know it better than anyone, Wilson. Play hard and maybe you get your shot. And by the way, you can call me Richie. Everybody calls me that."

"Hey, I like that nickname," Jones said. "Like, 'Richie Baseball', or somethin'. Your daddy probably called you that, right?"

He thought about Pat. He'd never called him anything but "Richie."

"Yeah. Something like that."

"You gonna be OK watching this game, Richie?" Wilson said, pointing at the screen. "Randy Johnson's out there, man."

"Oh, sure," he said, as coolly as possible. The game would be a tough ask for his team, beating arguably the game's best pitcher. But knowing what he knew, he thought he could handle it.

Wilson asked, "Think Donnie Baseball has one more season?"

He shrugged. "I was talking to a friend about it. Probably not. I'll be pretty sad. But I'll be OK in the long run."

Wilson patted his shoulder. "You a loyal young man, you know that? Steadfast. Just like your man. I like that."

"Hey, Rich," Jones said, pointing at a different TV screen. "Check it out. Pre-season. Nets and Celtics. Start of the championship run."[13]

Richie laughed. "What, champions of pre-season? They give out rings for that?"

Wilson guffawed. Jones shook his head.

As they laughed, he spotted Rachel across the room, listening to Toni and the other caseworkers. She was holding a drink in both hands, looking at him a little sideways. She gave him a wide, inviting, radiant smile, as if sharing a private joke. He smiled back. Then she set her drink down on a table, excused herself, looked at him one more time, and walked out the door.

"Excuse me, guys, be right back," he said after a few moments, then followed her.

It was the first cool October night. The parking lot was not lit at all, and trucks were still racing by on 9A, their brakes squealing. He walked blindly into the rows of cars, having trouble finding her.

"Hey, partner," he heard in front of him, like a beacon in the night.

She was leaning up against the side of her Honda, hands in her pockets. She'd switched over to jeans, a green sweater and tennis shoes. She didn't have her jacket, and she looked cold. He took off his sweatshirt and was about to put it around her, when she put her arms around his neck and pressed her lips against his, passionately, pulling his head closer into her own embrace. He held her tightly, gently spreading his hands across the smooth fabric of her sweater.

Her sweet, soft scent sent his mind far, far away. He couldn't hear the cars and buses speeding on the thoroughfare behind them.

When they separated, she said, "I was waiting for that all day."

"I was waiting for that all year," he said.

She laughed. "Well. We have two weeks to keep it under control."

"OK, then. I'm gonna walk in there and quit." And he started walking back to the bar. She grabbed his arm and pulled him into her again, kissing him once more.

"Thanks for quitting," he said, as he wrapped his Yankees sweatshirt around her.

She smirked. "I didn't quit, Richie. I moved on. It's a great opportunity."

"For me, yeah." They both laughed. "You sure about this thing?"

"Oh, yeah," she said, leaning now by his side. "Great place, great opportunity. Close to you, too. Maybe we can sneak out for lunch sometime."

"Who'm I gonna play Blind Basketball with now?"

She laughed. "Ellen might surprise you. You'll like her. Very smart, very capable, very kind. Good eye, good hands. Like someone else I know." She nudged his shoulder.

He blushed. "Congratulations on the job again, Rachel. You'll be great. You're so good at this. You have an instinct, always know what's right. And you love kids. I said it before: I learned from you."

"Thanks, Richie. You'll be great, too. I'm so glad you're taking my job. For a while I wasn't so sure you'd stay."

"Well," and he looked away. "Like I said, I kinda… checked out. Didn't care anymore. What they call 'phoning it in'. And it was stupid, you know, 'cause it was right after… you know. Johnny's Reef."

She nodded, and took Richie by the hand. "I'm sorry, Richie, I –"

He patted her hand. "No, no. You were absolutely right. I knew it the moment I said it. I just… liked you so much. I just… just wanted to spend more time with you. But we were coworkers. That wasn't a good idea. But I shoulda – I don't know… Been more focused. More attentive to my clients. That wasn't all that… mature of me. You know, it's… challenging, frustrating, crazy, this job. You handle it so well. Me, well… I'm working on it."

She hugged his arm a little tighter. "You don't have to worry about that anymore. I'm not your coworker, so you can ask me out again."

"Awesome. In that case, would –"

"Yes. Absolutely yes. I will go to the next round of the playoffs." She kissed him.

He laughed. "Of all the places to fall for someone."

"Bizarre. It was nuts. The wildest people I've ever seen in my life, and that's saying something. It was so exciting. Scary, nerve-wracking, a little scummy, but incredible, exhilarating. Watching you… I don't know… get your due, that was one of the most satisfying things I've ever experienced. I could live that night over again and again."

"Rachel, you made my dreams come true. And the playoff game was pretty good, too." They kissed again.

"Hey, no kissy-face on the job," Toni said.

Richie whirled around and looked at his boss.

"Well, Ms Petrocelli," Rachel said. "We're in the parking lot of a bar, so we're not at work." She stuck out her tongue.

Toni smiled and rolled her eyes. "Think you two can hold it together for two weeks?"

"Oh, sure, sure," Richie said nervously. "No problem. Sorry about this."

She laughed. "Don't be so nervous, Rich. Who do you think wrote her recommendation for the Blythedale job?"

He looked back at Rachel. She shrugged.

"How was the game, anyway?" Toni asked.

"Best game ever," Rachel said.

"I'd have to agree," Rich said, looking at her. "But how –"

"You don't ask questions of Johnny Two Times, pal."

Richie looked skyward. "I can't even believe this."

"She came all teary and crying in my office. I gave her a number for a cousin of mine. Now she owes me a favor."

"Well, transfer it over to me. I owe her like ten favors."

"Done," Toni said. "Stay on the job for a while. That's your favor."

"Too easy. No problem."

"Oh, by the way, I heard Wilson call you 'Richie'. Sorry about that. I tried to remind everyone to call you 'Rich'."

"Ah, it's OK," he waved. "Everyone's called me that since I was a kid."

"Yeah, but you're not a kid anymore. Either of you. I'll try to remember." She rubbed her hands for warmth. "OK. Game's gonna start soon, so come on back in a few, OK? No kissy-face, though."

"That a social work term?" he said.

"Smart-ass."

"If I were a real smart-ass, I'd think of something cleverer to say than 'thank you'."

She smiled. "I'm happy for you two. See you inside." And she left.

Rachel kissed him again. "Ready to watch the game, partner?"

"Eh," he said, "There are more important things than baseball."

"Ooh, I'm telling Queen Tina you said that, send you to the box seats."

"Please don't. They suck."

On a Saturday morning, two weeks after the Yankees lost the best-of-five series to the Mariners, a U-Haul van appeared in Richie's driveway.

Pat didn't own much stuff of his own. His stereo and computer were already at Marilyn's place in Chevy Chase. She also would never have allowed Pat to move the mismatched, frayed, dusty and decaying furniture in their apartment into her stylish condo, furnished to her exact taste, so the move would be easy. His stuff consisted mostly of his suits, his bike and some books. The rental van echoed even after they'd shuffled in his meager belongings.

Marilyn came along, again looking breezy and relaxed, wearing the same Yankee shirt he'd seen her wear before. She hugged Richie and said, "Sorry again about the Yankees. I was so sad. You doing OK?"

"Yeah, Marilyn. I'm fine. Thanks for asking. Oh, and thank your dad again for letting us watch the game at his house."

"Oh! That reminds me. He asked if you wanted to come over and watch the Giants game tomorrow."

"Really?"

"Yeah. Every now and then, he has some old college buddies come over. Uncle Danny, too, remember him? Big spread. Decent beer. You should!"

"You know what? I will. I'm not much of a football guy, but yeah, your dad's a nice guy. Tell him I'd love to."

Richie took a box to the van. He yelled, "Echo!" into the nearly-empty van.

"Wow, you really are pathetic," he said to Pat. "There are hobos with more stuff than you."

"Ha, jerk," Pat said. "It's all at Marilyn's place anyway."

"In a Hefty bag stuffed in her closet."

Marilyn snickered.

"Hey, don't take his side."

"Never, honey," she said. "Now go put your clothes in the glove compartment."

She and Richie burst out laughing. Pat smirked at them both, shaking his fist.

Just then, a hunter-green Prelude pulled in front of the house. Rachel appeared in a Don Mattingly t-shirt and jeans, her hair in a ponytail. Richie jogged out to greet her.

"Hey partner," she said, kissing him.

"Nice shirt," he said. "It'll be a collector's item soon. Come on, say hello."

He opened the door for her. "Hey, Pat!" she said, hugging him.

"Rachel, good to see you," Pat said. "Marilyn? Come meet Rachel."

Marilyn rounded the entrance to the living room. She blinked for just a beat. "Oh! Rachel! I've heard so much about you," she said, shaking her hand.

"Congratulations," Rachel said. "That's a nice ring."

"Oh, thanks. It actually belonged to my grandmother. Pat asked if he could borrow it until he had enough money for a ring, but I like this so much better, so I'm keeping it."

At this, Richie looked at Pat, eyes wide. Pat just shrugged.

"Wow, where's all your stuff, Pat?" Rachel said. "I took a peek inside the van. You get robbed or something?"

Everyone laughed but Pat.

It didn't take long to pack the whole van. Richie watched Pat. He watched him talk to Rachel about her job, vacuum the floor of what was his room, make a pot of coffee. As he talked to Rachel and Marilyn about the wedding, Pat poured a healthy cup and sat, casually reading the newspaper. Every now and then he caught him scanning the whole apartment, slowly, deliberately, hands on his hips. *He's taking forever,* Richie thought.

Good. Take all the time you need. In fact, stay a little –

No… go. It's time.

"Forget anything, Pat?" he said.

Pat didn't answer at first. "Hmm? Oh, yeah. Uh, I don't think so. Hey, don't forget, Con Ed is due soon."

"Yeah, I know. Sent a check already."

"Oh. What about Charlie?"

"Same thing. November 1. Asked him to call me when he gets it."

"Oh. OK. Looks like… ah… you got this. What're you gonna do with my room?"

"Shrine to Donnie Baseball."

Pat just stared.

"Ah, hell, Pat," Richie said, chuckling. "I don't know. I'll figure it out. Don't worry about it."

Pat grinned. "OK. I won't."

Richie looked at him. His eyes looked heavy, drooping at the corners. He had his hands in his pockets. He continued to scan the apartment with close scrutiny, like a potential homebuyer.

Marilyn was talking amiably with Rachel. Her legs were crossed and she leaned forward, listening closely to Rachel's story about

Game 2. They laughed together like old friends. At the end of Rachel's anecdote, Pat said, "Well, hon. Ready to go?"

"I am if you are. Take your time, hon. Take your time. Rachel, would you give me a hand with something?"

"Oh, sure," she said. She smiled at Richie, and they walked out together.

Pat drifted into the middle of the living room. Once again his eyes circled the room.

"Wow," he said. "Five years. Mom doubted us. Tried to split us up." He turned to Richie. "You know, I never told you this. But… all those years ago? Telling you, asking you to live with me? I was scared shitless. I didn't think I could do it. Take care of us both. All our bills. I was so scared I'd mess up. We'd end up in the poorhouse or something." He laughed a bit. "But look at you. You… you're a… a real grown-up now. Job, girlfriend, place of your own."

"Well," Richie said, "don't count your chickens just yet. Plenty of time for me to screw up, turn into a serial killer or something."

Pat chuckled. "We did it, man. Made a family, just us two."

"Stop talking past-tense, Pat. You're only a few hours away. I'll see you at Thanksgiving."

"Come on." And he gestured for them to go outside.

Marilyn and Rachel were waiting at the van, identical grins on their faces. Marilyn hugged Richie, gently, kissing him on the cheek. He felt a little tear brush his face.

RICHIE THE CASEWORKER Christopher Febles

Still embracing him, she whispered, "Richie. That chick is *gorgeous.*"

He laughed. "Yeah, I know."

"We're family now. You know that, right?"

"We were family a long time ago, Mar. But yeah. We are."

"So, we'll see you at Thanksgiving? We have plenty of room, remember."

"Sure, sure. Well, unless Rachel has to study."

"Ah, I can make it," Rachel said. "I'd love to."

Pat came over. Slowly, silently, he enveloped Richie. He'd never really gripped Pat quite so hard before, but he found himself holding on tight. He closed his eyes and took a long, shaky breath. Again he felt the moisture on his cheek.

"I love you, Richie," Pat whispered, the sound muffled by the embrace. "You and me, we're always family, understand? No matter how far apart. Always."

"I love you, too, Pat," Richie said, his eyes full and his voice wavering. "Thank you. Thank you, thank you, thank you."

They separated. Pat wiped his face on his sleeve. He gave Rachel a hug. "'Bye, Rachel. Take care of him, OK?"

She kissed his cheek. "He can take care of himself, but sure, I'll hang out with him."

Pat stood at the door of the van. He smiled at Richie and said, "Take care, you two social workers."

RICHIE THE CASEWORKER Christopher Febles

Richie gently pulled Rachel closer. "Social worker, this lady. Me, maybe one day. We'll see."

Pat chuckled and got in the van. He pulled into traffic, honked the horn, waved again, honked again, and waved as they pulled down the street. Richie and Rachel stood on the sidewalk as the van turned left and went out of sight.

Rachel looked up at him. "How you doing, partner?"

"Me? Oh, I'm great, I guess."

"So, show me that Don Mattingly ball you've been talking about."

"I can't."

"What? Why?"

"I gave it away."

She started. "You did?"

He pointed out into the street. "I put it in one of his duffel bags. He didn't have shit in there anyway, so it was easy. I figured, he gave me so much, it's the least I can do. I wanted him to have a little... memory of us, I guess. Dudes don't do that, and he'd have said no, stubborn bastard, so I had to sneak it on him. Not bad, huh?"

She laughed. "Yeah, not bad. But not as good as that errand a few weeks ago."

"Oh, never. Best kidnapping I ever had."

"Come on inside, partner. Let me kidnap you again for a little while."

Epilogue: Getting the "W"

October 1998

Richie heard the doorbell ring. He heard Marilyn yell, "I'll get it!" He watched her deftly sprint to the door in four-inch heels, dodging party guests and loose chairs. Over his shoulder he heard some polite greetings, some loud laughter, and then Marilyn calling him: "Richie? It's Mr and Mrs Wilson."

"Oh, good!" he said, drifting his way to the foyer. He shook Wilson's hand. "Hey, thanks for coming, all the way from Florida! Hello, Mrs Wilson, it's nice to meet you."

"Oh, you can call me Susan, dear," she said.

"Hey, young man!" Wilson said, patting Richie's shoulder. "So good to see you! How you been?"

"Good, good, you're just in time." He turned back to the party. "Is everybody else here? Pat? We ready?"

"Yeah, bro," Pat said, working his way through the partygoers to stand at Richie's side. His hair had thinned a bit, and he'd put on some weight, just a little on that athletic frame. He handed a short, thin jewelry box to Richie. "We're ready, Richie. Let's do this."

Richie cleared his throat. "Uh, excuse me, everyone! Excuse me? Could I have your attention, please?"

There were some murmurs, some shuffling, and soon it got quiet.

"Um, uh," he stammered. "Uh, I know you're here for something else, and uh, I'll try to make this quick, but Rachel? Would you come over here, please?"

Rachel turned. She'd let her hair down for this affair. She was wearing a satiny sleeveless sea-green dress with a blue cardigan Richie bought her for her birthday last year. She grinned, and the guests made a path for her to get to Richie. She looked around nervously.

"What is it, Richie?"

"Well… um… you know… you're the love of my life, Rachel. You're my best friend, my confidante, and we've been 'partners' for years now. You're basically like family now, ask anyone here. So… I… uh… just have to ask you," and he got down on one knee.

Rachel cocked her head, puzzled.

He again cleared his throat. "Would you… uh…" He opened the box Pat handed him. "Go to the World Series with me?"

Rachel shrieked. "OHMYGOD! OHMYGOD! YESYESYES! YES I WILL!" She took the box and gaped at the two glossy tickets inside. Then she threw her arms around Richie's neck and kissed him repeatedly.

A few partygoers, like Pat, Marilyn, Mr Harrington, Toni and Jones, all cheered. Wilson and a group of Rachel's coworkers laughed. Others clapped quietly, looking at each other confusedly. Marilyn turned to the group and explained what had just happened. Then they applauded and raised their glasses.

"I can't believe it!" Rachel exclaimed, as Richie clasped a lanyard around her neck which held her World Series ticket in a see-through holder. "Oh, Richie! I can't believe it! It's so amazing!"

"You earned it, partner. You put up with me for this long. I want you with me tonight. Let's relive one of our favorite moments. What do you say?"

She took his face in her hands and kissed him. "Of course. Of course I will. But, what about Pat?"

"Ah, it's OK," Pat said. "I had my chance in '96. It's your turn now, so you two kids enjoy."

"But," Marilyn said, "you're not dressed for it, obviously. So, we got you something." She nodded at Pat, who produced another box.

Rachel looked at them sideways. Richie grinned. She opened the box.

"Ohh, look, Richie!" she said. She pulled out a brand-new Yankees batting practice jersey with "21" and "O'Neill" on the back. The partygoers sighed.

""The Warrior," Richie said. "Your favorite player."

"Favorite current player. No one will ever take the place of Donnie Baseball."

Poor Donnie Baseball, thought Richie. 1995, a breakout year for Richie, had been Don Mattingly's last in baseball, his injuries catching up with him. In '96, while a million fans cheered as the Yankees held the World Series trophy over their heads at City Hall, Richie wondered if anyone remembered the floppy-haired kid with his lucky pen. That brought ME more luck than it did you, he thought.

He put his arm around Rachel. "No, never. He kinda brought us together."

Wilson had made his way to the happy couple. "Heeeeeey, that was pretty slick, youngblood. Pretty slick. Good to see you, young lady, and congrats again," and he kissed her cheek.

"Milton, what's going on?" Mrs Wilson said. "I thought this was an engagement party."

"Oh, it is, it is," Richie said. "See?"

Rachel produced her hand. On it was a silver band with what looked like a pinhole, or a distant star, or an old TV screen that had just been turned off. Mrs Wilson took the hand and squinted.

"See that little dot?" Richie said. "That's called a 'caseworker's diamond'. Practically invisible. It's about what I can afford."

"Aw, Richie," Rachel said. She looked at her hand. "All that matters is that it's from you. I love it."

"So, you are engaged," Mrs Wilson said.

"Yes," Richie said, as he squeezed his fiancée. "We took care of that already. The other thing, that was a... bonus, I guess."

"Heck of a bonus," Toni said, who'd joined in. "Nice job, Rich. Clever, like always."

"How did he propose, dear?" asked Mrs Wilson.

"Probably at the ballgame," Jones said, chuckling.

"Ohhhhhhh, no," Richie said, shaking his head. "No, no, no. I might be a Yankees geek, but I'm not that bad. Besides, can you imagine what the bleacher folks would say? I couldn't even repeat it here."

Rachel hugged his arm. "It was on the Brooklyn Bridge. It was a perfect night, not a cloud in the sky. You could see the whole skyline. So romantic."

"Once we get married, we're gonna put a combo lock up there."

The group said, "Awwww..."

"I didn't know you had it in you, ya mameluke," Pat said. Toni spit up a little, cracking up.

Rachel's mom came over. She had the same shiny blond hair, the same eyes and same teeth as her daughter. Mr Harrington sincerely thought they were sisters. She linked her arm with Rachel's. "I heard Rachel say that on the drive over. What's that mean, anyway?" she asked.

"Hey, Tony!" Richie yelled. "What's a mameluke?"

Tony, talking business with one of Pat's banking buddies, looked over. He really knew how to clean up. He'd lost twenty pounds, got a tan and wore a shiny green sharkskin suit. He'd shown up in a red Camaro, engine roaring through the Harrington's suburban neighborhood.

"You don't wanna know, Richie," he yelled back. "Just don't say the other thing, capisce?"

"I'm gonna try that out tonight," Rachel said. "'Go back to San Diego, ya mamelukes!'" The group laughed.

"That's my gal, she's a keeper," Richie said.

"Richie, are you sure about this? I mean, you and Pat... this is your thing. And geez, you went to a real stinker of a game in '96. They got clobbered."[14]

"What a disaster," Toni said, turning around. "I turned it off. You believe that? I turned off the World Series."

Stephanie, with Tajo in tow (Darlene called in her regrets), said to Toni, "You know? You could handle a junkie in your face, but you'd freak out during a bad Yankee game." Toni shrugged.

"He wanted to leave!" Richie yelled, pointing at Pat.

"What?!" shouted Pat. "You lie!"

"Don't deny it. 'Oh, this sucks, this team sucks, we're gonna get swept –'"

"Whooaaaa, back the heck up. I'd never say that, you little crud. Never!" Their play argument had drawn a crowd.

"Swear to God," Richie said, now addressing the guests. "Complaining, whining, he was a wreck. 'Let's go to Stan's and get wasted,' he says, in the fourth inning."

Jones turned in mid-handshake with Wilson. "You were gonna leave in the fourth? On your team, in the World Series? Shame on you, young man."

Pat threw up his hands. "It was 9-0! Time to get hammered, drown our sorrows!"

"Well, it turned out all right in the end," Toni said.

Pat smiled. "Yeah. It's your turn, Rachel. You're due."

Mrs Wilson asked, "And when's the date?"

"July 18,"[15] Richie said. "Sunday, so an odd date, but apparently we have the run of the place. Mr Harrington made all the arrangements at his club. And he's hosting this party. God, I love that guy."

"I guess Met fans aren't ALL that bad," Mr Harrington said from the kitchen.

"Ehhh," Pat, Toni and Richie all said in unison, laughing.

Wilson asked, "What time you lovebirds leaving?"

Richie checked his watch, then looked at Rachel. "Six?"

"Better make it 5:30," she said. "Gotta see BP, right?"

"Then let's get this show on the road," Mr Harrington said, handing out the champagne. "And hey: they better not stink it up tonight. My girl's going this time."

He meant Rachel, Richie thought.

Once everyone had a glass in hand, Pat boomed, "Hey, a toast to the happy couple! Years and years of happiness!"

Cheers ensued. Rachel put her head on Richie's shoulder. Hands reached out and touched them, hugged them.

After a few moments, Pat said, "Go on, Richie."

Richie stepped back. He took in a deep breath. He paused, could sense the eyes of the party on him. He raised his chin and met them all. There were Pat and Marilyn, of course, and Rachel's mom. Mr Harrington was still handing out glasses; some of his family came by. Then there were plenty of their coworkers, both from HSA and Blythedale. They all seemed frozen in their smiles. They'd be happy to watch him and Rachel all night.

"Wow," he said. "First, uh, let's thank the Harringtons once again for hosting. I don't know what I did to deserve it, but uh… I don't know. I, uh – this is like a second home, right? I mean, all the Giants games, that awesome Christmas party… hell, Mr Harrington, he invited me, us, all you HSA people, to watch the World Series here! Marilyn and Pat weren't even here! In '96, remember that? Remember how we went nuts when they won the Series?" There was a big cheer.

"Ohhhhh yeah," Toni said. She raised her glass to Mr Harrington. "You're a saint, buddy!"

Mr Harrington, arms folded, shook his head and grinned. "I don't know what I was thinking," he said.

Richie inhaled. He wrapped an arm around Rachel's waist. He loved her scent: warm, comforting, special.

"You know," he said, exhaling, "for the longest time, Pat was the only family I had. We had some pretty... mixed up parents. I guess... I guess they just couldn't handle it. So, really, from the time I was about, oh, nine or so, my mom and dad? That was Pat. He made me things I liked to eat, he told me stories, he let me tag along to all his baseball games. He's the reason I love the Yankees, he's why I loved Donnie Baseball. He even took care of me, took care of my bills, when I was in college. And, you know, in college I came home to Yonkers all the time. I had all the friends, all the family I needed right there. And yeah, he was my buddy, my partner in the bleachers. You saved my life, Pat. I love you."

There were murmurs and applause. Tears down his cheeks, Pat hugged him, whispering: "You're the best family I could ever have."

He continued: "And, you know, when Marilyn got the job in DC, I thought my family, the one good thing in my life, would be going away. I felt, I don't know... incomplete. All alone."

He paused. "But... I don't know, something happened. I flipped out, I lashed out. I let my anger push you all away." He had to swallow. Rachel slipped a hand into his, as she had that fateful night. Toni put a hand on his shoulder.

Shakily, he said, "And even though you had every right to turn your backs on me, you did the opposite. You grabbed me, turned me around, forced me to talk. Called me at all hours. Ran an 'errand' for me." He met Rachel's eyes, red and puffy, but smiling through her tears.

"I never expected to have a family like Pat anywhere but in Pat. But here you are. You're kind, you're fearless, you're dedicated. Your doors, your homes, are always open. You help me see the humor in everything. You give and give, and then you ask if you can give some more."

He looked down again into Rachel's eyes. They were the same shade of green as Pat's. How'd he not notice that?

"And this lady. My 'partner', my best friend. I fell for you that night in the Multipurpose room, that Valentine's party. You were the most beautiful caseworker I ever saw. I hung on your every word, every action that year, asking stupid questions and getting smart answers. And when I needed you the most, when I felt so alone, so scared, you spent an afternoon hearing my awful stories. You listened, you showed me you cared, helped me make it through those tough times. Since then it's been just like that magical night three years ago, the night all my dreams came true, or so I thought. I thought it couldn't get any better, but it did. The more I learned about you, the more I loved you. I can always count on you, always talk to you. You're amazing, tough, generous, kind, and I'll never feel alone again. I love you, 'partner'." He kissed her, and the gatherers applauded.

"So," he said, voice quavering, "here's a toast. A toast to finding family, to finding love in the wildest places. A homeless shelter. A children's hospital. A bachelor pad. A house on a hill. A stretch of lousy plastic seats filled with the craziest people you'll ever meet. I never thought I'd find it, but I did. You all helped me. I found love because of you. Here's a toast to you, my new family."

The "here-here's" were muffled through tears and sniffles. A line of well-wishers hugged the happy couple. Tony crushed Richie with a bear hug, saying, "Dio ti benedica, amico."

"Well, I guess you better get moving, kids," Toni said. "Gonna be a great game."

"Well," Rachel said, beaming at Richie, "it'll never be as great as our first playoff game."

"Oh, I love that story!" Stephanie said. "So romantic."

Mrs Wilson said, "It is? Oh, I'd love to hear it sometime."

"Yeah, Richie!" Marilyn said. "Let's hear it again!" A crowd gathered, anxious to hear it as well.

Richie grinned. "Sure. But for reasons she'll have to explain, I think Rachel should tell it."

"Oh, wow," Rachel said. "Richie, we might miss BP, partner. 'Cause have I got a story to tell."

Notes

1   Major League Baseball clubs can expand their rosters after September 1. Minor leaguers are then "called-up" to the majors at that point to give the roster some depth and get the player some big-league experience. Until 2021 clubs could have as many as forty players on the big-league roster in September.

2   No way is the author going to define every one of these words. Look it up.

3   It's a game played using baseball statistics. Trust the author: it's just one short rung up the nerd ladder from Dungeons and Dragons. For more information on how it works, try: https://imaginesports.com/news/who-invented-fantasy-baseball. And yes, the author played for many, many years. Shut up.

4   "It was one of the lowest points in baseball history, a time of anger, confusion and disgrace. In spring training of 1995, major league players were on strike, so teams were built with replacement players, a collection of minor leaguers, former major leaguers and anyone else who could play at all." - Tim Kurkjian in ESPN The Magazine (August 2002).

5   The reader is reminded that the opinions expressed by the characters in this book are not necessarily those of the author or the publisher. While the Mets have, in actuality, sucked on occasion, such a chant is hurtful to all those wonderful Mets fans the author has come to know over the years. Still room over here on the dark side, though.

6   Oh, please. Like you don't do seventy-five on the Sprain during rush hour. Pfft.

7   Women make up over 80% of the positions in the social work field, but even in 2021, men "occupied" - since it's now 2022. a greatly disproportionate number of leadership positions. Hard to believe that Toni would have been an anomaly even in 1995. There are lots of articles on this topic, but start with this: https://mswcareers.com/men-in-social-work/

[8]   In the final, clinching game of the 1976 American League Championship, first baseman Chris Chambliss hit a walk-off home run off the Royals' Mark Littell in the bottom of the ninth to send the Yankees to the World Series for the first time in twelve years. The game is perhaps less memorable for the outcome as for the pandemonium that ensued. Required watching for any Yankee fan: https://sabr.org/gamesproj/game/october-14-1976-chris-chambliss-home-run-delivers-pennant-to-the-bronx/

[9]   Gotta admit. Very impressive. Ugh. https://www.nba.com/history/top-moments/1995-jordan-return-double-nickel

[10]   Don Mattingly played 1,785 regular season games before making it to the postseason. There are 30 players who played in more games without ever playing in the playoffs. There are nine players in the Hall of Fame on that list, including one of the greatest shortstops in the game: "Mr Cub," Ernie Banks. https://www.baseball-reference.com/leaders/leaders_most_gamesnops.shtml

[11]   For all you Seinfeld fans out there: https://www.youtube.com/watch?v=cUwSxqnRW-8

[12]   Who saw that coming? Don't all get up at once. https://www.nytimes.com/2019/01/22/sports/baseball/mariano-rivera-hall-of-fame.html

[13]   Jones would make another outrageous claim a few years later: "Keith Van Horn is the next Larry Bird." But the Nets did go to the NBA Finals in 2002 and 2003, Jones claiming, "See? Called it!"

[14]   Ugh: https://www.baseball-reference.com/boxes/NYA/NYA199610200.shtml.

[15]   Ohhhhhh boy, did that make for an interesting reception. As the happy couple walked down the church steps, confetti flying, Pat, the best man, whispered to them: "Something special – I mean *really special* – is happening at the Stadium." At Mr Harrington's behest the club gladly rolled a big-screen TV into the reception room. When the game ended and the cheering died down, Pat made an impromptu toast. "The real perfection is right over there," gesturing his glass to Richie and Rachel. https://www.mlb.com/yankees/video/cone-remembers-his-perfect-game

Acknowledgements

As might be painfully obvious from the pages of this book, I have no formal creative writing education or training. I just got bored sometime during the early days of the COVID-19 pandemic, and started hammering away on the keyboard, like one of those million monkeys trying to bang out Shakespeare. Except you'd only have to go about two hundred monkeys deep for what I first wrote. So, it took a lot of help, a lot of guidance (excuse the pun) and free advice to give life to this thing, this blob of writing I cranked out on my dining room table / office. Now I can walk around calling myself a professional novelist. (You can stop laughing now.)

To Joanne Micallef and Faraxa Publishing, thanks for making a bucket list item come true, for having the patience to deal with my many questions.

To Sharyn November, my first editor, whom I met on Reedsy. com, thank you for your expertise and direction. I had all the enthusiasm but none of the brains, so meeting with you put some structure to my wild ideas.

To Richard Sheres, award-winning author of *Ingersoll* and *An Imperfect Certainty*, thanks for the confidence to strike out on my own.

To the Yankees media department, thanks for the help with some technical, historical elements. And thanks to the 1995 Yankees for all the inspiration. While we're at it, thanks to HELP USA and my friends at WestHELP Greenburgh, especially Lisa Lombardi, Debbie Jacobson, Delores Johnson, and Kim Markham-Grundman.

And thanks to everyone at http://www.baseball-reference.com: all along I thought this was a time-waster. But your handiwork is all over this book. Keep up the good work.

As for Regis High School...well. For all our ups and downs, for all the turmoil, the people there have been behind me every step of the way. I know lots of employers would have said, "Hey, that's not your job! Get back to work!" But instead, I heard things like, "Wow, that sounds great, when can I read it?" Or "What can I do to help?" I guess that's what our kids are always talking about: a community that cares.

So, at this magical place, special thanks go first to James Kennedy, Director of Development (please donate at http://www.regis.org). He read an early edition of the novel, gave me useful feedback, and put me in touch with alumni who could help. Among those were Jonathan Judge-Russo, Michael Izquierdo, and Craig DiFolco of the Regians in Media and Entertainment group. They offered good advice and told me to reach out to prominent literary alumni. That's when I heard from the great Phil Klay, author of the award-winning *Redeployment* and *Missionaries*, and the equally great Matt Thomas, author of the acclaimed *We Are Not Ourselves*. Each time I spoke to them I was energized, spurred onto a clear path toward completion. I also heard from a former student in the publishing business, Nick Thomas, and though now I feel even more like an old fart, his expertise was critical. Thanks as well to lots of my everyday colleagues for their support: Eric DiMichele, Anthony Andreassi, Dave Bonagura, Christian Talbot, Hee-Sun Hong, and Chris Rose.

But this thing started by me pestering my family and friends for early reads and special favors. I'm a card-carrying cheapskate, so of course, I got all this support and encouragement for free. I think.

My brother, George Febles, is the unquestioned master of constructive criticism. "If you wanted, you could do *this*," were all the words I needed. But he did so much more. That long phone call in August of 2020 became my personal course in "Plot Writing 101." My sister-in-law Nelsie Febles took it even further. She helped me shape the social work aspects of the book for accuracy, and picked out the minutest details, things I'd been too lazy to notice. She also pointed me to Evelyn Marron, a lifelong professional in the field of child protective services, who provided crucial expertise and advice on those subjects. My sister-in-law Susan Pon-Biscoe and my dear friend Diane Mingoia also read early drafts and provided some great ideas. I also had a long conversation about writing with my nephew Elijah Biscoe, a talk which showed me that while I had a lot to learn, I had no choice but to keep going.

My wife once told me I've picked good friends, and perhaps none better than the brilliant, generous, and patient Bryan Robinson. Not only would he give you the shirt off his back, he'd ask if you needed pants, too. To have his guidance on media and publicity has been a great gift from a guy who's a Hall-of-Fame-worthy gift giver. A few words at the end of a novel are not nearly enough to express my thanks for your friendship. Glad to see you're strong, bro. Stay that way.

Thanks as well to Ed Jennings at Fordham Prep. I happened to be talking up my book just before a track meet at Icahn, and he said, "Hey, I know this guy, parent of one of my students, he's written lots of books, you should talk to him." That guy turned out to be Joe Drape, New York Times journalist and best-selling author of *The Saint Makers* and *American Pharoah: The Untold Story of the Triple Crown Winner's Legendary Rise.* I'd never even met him and he talked to me like a favored teacher, the kind you eventually consider a mentor. The advice was great; the encouragement and support, invaluable. (Please read *The Saint Makers*, by the way. One of the best books of 2021 for my money.) Thanks, guys, and I'll see you on the tracks (the human and the equine).

Extra special thanks go to my wonderful daughter Rosemarie Febles. She didn't think less of me even though there were more curse words in the novel than she'd ever seen. She didn't mind that I took time away from playing Mario Kart and Minecraft to pound out page after page – she even drew me an inspiring cover page! All of her eight years in my life have been the happiest I've ever known.

But my first reader and my most trusted adviser was my beautiful wife, Shirley Pon. She encouraged me, listened to me, offered me smart suggestions. She actually read four different versions of this novel, tolerating my writing a love affair between another woman and a character that bore many similarities to her husband. "Thank God it was good," she said at one point. "I don't know what I'd have said if it wasn't." I'd never have accomplished this without knowing how much you love me. Rachel can't hold a candle to you, my dear.

Thank you all for your care, your wisdom and enthusiasm. Keep your phones handy, since I'll need you all for the next novel. Maybe this time I'll buy you all a hot dog.

About the Author

Christopher Febles has been a guidance counselor, college advisor, and track & field coach at Regis High School since 2008. He holds a Master's Degree in Social Work from Fordham University and has been working in the social services field since the early '90s. He's been a partial season ticket subscriber of the New York Yankees since 1996. He lives in Brooklyn with his wife Shirley and his daughter Rosemarie.

Richie the Caseworker is his first novel.

CPSIA information can be obtained
at www.ICGtesting.com
Printed in the USA
BVHW070720090123
655879BV00002B/195